For my lovely, devoted wife,
Janie Camp

And

In memory of my mentor,
Alexander Laing
1903-1976

ANGEL'S INFERNO

WILLIAM HJORTSBERG

NO EXIT PRESS

First published in the UK in 2020
by No Exit Press,
an imprint of Oldcastle Books Ltd,
Harpenden,
Herts, UK

noexit.co.uk
@noexitpress

ISBN
978-0-85730-413-1 (Print)
978-0-85730-414-8 (Epub)

2 4 6 8 10 9 7 5 3 1

Typeset in 11 on 13.9pt Minion Pro
by Avocet Typeset, Bideford, Devon, EX39 2BP

Printed and bound in Great Britain by Clays Ltd, Elcograf S.p.A.

Better to reign in Hell, than serve in Heav'n

John Milton, *Paradise Lost*

1

When the Devil laughs the whole damn world laughs with Him. Everyone gets a kick from another man's bad luck. Do unto others, not unto me. The cops wisecracking over my lover's corpse were all in on the joke. They dug Satan's eternal punchline. This bitch croaked and we're still alive enjoying the show. I slumped on the couch, staring down at my manacled hands. The coarse laughter in the bedroom echoed from another universe. A numb chill gripped me. I zipped my leather jacket up over the camera hanging around my neck, locking my fingers together. Looked like I was praying. A complete sham. There were no prayers left.

'Hey, Angel!' Lieutenant Sterne leaned out the bedroom doorway, big head blunt as a battering ram. A flashbulb popped behind him. 'Got your guns mixed up. The rod between your legs is for screwing. Stuck the wrong one into that bitch's pussy.'

Flashbulbs flared like lightning. Epiphany's bloody body gleamed in their lurid light. Wedged between her legs, my Smith & Wesson reflected the flashing Speed Graphics. A wave of hatred rose from the numbness in my gut. I choked it back, keeping things deadpan. Anger at these crooked cops and at the man who'd killed Epiphany and set me up to take the rap warmed my icy soul. Raw as a double shot of cheap bourbon. This square asshole Sterne with his dumb black shoes and white athletic socks should've shackled me from behind like some mad-dog killer.

Sergeant Deimos strolled in from the hallway. A smug smile brightened his five o'clock shadow. Looked like a cheap B-movie gangster. Black overcoat. Wide-brimmed fedora. I'd first laid eyes on him five days ago. Deimos had been dressed like a longshoreman then. I wore the work clothes now. Dungarees, knitted wool cap, war-surplus aviator jacket. Pair of handcuffs for that cool outlaw touch.

'What's the word, Eddie?' Sterne barked.

'Wagon's on the way.'

'Sooner the better. I want this bastard locked up tight. He snuffed out three people in the last week.'

'Six feet under sounds better.'

My gorge rose like a bad case of stage fright. 'I'm sick!' I yelled, hurrying for the bathroom close to the front door. 'Gonna throw up!'

Nothing like getting puked on to make the toughest cop duck aside. I slid on my knees across the tile floor to the toilet, heaving a gut-bucket of sour swill into the bowl. Deimos looked away. Policemen learn to live with the sight of blood. Vomit makes them queasy just like everybody else.

A second wave of nausea provided additional moments of privacy. I looked up under the ancient porcelain sink at the derringer secured with duct tape to the drain pipe high and out of sight. A.38 caliber Great Western copy of the classic Remington over-and-under. I'd taped it there a couple years ago after a heavyweight torpedo roughed me up and pushed me on my ass onto the john floor. The gorilla worked for a pair of Wall Street shysters who didn't like me snooping into their grift. I swore the next time trouble came knocking I'd have a secret surprise. Hitmen always let their marks take one last piss.

I lurched to my feet, grabbing the drain for balance. Played my ace in the hole, yanking the sneak piece free. Hunched over the sink, back turned on Deimos, I made a show of slurping cold water. Stupid flatfoot. Not interested in a sick man cleaning himself up.

Pressed my cuffed hands to my stomach, concealing the derringer. Three quick steps took me to the open bathroom door.

I stepped close to Deimos, showing him my heat. 'Try any cowboy shit,' I hissed, pressing the two-shot tight to his middle. 'I blow a hole through your liver.'

'Don't be stupid,' he whispered. A couple uniforms loitered in my living room, rubbernecking at what was lying on the bed.

'Out the door. Slow and easy.'

We were in the hallway. Not a second glance from two medical attendants bullshitting by a sheet-covered gurney. I guided Deimos past the central staircase to the fire exit. The door closed behind us on the landing. Told him to shrug off his overcoat.

'You'll never get away with it, Angel,' the detective sergeant said.

'Already have,' I said, frisking him down two-handed. Found his service revolver and pulled it free. I gripped the .38 caliber Smith & Wesson Bodyguard in my left hand and put the derringer into a side pocket where I found my own pair of lightweight aluminum cuffs. I yanked them out. 'Hands behind your back.' I jabbed him with the Bodyguard, getting my message across.

No more jive-ass back talk from Deimos. I snapped on the bracelets. Never trust a cop. Playing it safe, I ran my chained hands down his pant legs. He wore no ankle rig. I scooped up Deimos's heavy woolen overcoat and draped it over my manacled mitts, concealing the pistol that made me boss. 'Let's head downstairs,' I said.

We drifted down seven flights to the basement with no more gassing. The Chelsea Hotel's cavernous cellar housed ancient furnaces and boilers. Easy to imagine rodents roaming the shadows in this dank crypt. I'd never seen any but the super had told me horror stories about cat-sized monsters prowling the dark corners.

Scattered islands of light pooled under bare hanging bulbs. I knew my way around. Monthly lease-holding tenants stored things in obscure corners: old steamer trunks, unwanted luggage, cardboard boxes. Quick prods with the Smith & Wesson moved Deimos forward. I intended to gag him so he didn't scream his head off and give me up to the boys upstairs.

'Kneel!' I barked. Deimos didn't move. I smacked him upside the head with his own .38 and he bent to the floor easy as a choirboy settling at the altar rail. A grunted curse was the closest thing to a supplication he had in him. Dim bulbs cast blurred silhouettes in the gloom. I pulled up a dented footlocker and sat. Set the gun down, fishing my key ring from a jacket pocket. A standard handcuff key hung among the twirls. I had the bracelets unlocked in seconds. Snapped them on Deimos above my pair of S&W Peerless Model 4s.

'Do yourself a favor, Angel,' Deimos said. 'Give up while you're still breathing.'

I'd had enough of his lip. I shoved his pocket square deep into his mouth. He tried to spit it out then lunged back, almost throwing me off balance. I stuck the .38 in his back. 'Calm down, Sergeant. I'm holding the gun now.' I unfastened his ugly cop necktie and laid down the gun so I could wrap the tie around his yap. As I knotted it, a brick wall exploded in my face, the footlocker sliding out from beneath me. My head slammed against the concrete floor as the .38 skittered across the hard surface. Deimos who outweighed me by at least fifty pounds lay on top of me, his heavy shoulders and chest pinning my legs. He used his fat head as a battering ram on my kidneys. The tie had fallen off him and his enraged face looked grotesque as he tried to spit out the gag. Trying to kick free of him, I punched his head, his neck, his shoulders, but he just bore down on me. Sitting up, I landed a blow to his right eye and pulled free, springing to my feet.

Instinctively, I reached for the derringer in my pocket even though I knew I couldn't use it. The thunder of a gunshot in this windowless cavern would bring down all the cops, if they weren't already on their way to the basement looking for me. A kick from Deimos had me stumbling. I grabbed the cord from the light bulb socket above me, yanking it from the ceiling in a spray of sparks as I went down, dropping the derringer. Deimos had me pinned again, more securely now, and was slamming his head into my neck and jaw. Pain shot through me. I couldn't move. He could keep me there until his friends arrived. I managed to move my hands from beneath the gorilla-cop. I still had the socket cord. Pulling both ends tight, I slipped it around his neck when he raised his head and pulled the garrote tight. He leaned back, looking surprised, his eyes bulging as I twisted the cord tighter and tighter. He bucked like a bronco but the handkerchief still jammed in his mouth made things easier, muffling his gargled protests. I kept tightening the cord until he fell on top of me.

Interesting how death fills an empty space with its stillness. The body felt warm but nobody was home anymore. I shoved Deimos off me and rose to my feet. Stupid flatfoot. Shouldn't have fought back. I hadn't meant to kill him.

After collecting both guns, putting my derringer in my pocket and tucking the .38 into my waistband, I quickly searched the cop's clothing, turning up his wallet, a lead-filled leather sap, a pair of cuffs, and a lucky rabbit foot key chain. I shoved the take into his heavy topcoat, tossing Bugs Bunny away into the shadows.

Yanking Deimos's waistband sheath off his belt, I pushed in the .38 and hooked the rig inside my Levis. With my bulky flight jacket underneath, Deimos's overcoat fit just fine. His badge pinned to the wide lapel. I picked up the black fedora and put it on my head over my Navy watch cap.

I dragged the stiff to a far corner behind a stack of cardboard boxes and empty suitcases. Might be days before somebody found the dead cop. Let the rat feast begin.

I slipped out a door around the corner from the service entrance. Sheet iron steps led up away from the hotel entrance. Ascending halfway, I stood eye-level with the sidewalk. Two uniformed flatfoots worked on their pensions under the awning twenty feet away. Everything quiet as a hick town.

I climbed the remaining stairs, standing unnoticed on the landing. The safety gate facing the street was secured by a heavy chain. I waited until the cops looked away toward Seventh Avenue, and then swung a leg over the top rail. One of the uniforms turned his head, glancing in my direction.

I froze, straddling the fence. The cop stared straight at me, but must have seen nothing but shadows because a second later he looked away when a wailing ambulance raced down Seventh Avenue. I swung my other leg over and walked west on 23rd Street under the awning of the El Quijote restaurant. Halfway down the block, I unpinned Deimos's buzzer and slipped it into his overcoat pocket. I chanced a look back. No activity outside the Chelsea. The coast, as they like to say, was clear. I slipped off into the night. Just another stray cat on the prowl.

2

I caught an uptown cab on Eighth Avenue, telling the driver to drop me at the corner of 42nd and Seventh. A big-ass yellow Checker with folding jump seats and enough room in back for a man to stretch his legs and think. I had a lot to think about. My life had been turned upside down and inside out tonight. I'd just killed a cop. Who would believe I acted in self-defense when New York's Finest were convinced I'd killed three people in the last week? Who the hell was this client calling himself Louis Cyphre? Why was he setting me up to take the rap for his murder spree?

My world went to hell the moment Wall Street lawyer Herman Winesap called on behalf of his big-shot client, the elegant and elusive Louis Cyphre. Routine missing person caper that went south right from the start. Johnny Favorite. Superstar. Sang with the Spider Simpson band before the war. Took a powder from the private hospital upstate where he'd been a vegetable warehoused ever since getting hit on a USO stage during a Luftwaffe strafing in Tunisia. Everyone I talked to from his past got bumped off, up to and including his daughter, Epiphany Proudfoot. The investigation led me to a nest of Voodoo-worshipers and Satanists. Now some of them and Cyphre were trying to make me think *I* was Johnny Favorite. Partial amnesia from a war wound wasn't much help in the memory department.

No matter what was true and what was a pack of lies, I had to blow town on the double. To pull it off, I needed stuff from my office. If Cyphre had pinched everything when he'd broken in last night, I was fucked. Big risk going back. Figured the cops would get hip and check the joint out in maybe half an hour. I got nabbed a little after midnight. My Timex read twenty-three past the hour.

Money topped any get-away checklist. I kept two yards in double sawbucks as backup cash in my safe. With luck, it was still there. I pulled Deimos's wallet from his overcoat. Forty-seven bucks in greenbacks. Added his dough to the five spot and eight sorry aces in my worn billfold. Two hundred and sixty simoleons. A puny escape fund.

Passport was next on my list. Skipping the Apple meant putting an ocean between me and John Law. Ernie Cavalero, my onetime boss, always kept a passport handy. He took me on as his legman when I wandered into the Crossroads office healing from a war wound. Early am New Year's Day. Maybe fifteen, sixteen years ago. Can't remember exactly. A passport issued to Harold R Angel guaranteed putting my ass in the hot seat.

Ernie Cavalero always kept a blank passport ready for incognito travel. He had a contact on Pell Street in Chinatown. Mr Yin ran a legit import/export business for cover but made his real scratch dealing false identification. All the fake IDs crammed in my extra wallet came from him. Yin's passport deal included a little do-it-yourself kit in a metal box, tidy as a carved ivory puzzle ball.

'Here we are, Mister,' the cabby interrupted my musing. I gave him a couple bucks and didn't ask for change. The hack sped off. I waited out the red light, staring up at Times Tower. CASTRO BARS PLEDGE TO JOIN US IN WAR. The endless light-bulb headline parade wrapped around the triangular building. Everybody lies, I thought. Traffic light turned green.

Loitering prostitutes and panhandlers ignored me. Not an easy mark. I crossed 42nd, dropping Deimos's wallet into a wire trash container. Fishing for the key ring, I glanced into the window of the Funny Store, a novelty shop by my office building entrance. A row of cheap rubber masks hung from the edge of the top shelf.

Clowns, hobos, pirates, skulls. My all-time favorite, the Devil.

Ernie Cavalero considered himself a master of disguise. He picked up the art of stage makeup somewhere. Loved gluing on fake beards for stakeouts, posing as a homeless bum. Once, he daubed his mug in blackface for a job up in Harlem. I ribbed him about reading too much Sherlock Holmes as a kid. He returned the favor. Made me don a white wig and fake padded paunch for snooping undercover in a retirement home.

The door closed behind me, locking. I crossed the worn linoleum lobby and raced up the fire stairs to the third floor. Faster than the creaking elevator. Ernie worked hard teaching me pancake stick and spirit gum. When I took over the business the year before he passed, I had no further use for the stuff but kept his old makeup kit around as a cornball memento. It might save my ass before this caper played out.

Gold leaf lettering spelled CROSSROADS DETECTIVE AGENCY on the pebbled-glass front door panel. The lights were off inside, the way I'd left things about fifty minutes ago. I never locked the outer office door in case clients came at odd hours. This time, I drew the deadbolt. Wanted an edge if the cops showed up.

Light from the hallway spilled onto my tan Naugahyde couch and the partition dividing the room where Louis Cyphre had forced the lock on the inner door a couple hours ago. Outside my big window, a carnival neon blaze from Times Square lit up the place. I could find my way around but not well enough to get things done in a hurry. I switched on the overhead fluorescent lights.

The safe's heavy iron door hung open like a broken promise. Cyphre had cracked it, taking what he needed to frame me for murdering millionaire businessman Ethan Krusemark's daughter Margaret, a high-society astrologer. Johnny Favorite had been engaged to her years ago. I'd found her body in her apartment high above Carnegie Hall. Someone had cut out her heart. Yesterday's news.

The brown envelope with my last couple centuries lay far back inside the safe. I grabbed it in an adrenalin surge of hope. The bread was all still there along with several fake driving licenses from different states. I stored evidence in an old tin cashbox. Spent pistol shells, fingerprints lifted on transparent tape, drug packets, bullets pried out of plaster walls, that sort of thing. It also contained fifteen tiny film cartridges, shot with a tripod copy stand and a subminiature Minox A the night before last in Krusemark's fancy office over at the Chrysler Building. I recorded every document I'd dug from his files. A treasure trove of hidden crime.

Soft as a worn fielder's mitt, my leather Ghurka bag slumped beside the safe, packed with a change of clothing for whenever I had to blow town on a job with no time to pack. I shoved in the cash envelope, along with Mr Yin's passport alteration kit. Several green passports bound together with a rubber band gave me a draw to an inside straight. The newest Yin forgery went into the Ghurka bag along with my legit ticket. Never faked a passport before. Wanted to make sure I did it right.

Two half-empty cartons of pistol ammunition remained in the safe. Beneath them, an envelope from the law firm of McIntosh, Winesap and Spy, attorneys for Louis Cyphre. It contained their check for $500 made out to Crossroads. My retainer for tracking down the missing swing band crooner Johnny Favorite. I felt I was getting close, maybe too close. Too bad I hadn't cashed the check. It was a one-way ticket to the electric chair now. I tossed it into the wastebasket.

The .45 caliber rounds were for the Colt Commander the cops took off me at the Chelsea. I dumped them in the trash. Twenty .38 special shells went into my overnight bag. I emptied the pockets of Deimos's overcoat and my flight jacket, keeping only his black-jack and badge and my three rolls of exposed 35mm Tri-X film. I'd shot the film at a Palm Sunday Black Mass I'd secretly attended last night in an abandoned subway station on the Lexington Avenue IRT Line. A virgin deflowered on the makeshift altar, her tits washed in a throat-slit baby's blood. I had twenty-four exposures of Ethan Krusemark and other naked Satanists howling and screwing in their animal masks. Got into a beef with him later when he fed me some story about Johnny Favorite eating a young soldier's heart so he could switch psychic identities with the guy. Krusemark fell on the third rail. Fried him crisp as a potato chip. More food for the rats.

I did a quick rummage through the desk drawers. All useless crap from a past no longer mine. I dumped it all in the waste basket along with everything in my billfold that bore the name Harold Angel, saving only the invitation to the Black Mass and a case I took off a pillow I kept in the bottom drawer for when I was too drunk to go home.

My time had run out. I slapped the postage on a manila envelope, addressed it to Frank Hogan, District Attorney of New York County, 100 Centre Street, and stuffed in the 35mm film, the Minox cartridges and the Black Mass invitation, adding Krusemark's business card before sealing the flap. Everything cleaned of my prints.

I filled a cigarette lighter with fluid, squirting the rest into the trash container. Struck a match and set the folded cover on fire. When the matchbook flared, I let it fall. The basket went off with a *whoosh* like a midget volcano.

With the Ghurka bag slung over my shoulder, I grabbed the manila envelope and the fishing tackle box containing Ernie's makeup kit. Looking back as I made the stairs, I saw the little bonfire dancing behind the blurred glass panel in my office door. There goes Harry Angel. Up in smoke.

3

I hit the street, heading uptown past the Rialto toward the Paramount Theater where Johnny Favorite had had the chicks dancing in the aisles back before anyone called them bobby-soxers. Miles of neon, millions of light bulbs. Times Square, bright as noon. Remnants of the Sunday night crowd in for a good time strolled along rubbernecking. Still plenty of action on the Great White Way at one am.

Reaching the corner, I heard the .45 caliber rounds explode in my office. Sounded like distant firecrackers. I glanced over my shoulder and saw a bright orange glow light up the third-story casement windows of the Crossroads Detective Agency. Flames wavered inside my office. Going out in a blaze of glory. No one else seemed to notice. Didn't mean shit to me. Let the whole damn building burn to the ground.

I waited for the light on 44th by Walgreen Drug across from the Hotel Astor where Seventh Avenue intersected Broadway and the square became an X. Crossing below the hourglass neck, I saw Disney's *Sleeping Beauty* still played at the Criterion. Further up Broadway past Bond Clothes, Marilyn Monroe starred at the new Loew's State in *Some Like it Hot*, set to open Easter Sunday weekend. Things were plenty hot enough for me.

I glanced around by the Elpine hotdog stand at the corner of the Hotel Claridge and spotted a mailbox. I jaywalked over, and dropped the fat manila envelope into the chute. Too bad

Krusemark had croaked and would never feel the heat.

Broadway was already ancient history. I walked east on 44th. After the brilliant glare of Times Square the shadowy side street provided welcome darkness. An almost-full moon hung in the clear sky overhead, a display lost from sight under the main stem dazzle. Rounding the corner on Sixth Avenue, I came to the Hippodrome Garage where I parked my car. The place was named for a famous turn-of-the-century theater. In the 1920s, Houdini made an elephant disappear onstage. My own disappearing act wouldn't get as much applause. Unlike the magician's smoke and mirrors it was the real deal.

Climbing the stairs to Level Four had me pondering my next move. Two hundred and sixty bucks was better than nothing. If I wanted to pull a real Houdini I'd need a lot more bread. My 1953 Chevy Bel Air two-door sat parked far back in a corner space affording protection on one side. I unlocked the trunk, dropping in the Ghurka bag and fishing tackle box. Just an average Joe heading off for some down time in the sticks. I took a screwdriver and pair of pliers from the tool kit and quickly removed my license plate. After midnight always best for petty crime. Moving five cars down to a new model red Caddy with tailfins towering like Flash Gordon's space ship, I swapped license plates in under three minutes.

I drove east one block on 44th to Fifth Avenue and turned downtown. At 42nd Street, I swung left toward Grand Central. Passing the terminal, I thought how easy it might have been to catch a train. The cops surely had this place and Penn Station already staked out. I cruised past Lexington Avenue and the Chrysler Building, keeping an eye peeled for a parking space. Just beyond Third, I found one with no problem. I locked the Chevy and strolled back west, humming an old Louis Jordan jump-jive tune slightly off key.

I walked past the 42nd Street entry to the Chrysler Building figuring it was closed. Most of the skyscraper was dark. I saw a scattering of office lights on the upper floors. At the main 405 Lex entrance both revolving doors were locked for the weekend. The wide stainless steel and glass central entrance was open and I let myself in. The lobby retained a bygone magnificence even under dim night-time utility lights. Ceiling murals masked by shadow. Red marble walls glowing with inner fire. Somewhere, greedy developers schemed to tear the place down.

A uniformed guard behind the reception desk eyed me with suspicion. I glared hard at him as I approached. 'Detective Sergeant Deimos,' I snarled, hauling out my wallet and flashing the dead man's badge. 'I'm investigating a complaint on the 45th floor. Let me see the sign-in register.'

'Who called –'

I cut him off with an angry look. 'The register,' I said.

'Be my guest,' the rent-a-cop replied, pushing a clipboard my way.

I pretended to study it for a moment then scrawled some bullshit signature and my time of arrival, 1:25 am, beside it.

'Last car on the end's a local. Only one working,' the guard said.

A curt nod and I headed for the elevator bank. The door to the end car was open. I stepped in, punching button 45. I gave the guard the correct floor in case he checked the master annunciator panel to see where I got off. My destination was Krusemark Maritime, Inc. I'd shot all that Minox film there two days ago after an overnight stay at Bellevue, courtesy of a couple goons Krusemark set on me to discourage further snooping. Getting beat up stimulates my curiosity.

I knew a guy who was head of key control at a big outfit handling security for most of the important midtown office towers. He owed me one and loaned me a sub-master to the 45th floor of the Chrysler Building for the day. I made a copy before mailing the original back to him. The corridors high upstairs were fairly drab compared to the opulent lobby, rows of mostly single-room offices housed behind dark wooden doors framing pebbled-glass panels.

Uniform gilt lettering identified the occupants. When I got off the elevator I saw the lights on in two separate offices down the long hallway. Good news. Probably accountants working late during tax season. Made me look legit to the guard downstairs.

Krusemark's headquarters occupied a big corner office with an imposing bronze and glass entryway meant to suggest the security of Fort Knox. A sub-master opens every door on the designated floor of a building. I slipped mine into the lock and I was inside easy as Ali Baba and his magic words. Two previous trips this week had taught me the layout and I passed quickly through the dark outer rooms to the big mahogany door with raised bronze letters spelling out ETHAN KRUSEMARK.

I turned on the lights in Krusemark's private office. Everything looked just as I'd left it on Saturday. The millionaire shipbuilder kept some excellent old cognac in his alcove bar. I poured a healthy splash into a monogrammed snifter. On my last visit, I wore surgical gloves but no longer gave a damn about fingerprints.

First place I checked was the big marble-slab desk. Not expecting to find anything new, I unlatched the hidden drawer underneath. It slid open. A couple Dunhill pens, a boxed Parker 38 with an overlay of intertwined gold snakes and a sterling silver Waterman. All valuable. I grabbed them and an antique gold-and-ivory mounted dirk. Yanking the pillowcase free from under my belt, I dumped the loot inside.

There had to be something more in Krusemark's office. I glanced at the French Impressionists gracing his walls. Art was never my strong suit. I once traced a small stolen Rubens all the way from a Park Avenue duplex to a trash-filled basement in Baltimore. To me, these paintings looked like greeting card illustrations. I had no clue what they might be worth. Probably a bundle. Too big to hide under the black overcoat. I'd looked behind all of them on my last visit.

The thought of unseen treasure sitting under my nose made me want a second look. I took the canvases down one by one.

Beneath the third, I uncovered something I'd missed before. The geometric wallpaper pattern concealed the edges of a movable panel. A picture hook served as a pull. I tugged on it. The panel opened, exposing a compact wall safe. Playing a hunch, I spun the combination dial right, left and right again, stopping at six each time. 666. The number of the Beast from the Book of Revelation. Epiphany taught me that one. I pulled on the dial and the safe door swung open.

I found a big stack of cash, about forty large in bundles of C-notes, and dumped it by the handful on the desk. The sight of so much mazuma all in one pile kicked the breath out of me. I sat down and drained the brandy. Booze burned away exhilaration's sudden chill. I'd planned on using the 45th floor sub-master in every unoccupied office, popping petty cash boxes in hopes of scrounging up another couple hundred bucks. That caper was no longer worth the sweat. I lived in fat city now.

Back at the wall safe for a second look, I pulled out a slim red silk-bound book, a gold-tooled leather jewelry box and a small black velvet bag containing some sort of antique silver coin. I pushed a small gilded button on the flat morocco container, popping the lid open. Hanging from a golden chain inside, a gold medallion glittered with cold menace. Set with rubies, emeralds and pink diamonds, the half-dollar-sized pendant depicted an inverted pentagram enclosing the engraved head of a demonic goat. Hebrew letters surrounded the satanic image. Louis Cyphre wore the same sort of inverted star as a lapel pin. I asked him about it at lunch last Thursday. Cyphre said he had it on upside-down, claiming it was the insignia of some patriotic organization. 'In France I always wear the tricolor,' he joked.

I dumped all the cabbage, the boxed necklace, the silver coin in the velvet sack and the little red book into my pillowcase. I switched off the lights and was surrounded by the diamond-sparkle of midtown Manhattan outside the office windows. I'd never see this view again. I rolled the pillowcase into a tight bundle and stuffed it under my flight jacket. Leaving my prints behind no longer seemed like such a cute idea. I found a linen hand towel in Krusemark's private bathroom and wiped down everything I'd touched. After closing and locking the safe, I rehung the paintings and washed the brandy snifter clean, returning it to the mirrored shelf.

The plate-glass front entrance closed and locked behind me in the deserted hallway. I took a little extra time making sure the ornate bronze trident door handle was free of my prints. Krusemark's monogrammed hand towel went into my coat pocket as a souvenir.

The night watchman had his nose stuck in a copy of *Nugget* and didn't have a clue as I rubber-soled up and rapped my knuckles on the desk counter. 'That was quick,' he blurted, stashing his stroke book underneath. He slid the clipboard toward me.

'Much ado about nothing,' I said, drawing a puzzled look from the guard as I jotted 1:47 pm in the Departure column beside my fake John Henry.

Walking east on 42nd, I unhooked Deimos's tin from my wallet. His badge marked me now. I tossed it down a storm drain at the corner of Third Avenue. Just as I reached the Chevy, a wino bum stumbled toward me, mitt extended for a handout. In a snap decision, I peeled off Deimos's topcoat. 'Try it on,' I said, handing it over, tossing him the black fedora as a bonus.

The threads fit the beggar worse than me, sleeves hanging to his fingertips, hat wobbling over his ears. 'Thanks, mister,' he muttered. 'Where'd you get these?' Even he suspected something was not legit.

'Rummage sale at the morgue,' I jived, getting into the car.

As I drove north into Spanish Harlem, I whistled Artie Shaw's 'Stardust' solo somehow remembering every perfect note.

4

I needed to get off the island of Manhattan. Most of the bridges out of town required a toll and toll booths might put me behind the eight ball. Toll-takers saw every passing driver. If the cops put out a BOLO with my description, a toll collector might likely make me. The Willis Avenue Bridge, a northbound one-way swing bridge crossing the Harlem River into the Bronx, had no toll because traffic backed up whenever the bridge opened for the passage of barges and freighters.

I pulled onto the bridge at 124th Street. The hum of my tires on the metal road grating sounded sweeter than Bunny Berrigan's trumpet. When I hit the Bronx, I continued up Willis Avenue and turned off the overpass down onto the old section of the six-lane Major Deegan Expressway. I made good time, staying at the speed limit, passing Yankee Stadium on my right.

A couple hours ago, my plan had been to drive up to Albany, ditch the Chevy and board the Empire State Express to Detroit where I could slip across into Canada. Things felt different now. The golden goose had laid a 24-karat nest egg in my lap. The last place on earth the law would ever look for a bird on the lam was traveling first class. My new scheme involved making it to Boston and catching the first possible overseas flight.

Driving north, I lit a Lucky. As I inhaled, my mind drifted back to the terrible sight of Epiphany lying dead in my room. She was a sweet kid who didn't deserve to get butchered by a monster like

Cyphre. Her father, Johnny Favorite, supposedly had amnesia due to a head injury he'd suffered in North Africa during the war. I'd had a little taste of the big blackout myself when I was injured overseas. I got my boiled potato nose from a botched plastic surgery job. The beauty part was I got hit at Oran in Algeria. Shot by the fucking French. No big deal. Thousands of guys fought in North Africa. Who knows how many were wounded around the same time. Louis Cyphre parlayed my memory loss into making me think I was Johnny Favorite, a cat who had sold his soul to the Devil in return for big-time fame.

Maybe I was Johnny Favorite. What fucking difference did it make? I can't remember a damn thing anyway. It didn't turn Cyphre into Satan. Never mind his double acrostic name. Calling yourself Louis Cyphre doesn't make you Lucifer, except to suckers with too much hoodoo in their voodoo. I'd seen Cyphre in the flesh, watched him eat fancy lunches and smoke expensive cigars. He was a tricky magician sure as shit but still remained flesh and blood. A man who breathed and dreamed like any other patsy. Let's see how metaphysical he was when I pumped hot lead into his belly. A shyster's phone call got me into this mess. A couple slugs from my .38 would set me free.

Louis Cyphre, man of mystery. I'd seen him less than three hours ago, right before he killed Epiphany. Too bad I couldn't stick around and hunt him down here – if he was still here. I had a good idea of where he would go eventually. His lawyer Winesap told me Cyphre traveled under a French passport. 'In France I always wear the tricolor,' Cyphre said at lunch. I planned on finding him. La Belle Paris! City of light, laughter and sin. If the Devil was human why wouldn't he choose to be a Frenchman? Sophisticated and suave. Fabulously rich. A man about town, full of parley-voo and savoir-faire. See Paris and die. Why the hell not? Made sense to me.

No bookie would give my chances of finding Cyphre better than a hundred to one. Even with the odds against me, I knew I'd track the bastard down. A guy pretending to be the Devil stands out in a crowd.

I stopped for the night in Hartford. I wasn't looking for some flea bag where cops snooped for fugitives. I could afford the best hotel in town. The Hotel Bond looked posh enough for me. The next morning, after shaving my black mustache, I used the contents of Ernie Cavalero's tackle box to cover up the wounds Krusemark's goons had given me a few days ago. Lieutenant Sterne had paid me a visit in Bellevue and seen the injuries, now doubtless part of my official description. Ernie's blond wig covered the shaved patch above my left temple where nine stitches zigzagged in an uneven line. My left ear, badly lacerated from the kid's blackjack, and my split lip I painted with flexible collodion, amazing stuff that is kind of an invisible Band-Aid.

After a shopping spree that included stops at a fine men's clothing store, a camera shop, a sporting goods store, a luggage shop and a bookstore, I was a new man. Dressed in suit pants, black shoes and an Aquascutum raincoat, I ditched the Bel Air in a long-term parking garage, shelling out thirty bucks for three months in advance, and boarded the 5:39 train to Boston. I stuck my ticket on the seat back for the conductor and settled in for a closer look at the newspapers I'd bought that morning.

I re-read the three-paragraph article headlined **PRIVATE EYE WANTED** on page five of the *New York Daily News*. The article said a private investigator named Harold R Angel was suspected in three brutal Manhattan murders committed during the previous week. His whereabouts were currently unknown. An arson fire at the office of the Crossroads Detective Agency at 1481 Broadway was believed to have been set by Angel. Only an emergency call from a concerned citizen and the prompt response of firefighters had saved the entire building from destruction.

No mention in the paper of Dr Albert Fowler in Poughkeepsie, the first of Cyphre's victims, but that death was officially a suicide.

A small photograph of me accompanied the article. Taken twelve years ago when I applied for my first PI ticket. I sported a GI-style crew cut back then. Aside from the tuberous nose, the picture looked nothing like me.

Detective Sergeant Deimos didn't make the story. Nothing about my escape from police custody. I figured this revised version of events had been decreed from the commissioner himself. Top brass didn't want the press to know how badly their boys in blue had screwed up. Embarrassing for the big shots. Big black mark on New York's Finest. Better to make things sound like an ongoing investigation, a dragnet closing inexorably around the suspect. Cops and politicians always cover their asses when the shit hits the air-conditioner. I didn't see anything about me or the string of New York homicides in the *Hartford Courant*. This was a good thing. The less said about a gumshoe on the lam the better my odds of a clean getaway.

As the rushing landscape outside grew dark, I pulled my new passport out of the handsome new wallet I'd bought. Thanks to Mr Yin's handy kit, I was now John X Favorite, born June 2, 1920. Smart money might make using Favorite's name a dumb call. I figured it a wise bet. Only Herman Winesap and Louis Cyphre knew Harry Angel had been hired to find Johnny Favorite. Winesap was dead. With any luck, I'd soon add Mr Cyphre's name to the obituaries.

A couple minutes before nine, I entered the splendid lobby of the Ritz-Carlton in the heart of the Back Bay where I'd reserved a room. The man at the desk treated me like visiting royalty. 'Welcome to Boston, Mr Favorite. We have room 925 ready for you.'

When I asked about a nearby travel agency, the polite gentleman in the gray suit said, 'Our concierge will be happy to help assist you with any travel plans.'

Concierge. I liked the sound of that. Almost a preview of Paris. I said I'd like to leave my bags at the desk while I ate. The diplomatic deskman told me he'd send them up to my room. Big tippers get the best service so I slipped him a fin, adding a buck for the bellhop, and walked across the gleaming marble lobby to the concierge desk. Another diplomat seated there told me he'd be happy to make my plane reservations. I said I wanted to fly first class to Paris ASAP. No problem. He'd get right to work on it.

'Would you like me to arrange hotel reservations in Paris?' the concierge asked. 'Do you have a preferred place to stay?'

'Let's keep it simple,' I replied. 'Book me in at the Ritz.'

The dining room looked about half-full. After checking my hat and coat with the twist at the door, I was shown to a two-top and ordered a double Manhattan, straight up. My favorite drink for as long as I could remember. Probably longer. Harry Angel had been a rookie cop in Madison, Wisconsin, before he went in the army. Fancy mixed drinks didn't seem like his thing. Beer sounded more like it. Manhattans better suited Johnny Favorite's nightclub tastes. But sometimes people surprise you.

I followed my cocktail with a dozen Wellfleet oysters, a whole steamed Maine lobster and a Caesar salad tossed tableside, all washed down with a fine crisp bottle of Sancerre Blanc. This was living large. Johnny Favorite sold his soul for the high life. Harry Angel made do with hot pastrami sandwiches, always pinched by an occasional splurge. I liked it much better here on the sunny side of Easy Street.

I put the bill on my tab. The concierge approached me in the lobby on my way out. 'Excuse me, Mr Favorite,' he said, handing me a small square envelope embossed with the Ritz-Carlton crest. 'I'm afraid the only direct Boston to Paris flights are on Fridays and Saturdays. Knowing you wanted to leave right away, I've made a reservation for you tomorrow on TWA out of New York.'

'But…' This was bad news.

'Not to worry. There's an American flight leaving Logan at noon. It gets you into LaGuardia at 1:45. Plenty of time for a cab ride to Idlewild. The Paris flight departs at six. I've written down all the flight numbers and departure times.'

I thanked him and walked to the elevators. Going back to New York struck me as a dumb move. All the local airports would be staked-out by now. On the other hand, bold bets often paid off in spades. I had my disguise. The cops wouldn't be watching in-coming flights at LaGuardia. And they'd never figure on me traveling first class, dressed like a swell. Sticking around Boston for three days seemed a riskier option. Chances of getting nabbed increased the longer I holed up in one place. I liked the notion of taking a powder right away.

My bags waited in number 925, the swankiest pad where Harry Angel ever hung his hat. Johnny Favorite on the other hand lived the life of Riley. A high pillow who took boss cribs like this for granted. Corner room furnished with replica French antiques. Brocade bed-covers turned back beneath a gilded baroque headboard. As if long accustomed to such luxury, I checked the Continental breakfast on the order card for a 7:30 am delivery, hung it on the outside doorknob and strolled down the hall to the fire stairs entrance. Always good to know the back way out in case of emergencies.

I tossed the .38 on the bed and dumped the Ghurka bag's contents out on the bedspread, putting the latex surgical gloves and hair dye I'd bought in Hartford into the shoebox with my makeup. Needing to camouflage any contraband in case French customs examined my luggage, I planned to gift-wrap anything suspicious. Presents for friends. A low-level official might hesitate before ripping open the packages of some fat-cat executive.

The phone rang as I packaged the blackjack, making me jump and grab for my heater. Who in hell would be calling? It was the concierge. 'I'm very sorry, Mr Favorite,' he said, 'the Hotel Ritz is completely booked for Wednesday night. I can check the availability of comparable establishments in the area if you'd like.' I said that would be aces.

After gift-wrapping my sap, I considered the small silk-bound book beside me on the bed. Maybe I should toss it? Krusemark kept it locked in his safe so it had to be worth something. I took a look. Small and narrow, about two-and-a-half by five inches, the slim volume had a faded gilt inverted pentagram embossed on the front cover. Flipping through the pages, I saw dozens of intricate arcane symbols, each accompanied by printed passages in Latin, Greek and Hebrew. All were set in an archaic typeface even someone hip to the lingo might find difficult to read. The signs of the zodiac I knew. The rest was pure mumbo-jumbo. Some kind of satanic guidebook, I guessed. Figuring it might come in handy, I wrapped the little volume in silver paper.

Half an hour later, I had everything wrapped and stashed in the bag. After double-locking the door and drawing the security chain, I wiped off the pan stick and lip rouge, washing the collodion from my ear. Facing my reflection in the mirror, I wondered who was the real me. The bleary-eyed ex-private dick staring back out of the glass, the blond big shot I'd been ten minutes ago or maybe an unknown pretty boy crooner with a taste for Devil worship. The truth lay in the near-forgotten past. Deep down in what was left of my soul, I knew the time was coming when I might recognize that the monster grinning out of the mirror was truly Johnny Favorite.

5

The next morning, the courtly ambassador behind the front desk handed me a small envelope. Inside, I found a card with a Ritz-Carlton letterhead from the concierge. 'Wednesday night reservations have been made for you at the Vendôme, 1 Place Vendôme, in the 1st arrondissement. On the same city square as the Ritz. A smaller hotel but very chic.' I put the card into my satchel and slipped a five spot into the envelope. 'See that the concierge on duty last night gets this,' I told the desk clerk, handing him the envelope. 'I'll be back next month.' That last bit meant to insure he didn't pocket the tip.

I got to Logan a little before eleven. Only a couple travelers stood on line ahead of me at the American Airlines counter. I checked my bags and paid $14.05 for the one-way ticket. There was a forty-five minute wait before boarding. I spent my time leafing through *Time* magazine, feeling conspicuous as a circus clown in my wig and makeup. No one gave me a second glance. To the other passengers, I was just another square businessman like them.

Flight 417 left ten minutes late. A favorable tail wind made up the time and we landed in LaGuardia at 1:48 pm. I waited for my luggage, trying not to look over my shoulder. Just as I figured, no one was staking out Arrivals. Plainclothes cops were just as easy to spot as the jerks in uniform. Not a flatfoot in sight.

It was a beautiful New York day in the mid-fifties. Blue skies and no wind. I grabbed a cab right away with no waiting. Two in the afternoon was not the rush hour. As the driver hustled my bags into the trunk, I watched one of the boys in blue standing off by the Departures loading zone. He never looked my way.

All along the drive, the Grand Central Parkway connecting into the Van Wyck Expressway, I stared out the window at the city I thought I'd never see again, thinking about what I'd do if things went wrong. Suppose I got behind the eight ball at the airport? No way I'd go down alone. Shooting the works made sense to me. I had five lugs in my heater. Another ten in the speedloaders. Make every last round count. Take a couple coppers along with me before buying the big one. Cash out like a winner. Better than frying up at Sing Sing.

The cab ride took less than fifteen minutes. We pulled into Idlewild about a quarter to three. The tail end of the parkway curved through Terminal City, an enormous unfinished airport expansion designed to accommodate the coming jet age. The cab dropped me off at the temporary terminal. I paid, tipping the driver after he wrestled my luggage from the trunk. Four uniforms stood along the lengthy departure zone. One of them gave me a hard stare. I ignored him, gathering up my stuff and heading for the terminal building. Crossing the entrance hall toward the TWA counter, I clocked a couple undercover fuzz. The one closest to me, a shambling oaf in an ill-fitting gray suit, pretended to read a newspaper. I figured he had a printout of my photo hidden inside. He tried playing it cool but there was no hiding his expressionless cop stare. I paused, setting down my suitcase. The Ghurka hung from my left shoulder, the new satchel from my right. My raincoat and jacket were unbuttoned. The .38 was an easy reach even with the hanging bags. If he started my way, I'd blow him down.

The dick stuck his big shnozzle back into the scandal sheet. I picked up the two-suiter and continued on to the first class line. I knew he still watched me. I felt it even with my back turned. Only a couple people stood ahead waiting to check in. I put my bags down and chanced a look, gun hand free for a quick draw.

The copper was giving a new passenger the up-and-down and I relaxed just a bit. The line for coach seats wound through a rope-enclosed maze like payday at the corner bank. Yesterday, I'd have been standing in there with the rest of the cattle.

I set my luggage on the scale as the pretty gal at the counter checked my reservation and asked to see my passport, barely giving it a glance before sliding it back. She was a looker all right. 'Smoking?' she asked.

I said yes, requesting an aisle seat. I paid $455 cash for my ticket. When the babe gave me change from the five centuries, she told me TWA was pleased to invite me to their Ambassador Club, a first class lounge, where I might relax in comfort before departure. 'Complimentary cocktails,' she said with a pert smile, as she handed me my boarding pass.

I thanked her and strolled off, pretending to study the ticket jacket while glancing sideways at the plainclothes cop who faked reading his newspaper. He gave me a quick eyeball before sizing up the other passengers walking in from the loading zone. My flight didn't board for another two and a half hours. No way I was cooling my heels in the Ambassador Club where some asshole might corner me for bullshit chit-chat.

I bought a copy of the *News* at a magazine stand and found my way to the Kitty Hawk, a plastic airport bar and grill with framed photos of biplanes and Eddie Rickenbacker on the walls. The place was packed, couples sitting at little round tables, a line of standing travelers chowing down in a hurry at a narrow counter along one side. The bar was a rectangular island in the middle of the room. I wedged in between two squares at the far end with my hat, coat and satchel bundled on my lap.

The tabloid's banner headline read:

**TRAIL 300 GIRLS
IN SIN FILMS
Police Break Code on Names**

I folded the paper to page three. There it was at the bottom, **Cop Missing in PI Murder Case**. 'What can I getcha?' the bartender barked before I read any further. I ordered a draft of whatever they were pouring along with a ham and Swiss on rye, hold the lettuce.

My new reading glasses were more than a disguise, the specs really helped with the small print. The article reported the 'unexplained disappearance' of homicide Detective Sergeant Edelio Deimos, age 36, during the early Monday morning 'vanishing act' escape of Harold R Angel, a private investigator under arrest for several recent murders. The police department's official position maintained Deimos was the fugitive's hostage, although when pressed by reporters, their spokesperson admitted that the possibility of him being an accomplice could not be ruled out.

The bartender set a beer at my elbow. I dropped a buck on the bar top and slurped off the head, focusing on the scandal sheet while he grabbed my money and brought back change.

I read the story over slowly a second time, savoring a quote from an unidentified patrolman. 'It was like magic. This Angel must be some kind of Houdini. We had him in cuffs, surrounded by officers, and then, poof, he's gone.' Good news for me. They still hadn't found Deimos's body by the morning edition deadline. If the law considered him missing, the coppers were looking for two suspects traveling together. With Deimos my hostage, they'd figure I'd keep him close and alive for security. I knew the bulls preferred believing that fiction instead of one of their own selling them out.

My food arrived and I ordered another brew. Folding the *News* to the sports section, I read about the ass-kicking the St Louis Hawks gave to the Minneapolis Lakers, 127 to 97, in the third game of the Western Division NBA playoffs as I ate my sandwich.

'Hey you! Angel!' A loud voice called out somewhere along the bar. The words stabbed through me like an icepick. I froze, not looking up from the newspaper, pretending to still read about basketball. 'I'm talking to you, Blondie! Don't high-hat me. You were in my office twice last week. Shaving the 'stache makes the nose look worse.'

I chanced a look over the top edge of the *News* and spotted the loudmouth jerk sitting kitty-corner across the end of the bar, a pipsqueak four-eyed creep with curly red hair and freckles. He looked like a drunken ventriloquist's dummy. It was Warren Wagner Jr, a third-rate talent agent. His father had been Johnny Favorite's manager back before the war when he was a rising star. Junior recently started representing Louis Cyphre, aka Dr Cipher, flea circus magician. Having this little shit show up out of the blue was really bad news.

I ignored him, turning back to my newspaper. Emboldened by booze, the asshole agent was not to be denied. 'Hey, Angel, Harry Angel,' he shouted, 'you don't fool me with your phony wig.' Rudeness was the essential tool of his jerk-off trade. No one else sitting around me seemed to know at whom the pint-sized idiot was yelling. Wagner lurched to his feet and came around the corner of the bar carrying his briefcase. 'I been in show business all my life and can smell greasepaint a mile away.'

He was bellowing as he staggered toward me. I knew I better split before the scene got out of hand and stood up, sticking the *News* and my satchel under my arm.

'People are looking for you,' Wagner said with a big smirk. 'Flip over five simoleons and I never saw you here.'

'You've made a mistake,' I said, walking away. 'I've never seen you before in my life.'

'Bullshit!'

I made a beeline for the men's room, pulling the pigskin gloves from my coat pockets. Stay cool, I told myself as I tugged them on and pushed open the bathroom door.

'Angel...?' The ten-percenter staggered behind me.

A short tile wall provided privacy from the tables outside. I ducked around it and stood with my back against a cloth towel dispenser. My newspaper fluttered to the floor when I unzipped the satchel. A counter with four sinks stretched toward three toilet stalls. Four urinals stood on the opposite wall to my left. 'Do yourself a favor, dickhead,' I thought. 'Don't come in here.'

Hearing the door open, I reached inside my satchel and gripped the dirk's gift-wrapped handle. 'Peek-a-boo!' Wagner crooned, coming around the corner without seeing me. In one motion, I tossed the satchel aside onto the counter and grabbed the little man from behind, clamping my gloved left hand over his mouth and yanking him back against my chest. The toes of his shoes tapped on the tiled floor as I drove the dirk through the wrapping paper upwards under his sternum. I angled the blade to the left, seeking the agent's heart, if he had one. 'Surprise,' I whispered in his ear.

Wagner's muffled protests continued under my grip, his tiny feet doing a pathetic dance against the bathroom floor as I worked the blade back and forth inside his chest. The scuffed briefcase dropped from his hand. He grabbed feebly for the knife as we turned a slow circle in our death waltz.

I didn't want anyone walking in on us and dragged Wagner toward the stalls. The door to the one in the middle hung ajar. I elbowed it open, hauling the limp body inside. When I let go of his mouth, Wagner's head slumped forward, a gargling strangled sound escaping from his throat. He was way beyond screaming for help. I closed the stall door, flipping the latch to lock it.

Wagner grew heavier in my grasp and I knew he was gone. They don't call it dead weight for nothing. The last customer to use the stall left the toilet seat up so I swung the stiff around and sat it down in the bowl. Wagner's ass went in deep enough to hold his sagging body upright when I let go of the dirk. His head hung down like that of a sleeping drunk. Holding him by the shoulder to steady the body, I tugged my knife free. There hadn't been any blood to speak of but a sudden crimson rose bloomed on his white shirtfront. I watched for a moment to see if it dripped down onto the floor. If Wagner bled like a stuck pig, I wanted it all to flow into the toilet. I pushed his legs apart positioning his feet more realistically and rechecked the stall door. Getting down on my hands and knees, I crawled under the partition into the adjacent stall.

There was blood on the dirk's blade. I stepped out to the sink and rinsed the knife, wiping it dry on the towel looping from the dispenser. Murder seemed so damned easy. After putting my weapon back in the satchel, I rolled the shreds of blood-stained wrapping paper inside the *News*.

Wagner's briefcase was worth investigating. I set it on the counter, checking my reflection in the tall mirror running the length of the sinks. As far as I could see, there was no blood on my clothing. Just as I snapped open the briefcase, some citizen strolled into the men's room and took a position at one of the urinals. Keeping an occasional eye on him in the mirror, I shuffled through the agent's paperwork. In a central divider, I came across several client photographs, 8 by 10 glossies stamped WARREN WAGNER ASSOCIATES on the back.

The first was signed 'Muggsy O'Keefe' in florid script. This was the old midget I'd seen in Wagner's office last Friday. The one who'd starred in all the 'Hell's Kitchen Kid' comedy shorts back in the early thirties. Others I didn't recognize. A banjo player, some guy dressed as a Cossack juggling scimitars, a chick singer with buckteeth. I pulled out the next photo. Louis Cyphre in his old-fashioned vaudeville soup-and-fish. The fellow at the john zipped up and came over to wash his hands. He didn't even glance at me but I shoved Cyphre's glossy back into the briefcase to play it safe.

Another stranger wandered in as the guy next to me finished using the towel machine. This cat headed straight for the first stall and locked himself inside. It was getting to be like Grand Central Station. Seeking privacy, I gathered all my stuff and made for the third stall. From under the closed doors, Wagner's spread feet looked just as lifelike as those of the guy sitting next to him.

Alone in the solitude of my cubicle, I sat on the throne, resuming my investigation of the agent's briefcase. Flatulent trombone blasts echoed from two doors down. I slipped Cyphre's photo into one of the partitions in my satchel. There was also a copy of the small cardboard poster showing Cyphre dressed up like a swami in his guise as 'EL ÇIFR, MASTER OF THE UNKNOWN.' I added this to the satchel and thumbed a sheaf of contract forms and correspondence, finding lists of Paris venues, two short letters from Cyphre and a small dog-eared address book. These went in the satchel. I leafed through the other file pockets in the bag but came up empty-handed. When I finally heard a toilet flush, I waited a couple more minutes before sticking my head out of the stall.

The coast was clear. I shoved Wagner's briefcase under the partition into the stall with his corpse. I figured his body would not be found until the janitor came to mop up after midnight. Anybody using the john would spot his feet and take him for just another guy on the crapper. I let myself out and breezed, adrenalin pulsing through my veins.

Not a single head turned in the Kitty Hawk to mark my departure. The Ambassador Club now struck me as the safest of all hideouts. It's always when you're sure nothing can go wrong that you land in deep shit. I had to ditch the bloody gift paper and drilled across the foyer, chancing that one of the flatfoots on stakeout might mark my return. Far from the Kitty Hawk, I tossed the rolled-up *Daily News* into a trash container and headed for passport control and the boarding gates.

After presenting my ticket jacket and passport, freshly marked with a genuine departure stamp, I was admitted to the international departure area. The naked dirk in my satchel troubled me. I could almost see the blade with Superman's X-ray vision. The gift-wrapping ploy was maybe a dumb con but I had a hunch it was just stupid enough to do the trick. I needed another phony present. The

Duty Free Shop fit the bill. Browsing inside, I bought four cartons of Luckies, which a sign informed me was the maximum allowed for France. For a pack a day man, this meant feeding my habit for another month. It felt like placing a bet that I'd live that long.

I had no idea what else I was looking for until I spotted a narrow gilt-paper covered box of chocolate cordials. When I bought the candy, I asked to have it gift wrapped, obviously a routine request. Five minutes later, I dumped the candy in the trashcan of one of the Ambassador Club's fancy private toilet compartments and the dirk fit perfectly in the box, which I carefully re-wrapped.

After a couple of double bourbons on the rocks, I found my gate just as someone on the PA said TWA Flight 830 to Paris was boarding its first class passengers. Joining the short line forming at the door, I half expected a squad of cops to come rushing in to collar me. When my turn came, I handed my jacket pass to the uniformed attendant who tore the top coupon from the ticket, handing it back with a smile. 'Have a nice flight,' she said.

I went through the doorway and down the stairs to the tarmac. In some dark corner of my mind I craved a final last-minute twilight of the gods shootout. Was I secretly afraid of confronting Cyphre? I reached the boarding ramp and started up. A glam young stewardess stood in the open hatchway of the Lockheed Super G Constellation, ready to greet me. For the first time since Sunday night when I found Harry Angel's dog tags hidden in Margaret Krusemark's ancient alabaster canopic urn and confronted the bizarre possibility that Johnny Favorite and I were somehow connected, all dread and doubt were gone. My tainted soul soared free as a high-flying bird.

6

The flight to Paris would take twelve hours, the first half-day of my new life. Stepping aboard, shrugging off my hat and coat for the hostess to hang in the closet, I felt like a snake shedding his old unwanted skin. I had never flown first class before and it came as a gasser surprise when the stew asked if I'd like a drink the moment I buckled my seatbelt. I ordered a Manhattan with no fruit. Only a premix but perfectly chilled in a tall stemmed glass. I sipped my cocktail as the tourist class passengers shuffled forward in a bovine procession through the lounge. I had only been an upper-crust citizen for two days and was already a snob, regarding my fellow travelers seated up front as inherently inferior. When the last of them straggled onto the plane, the stewardess closed the curtains marking the boundary of our distinct worlds. I enjoyed a smug boozy satisfaction.

The starboard window seat beside me was unoccupied. Just before takeoff I unbuckled and slid over. As the Constellation angled into the night sky above Long Island Sound, I stared out at lower Manhattan, a dark cluster of distant towers delineated only by the random diamond-point scattering of lights. Already the city was gone, a nocturnal fantasia dissolving into memory. We climbed higher, clouds streaming past, and soon the continent was lost to me, swallowed up in darkness. My old life disappeared with it, a shadow left behind in shadowland.

When the smoking lights went on and everyone unfastened their seatbelts, the stewardess announced cocktails and *hors d'oeuvres* would be served in the first class lounge. I joined the others making for the little area just past the entryway and coat closets where a cluster of couches broke the monotony of row seating. The two married couples sat together, broads already chattering away like sorority sisters. I found myself next to a dapper gent with wavy pewter-colored hair who had the seat across the aisle from me. He lit up a coffin nail that stank like burning carpet and croaked at me in frog talk.

'No comprendo,' I said.

'Are you going to Paris for business or pleasure?' he asked in English, sounding just like Charles Boyer.

'A little of both.'

'Will you be staying long?

'As long as it takes.'

The stewardess wheeled in a serving cart rattling with glassware and liquor bottles, interrupting our fumbling conversation. She served drinks and appetizers. I had a second Manhattan and a small plate with Beluga caviar, goose liver pâté, smoked salmon and tiny toast points. Everything tasted boss. I was feeling no pain. My companion sipped champagne from a slender flute. 'My name is Christian D'Auburan,' he said with a smile.

I introduced myself as John Favorite. Lucky for me it didn't ring any bells and there was no bullshitting about those long-gone swing band days I couldn't remember. This was the social hour and I decided to be sociable, asking, 'What do you do for a living Mon-sewer D'Auburan? Pardon my French.'

'I am *un agent immobilier*, Mee-steer Favorite,' he grinned. '*Pardonnez-moi mon Anglais.*'

'I don't savvy. What is it you do?'

'I'm an estate agent.'

I still didn't get it. Maybe he was mixed up in legal shit like wills and contracts, planning rich peoples' estates. I wasn't asking again. Didn't want to come off as some kind of American moron.

'And what is your profession?' D'Auburan asked, spreading pate onto a triangle of toast.

'I'm kind of a producer.'

'*Un producteur?*' He eyed me more closely.

'Show business,' I said. 'Like a talent scout. As a matter of fact,' I reached down for my satchel and unzipped it, extracting the glossy photo of Louis Cyphre, 'I'm looking for this bird.'

'I do not know *cet oiseau.*'

'Name's Dr Cipher. He's a very skilled magician.' I pulled out the el Çifr poster. 'Sometimes he puts on a kind of religious minstrel show. El Çifr, man of mystery.'

'A bird of many feathers, it seems.' D'Auburan studied the little poster then looked up and studied me, his gaze settling on my new blond hair. He just smiled when our eyes met. 'Paris has clubs and theaters which feature magic and illusion. Perhaps helpful to you?'

I said that would be aces and got out my old leather-bound pocket notebook and one of Krusemark's fancy fountain pens. D'Auburan regarded the golden serpent-entwined Parker 38 with an appraiser's eye and started spewing names and addresses, all of which he had to spell for me. It was all gibberish to me. As I wrote it all down, I worried, with my luck, this frog could be an undercover cop.

After the information exchange, we found we had little to talk about yet I made an extra effort to keep up my end of the mindless banter of strangers thrown together by chance until the stewardess came over and suggested we return to our seats because dinner was about to be served.

'In case you are interested in finding a flat in Paris,' D'Auburan said, handing me an embossed calling card. 'Please do not hesitate to call.'

'Thanks.' So, the guy was just a real estate agent hustling up business. I filed his card away in my passport wallet.

My experience with airline food was almost nil, mostly

little bags of peanuts and once, on a flight to Chicago, a choice between chicken à la king and beef stroganoff so I was startled when the stewardess handed me a menu and brought a white-linen covered tray set with a full service, including china and crystal glasses.

After a wonderful meal of thick sliced beef tenderloin, hearts of palm salad and a cheese plate, well matched by three glasses of Margaux, I opened my satchel and got out the stuff I took from Warren Wagner Jr. The wad of single-page contracts proved of little interest. I found one for Louis Cyphre. It was like all the others except for the signature and date. Cyphre had signed with Wagner only two weeks ago, right before he hired me to find Johnny Favorite.

What was his grift? Did he become Wagner's client because the agent's father had been Johnny Favorite's manager? What did Cyphre gain from it? Too much booze in my bean to puzzle this one out. I turned my blurred attention to two short letters, both typed on hotel stationery. The most recent was posted on March 3 from the Imperial Hotel in Tokyo. It said: 'Dear Wagner, I will be in New York for two weeks before Easter. See if there is an opening at Hubert's during that period.' He signed it, Dr Cipher.

I recalled Cyphre's clever performance with the dancing mice at Hubert's Flea Circus on 42nd Street. He claimed to have the soul of an ancient Spanish sailor trapped in a bottle. Had it only been five days ago? A whole lifetime had slipped away since then. Harry Angel, private eye and murder suspect, washed down the drain like unwanted filth. The other bit of correspondence, dated January 19, was typed on stationery from the Bristol Hotel Kempinski on the Kurfürstendamm in West Berlin. It was a letter of inquiry. Cyphre said he was a 'professional magician' seeking representation for bookings in 'small venues in major east coast cities,' his florid Dr Cipher signature boldly scrawled at the bottom of the page.

I already knew the gist of these letters but they provided a fresh glimpse into Louis Cyphre's globe-trotting life. No way I'd ever catch up to him chasing him around the world. I figured he had to have a base. Everybody does. Cyphre carried a French passport, so Paris made sense. This is where Warren Wagner Jr's cheap address book proved most valuable. The agent had written down several contacts for his new client. Two were in care of banks in Rome and Paris. Another was the 1-2-3 Hotel on 46th Street, which I knew had been only a transient way station for Cyphre. Three names and addresses in Paris, along with a list of clubs where he'd performed as Dr Cipher.

Probably Cyphre lived his secret life in hotels. Much harder to trace him that way. He collected his accumulated mail at banks or his attorney's office. The 1-2-3 was only a grade above a flophouse while the Berlin and Tokyo hotels were both five-star joints. Cyphre must like mixing them up, his trail that much colder. How do you look for some bird nesting one night at the Ritz and flying off to a welfare mission the next?

The stewardess passed along the aisle, handing out blankets and pillows to the passengers. Several of my fellow travelers had already extended their 'Siesta Sleeper Seats,' settling down for the night. I decided to bunk down by the window and avoid being disturbed by any aisle traffic during the night. I pulled the window curtains closed although there was nothing but blackness outside, kicked off my shoes and tucked myself in. The mask made me pause. Something about being blindfolded didn't sit right. The cabin lights had dimmed but D'Auburan and a couple others were still reading. The little beacons above their heads proved an annoying distraction. I figured I was in no immediate danger and tied the mask over my eyes. Almost right away, lulled by the throbbing engines, I fell into a deep sleep.

Toward morning, teetering on the edge of consciousness, a vivid dream occupied my mind. Much closer to memory than my usual horrific nocturnal hallucinations, the reverie found me on the band bus racing somewhere through the unknown night-time heart of mid-America. The whole outfit was there. Spider, Ben Hogarth, Choo-Choo and Lenny Pinsky, the new cat on bass, sat in the back, playing poker on an upended drum case. Looking around, I saw Red Diffendorf and Carl Walinski, the two 'bone wizards, sleeping like babies. Tiger Man, George Van Eps and Fingers Fagan slouched down, sharing a secret fifth of rot gut. The horn trio, Wing Nut, Harry 'Big Hesch' Geller and Sam the Man traded blues riffs on their mouthpieces. Their sad lonesome sound said it all.

The dream felt so real. I searched the shadowy bus for the rest of the gang. Always a loner, Vernon Hyde, who blew alto and tenor, slouched up front by the driver working on a crossword puzzle. Nose buried in a fat book, piano man Dodo Mamarosa sat beside the Swedish bari sax player we all called Peanut. Dodo had just turned fifteen, a skinny kid with a five o'clock shadow making him look years older. Hard to believe when you heard him tickle the ivories.

Made me happy being back with the only family I'd ever known. I loved those guys. They were my brothers. Fellow hepcat troubadours living the gypsy life. Only one thing set us apart. Ambition. The other musicians lived paycheck to paycheck, jumping from one band to the next. Maybe some aspired to fronting their own outfits someday. Most were born sidemen and would die that way. I wanted more. Bing Crosby rose up in the twenties from the ranks of the Paul Whiteman Orchestra to become a movie star with his own radio show. He was a crooner just like me.

The dream shifted. No longer a passenger, I stood front and center on the bandstand wearing my tux, the boys ranked behind me like a penguin symphony. Spider kicked things off with a steady throbbing tom-tom. After the reed section blew four bars of the melody, I launched into Cole Porter's 'Night and Day.' It was my first big hit, reaching number three on the charts. Not bad for a song already nine years old.

We were in some Midwest hotel ballroom verdant with potted ferns, Chi-town or Cincinnati maybe. I couldn't remember. After a couple months on the road, they all start looking alike. This was an earlier memory. Dodo hadn't joined the band yet and KC Bates pounded the eighty-eight. The audience sat at small round tables beyond a polished dance floor, everyone dressed like swells in formal evening clothes. They inhabited a separate universe from the band who sat itching in second-hand monkey suits. Several couples slow danced at my feet as I sang the familiar lyrics. I stared soulfully at the best-looking dancers, letting them know every word came straight from my heart. All at once, I saw him sitting at the best table in the joint. Louis Cyphre. All decked out in white tie and tails like Fred Astaire.

He smiled at me, raising his champagne glass in a silent toast. I didn't know who he was back then. From the way he stared at me, I knew he dug my act. Some big-shot mogul. Maybe the head of a movie studio or a Broadway producer. Everything about him reeked of money and power. Best of all, his eye was on me. I'd have a drink with him later during the break. I didn't know our meeting would change my life forever.

I woke up with a gasp, panicking when I opened my eyes to complete blackness. Remembering the mask, I tore it off, blinking at my unfamiliar surroundings. I was back in first class, a million miles from the band bus. This had been no dream. Every detail was born from primal memory. A week ago, I couldn't tell you the lineup of the Spider Simpson Orchestra or begin to describe what they looked like. In the dream, I remembered every face with photographic clarity. Harry Angel heard Cyphre's name for the first time twelve days ago. But now I remembered meeting the Lord of the Underworld for the first time in November of 1939. The gig went down at the Palmer House in Chicago. After the last

set, I had a drink with Cyphre and he took me off to some fancy
society party on Michigan Avenue's Near North Side. I didn't
know it at the time but all the guests were Satanists. It was the
beginning of my new life.

I pulled back the window curtain and saw daylight gilding the
clouds below. My unconscious mind must be playing tricks on me,
making me think a dream was a memory. Cyphre had looked the
same twenty years ago as he did last week. It didn't make sense. I
needed more sleep.

About an hour later, the stewardess hooked up the meal tables
and served us breakfast. As I ate, I tried to bring back more of the
details of that posh Chicago party. It was like watching something
through a fog, my thoughts lost in the clouds I stared down upon.
Cyphre had introduced me to many of the guests, important people
in radio and film, producers and studio executives, advertising big
shots. I struggled to remember the faces but they all came back a
blur.

Cyphre promised me an RCA recording contract that night.
When I told him Spider Simpson had signed with Savoy, he said
he'd make all necessary arrangements. My version of 'Night and
Day' would create a sensation. Before the evening ended, I inked
my first agreement with him. I remember Cyphre loaned me his
fountain pen, my signature florid in purple ink. If what Krusemark
had told me was true, the next contract I signed with the Prince of
Darkness was written with my own blood.

My hand shook as I raised the coffee cup to my mouth.
Krusemark's cockamamie story about Johnny Favorite cutting
out a soldier's heart and eating it could be true. Many of the
people I'd talked to during the investigation told me Favorite
was involved in the occult, a devotee of the dark arts. He had
found a ceremony he could perform to switch psychic identities
with someone so he could duck out on his bargain with the
Devil. I'd found Harry Angel's dog tags last night in the canopic
urn where Krusemark said his daughter had hidden the soldier's

identity. I'd thought it was a set-up. Now I wasn't so sure.

Once the stewardess cleared the breakfast trays, leaving the service tables in place, she handed out French entry and customs declaration forms. I gladly turned my attention to this mundane task. Everything seemed simple enough. There was no limit on how much currency could legally be brought into the country, so my money belt bankroll was strictly legit. Smuggling in gift-wrapped contraband was another story. The gat I wore under my shirt took me another step closer to the guillotine.

I uncapped Krusemark's fancy pen and filled in the blanks. It was a lark, really. I was a businessman, strictly on the level, who had nothing to hide. Along with personal information, they asked where visitors would be staying in France. I felt smug writing down 'Hotel Vendôme, Paris.' Glancing over at D'Auburan, I found him gazing at me. He quickly smiled and looked back down at his book. I nodded and returned to my fraudulent paperwork.

After the stewardess gathered up the forms, I stared out the window. In another hour, the coastline of Europe stretched below me, dun and featureless below the ragged clouds. Had Johnny Favorite been here before? Harry Angel had only made it as far as North Africa. Was this my first trip to the Old Country?

We began our descent, so imperceptible I'd never have noticed if the stewardess hadn't made an announcement instructing us to extinguish all cigarettes and fasten our seatbelts. Soon the runway was in sight, our plane leveled off and we cruised down for a near-perfect landing.

Passport control posed my first challenge. A few passengers stood ahead of me and I waited in the queue for my turn. My makeup and wig had to be a dead giveaway. I felt like a black man at a KKK cross burning. Wasn't long before I toed the white line. The woman ahead of me finished and I stepped up to the counter, handing my passport to the blue-uniformed official. He glanced at me and studied my photograph. 'What is the purpose of your visit to France, *Monsieur* Fah-for-eet?' he asked.

'I'm looking to get a decent meal for a change,' I answered with a good-natured smile.

'That I can guarantee you.'

He stamped my passport, sliding it back to me, and I was on my way, legally admitted to Frogistan.

7

One thing I learned in almost fifteen years as a private dick. Never trust your first impressions about anything. From the taxicab window on the drive north from Orly Airport to the city, France struck me as a dull and dreary place, the flat suburban landscape sodden with rain, a monotonous succession of bleak middle-class homes bland as Wonder Bread. Strictly from Squaresville. Instead of brooding on the nothing view, I occupied my time comparing the texts of my two *guides verts*. I spent my first 475 francs in an Orly terminal bookshop where I spotted the English language version of the green Michelin guide. Most of the entries appeared identical and I gave myself an impromptu language lesson, comparing the French text with its matching English translation.

It did me no good. I couldn't pronounce the strange words. 'Hinky, dinky, par-lay-voo,' kept running through my mind like an insane nursery rhyme. When we rolled into the outskirts of the city, I crammed the guidebooks back into my satchel and gave my full attention to the view out the window. Things looked a lot better the closer we got to the center of town; tree-lined boulevards, rows of handsome old buildings, a never-ending succession of bars, cafés and restaurants. A surprising number of bicycles wove between the haphazard traffic.

We hung a left when we hit the river and the full magic of the place hit me like my first sight of the 1939 World's Fair with its futuristic vision of tomorrow's miracles. Except this was the city of yesterday in the land of once upon a time. The street paralleled the river and when the cab rounded a bend there stood the Eiffel Tower, a monument at once utterly familiar and completely alien. I knew in that moment I'd come home at last.

A right turn took us across the river over a humped fairyland bridge. I saw narrow glass-roofed boats moving against the current and old men with fishing poles sitting along the stone embankments. The guidebook told me it was the Seine, but gave no clue how to pronounce the river's damn name. I remembered it to be something like 'Zen.' Good name for a river. Better than Styx.

We passed through a large formal garden along the riverbank. Took a left on a busy street running beside it. A right turn four blocks later straight into a large rectangular square. Interconnected identical four-story houses from centuries ago on all sides. Dead center, a bronze column towered above rows of luxury automobiles parked ten deep on the pavement like a fat cat's used car lot. Some dead big shot from long ago perched on top.

'*Place Vendôme*,' the driver announced, taking me on a tour all around the square. Pulled up in front of my hotel at number one, just across from where we'd first entered. The Vendôme proved a palatial gem, more like the town residence of a grand duke. Made the exaggerated splendor of the Ritz-Carlton in Boston feel rude and plastic. The staff all spoke perfect English. Impeccable manners.

According to the red Michelin guide, my room on the third floor was one of only thirty-five in the hotel. Looked down onto the Place Vendôme, providing a better view than the one of 23rd Street from my pad at the Chelsea. I unpacked and put everything away, using only a single drawer in the ornate dresser. My suits, bathrobe and flight jacket took no more space in the antique armoire than lonely ghosts haunting an empty house. I lived in Cyphre's world now. I needed to dress the part.

It amused me to think how easily I'd adapted to a life of privilege. Like some playboy trust-funder, I didn't earn my money so spending it lavishly seemed of little consequence. Easy come easy go, always the remittance man's mantra. I felt I belonged here by birthright, completely at home in my luxurious surroundings, as if I'd been accustomed to antique furniture, oil paintings in gilded frames, damask wallpaper and heavy velour drapes all my life.

I felt safe in this splendid room, one of thousands like it in an unfamiliar country. Not speaking the language was an asset, not a liability. Rather than setting me apart, being a foreigner rendered me invisible. No one would ever take notice of yet another American tourist, one more anonymous sparrow in a huge identical flock. Putting my theory to the test, I decided to walk the streets of Paris. I needed to get the feel of the city. Seeking the anonymity of a tourist, I fitted the new lens onto the Leica and hung the camera around my neck. I slipped the derringer into my leather satchel. The little two-shot had saved my ass twice already. I figured it brought me luck.

Before leaving the hotel, I took a look around, prowling the corridors and snooping into the service stairs. Didn't take long to plot an alternate exit route avoiding the lobby should the need arise. On my way out, the doorman asked if I wanted an umbrella. He didn't use the word 'umbrella.' Said something sounding like 'para-plea.' Knew what he meant when he pointed to a tall bronze urn stuffed with furled bumbershoots like a vase of black flowers. 'No thanks,' I said, walking out into the misty drizzle. Phrase book told me it should have been, 'Non, merci.' Best not to let on I understood any French.

I angled across the neck of the Place Vendôme to the even-numbered side of rue Castiglione. I could pronounce this one thanks to a couple mob wop pals back in the Apple. The sidewalks along the next two blocks leading to the river were protected from rain by arcades paved with colorful cracked tiles. Broad tiled circles enclosed the mosaic names of the shops alongside. Near the corner of rue de Rivoli across from the park, the tiles read SULKA. Waiting out the traffic light, I stared in the window at pricey silk neckties and tailored shirts. I needed luxurious threads like these if I wanted to beat the Devil at his own game.

Amused by the absurd notion that I might bump into Louis Cyphre just strolling about, I crossed to a long tree-lined terrace overlooking the broad park and the river beyond. To the west, around a downstream bend in the Seine, the Eiffel Tower tapered skyward above the recumbent city sprawling around it. I descended a broad set of steps into what my guidebook called the *Jardin des Tuileries*, however the hell you pronounced it. I passed a pair of winged statuary horses as I walked out onto the Place de la Concorde. The square had as its centerpiece an ancient Egyptian obelisk looking like the twin to Cleopatra's Needle in Central Park.

I stared at a stretch of empty pavement where my Michelin said the guillotine once stood, trying to imagine the cheering crowds watching day after day as more than a thousand knelt beneath the 'nation's razor.' The same surrounding buildings had looked down on the executions. In my mind's eye, I saw the flash of the falling blade, a vivid spray of blood, the executioner holding the dripping head, startled staring eyes. They say the brain lives on for minutes after decapitation. If Louis Cyphre was everything he claimed to be he must have had a ringside seat for these festivities.

I turned up my raincoat collar and crossed the square, looking up the Champs-Élysées. Shrouded behind a gray curtain of mist and rain in the distance, the Arc de Triomphe looked smudged, a hasty discarded charcoal sketch. Walking north past a jetting fountain, I strolled along the rue Royale toward a classical Greek temple sitting in the middle of the road. It turned out to be a church called La Madeleine. Perched above a high set of broad steps and enclosed by surrounding Corinthian columns, it looked like a courthouse.

On the walk back to the Place Vendôme, I went into La Tabatière d'Or, a fancy tobacco shop with a Kodak decal pasted to the window. Using my little dictionary, I made arrangements with the proprietor to have twenty copies made of the 8x10 glossy of Dr Cipher and the cardboard poster of el Çifr. I hated to part with the photos but I knew copies would be useful in my search. The old man told me the duplicates would be ready tomorrow. I checked every news kiosk I passed for a New York newspaper. No luck. All I could find in English was the Paris *Herald Tribune*. The NYPD's dragnet for Harry Angel didn't rate international coverage but the death of shipping millionaire Ethan Krusemark did. I bought the *Tribune* and tucked it into my satchel.

The gray sky and steady drizzle didn't mar the old-world elegance of my surroundings. The city felt adrift in time. While Manhattan was an ever-evolving dynamo, continuously renewing itself in a frenzy of demolition and construction, Paris was different, tranquil and abiding, a lost world hidden inside long-forgotten dreams. Everything about this town suggested a bygone era. Ghosts lived here, haunting the present with their memories. Just the place for someone claiming to be the Devil.

I strolled back into the hotel at quarter past four, bedraggled after walking in the rain. My shoes were soaked, my pant legs wet to the knees. 'I love Paris when it drizzles,' I joked to the man behind the concierge desk.

'Two months ago it flooded,' he frowned. 'The Seine up onto the street.'

I asked him to send a bucket of ice to my room. Breakfast on the plane had been my last meal. I mentioned this when inquiring about a dinner reservation for the hotel restaurant. Polite as Alphonse holding the door open for Gaston, the concierge suggested nothing earlier than seven o'clock 'unless you wish to dine in an empty room.' He said room service had an excellent mixed *charcuterie*. To save me from starvation, he'd have them bring up a tray and some bread with the ice.

The charcuterie turned out to be a mixed bag of cold cuts, dry sausages white with mold and various pâtés. I filled a water glass with ice cubes and poured a tall drink from my flask. Everything tasted first-rate, best deli food ever. I flipped through the *Herald Tribune*. Nothing about Krusemark. Maybe his body hadn't been found yet.

Thinking about Krusemark reminded me that I had his silver coin, which was probably worth a bundle. I took the small black velvet bag from my satchel and opened it. The coin was a bit smaller than a half-dollar. Twice as thick and slightly concave. Worn from centuries of use, the front side depicted the profile of some long-dead potentate. The reverse showed a standing eagle flanked by Greek letters. Way back in the distant past somebody had die-stamped Roman numerals into the silver surface. Like a tattoo, a cryptic I.I. adorned the cheek of the royal portrait. On the reverse, XIII branded the eagle's breast.

Krusemark had kept this trophy in his safe. It possessed either great monetary worth or some hocus-pocus mumbo-jumbo valued in the black magic world of Devil-worshipers. I wanted it locked up tight. I made a graphite rubbing of both sides, using a lead pencil and a sheet of hotel stationery and slipped the sheet into the Cyphre file in my satchel.

I moved on to more pressing matters, getting the Paris telephone directory out of a desk drawer. I shuffled through the pages, looking in the 'C' section. I found no listing in the phone book for Louis Cyphre. Ditto el Çifr and Dr Cipher. I pulled Warren Wagner Jr's ratty address book from my satchel, turning to the Cyphre entries. His Paris address was c/o Morgan Guaranty Trust, 14 Place Vendôme. Bingo! Right in my neighborhood.

On a sheet of hotel stationery I wrote down the contact information, including the bank's phone number. Working through Wagner's address book, I wrote down every name located in Paris. There were nine in all. Six were either restaurants or nightclubs. I double-checked each in the phone directory. I couldn't find two of the bars and figured they'd gone out of business.

Long shots, every one but they were my only leads. You can only play the hand you're dealt. Housekeeping had stacked a couple magazines on a back corner of the desk. One was *La Semaine à Paris*. Like *Cue* magazine back home, it contained a weekly listing of everything happening in town, all the movies, shows, art exhibitions, musical performances, the top restaurants and cabarets, and sporting events. It was all in French but I got the gist of things.

I leafed through the newsprint pages, comparing the club and cabaret names with those on Wagner's list. I found them all, scattered across town. A place called the Blue Note caught my eye. Not one of Warren Wagner's spots. A drummer named Kenny Clarke and his group were featured there. Back in '53, I heard him play with the Modern Jazz Quartet at Bop City in the Brill Building on Broadway where Wagner had his office. Seeing Clarke's name in print ignited glimmers of more distant memories. Maybe he'd be able to help me piece together my past.

Dressed for the evening in my gray suit, pale blue shirt and a maroon silk tie, I had an excellent meal, duckling *ragoût* with olives, and a superb '48 Margaux in the Vendôme dining room then headed for the Blue Note.

The club's lighted rectangular sign thrust out above the entrance in rue d'Artois and provided the only ground-level illumination on the narrow residential street. I went inside, taking a seat at the bar in back. After setting fire to a Lucky, I ordered a Manhattan. The first set had already started, a trio session with Kenny Clarke at the drum kit, some white cat playing bass and an intense little soul brother noodling bebop intricacy out of the eighty-eight. I never cared much for the discordant frenzy of bop but this group, driven by Clarke's relentless hi-hat, really swung. The piano man was a wizard, a kind of off-beat Art Tatum. By their third tune, my mind stepped backward through a time machine into the past – to 1939 when I first met Kenny 'Klook' Clarke.

When the session ended, the musicians wandered among the tables, stopping for a greeting here and there. They didn't linger long. Their obvious destination was the bar.

'How's it going, Klook?' I said as the drummer took the stool next to mine.

'I know you, man?' Clarke frowned.

'Johnny Favorite. Used to croon with Spider Simpson's outfit. Met you back in '39 when you played for Claude Hopkins. There was a battle of the bands at the old Roseland on Broadway.'

'I remember that night.' A grin replaced the frown. 'Kicked Spider's sorry ass all the way back to crackerland. Don't recall you as a towhead.'

'Spider made me dye it black. Wanted me to look more like the dago big band crooners so popular back then. He said they were sexier.'

'Lady Day had to wear blackface when she sang with Basie. Folks thought she looked too ofay.'

The bartender set drinks in front of Clarke and the piano player. I pointed to my change on the bar, signaling the tab was mine. 'Caught you off and on up at Minton's just before the war,' I said. 'You and Monk. Charlie Christian sat in when Goodman wasn't cracking the whip. Don Byas. Dizzy.' The long-forgotten names came drifting back out of the shadows, written on cigarette smoke in numberless dimly lit clubs.

'Yeah, man. Groovy times. You'd fall by with this foxy high yellow bitch.'

'Evangeline Proudfoot.'

'That's right. Say, what happened to you, man? Thought you hit it big. Haven't heard a sound in years.'

'Got out of the music business,' I said. 'Went into another line of work.'

'Bad move. Could've been some kind of star.' Clarke swiveled left toward his band mate. 'Look here, Bud,' he said to the piano player, 'this here motherfucker's Johnny Favorite. 'Member him?'

The dark little man said nothing, staring at me with lidded bloodshot eyes. He lifted his glass with a nod of thanks. I reached my drink over and we clinked.

'Bud Powell,' Klook said, cutting the introduction short as possible. 'First trip to Gay Paree, Johnny?'

'I was here once with Spider way back. Don't remember much of it.'

'Shit! Them big band days. One-nighters. Barnstorming. What's to remember? Every gig the same. Fuck that shit. You'll dig it here.'

'Already am. Only been a day.' I wished now I still had Cyphre's photo with me. 'Any chance you know a cat named Louis Cyphre?' I asked. 'Middle-aged. Jet-black hair combed straight back. Wears a mustache and square-cut goatee whiter than snow. Works a magic act under the name Dr Cipher.'

'No way. Should I?

'Sometimes he appears in blackface calling himself el Çifr.'

The drummer gave it extra attention. 'What is he? Some kind of mullah?'

'More like a dime-store Houdini. Lives in Paris, I think. Ever seen him around?'

'Sorry, man.'

'Maybe you could hip me to some of the joints where he might hang out? Any clubs in Paris feature voodoo ceremonies?'

'Voodoo?'

'Yeah. Drumming. Dancing. Haitian mumbo-jumbo.'

'There's a joint called *La Cabane Cubaine*, you know. Mostly rumbas and sambas. Dinner dancing. Shit like that.'

'Baron Samedi,' Bud Powell mumbled, staring straight ahead.

'Say what?' Klook turned toward him.

'Baron Samedi, over near les Halles.'

'Solid.' Clarke looked at me. 'Bud's on the money. There's this dive called Baron Samedi, over next door in the 1st. Close by the big central food market. Haitian place. Serves Creole food. Voodoo floor show. All that zombie shit. Hear tell they drink chicken blood and fuck knows what all.'

'Thanks, man. I'll check it out.'

Kenny Clarke studied me for a moment like a cop. 'Come to think of it,' he said, 'wasn't that sweet Evangeline s'posed to be some kind of voodoo queen herself?'

'Something like that,' I admitted.

'Heard all sort of shit about you. How you one time used to carry a skull around in your luggage.'

'So they say. Don't really recall.'

'Bullshit!' Clarke came on full cop now. 'No way you forget shit like that.'

'I got fucked up in the war,' I said. 'Memory loss. Didn't really remember you until tonight when I heard the trio play "Cherokee." All at once it clicked.'

Klook regarded me more sympathetically. 'Fuckin' war,' he said, placing a big hand on my shoulder. 'Bud got his head messed up back then, too. Maybe you two motherfuckers be the lucky ones. Sometimes I'd like to forget all that shit myself.'

'No way, man,' I said. 'Forget too much, you forgive too much.'

'Amen, brother,' Klook said.

8

I dreamed of Epiphany dancing naked in Central Park, blood streaming over her breasts as she whirled among a chanting crowd in a frenzied bambouché. In my dream she didn't clutch a decapitated chicken. A severed human head hung by the hair from her upstretched hands, gore raining across her ecstatic face. It was my head. Nightmares usually have me waking in a cold sweat, a silent scream caught in my throat. This time, I laughed my head off. No joke. In the dream, my dangling, dripping head howled with manic laughter. I woke up happy to find my mug still attached to my body.

I got to work immediately. First, I cocooned the blond wig with the others inside the shoebox. Wigs topped my pain-in-the-ass list. Most of the heads that rolled during the terror wore wigs. No more wigs. I followed the simple instructions on the Miss Clairol hair coloring kit I'd bought in Hartford. The dye job eliminated my need for a wig. My passport photo was backdated by a year. A trip to the barber explained any difference.

While I sat at the desk waiting for my hair to dry, I scrolled a sheet of hotel stationery into the typewriter I'd asked the concierge to deliver to my room last night and began the first of several letters, starting with Wagner's three Parisian address book contacts. I wrote each of them essentially the same letter, saying I was Wagner's associate in the city on business and hoped they might put me in touch with Louis Cyphre. I signed them all, 'John

X Favorite,' and planned to fold a copy of both the Dr Cipher and el Çifr photos in with each letter after I picked up the copies.

All decked out in the double-breasted suit, Windsor-knotted red foulard tie, trim pocket square, I felt ready to confront any stuffed-shirt banker. With the five-shot clipped to my belt I felt prepared for confrontation. Didn't expect the OK Corral.

I asked the concierge in the lobby to make a lunch reservation for me at the Ritz at one o'clock sharp and to recommend a good local dentist who spoke English. Needed my temporary caps replaced with something permanent. Didn't mention getting kicked in the mouth. He said 'oui' to both requests, telling me to ask for Michel, the headwaiter at the Ritz to insure better service, and that he'd have the information about the dentist for me later in the day. On my way out the door, I pulled a loaner umbrella from the bronze urn.

The entrance to the Morgan Guaranty Trust at number 14 looked more or less the same as all the other arched portals along the unified façade surrounding Place Vendôme. No more swank or formal than Guerlain, Schiaparelli or Caron. Inside, it felt stuffy and uptight just like fancy-pants banks the world over. I told a gentleman in a three-piece gray suit I wanted to rent a deposit box and the cog wheels of efficiency shifted into gear. Seated at a partner's desk, I presented my passport for official inspection and filled out several forms with the aid of a translator. My drugstore cheaters made reading the fine print a snap.

Everything looked to be in order. I was given a key. Asked if I had any valuables I wished to secure, I replied, 'Wcc,' and was escorted to a small private chamber furnished with a table and chair. The bank attendant left and returned moments later carrying an oblong metal deposit box. He placed it on the table and departed. I turned my new key in the lock. Opening the lid, I half expected to find something unpleasant inside. The container was as empty as my soul. I placed the velvet bag containing the silver coin inside. Hanging my suit jacket over the back of the chair, I unbuttoned my shirt without taking off the tie. I unzipped the money belt, hauling out all four bundles of cash. Removing five grand for immediate use, I dumped the rest into the box, put my jacket back on and rang the buzzer for the guard.

Before leaving the marbled halls of Morgan Guaranty Trust, I changed my American dough into frog paper. It came to just under two and a half million francs. I slipped the moola into my satchel as the gent in the three-piece suit stepped back up and thanked me for doing business with his bank. I said a friend recommended the place. 'Louis Cyphre.' I gave it my best showbiz shot. Sounded something like 'Louee Seafair.' 'He gets his mail here. Do you know him?'

'I'm sorry, *monsieur*. Our policy is never to reveal the names of our clients.'

'Mine, too,' I said and split.

I drilled through the parking lot of limos across the square and out of the Place Vendôme. Couple minutes before one. Headed for the tabac on the corner of rue des Capucines and picked up the forty prints I'd ordered yesterday and slipped everything into my satchel.

The Ritz was at number 15 directly opposite my bank. L'Espadon looked fit for all the kings who'd ever dined there. Sumptuous peachy-cream walls, tall arched windows draped in swags of gold and blue, the high ceiling painted to resemble puffy clouds drifting across a summer sky. I asked for Michel. The tuxedo-clad headwaiter approached with the aplomb of an ambassador. I gave him my name and he awarded me with the trace of a smile. 'Right this way, Mr Favorite,' he said in unaccented English, guiding me to a perfectly appointed table off to the side of the room.

Michel pulled out a chair and I slipped him a *f*500 note. We were true amigos now. I had the *f*1300 prix-fixe luncheon, an excellent meal, Dover sole boned tableside by the waiter, *asperge hollandaise* and a delicate mixed green salad, all washed down with a tasty bottle of Pouilly-Fuissé. The wine cost extra. Learning the French word for asparagus came as a bonus.

On my way out, I stopped for a word with Michel and told him how much I enjoyed my lunch.

'You are always welcome here, *Monsieur* Favorite.'

I thanked him, saying I was a producer in Paris hoping to connect with a great talent I'd never met and knew only by his stage name. 'Perhaps you know him?' I said, showing the headwaiter my Dr Cipher glossy with another ƒ500 note tucked discreetly behind it. Michel made the bill disappear with a deft sleight-of-hand as he studied the photo.

'Ah, yes,' he said. 'A very good customer. Not so much for some time. Perhaps several months since I have last seen him.'

'Do you know his name?'

'Of course. It is *Monsieur* Natas. Always requests the table in the far corner.'

I inquired how the name was spelled and Michel wrote it out for me on the back of his card. 'Ask for me whenever you need a table,' he said, handing it over. 'I will make certain that you have the best.'

Back at the Hotel Vendôme, I stopped at the concierge desk and asked for a ten o'clock reservation at Baron Samedi. I needed a taxi to get me there on time.

'*Pas de problème*,' he said, switching immediately back into perfect English. 'You don't have to travel out of the first. Very close. Fifteen minutes should be sufficient.'

The concierge handed me a card. 'Here is your dental appointment. Tomorrow at noon with Dr Mussey. His office is not three blocks from here. An easy walk.'

Up in my room, I got out the phone book and searched the 'N' section, finding nine people named Natas living in Paris. I wrote down all the names, addresses and phone numbers. Some used only their first initials, making gender determination impossible. For a moment, I thought of calling them all but quickly rejected the notion, wanting to hang onto the element of surprise.

Time to perfect my disguise. Grabbing a loaner umbrella in the lobby, I headed straight for A Sulka & Company. I'd read someplace that the Prince of Wales and Clark Gable shopped there. Stepping inside, I saw why. If selling your soul to the Devil meant being a customer here after lunch at the Ritz maybe it wasn't such a bad deal after all. The polished honey-blond wooden walls glowed like slabs of amber. Immaculate beige rugs defied footprints from the wet sidewalk outside. The goods were discreetly stored in alcoves and displayed on island cubes of the same golden wood. Silk neckties hung in long even rows like shelved books.

I stood for a while taking it all in. After a short interval, a young man clad in the best the shop had to offer glided up to me and murmured something in French. 'Do you speak English?' I asked.

Of course, he did. Probably just one of half a dozen languages at his command. He wanted to know how he might be of service. A purple wen the size of a raisin bloomed on his pale cheek. I wanted to lean forward and bite it off. Would it be soft and chewy like a jujube? Where the hell did that thought come from? I wondered. The clerk politely repeated his question. Prying my eyes off the birthmark on his face, I said I needed shirts, ties, socks, maybe a jacket; shoes if the store carried them. Fruit-face's artificial smile grew bright as a hooker checking her john's wallet before turning the first trick.

Easy spending dough in a classy joint like this. In under half an hour, I'd bought a couple sports jackets, (a camel hair and one in blue windowpane cashmere), six shirts and neckties, a bunch of socks and half a dozen pairs of silk boxers like Al Capone used to wear. The whole time, I clocked the suave salesman, thinking about eating him alive, ripping into his flesh with sharp canine teeth.

Now I knew what Krusemark had told me was true. I ate Harold Angel's heart. Some innocent young GI fresh out of a VA hospital. Picked him up in Times Square, New Year's Eve, 1942. Two dogfaces on leave sharing a few brews. Got the kid drunk and took him back to my apartment at the Waldorf Towers. Killed him in a secret ceremonial room. Some black magic soul-switching ritual. Don't really remember the mumbo-jumbo. Can't even recall what my fancy pad looked like. Ethan Krusemark was there to help me. And his daughter Maggie, my fiancée. I became Harry Angel for the next sixteen years. My secret life as a gumshoe. Didn't do me a whole lot of good in the end. Still the same old Johnny, thinking about sinking my choppers into this little creep's liver while he showed me a couple cashmere sweaters.

Instead of making a meal of him, I bought a fly suede windbreaker, anticipating the famous springtime in Paris. In the far backroom, I spotted a decapitated torso togged out in a primo tux and thought someday soon I might need some boss evening clothes to facilitate my pursuit of Louis Cyphre. Being part of his world required dressing for the part. My shopping spree set me back close to a grand. ƒ440,000. Fuck the Devil. I just sold my soul to Mammon.

The edible young clerk asked where I was staying. When I told him the Hotel Vendôme, he said Sulka's would be pleased to deliver my purchases free of charge. 'Très bien, merci,' I replied and left the store.

Rain continued drizzling down. No need for the umbrella under the cover of the arcades. I opened it again when I turned left on rue St Honoré walking past my hotel to the opposite end of the square. My shopping spree was not over yet. The concierge had tipped me off to a department store called Aux Trois Quartiers on the Boulevard de la Madeleine where I figured I could pick up jeans, khakis, hiking boots, and other basic items and to Le Mistral, a bookstore across the river that sold American newspapers.

On the taxi ride back to the Vendôme I scanned a day-old copy of the New York *Daily News,* the most recent edition available. I saw a squib about talent agent Warren Wagner Jr who was found stabbed to death in a men's room at Idlewild. The police were investigating. I wished I'd taken his wallet so it looked like a straightforward robbery. But there was no way they could finger me for the crime. I kept reading. No updates on Lieutenant Sterne's pursuit of fugitive Harry Angel and nothing about Deimos. No obituary for Krusemark in either paper.

Back in my room, I found the elegant Sulka boxes stacked in an embossed ziggurat on the bed. As I unpacked boxes and emptied shopping bags, I savored the touch and aroma of every garment I hung in the armoire. They felt and smelled like success. Tigers know one another by their bright stripes and bold musk. The wealthy and powerful recognized their equals with a sniff of expensive cologne or the cut of their clothes. Harry Angel didn't give a shit about what he wore. His idea of the perfect necktie was one without grease spots. He thought a wardrobe was what I now called an armoire. The cat I was four days ago had been a total square.

I saw it all in a flash like the puzzle-solving climax to an Agatha Christie novel, many pieces dovetailing together. The Johnny Favorite caper had been Harry's biggest job. He was a two-bit gumshoe, tracing runaway teenagers, snooping on adulterous lovers, buying off blackmailers and unraveling the seedy tangle of some grifter's lay. Angel thought he was in the know when all along he'd been the biggest sap of them all, believing swells like Ethan Krusemark were just well-dressed hoodlums with deep pockets. His biggest mistake was thinking a .38 made all men equal. The dumb sap lived in a fantasy world where cheap detectives ranked right up there with the Rockefellers and Vanderbilts. Johnny Favorite had known better all along. He understood the rich were different from the nine-to-five slobs and wanted access to their inner sanctum. That's why he, no, I sold my soul.

Fingering my boss new threads, I thought about how Johnny's little deal had nearly paid off. He'd had money to burn, a couple million-selling hit records, been engaged to a millionaire's daughter and been about to embark on a glorious solo career. Then came the war, amnesia, seventeen years of living another man's life, and Louis Cyphre. No way in hell Cyphre was the real Lucifer. Probably some con man I knew back in my Devil-worshiping days. A member of my coven or whatever the hell they called it. I didn't know his grift but he'd already done me a big favor. I was forty grand to the good, living large in Paris and back to my old self again.

Even my lost years as a private dick came in handy. Trained in the art of snooping, I knew I'd track Cyphre down some day soon. Learn all I needed to know about the ins and outs of his con. How and why it involved me. What sort of payoff was in it for Cyphre? Maybe I'd fatten my bankroll along the way. Once I knew the score, after Cyphre spilled his guts to me, I'd kill him.

Around nine-thirty, I dressed for the evening. I wore tan slacks with an assortment of Sulka goodies: alligator loafers and the blue windowpane sports jacket, a deep indigo silk shirt and maroon necktie. Checking myself out in the armoire mirror, I looked trim and sharp, never mind Deimos's .38 on my hip – only suckers trusted on luck for security – and a fat money belt strapped under my shirt. The satchel seemed OK. Carrying a briefcase said I was just another square working late. I felt the full impact of my metamorphosis. Last week, I'd been a two-bit shamus and dressed like one, wrinkled suits and greasy ties. The reflected swell staring back at me was a star. Johnny Favorite back from the dead.

9

The doorman waved a taxi over from in front of the Ritz. I removed my cheaters and slipped them into my breast pocket. Useful as reading glasses but I no longer needed that part of my disguise. I tried some French on the cabby, rolling my Rs like gargling when I told him the club's name and street address. The guy seemed to understand, heading off without a word. I gave the first of several memorized phrases a shot. '*Le nuit en Paris c'est magnifique.*'

That really got him going. *Vive la belle France!* The cabby was my best buddy now, babbling away about the wonders of nocturnal Paris until we pulled up in front of Bijou's Baron Samedi on rue des Innocents. I never got to use my line about the glories of daytime Paris.

Shaped from bent neon tubing, the nightclub's name scrolled in vivid scarlet above an entrance painted to look like a bamboo gate. On either end, twin caricatures of a skull wearing a top hat and shades grinned down at me. Inside, the joint was black as midnight aside from some candles and a couple distant torches. I checked my coat and hat as my eyes grew accustomed to the dark, making out several silhouetted palm trees. The walls and ceiling were covered in woven grass mats with bamboo beams and pilasters. Glittering flags sparkled in the half-light along with the ivory glow of hanging animal skulls. It reminded me of Trader Vic's in the Savoy Plaza Hotel except this was a whole lot more creepy than tiki.

A tall, emaciated Negro approached. He wore a cutaway with an opera hat and sunglasses, his face chalked white. A sequined skull and crossbones was stitched onto the front of his silk hat. He was the maître d'. I told him my name, saying the Vendôme had made a reservation. He nodded without a word and showed me to an excellent table beside the raised dance floor.

A distant throb, the pulse of drums muffled by water's purling fall, seeped into my brain. I figured it was all recorded sound until my eyes made out the shimmer of an artificial waterfall splashing down a back wall. What I first took for a dance floor was in fact a low stage designed to resemble a voodoo peristyle. A central pillar Epiphany called the *poto mitan* rose thick as a tree trunk, reaching up out of a circular black-and-white-tiled base. Painted carvings of twin intertwining snakes coiled up the smooth polished mahogany column.

When my vision adjusted to the twilight, I saw tables surrounding the stage on three sides. A multitude of sequined banners emblazoned with *vèvè* and other voodoo symbols hung from the bamboo rafters. All along the far walls, vivid folk murals depicted the various voodoo spirits known as loa. I recognized crude colorful depictions of Papa Legba, Damballa, Erzulie, Baron Samedi and Agwé.

Voodoo altars stood between the paintings, each one dedicated to an individual loa. Shelves crowded with animal skulls, swords, beads, dolls tied to tiny chairs, candles, plaster saints and crude carved idols studded with rusty nails. Each jostled for attention among rival displays of tawdry magnificence, all of them powerful and vibrant with faith. I felt an improbable connection. Deep down, I believed in these spirits. Worshiping them remained half-lost in memory. An essential belief lingered. Once upon a time, the mambo Evangeline Proudfoot had been my main squeeze.

Someone set down a glass-cupped votive candle and my table burst into light. Everything I observed in the dark was lost beyond a soft glow of candle flame. Behind me, a pop, loud as an unexpected gunshot, had me spinning around, making a grab for my gat. I came face to face with a waiter holding a foaming bottle of Mumm. Lucky, I didn't show him any heat. He grinned like Stepin Fetchit. Got a big kick out of making me jump.

A striking black woman stood beside him, a champagne flute in each hand. She wore a snug strapless silver sequined sheath dress so tight she might have been poured inside like molasses. Her close-cropped gray hair looked somewhere between pewter and wood smoke. Fine wrinkle-free ebony features. Ample cleavage revealed breasts high and firm as a teenage prom queen. Barely visible against her dark skin, a tattoo on her right boob peeked above the low-cut gown. Looked to be a cartoon top hat. Maybe her club's skull logo. I guessed her age around fifty.

The waiter filled our glasses with champagne. She sat down and pushed an effervescent wineglass toward me. '*Bon soir*,' she crooned, her voice ripe and throaty.

I lifted my glass. 'Bottoms up.'

She effortlessly switched gears into English. 'New customers get complimentary bubbly.' And back to French. '*Être au frais du patron.* On the house.'

'This your gin mill?' We touched glasses. 'You must be Bijou.'

'Bijou Jolicoeur.' She smiled, sipping champagne. 'Your first experience at a *cérémonie voudon*? *Monsieur...*?'

'Favorite,' I told her. 'Johnny Favorite. Know a little something about voodoo. Been in a hounfort back in New York.' More than once maybe. Went down with Evangeline back when I was a rising star.

'Johnny Favorite...' She savored my name. 'Familiar to me. Why? I cannot say.'

'Used to be in show business. Crooned with a big band before the war. Spider Simpson's orchestra. He played drums. Remember him?'

'No,' Bijou's smile twisted into a smirk. 'All the same... I remember you.'

'How's that? You had no idea I was a singer.'

'*Vraiment.* I knew you to be a celebrity, only that, *un blanc,* yet a devotee of *voudon.*'

'Where'd you hear that stuff? Walter Winchell?'

'I do not know any Wind Chill.' Bijou's obsidian eyes bored into mine. 'You are familiar to me because of my *milieu.* I was born in Jacmel, Haiti.' She pronounced her homeland as three syllables, Hi-E-Tee. 'My birthday was auspicious. The very day in December when President for Life, Pierre Nord Alexis was overthrown.'

'When was that?'

'A gentleman never asks such a question.' Her smile suggested a cat's pleasure before devouring a mouse. 'Do some research. Check the history books.'

'Not much of a scholar.'

'So I see. You are a man of action, *sans doute.*'

'I take care of myself when the chips are down.'

'A most admirable quality.'

'Don't know about that.' I savored a long slow sip. 'Maybe I do. Who knows? Have a little problem with memory.'

'You are blessed. Most of life is best forgotten. I wanted a new life and came to *Paris* when I was fifteen. With a man, of course.' Bijou gave me a coy smile. 'A much older man.'

'Whatever it takes.' A memory of Epiphany's smooth young cinnamon body stabbed through me. I pulled a couple pills from my cigarette case and offered one to Bijou. 'Smoke?'

'*Merci.* I enjoy American cigarettes.' She held the Lucky upright like a pencil between her fingertips, dark eyes darting. '*Andre!*' she called. The uniformed waiter materialized on cue out of the shadows. '*Portez moi un fume-cigarette... Vite!*' The fellow scurried into darkness, returning with a slender ivory and gold cigarette holder. Bijou deftly fitted in her cancer stick. I snapped my lighter, holding it toward her. She leaned into the flame. Her head bent and I saw the engraving on her *petit* gold medallion. It hung between her breasts on a slender chain. An inverted pentagram enclosed the horned head of a goat. My kind of gal.

I watched her easy exhale. 'Tell me your youthful night-time adventures in Paris.' My eyes never wavered as I drained the champagne. 'You were a wild voodoo child just like my daughter.'

'*Peut-être*... Instinct always trumps intellect.' Bijou Jolicoeur's smile looked real for the first time as she exhaled a long plume of smoke.

'Must have been strange, coming straight from the islands. Where did you go to celebrate voodoo?'

'Small societies all over the city. Many blacks lived in Paris. Africans. West Indians. *Les Américains.* Never hard to find *une célébration* if you are one of the faithful.' Bijou stubbed out her cigarette. 'That is how I first learned your name. Bar-room gossip. When you hear about a rich, young white American involved with *voudon*, you don't forget.'

'I was famous back then, I suppose. The war stole it from me. Big deal. Can't hurt if you don't remember. Used to star in fancy floor shows just like yours.'

'The *cérémonie* you see here tonight is authentic, not *un spectacle du cabaret.*'

'OK. I stand corrected. My backdoor frail before the war was a mambo in Harlem. Evangeline Proudfoot. *Connnaissez-vous elle?*' Took a stab at it in French, trying to ask if she knew her.

'Proudfoot? *C'est un nom anglais.* I do not know any English-speaking practitioners until you. Spanish, yes. Portuguese. Cubans are devotees of Santeria. Brazilians follow Macumba. *Voudon* thrives in most English-speaking islands. Jamaica, St Kitts, Barbados. They call it Obeah.' Bijou rose to her feet like a queen. 'I enjoyed making your acquaintance, *Monsieur* Favorite. I have a business to run. If you plan on dining before *le cérémonie*, I recommend the goat. *Très délicieux.* We are the only place in Paris where it is served.'

I stood and kissed her extended hand, a commoner saluting

royalty. '*Enchanté*,' I said, giving my uncertain French a workout. 'If you have the time, perhaps you'll join me later for a nightcap.'

'*Un casque à mèche*?' She smiled like she meant it. 'I would be delighted.' With that she was gone, a silver mist swallowed by darkness. A waiter appeared in her place, quick as a magic trick. I ordered a chilled bottle of Vouvray with my meal. I gave the goat a pass, choosing shrimp creole. The food was delicious. It came with corn bread and a crisp green salad. They ate like this in Harlem. I was mopping up around 11:30 when the show started. A man dressed all in white with a red sash around his waist came out on stage. I knew from Epiphany he was the La Place, a kind of mystic master of ceremonies. He formed intricate designs on the floor around the peristyle's central column, carefully drizzling a thin stream of flour from his hand. He created *vèvè*, representing the individual spirits that Epiphany called loa. Those depicted would be invoked during the ritual. I can't vouch for the magic. Judged as art, the *vèvè* looked better than anything done by Jackson Pollock.

The insistent throbbing grew louder offstage as three bare-chested black men carried in handmade drums carved from single logs and began pounding out an intricate interweaving percussive pattern augmented by the steady throb backstage. A shrill tin whistle stabbed through the drum thunder, answered immediately by the crack of a whip. This signaled the entrance of a procession led by the hungan dressed as Baron Samedi in an *Amos 'n' Andy* mortician's getup, battered top hat and black frock coat glittering with costume jewel medals. He held a cane carved with tiny skulls in one hand, cracking a bullwhip with the other, a trilling police whistle clenched between his teeth.

The La Place followed the hungan, carrying an upturned saber with both hands. Behind him, a barefoot chorus of ten lovely mulatto girls bearing torches sashayed onstage clad in long white dresses, their hair bound in white silk turbans. A skinny guy leading a goat on a rope brought up the rear. The girls swirled past the *poto mitan*, each placing her torch into receptacles set equidistant around the circumference of the circular stage. The central column had been heaped at its base with fruit, cakes, bowls of cooked rice, loaves of bread, sugar cane, bottles of wine and rum.

The goat-keeper tied the hapless creature to a bolt screwed above the offerings and took his position in line with the band, shaking a pair of gourd maracas. The initial cacophony melded into an intricate polyrhythm punctuated by whip-cracks and whistle trills. The girls started dancing, clapping their hands above their heads and chanting in perfect syncopation. I sat transfixed by the complex pulsing rhythms.

Bijou was right on the money. This was no nightclub extravaganza. It felt as real as when I hid in the shadows a week ago, watching Epiphany preside over a wild voodoo shindig in Central Park. Showbiz loved timing, pizzazz, punch lines, schtick. None of this was on display in the wild cavorting bacchanal I observed from my ringside table. In place of well-rehearsed artifice, raw, primal passion exploded before me.

As the frenzied drumming and dancing grew wilder and wilder, the hungan lit two cigarettes and placed them backwards in his mouth. He hopped up and down, puffing until his ballooning cheeks glowed red from within, exhaling streams of smoke through his nostrils like a fire-breathing dragon. The La Place also transformed himself, hobbling around the peristyle like a cripple. He had changed into Papa Legba, the gatekeeper, guardian of all crossroads, my patron loa. Epiphany taught me he was the first and last of the 'invisibles' invoked at a ceremony because he granted permission for mortals to cross over into the spirit world.

The girls went into cosmic overdrive, their movements more like the spastic gyrations of maniacs than anything remotely resembling dance. One tore off her turban, yanking out tufts of hair and tossing them into the air like handfuls of grass. Another fell to the floor, writhing spasmodically, her body bending into impossible positions. A lean mocha beauty ripped open the front of her dress, grasping her breasts in both hands, squeezing them until milk spewed from her nipples.

The hypnotic bacchanal went on for over two hours. It wasn't exactly entertainment but remained fascinating to the end. Like having a front-row seat at a public execution. By 2:00 am, the musicians and dancers were drenched in sweat, clothing stuck fast to their lithe young bodies. Several faces ran with blood where the women had scratched themselves in their frenzy. For the grand finale, the La Place slit the goat's throat with a single shocking slice of his saber. Two girls knelt before the dying animal, holding either side of a large copper bowl to catch the gushing gore.

The audience sat in stunned silence until the sound of someone clapping reminded everyone that what we had just seen was meant to be a show. The applause built into an ovation. The celebrants took no bows. Instead of a curtain call, the dancers and musicians collected the food offerings that surrounded the *poto mitan* and circulated through the nightclub, sharing them with the patrons. Their way of saying we were all participants, not merely spectators. We shared in the sacrifice. Our hands, too, dripped red with blood.

I ordered a snifter of Rémy, watching Bijou as she moved from table to table chatting up her customers. Figured she'd forgotten all about our promised nightcap and was about to call for *l'addition* when she came over and sat down beside me. 'What are you drinking?' she asked.

'Cognac.'

'I have something else in mind if you care to join me.'

'Why not?' I said. She waved to an elaborately uniformed waiter, holding up two fingers in a secret signal. The generalissimo was back in a flash with an unlabeled bottle and a couple shot glasses. He filled each to the brim with some sort of clear liquor and left the bottle, making himself scarce. '*Qu'est-ce que c'est?*' I asked, experimenting with a recently memorized phrase from my lingo book.

'*Kleren*,' Bijou said. 'A drink made by *les paysans Haïtiens. Alcool de contrebande*.'

'Moonshine.'

'*Vraiment*.' She lifted her glass. I hoisted mine and we clinked. '*Santé*,' she said, draining her shot in a single swallow.

I did the same. It went down like flaming gasoline. Had to be better than 180 proof. I winced from the gut burn. She smiled like a sly kitten. 'Why do you carry *une serviette* at night.' Bijou poured each of us another belt. 'Is your business so important you can not leave it at home for an evening of pleasure?'

I knew she referred to my satchel. 'Many things don't fit in my pockets,' I said. 'Guide books. Dictionary. Street maps.' I unzipped it and pulled out a copy of the Dr Cipher photo. 'Know this man?'

'*Non... Pourquoi*?'

'I'm looking for him. We have a debt to settle. Sometimes he dresses like this.' I showed Bijou a print of the el Çifr poster.

'*Çifr*,' she said without hesitation.

'You recognize him?'

'Only by reputation. *Il est un médium très célèbre*.'

'Medium?'

'*Oui*. He conducts *la séance de spiritisme* for the very wealthy.'

'How do I get in touch with him?'

'*Je ne sais pas*. I am neither rich nor spiritual.'

'What about all this?'

'It pays the rent.'

'You don't believe in *voudon*?'

'*Comme une jeune fille, naturellement*. As a mature woman of property, I believe in a higher power.'

'So do I,' I said, unfastening the middle buttons on my shirtfront and pulling out the engraved gold medallion I wore. 'The All-Powerful protects the faithful.'

Bijou stared at the inverted pentagram, as stunned by my disclosure as a gambler when the bet goes wrong. Her hand moved instinctively to cover her own satanic ornament. 'I knew you are familiar with *voudon* but you… One of us?' she stammered.

I looked deep into eyes gone wild with fear. 'I am anointed,' I said. 'Did you take me for some silly cross-wearing Christian? I believe in sacrifice, not worshiping the victim. Sunday is Easter. A Black Sabbath will be conducted somewhere. Missa Negra. I want to go. I insist on attending.'

'In a city as big as Paris such an occasion demands *un grand sabbat*.' Bijou knocked back her second shot of *kleren* and poured a third.

'Are you going?' I placed my hand gently on top of hers.

'Of course.'

'Take me.'

'*Quoi?*'

'Take me along with you.'

'I would like to… very much… but such things are not so simple. First, I must receive permission from a higher authority.'

'When can that be done?'

'Tonight, if possible, after I close. Where can I find you?'

'The Vendôme.'

'*À bientôt.*' With that, she quickly leaned forward and kissed me hard on the mouth before sauntering into the shadows.

I couldn't find a cab anywhere. It took me forty-five minutes to find my way back to the hotel. I didn't mind the walk, tasting Bijou's lipstick every step of the way.

10

The telephone's insistent ring tore me out of a dream around eleven. '*Bonjour, chéri,*' Bijou whispered. '*Que faites-vous?*'

'Dreaming of you,' I lied.

'*Quel flemmard!* Still in bed at this hour.'

'Cool it, babe. I didn't hit the sack until four.'

'What does this mean? Hit the sack?'

'Go to bed.'

'Oooo… *Pauvre bébé.*'

'That's plenty of shut-eye for me. What's up?'

'*Très bonnes nouvelles.* You have been approved. I am permitted to bring you as a guest *avec moi au grand sabbat.*'

I reached for my smokes on the bedside table and burned a Lucky. 'Cool,' I said, exhaling. 'What's the plan?'

'*Dimanche. Arrivez chez mois à minuit moins trois heures.*'

'On Sunday,' I repeated, playing it safe. 'Three hours before midnight.'

'*Exactement.* You know what to bring. Best if you found a pair of Wellingtons.'

'What?'

'Rubber boots. Very wet where we are going.'

'OK. Be there at nine. You're a sweetheart. Owe you big for this one.'

'*Vraiment.* I will think of some delicious way for you to pay back the debt.' She hung up without saying goodbye.

Bijou's phone call alerted me to my dental appointment. I had an hour and was showered, shaved, dressed and down in the lobby in half that time. A stop at the concierge desk for directions also yielded the names and addresses of a sporting goods store and a costume rental shop. No rain yet today. I had my new folding umbrella in my coat pocket just in case. A sullen sun the color of a communion wafer sulked in the overcast sky. Maybe it promised hope of brighter days to come.

After Dr Mussey fitted me with a new set of temporary caps and I made an appointment to return the week after next to have him finish the job, I made a beeline for the coin shop I'd passed on the way to the dentist. No larger than a cigar store, the place felt like a musty corner of grandma's attic. An old party with an upswept white mustache and pince nez hanging on a black satin ribbon presided over an antique display case where gold and silver coins gleamed on black velvet. I complimented Monsieur Laroque on his perfect English. The novocaine made me feel like my mouth was stuffed with cotton. Laroque said languages came easily to him. He spoke nine, plus owning a reader's savvy of Latin, Greek and Hebrew.

'Glad to hear it,' I said, spreading my graphite rubbing of Krusemark's coin out on the counter top. 'Tell me about this.'

He squinted down through his old-fashioned cheaters. 'Tetradrachm of Tyre,' he mumbled without hesitation. 'Called also a Tyrian shekel. Tyre was an ancient Phoenician city on the coast of what is now Lebanon. This coin dates between 31 and 30 BC. Approximately 0.5 troy ounces of silver. I would need to examine the actual coin to ascertain its true weight.'

'What's it worth?'

'Tyrian tetradrachm are not particularly rare. A fine example might fetch a thousand francs. This one has been disfigured. On the obverse, letters have been die-stamped across the face of Melqart.'

'Melqart?'

'The tutelary god of Tyre, often equated with Ba'al.'

'I thought it was some dead king.'

'When Herodotus visited the Temple of Melqart in Tyre, he found it rededicated to Heracles.'

'Tough being a god.'

'*Regardez...* on the reverse, the Egyptian eagle also disfigured with numerals.'

'Has it any value?'

'The market price of silver. Make that your bottom line. A true collector would have no interest in it.'

'*Merci*,' I said, leaving the shop. If Krusemark's coin wasn't worth anything why had he kept it locked in his wall safe?

It was nearly 3 pm by the time I rented my outfit for the Black Mass – a floor-length red robe and wolf mask – from a costume shop near the Bastille and purchased a Catholic prayer book in Latin, a Latin-French dictionary (no English available), and the latest edition of the *Daily News*. While digging into my lunch of *poulet rôti* at a bistro near the bookstore, I saw the double headline on page two. **MURDERED COP TIED TO FUGITIVE PI WANTED IN TRIPLE-HOMICIDE CASE.** They'd found Deimos's body in the basement of the Chelsea on Tuesday night. The cops were expanding their dragnet for Harold R Angel but were tight-lipped about the progress of their search. No skin off my back. No way they'd track the gumshoe to Paris. I ordered another glass of Côtes du Rhône and turned to the sports pages.

By 4:35 twilight wrapped a damp gray shawl over the city. I figured it was too late to look for the sporting goods place and hailed a cab. Settled in, I pulled the list of Natas addresses from my satchel, using the pocket flashlight to find the one in Montmartre. 'You are American?', the driver asked as we pulled away from the curb.

'As apple pie.'

'Good people, the Americans.' The cab swung out onto a broad boulevard. It was too dark to read the name on the street sign. 'I like them. You were in the war?'

'For a short time.'

'Myself as well. As short as possible. I was in the army. Stationed in North Africa when Paris fell. Algeria. In that one day everything changed and I was serving the damn Vichy government. You Americans took me prisoner during the invasion at Oran.'

'I was wounded in Oran,' I said. This was a lie. Harry Angel had been wounded in Oran. For sixteen years, I'd lived an imaginary life. What did one more lie matter?

'Maybe I surrendered to you,' the driver chuckled.

'Maybe you shot me.'

'Never! I never fired one shot. I lay there with my head in the sand until the fighting was over. Next thing, I work for the 1st US Ranger Battalion as translator. I am good with language. Speak OK Arabic.' The cabby went on and on about his wartime experiences. I let it all roll over me, not really listening. I was remembering...

When I got drafted the army's brass figured they'd landed a star and assigned me to the Special Entertainment Services Branch. There must have been some kind of basic training but I couldn't remember it. Got shipped to North Africa, arriving early in March of '43. Right after the battle at Kasserine Pass in Tunisia where our guys got their butts kicked in their first engagement with the krauts. In the end, helped by the Brits, we held the ridge line. Supposed to have been all quiet by the time I got there three weeks later. I remembered this only in bits and pieces like fragments of a movie randomly cut together. They sent me and a quartet up to Thala, along with a chick singer and some comic who did magic tricks.

A crude stage had been rigged on top of several empty oil drums. I remember the heat and the stink of petroleum. An iridescent rainbow ribbon of spilled diesel snaked through the desert sand. I sang a duet with the blonde (what the hell was her name?) and the guys, hundreds of them, sat cross-legged in their fatigues staring up at us. 'Begin the Beguine,' I think it was. I saw a flash high in the sky. A lone gull-winged Stuka dive-bomber came down out of the glaring sun. That was it. I still hear the plane's Jericho trumpet siren screaming. Boom! Sixteen years lost. Was it all a dream? Some nightmare from Hell?

'... and after the war everyone is big hero. All the collaborators say they fought with the Resistance. We are a nation of liars and cheese-makers.' The cab driver's blather tore through the tattered faded curtain of my distant lost memories. I sat in a Paris taxicab trying to figure out what was real.

'Easy to be an armchair hero,' I said.

'All covered in flannel like Tartarin,' the cabby replied, voice corrosive with contempt. Didn't know what he meant so I kept my trap shut.

The cab turned off another broad boulevard and wove uphill through Montmartre, a dense maze of narrow streets, pulling to a stop on rue Berthe. 'Are you by chance an artist?' he asked.

Curious question. 'Sort of,' I replied. 'Used to be a singer.'

'Opera?'

'Swing band.'

'Jazz?'

'Sort of.'

'I do not care for jazz music.' The driver rolled down his window. 'Much too... frantic.' He pointed across the cobbled street at a small triangular plaza where three bare-limbed horse chestnut trees reached starkly up out of the pavement. 'You have an artistic spirit, all the same,' he said. 'See the little building in the corner. Bateau-Lavoir. Great artists lived there fifty years ago. Matisse, Georges Braque, Modigliani, Juan Gris, Jean Cocteau. Many more. Pablo Picasso created the first work of Cubism in the Bateau-Lavoir.' The cab pulled forward around a sharp corner onto rue Ravignan, stopping in front of a beige apartment house halfway up the hill on the right across from a vine-draped brown

fieldstone mansion. '*Nous sommes ici*,' the driver said, telling me
we were here.

'Why was it named for a boat?'

'On the other side, the hill climbs very steep. There the building
stands three levels tall. Mostly wood. Poorly constructed. It looked
to the artists like the old laundry barges tied up along the Seine.'

'Maybe they took in washing.' I reached for my billfold.

The driver waved me off. 'No charge,' he said with a grin. 'Two
veterans of Oran.'

I stepped out with a comrade's wave, watching him drive off.
Once again, I'd profited from a lie. A detective made his living
pretending to be someone else, disguises, fake IDs, verbal dexterity.
All a hoax. I stared down the street. Picasso's career began in a
slum laundry boat shit-house. Maybe old Pablo sold his own soul
to the Devil. What did it matter if Satan gave Picasso fifty years
of fame and fortune while dealing Johnny Favorite a deuce from
the bottom of the deck? You pay your money and you take your
chance.

I opened my coat, providing easy access to the .38 and rapped
on the door of number 20. The sound of shuffling footsteps inside
told me someone was home. After a count of ten, I knocked again,
louder this time like the cops. The door swung open a crack. A
wizened white-haired crone peered out at me. She might have
been Mother Goose with her long apron and warty nose.

'*Je cherche Monsieur Natas*,' I said.

'*Il n'est pas ici*,' the wizened biddy croaked.

I asked where I might find him, not sure if I got the words right.
The old woman who lived in a shoe looked me up and down. I got
the impression that my fancy Sulka outfit didn't score any points
with her. After an eternity, she rasped '*Monsieur Natas est au
cabaret de Lapin Agile*,' and shut the door in my face.

When she mentioned the cabaret, the crone's ancient watery
eyes had flicked to the right. I guessed it was somewhere in that
direction and wandered up the street into darkness trying to make

sense out of the name. I thought I heard the crone say the word for bread but *'pain'* was masculine and she said *'la pain,'* so I must have gotten it wrong. I walked up the narrow street, the cobblestones rippling before me in semicircular waves. I felt no longer in Paris but wandering in some mountainside country village.

I spotted a fellow walking a pug dog dressed in a little plaid coat. I asked for directions. *'Ah, oui,'* the man muttered, *'Lapin Agile.'* He pointed toward a white tower with an enlarged top thrusting into the night sky. *'L'ancien chau d'eau,'* he called it. The rue des Saules began there. It would take me to the cabaret.

The dog walker proved right on the money. Rue des Saules angled downhill past a two-story pink cottage with green shutters, a café called La Maison Rose. All along the next block, an iron fence enclosed a vineyard on my right. Bare gnarled grape vines wired-up in rows along an inclining grassy slope under the streetlights. Seemed impossible. Imagine an apple orchard in Manhattan. Crowning the top of the butte, bone-white in a blaze of spotlights, the Byzantine dome of the Sacré-Coeur basilica towered above the quaint neighborhood like a surreal dream.

Down the steep hill, I saw light spilling from another old pink cottage. A large tree grew out of the paving stones in front. At the intersection with rue Saint-Vincent, three large granite bollards bulged up out of the cobblestones, preventing motor vehicles from continuing farther down des Saules.

A painted sign above the cabaret's entrance gave me another language lesson. It depicted a cap-wearing rabbit balancing a bottle of wine on one paw as he jumped out of a sauce pan. *'Lapin,'* meant rabbit. The agile rabbit. *Très simple.* I stepped up past the weathered rustic fence out front and went inside.

The little dive was dark and shabby. Many framed paintings plastered the drab mud-colored walls like an avant-garde patchwork quilt. A shabby senior citizen noodled away on a battered upright piano. Long slab-like tables stood about the room surrounded by backless wooden stools. Aside from a couple solitary drunks, most were unoccupied. In the corner to my right, a noisy cluster of beatnik-types shouted and laughed, waving tumblers of red wine. They seemed my best bet.

'Natas...?' I said loudly. 'I'm looking for a man named Natas.'

The group fell silent and stared dubiously at me, put off either by my English or my upscale wardrobe. I looked as out-of-place in this arty pigsty as a banker in a barrelhouse. 'I am Viktor Natas!' announced a mangy bearded string bean wearing a black turtleneck sweater. He rose to his feet. His scruffy hair almost covered his ears. He might have been about thirty. Hard to tell under the beard. 'Are you a patron of the arts?'

'Are you an artist?' I asked.

'I am a genius. *Cette boîte est un temple du génie!*'

'A temple of genius?' I repeated to show I was hip to the lingo. Maybe my sarcasm got lost in translation.

'*D'accord!* Modigliani. Apollinaire. Picasso. Hemingway. Kipling. Toulouse-Lautrec. Utrillo. Henry Miller. All drank here. Each one a genius!' Natas sat, gesturing toward an unoccupied stool. 'Join us,' he said. '*Monsieur...?*'

'Favorite.' I sat down, placing my satchel on the floor beside me. This bird was the wrong gee and I probably should have split. Not planning on staying long, I didn't take off my hat and coat.

'*Paulo,*' Natas called out. '*Un verre pour notre ami Favori.*' He sat beside me. 'You made the right choice to come here. Look around you. The Twentieth Century was born in this very room.' I let that one pass. This cat was so full of himself there was no space in the conversation for anyone else. 'You see that painting?' He pointed to a large canvas of an unhappy man wearing fool's motley having a drink beside a pale woman who ignores him. 'It is a reproduction. Picasso painted the original fifty years ago. That is the maestro himself dressed as Harlequin. The bitch next to him was his mistress. It depicts the Lapin Agile. Picasso once settled his bar tab with this painting.'

A lean gent in his late fifties set an empty tumbler in front of me. '*Merci, Paulo,*' Natas said without taking his focus off me. He filled my glass with red wine. 'That jackass in the background playing the guitar,' he pointed at the Picasso, 'is Frédé Gérard, Paulo's father. He sold the painting for 10,000 francs! Twenty fucking dollars. Today, it is worth millions!'

'Not bad for a round of drinks,' I said.

Viktor Natas rose again grandly to his feet. 'I, too, have settled accounts here with my art.' He gestured toward a small work on the wall behind us. It was black and white. A pattern of diamond shapes, triangles and squares that seemed to move if you stared at it long enough.

'Interesting,' I lied.

' Would you care to come to my studio and see my latest work?'

'No, thanks. Don't much care for art.'

'What? Why come here then?'

'Looking for a man named Natas.'

'I am Natas!'

'You're the wrong Natas.'

'*Impossible!* I am the most right Natas. I am the now and forever Natas!'

I reached down for my satchel, pulled out the photo of Louis Cyphre in his stage tails and showed it to this skinny bearded bag of hot air. '*Ici est le même Natas qui je cherche,*' I said, giving him the benefit of my imperfect French.

'*Lui?*' Natas stared at the photo. 'What is he?'

'A magician.' I tugged out a photo print of the el Çifr poster. 'Sometimes he dresses up like this.'

The painter examined both pictures with a critical eye. 'He is a Natas?'

'So I've been told. He also goes by other names.'

'A stage performer?'

I nodded. 'Occasionally. In New York, he played at a flea circus just off Times Square.'

Natas clapped his hands. '*Eh bien!* I know just the place to look.

Le Cirque Medrano. What will you give me if I take you there?'

This pompous clown thought I couldn't find a circus in Paris? 'I'll buy you dinner,' I said, draining my wine. 'You pick the restaurant.' What the hell? The jerk might come in handy.

11

I stared out at a blurred rush of neon advertising until the taxi pulled up in front of a multi-sided structure with a tent-shaped roof on Boulevard Rochechouart. Tall letters vertically spelled MEDRANO along the side of a neoclassical portico sporting four Corinthian half-columns. All the lights were out. No show tonight, Natas told me. Painted canvas banners and a huge streetside billboard advertised FERNAND RAYNAUD, the headliner. Some sort of comedian.

'At same location one hundred years,' Natas boasted. 'Inspiration always to great artists. Degas, Renoir, Seurat, Léger, Lautrec, van Dongen, Picasso; all painted *le Cirque Medrano*.'

Natas led me down rue des Martyrs to the stage door by an open space where I guessed they corralled horses and other circus animals. The hefty party on duty greeted him like a long-lost brother, gathering the scruffy artist into an enormous bear hug. They jabbered at each other in a frog-frenzy too rapid for me to understand. Natas grinned with idiotic enthusiasm. The linebacker doorman retreated into the shadows, gesturing for us to stay put.

'I work here time to time,' Natas said. 'You know. Behind the scenes. Roustabout.' The corridor walls were lined with posters and photographs of famed circus performers. I walked along looking at the portraits of clowns, acrobats and equestrians. Even recognized a couple. Deadpan Buster Keaton in the center of the single ring. Maurice Chevalier tipping his top hat with a wink and a smile. Josephine Baker preening in full plumage. At the end of the row, colored art prints flowered, bright blossoms among the monochrome display. I stared at the image of a female aerialist dangling from her teeth high under the girder-grid of the circus roof.

'*Miss La-La*,' Natas said behind me. 'Degas. Beside her is a Picasso: *Les Saltimbanques*. Rose Period.' The artist tapped the glass covering another print. 'The great Medrano masterpiece. Georges Seurat. Unfinished when he died. Thirty-one years of age. The original hangs in the Jeu de Paume.'

A long-faced man with a receding hairline and pencil-thin mustache came down the hall. Viktor Natas greeted him as '*Monsieur Medrano*.' He wore a conservative gray suit instead of the garish plaid I expected of a circus impresario. '*Bon soir, mon vieux!*' Medrano placed an avuncular hand on the skinny painter's shoulder. Natas so overwhelmed he blew his stammered attempt at an introduction.

'Jérome Medrano,' the elegant man said, extending his hand.

'Favorite,' I replied with a firm shake. 'Johnny Favorite.'

'That name is familiar to me. Are you by chance an entertainer?'

'Used to be. Once upon a time back before the war. I was a crooner with a swing band.'

'*Bien sûr.* Spider Simpson.' The circus boss smiled. 'You were very good. Promising. What happened to you?'

'Real life. Got injured pretty bad. Woke up in a hospital back in the States and the dream was over.'

'*Quel dommage!* I assume you are not asking to sing?'

'No way in hell.' I unzipped my satchel. 'Wanted to find out if you knew this guy.' I showed him the photo of Cyphre.

'Ah…' Medrano's eyes lit up. 'Fra Diavolo. *Il est le mieux.*'

'He's performed here?'

'Not often enough. A true master of illusion.'

'You call him Diavolo.'

'*Certainement.* Fra Diavolo. The name of his act.'

'And his real name? Is it Natas? Or Louis Cyphre?'

A thin smile sliced across Medrano's features. 'Why should you care about his name, Mr Favorite?'

'I… I was thinking of maybe trying for a comeback. Putting together a big variety show. Singers, dancers, all kinds of talent. Saw him… Fra Diavolo perform once and want him on the bill.'

The smile widened into a silent laugh. 'I can't promise you success with that ambition. The last time Diavolo worked here was more than two years ago. His offstage name is Nicola Dumas.'

'Where do I get in touch with him?'

'I have no way of knowing. My only address for Dumas is in care of his bank.' Medrano opened his cigarette case and offered us a smoke. We both declined and he tapped one down and lit up, exhaling through his nose.

Something felt wrong here. 'How do you book his act if you don't know how to find him?' I left any hint of threat out of my voice.

'You must understand. Fra Diavolo is unique, one among millions. I would wait ten years to sign him again. And that's all I can do. Wait. One day, he will call out of blue air. Ask to perform. One night only. Maybe I get two days notice. Three at most. I always say yes. Even open the circus for an extra day or two. What choice have I? No other act can compare.'

I feigned a show of confusion, as I suppressed my elation. I'd found Cyphre. Medrano knew him. He performed at this family-owned circus. All I had to do was wait him out. 'You haven't heard from this guy Dumas, Diavolo, Cyphre, whatever he calls himself, in over two years and still as far as you know he might call tomorrow asking for an opportunity to perform?'

'*Certainement.* I lose no sleep waiting for him to call. I know he will. He's performed at the Medrano since my father's time.'

'What?'

'Fra Diavolo's first appearance here was in 1896. I know this sounds impossible. I suspect it's not the same man. Perhaps his son. Carrying on the family tradition just like the Fratellinis. I don't care. Fra Diavolo's performance never falls short of amazing.'

I took a moment to digest what he said. 'Will you do me a favor?' I asked with all the faked sincerity I could muster. 'If you hear from Fra Diavolo. Whenever you next hear from him. I'd be very grateful if you'd let me know.'

'Of course, *Monsieur* Favorite. Much as I might wish it, Cirque Medrano has no exclusive contract with this most amazing magician.'

I coughed out a polite fake laugh. 'I know it's a long shot. Isn't that the secret heart of show business? I'm staying at the Hotel Vendôme. At the very least, I'd like to catch his act one more time.'

Medrano stubbed out his cigarette in a sand-filled fire bucket. 'If I hear from him you will hear from me. I should be delighted to have you attend as my guest on any occasion.' He pulled a card from a small leather folder and handed it to me. 'Call me at this number should you change your residence. It is my private line.'

'Many thanks.' I slipped Medrano's card into my billfold. 'I know it's a bit of a wild goose chase.'

The circus impresario smiled. 'One must chase the goose to cook the goose,' he said.

I handed Medrano the photograph of Dr Cipher. 'A gift. Add it to your rogues' gallery?'

'Rogues' gallery? *Je ne comprends pas.*'

'Hang it on the wall with all the others. Maybe it'll bring him back like some lucky charm.'

'*Bien sûr.*'

Before I left, I asked the impresario if he knew of any Paris nightclubs where magicians performed. Medrano gave me three names. One of the clubs, Sphinx on rue Pigalle, was also on Warren Wagner's list.

'*Merci bien,*' I called after his retreating shadow. Once darkness swallowed Medrano, I retraced my steps along the corridor, studying the portraits of those who had performed at the circus, wondering if somehow Cyphre might have left his mug shot behind.

'So this magician you seek is not a Natas,' the bearded painter said, hovering by my side.

'Not this time around,' I said, checking out the long rogues' gallery of circus folk. Not a single photo of Dr Cipher or Fra Diavolo among them.

Outside, the night air tasted crisp and cold. Viktor Natas led me to his restaurant of choice, Aux Merveilles des Mers, a posh fish joint. He ordered bouillabaisse, a house specialty, asking for it with lobster, which doubled the price. The painter was all smiles. I asked for a dozen oysters, *Claires spéciales,* on the half shell along with a bottle of Pouilly Fumé to share with the young painter.

Natas had earned his pricey meal. He led me to Medrano's circus where Cyphre performed and might reappear at any time. Knowing it could happen tomorrow gave me hope. I had eight more Natas addresses on my list from the phone book. My quarry might be any one of them. Everything began making sense. These flea circus magic turns were no one-time thing for Cyphre. He got off on it. Probably performing in some Cairo or Bangkok dive at this very moment. Didn't he strut his stuff as el Çifre up in Harlem? My bet was the Medrano wasn't the only Paris venue where he worked his hocus-pocus. I'd start with the nightspots featuring magicians that Medrano had mentioned. Wouldn't take much to run them all down. Legwork was my business.

Natas tried cajoling me into coming to his studio. I slipped him ƒ500 for cab fare and said I wanted to call it a night. I knew he'd walk home and spend the dough on booze. That was OK by me. Pleasure trumps convenience every time.

12

Having crashed my first Black Mass a week ago, I knew what to expect on Sunday night. Nonetheless, after futilely looking for Louis Cyphre at three of the Natas addresses nearby in the 1st arrondissement, I spent a good part of Saturday reviewing everything I'd seen in the abandoned New York City subway station over and over in my mind to refresh my memory. It had to look like I was in the know. Over and over I practiced saying the Latin Lord's Prayer backwards. I had only sixty words to memorize. Didn't need a Harvard degree for that. The tricky part was pronunciation. My new dictionary used the sounds of French to illustrate Latin phonetics. I needed the pronunciation guide in the French/English book I'd bought in Hartford to sort things out. Each word took twice the time. As a shortcut, I wrote the backwards prayer out phonetically, one word at a time. Sipping wine made a boring task less of a chore.

Out of the wild blue yonder something clicked. Johnny Favorite knew the lyrics to hundreds of songs, not just the words but the tunes and specific arrangements. They were all still inside my head. I remembered scat singing at after-hours jam sessions. Hearing a little jump tune in my noggin, I started scatting the prayer, turning the nonsense syllables into rhythm and melody. Worked like a charm.

Once I'd been a headliner. Still had the juice to stand front and center in the spotlight. Remembering my time as a crooner might bring back all knowledge of the dark arts. People said I'd been a master magician. If I remembered Cole Porter and Lorenz Hart lyrics, why not every invocation and satanic spell I'd ever learned? They still lived as part of me, lurking deep inside. Buoyed by song, every last forgotten fragment of my past might rise to the surface like some gas-bloated corpse from the dark depths of oblivion.

At quarter to nine on Sunday night I took a taxi to Baron Samedi. Bijou stood outside her club, wearing dark slacks and a chic tailored peacoat. A round black leather hatbox sat beside her fashionably shod feet. I told the driver to pull over and she climbed in, kissing my cheeks with extravagant Gallic enthusiasm.

Bijou barked a new address at the cabby in rapid-fire frog-babble. He grunted a monosyllabic reply and we sped off into the unknown dark. '*Puis*... 'ave you been a good boy?' she asked.

'Keeping busy,' I said.

'*Menteur.*' She called me a liar. 'I do not believe you.'

'Satan loves a lazy man.'

'You must certainly be his darling.'

'I hope so.'

The cab crossed the river at some point. After that, it was all unfamiliar territory to me. Bijou took my hand and twined her fingers between mine. We didn't speak again until the taxi dropped us off in a part of town I'd never seen before.

'*Allez.*' Bijou led me across an unknown street toward a cylindrical metal structure on the opposite sidewalk. Painted green and crowned by an ornate antique cupola, it boasted cast-iron Ionic columns on either side of an open entrance. 'What's this?' I asked.

'*Vespasienne.*'

'Some kind of toilet?

'*Vraiment. Un pissoir.*'

I followed Bijou inside. The place reeked of urine. A bare bulb high in the hollow dome overhead cast a pale light over the sordid space. Dried vomit caked a wall above the urinal trough like fungus. 'Nice,' I said. 'Isn't this for gents only?'

'Not tonight.' Bijou bent down, taking an old-fashioned key from her pocket. She turned it in an antique padlock secured to a hasp on a sidewalk grate.

'Where are we?'

'You don't need to know.' She slipped the padlock into her pocket. 'This is my portal. Mine alone. The others have their own way in. *'Votre assistance, s'il vous plaît.'* We bent together and I helped her swing the heavy hinged iron grate upright. Inside the opening, a metal ladder mounted to the masonry wall dropped deep into the pitch black. 'Best to put on your Wellingtons now,' Bijou said.

After we'd pulled on the rubber boots and packed our street shoes, Bijou produced a small flashlight. *'Allumez votre torche,'* she commanded, switching hers on and starting down into darkness. I followed, my own pocket light moving from rung to rung. The sounds of running water purled from the subterranean depths. Just as my head dropped below street level, she called out, *'Fermez la grille!'* There was no please this time. I reached up and pulled the grate back into place behind me.

It was slow going. I slung the Ghurka bag over my shoulder by its strap. Holding even a small flashlight in one hand made gripping the rungs difficult. I wondered how Bijou managed with the clumsy hatbox and saw she'd turned off her light. I did the same, slipping the little torch back into my pocket. The ladder led down for at least fifty feet along a shaft opening onto the side wall of an arching tunnel large enough to accommodate a freight train.

The final rung jutted a yard or so above the bottom, making for an awkward drop to the muddy floor. Bijou switched her flashlight back on to make it easier for me. A stream of water flowed along a channel running straight down the center of the tunnel. I accompanied Bijou on the right-hand walkway, our flashlight beams probing the shadows. We didn't talk. The walls glistened with moisture. An odor of damp decay and mold hung heavy in the cloistered air.

A hundred yards farther along, Bijou flashed her light at a constricted side passage. 'This way,' she said. Impossible walking two abreast in here. I stayed a couple paces behind her until we came to a broad set of steps carved from the natural rock. She paused at the top, waving her light beam around the large chamber before us. 'These are ancient quarries,' Bijou remarked. 'Some date back to when Paris was a Roman city. Others to the time of Clovis.'

'Didn't the Resistance hide out down here?'

'The Boche as well. They built bunkers beneath the city. *La Résistance* had their secret command posts elsewhere underground. The caverns are vast. No one knows how big.' Bijou descended the steps. I walked one step back like a royal consort to the Queen of Hell. We crossed the empty quarried hall. The sound of falling water echoed in the distance. Another brief passage at the chamber's far end brought us to more stairs chiseled into the stone. They looked desperately narrow, less than two feet across with treads maybe eight inches wide. A long plume of water plunged beside them into blackness. There was no guardrail. Bijou started down without hesitation, moving with an easy grace.

She knows the way, I thought, trying not to fall by pressing my left hand against the moist rock wall for balance. I held the torch in my right to light the way. The steps were wet and slick, an invitation to disaster. Bijou waited for me at the bottom. My light revealed her amused smile. '*Trop difficile?*' she teased as I slipped on the last step and caught her arm.

'I'm OK,' I said, trailing after her as she rounded another corner. Bijou waited until I caught up, her flashlight stabbing into a grotesque corridor, the shadowy walls a long mosaic of ancient bones. '*Les Catacombes*,' she said. 'Above our heads is the Montparnasse Cemetery but many more bodies are housed down here.'

We walked along the decorative ossuary, bones stacked in

geometric patterns, the joints of femurs thrusting forth like the scrolled ends of violins, hollow-eyed skulls inserted in contrasting designs, forming crosses, stars, diamonds. 'Plague victims?' I asked.

'*Quelques, peut-être.* In the decades before *la Révolution* the city expanded. Many graveyards and too many bodies on the outskirts of the old city. They popped out of the ground like mushrooms. *Atroce!* What could the city fathers do? They dug up *tous les cadavres* and carried them down into the old quarries. Millions of bodies. There are more dead sleeping beneath the streets of Paris than live ones above. *Quelle grande bouffe!*'

I dug it. My kind of joke. Bijou and I walked along this gallery of death without further comment. The grinning skulls remained eloquent in their silence, providing a stark rebuke to the living. Remember us, the bleached bones mutely proclaimed. Our end awaits you. Soon you will join us underground.

This tunnel did not follow a straight path but zigged and zagged as if engineered by a psychotic. All along the way, other openings led to new corridors. It occurred to me that without Bijou I'd become hopelessly and forever lost in the underworld, a rat trapped in a never-ending maze. And then, just when I thought the morbid journey might last forever, the corridor abruptly dropped deeper underground, carved steps angling from landing to landing into the mysterious depths. From far below came an eerie shrieking noise and I knew we had at last reached our destination.

The stairs led to another round chamber. Along with many pairs of rubber boots, numerous briefcases, small duffel bags and rucksacks lay scattered about the floor. 'Here is where we disrobe,' Bijou said. She turned her back on me, tugging off her Wellingtons before unbuttoning her jacket.

I got busy undressing and stashed my wallet in the toe of my right rubber boot. The chill damp air encouraged a speedy change. I draped the red cape over my shoulders, stuffing my rolled-up clothing into the Ghurka bag. Krusemark's dirk hung from the leather belt I buckled about my naked waist. I clipped the .38 to it at the small of my back, angled for a right-hand draw. The weighted sap dangled from my left wrist on its braided thong. No telling what might go down at a Black Mass. I once ate a man's still-beating heart and didn't want to take any chances in a howling pack of fellow Devil-worshipers.

Adjusting my wolf mask and pulling the red cape's hood up over the top of my head, I turned to find Bijou watching me. She wore a leopard-spotted cape and cheetah mask. Like mine, her cape completely cloaked her body. What little I saw struck a nerve. The cat mask and cloak transformed Bijou completely. She had become both menacing and anonymous, a dangerous combination. I hoped my lupine outfit conveyed the same mysterious dread. Without saying a word, Bijou turned away and I followed her out of the dressing chamber.

We walked the length of a short tunnel ending on a jagged stone ledge jutting out over a cavernous chamber the size of a basketball court. Several wall torches below cast a wavering light over the gathered congregation, about three times the size of the crowd at the Black Mass in New York. Why not? It was Easter Sunday, the holiest day in the church's calendar. People wore masks and swirling capes. Some wore black, somber crows amid a field of flowers. Every hue of the rainbow was on display, along with tiger stripes, snake-skin prints and the vivid parti-color of parrots. A menagerie of masks celebrated the savage spectrum of the animal kingdom, lions, bears, crocs, hawks, sharks, all snorting and screeching as they mingled in the flickering firelight. Their primitive animal noises complementing the high-pitched shrieking that occasionally rent the air. I realized now it wasn't a baby's wailing or a human scream. '*Qu'est-ce que c'est?*' I asked Bijou.

'*Un sacrifice plus fort pour la Pâques – un coq negre.*'

A more powerful sacrifice for Easter, a black rooster, she told me as she started down a circular iron staircase bolted to the quarried stone face at the far end of the ledge. Fine by me that I wouldn't have to watch the slaughter of another innocent infant, as I had in New York. Following Bijou, I caught a sideways glimpse of the large inverted cross mounted with spikes to the chamber's far wall. All around, Gnostic symbols adorned the rough rock surface in a frenzy of red paint. The upside-down cross hung above a massive rectangular altar carved directly from the stone. Probably intended as a cathedral building block but left unfinished in the quarry for reasons lost in time. A black cloth covered the altar and dozens of squat black candles flickered on the ground along its perimeter. I'd learned a week ago they were made from human fat. I didn't see the rooster. The star of the show no doubt was waiting offstage to make his dramatic entrance. A closer look at the altar revealed two husky figures wearing black robes and black ski masks. The menacing duo stood in the dark shadows behind the altar.

Stepping off the spiral stairs, I watched Bijou move away into the crowd of masqueraders. She had no interest in being seen as my companion tonight. I didn't give a damn. I wasn't here to be her fucking date. My purpose was to observe and to see what I could find out about Cyphre. He might be here. As I wandered anonymously through the grunting, shuffling pack of naked strangers, I felt a soaring exhilaration as if I'd found my way home. I spotted two worshipers, one wearing a hawk mask, the other decked out as a lion, whose body types matched Louis Cyphre's. As I headed toward the hawk to rip off his mask, the garish crowd around me seemed to become something other than human. The wild joy of complete freedom took hold of me. Power surged through my body, strong and savage as the wolf I portrayed. All those around me made guttural animal noises summoning the beasts within them. Exultant, I threw back my head and howled.

The discordant screech of an out-of-tune pipe organ cut through the zoo noises. A mangled melody echoed in the cavern. Badly played Bach or Handel or some other Baroque cat turning over in his grave. I figured it had to be a recording. Several masked parishioners shrieked in ecstasy and then everyone began chanting in Latin, each worshiper dancing in place to a private beat. Everyone had their own individual chant. This was fine by me. No one would notice if my backward prayer sounded different from all the others. 'Amen,' I chanted, 'malo a nos libera sed.' The rote words flowed out of me and I let pure rhythm carry me along, falling into a dervish trance state. 'Tentationem in inducas nos ne et.' Hypnotic as talking in tongues.

Through the curtain of whirling capes, I spotted the priest naked beneath his purple chasuble, a scrawny old bald party wearing thick glasses with one of those short gray beards that look like a crew cut turned upside-down. His hands were pressed together in prayer. He was followed by a naked acolyte carrying a huge screeching black rooster by its feet. With the bird flapping its wings and pecking furiously, the expressionless boy held it at arm's length. Another naked acolyte trailed him, his swinging censer emitting clouds of sweet-smelling opium smoke. The tail end of the procession included another bare-ass pair of pretty boys flanking a naked adolescent girl shuffling like a sleepwalker. She was a little brunette with tiny tits and an addict's lidded eyes.

'Nobis dimitte et, hodie nobis da quotidianum nostrum,' I chanted as I watched them settle the little broad on the altar, placing a flaming black candle in each of her outstretched hands. All around me the depraved momentum grew. I was part of it, chanting louder and louder. 'Tua voluntas fiat. Tuum regnum adveniat.' The acolyte handed the frantic black rooster to the priest who accepted it and reached for the sacrificial dagger.

I pushed through the crowd, howling my prayer like a demented wolf. Seizing the rooster by one leg, I yanked it from the priest's grasp. With my other hand, I drew Krusemark's dirk from the tooled leather sheath. Turning to face the masked congregation, I cut off the cock's head with a single slice and silenced its awful screeching. Blood pumped from the neck in rhythmic spurts, spraying across my naked chest. '*Caelis in es qui, noster pater,*' I screamed, hurling the dying animal at the priest.

He caught the gory bundle awkwardly, his astonished expression revealing a fear of the unexpected. Blood splashed across his bare hairless chest. 'Tell our Lord Satan I'm back,' I screamed. 'Tell Him Johnny Favorite is back!'

13

Adrenalin electrified my senses. I saw everything fresh and clean with an exaggerated clarity known only to madmen and fanatics. It felt like being reborn. I wiped the blood from the dirk's blade with my cloak and thrust the dagger into its sheath. Someone grabbed my arms from behind. Trembling with violent sexual energy, I shook loose of his grip and grabbed my sap as I turned, beating the big guy in black over the head. He staggered away, clutching his head. The other sentinel came at me. Power vibrated through my body, enhanced by the roaring adoration of the assembled devotees. The priest and the naked boys scuttled away from the altar as the husky black-robed figure and I danced, sizing each other up. He took a swing at my face, but I dodged it, straightening up quickly enough to land a swift kick to his groin. He fell back and the crowd howled wildly. I had done something unexpected. Awed by my bold action, they would follow me anywhere.

Howling like a feral pack, masked men and women flung open their robes and coupled where they stood. The orgy had begun. The usurped priest looked on in disbelief. I'd upset the order of things. Even Devil-worshipers followed a protocol. Their formal ritual had been disrupted, the liturgy discarded. What had been intended as controlled chaos dissolved into insane mania. I threw back my cloak and strode toward the altar where the somnolent virgin lay. The priest, still clutching the dead rooster, stepped forward, staring in awe at the bejeweled golden devil ornament hanging around my neck.

My erection throbbed with the pulsing of my heart. I didn't give a shit about symbolic sacrifice. I desired something more than what this virgin had to offer. Looking across the copulating crowd, I saw just what I wanted. She was cloaked like a leopard and wore a cheetah's mask. A stocky man disguised as a bull advanced upon her.

I pushed past couples tangled together in a frenzy of flapping capes. The burly bovine bastard reached his hairy mitts out toward Bijou as I came up behind him. I swung the weighted leather sap full force with my left hand and caught him square in the back of his hooded head. He dropped like a sandbag opening the trap on a gallows. One horn broke off his papier-mâché mask when he hit the ground.

Bijou's wide white eyes gleamed through the openings in her mask. I spread open her cloak as if parting a curtain. Sumptuous body gleaming with torchlight. Ebony breasts round and ripe. I got it right. Her faint tattoo depicted Baron Samedi, a grinning top hat-clad skull.

Reaching between her smooth thighs, I cupped my hand over her midnight pelt. Moisture flowed into my palm. I pushed my mask up above my mouth and licked the nectar from my fingers. Bijou gripped my rigid cock, pulling me closer. I grabbed her butt with both hands and hoisted her up against the rough wall. She wrapped her legs around my waist as I entered her. A cry caught in the back of Bijou's throat. She moaned. A dove-like croon grew louder with each driving thrust. Bijou yanked off her mask and kissed me. Full, deep, probing. I came and came and came.

Panting, I eased her down beside me. The lingering kiss continued, our damp bodies pressed together beneath our cloaks. Bijou broke away. 'We must go,' she said. '*Maintenant!*' Glancing over my shoulder, beyond the orgiastic shadow dancers behind me, I saw one of the big men in black pulling out of the virgin. The other was moving through the crowd toward me.

'*Vite!*' Bijou commanded, tugging me by my hand. I let her lead me away from the bacchanal and we hurried up the spiral staircase, our bare feet making no sound on the metal treads.

We dressed quickly in the circular room. Inspired by Bijou's urgency, I wasted no time and was packed and ready to go even as she bent to pull on her Wellingtons. Before anyone else joined us, we hurried up the steps carved into the wall, flashlights and satchels in hand. Back in the safety of the tunnels, I tried drawing Bijou into an embrace but she pulled away. 'Not now,' she hissed, looking anxiously back the way we had come. 'You are a dangerous man. *Un fou!*'

I lost track of our labyrinthine route until we were about to leave the bone tunnel. Some primal impulse made me tug a skull free from the wall. '*Qu'est-ce que tu fais?*' Bijou demanded, angry as a fifth-grade teacher.

'Used to travel with one of these when I sang for Spider's band,' I said. 'A little souvenir of a night worth remembering.' Grinning at Bijou, I slipped the skull into my Ghurka bag.

'*Comme un voleur dans le nuit,*' she said.

'*D'accord!*'

I got the silent treatment from her until we were back at street level. Not a word of thanks when I helped her up onto the ladder for the final climb. Bijou snapped the padlock shut on the pissoir grate and took my hand as we stepped out of the foul-smelling toilet. 'I hope your blasphemy will not cost you favor with the Son of the Morning,' she said. 'Your athame will not be of any help to you then.'

'What's an athame?'

'You do not know this? What sort of warlock does not know the name for his sacrificial dagger?

'Maybe one who's lost his way.'

Bijou regarded me closely. There was fear in her eyes. 'You are at great risk.'

'Haven't got time to play it safe.'

'You may not have any time at all.' She ran away into the darkness so she didn't hear me say, 'I'll take my chances. Lord Satan loves a gambler.'

14

When I got out of bed the next morning, I spotted an envelope lying on the rug just inside the door. I picked it up. The flap wasn't sealed. I pulled out an invoice on heavy Vendôme stationery. The tab for five nights came to f126,300, including all room service and a twenty percent service charge. At this rate, it would cost me a grand a month to keep on living this high. I knew what I had to do. But first I luxuriated under the steaming spray of the shower. I had no illusions about cleansing myself of last night's evil. Blood washed off. The residue of black magic remained indelible on your soul.

After calling Christian D'Auburan, the estate agent I'd met on the flight to Paris, and making an appointment for him to show me some rental properties that morning, I went down to the lobby to settle my bill.

Sipping an espresso while I waited for D'Auburan, I thought about how I'd just blown over two grand in five days. Acting like a stickup artist on the lam was not the way to go. Suckers like Dillinger and Baby Face Nelson made a big score and headed straight for the track to lose a bundle. They knew their days were numbered. Living on borrowed time makes a man reckless. I intended to track down Cyphre fast before his trail got cold, but no matter how long it took to find him I wasn't going to quit.

'Mr Favorite…' Christian D'Auburan's velvet voice interrupted my thoughts.

'Make it Johnny,' I said, getting to my feet and extending a hand.

'Chris,' he replied as we shook. He looked hard at me. 'You look different.'

'*Une nouvelle coupe.*' I'd prepared for this one, learning how to say new haircut in French.

'*Très chic,*' he said. 'My car is just outside.'

D'Auburan owned a nice ride, a sleek black Citroen sedan with a sloping shark-snout hood that looked ready to break the sound barrier. We slid out of Place Vendôme and into the traffic along rue de Rivoli with Chris keeping up a flow of casual banter just like we'd been best pals forever.

Over the course of the morning, we looked at four or five apartments, flats as D'Auburan called them. They all shared the same basic flaw. A concierge. Squinty-eyed harridans in ill-fitting house dresses. They came in different sizes and shapes but were all snooping busybodies. They bore no resemblance to the helpful fellow at the Vendôme who knew how to find a dentist and wrote detailed lists of good restaurants. The main thing I required was the ability to come and go without observation. I needed to keep my business private. Easy explaining this to Chris over an excellent lunch at Fouquet's on the Champs-Élysées.

'*Bien sûr.* I know a little place. Might be perfect for you,' D'Auburan said. 'Except it is over on the Left Bank in the 7th.'

'What difference does that make?'

'I don't know. The neighborhood is a little bit, how do you call it? *Bohème.*'

'*Tant mieux,*' I said showing off my limited French. 'So much the better.' Not a hundred percent sure, I echoed the phrase in English to prove I knew what I was talking about. 'Remember that magician I asked about on the flight over?'

'In a way.'

I pulled the two photographs from my satchel and handed them to him. 'Why don't you keep these? I made copies. You meet a lot of people in your game. Maybe one of them has seen him lately.'

'Perhaps.' D'Auburan studied the photo of the el Çifr poster. 'Have you been to those nightclubs I suggested?'

'I'm working on it. Checked out the Cirque Medrano the other day. Dr Cipher performed there calling himself Fra Diavolo.'

'Really? My children love that place.'

'Keep them away from this character. He's bad news.'

Driving to the other side of town, D'Auburan cheerfully described the sites along the way. We crossed the Seine by way of an island he said was called the Île de la Cité, pointing out Notre-Dame cathedral as we sped onto a second bridge span. No-ter dame, I thought. We turned right toward a street running along the river. Chris waved at a tree-lined boulevard across the wide plaza he identified as the Place Saint-Michel. '*Boul' Mich*,' he called out cheerfully. 'Center of the Latin Quarter.'

I'd been on this riverside street once before on the drive in from the airport. Everything had looked so different and unfamiliar a week ago. This time around, I ignored the distant Eiffel Tower in favor of a row of booksellers operating out of little wooden shacks very much like New York City newsstands. Things didn't look all that different over here on the Left Bank. Having worked many runaway cases in Greenwich Village, I'd had my fill of bohemian riffraff. None of that on display in this picture postcard setting.

Several blocks later, I saw the Tuileries Garden across the river and D'Auburan hung a sharply angled left. 'Boulevard Saint-Germain,' he told me. We continued with the flow of one-way traffic, passing an intersection with Boulevard Raspail. A bit farther along the car slowed alongside a uniform row of gray 19th-century buildings. D'Auburan turned right through an arched fin de siècle carriageway entrance into a cobbled inner courtyard, pulling up in front of a two-story cottage encased in blue Delft tiles. '*Voilà!*' The little house looked like something out of a fairy tale. It sat off in the far left corner of the courtyard.

'A farmhouse built during the reign of Louis XVI,' Chris said as we climbed out of his Buck Rogers car. 'All mortise and tenon. Wooden pegs. Not a nail in the place. The tiles were added sometime before the Revolution. In the middle of the last century, the city expanded and swallowed it up. A butterfly trapped in amber.' I wondered if D'Auburan used this butterfly line on all his potential clients. 'A special place,' he went on, dropping the poetry in favor of an old-fashioned sales pitch. 'Not for everyone. Perfect for the connoisseur who can appreciate such a gem.'

I thought he was spreading it on pretty thick. 'No concierge?' I asked as we walked to the wide front door with ancient wrought-iron strap hinges.

'None. You will be on your own.' D'Auburan reached above his head to the lintel and pulled on a carved rosette above the right side jamb. It came away to reveal a hollow space from which he extracted an old-fashioned iron key three times the size of anything still in ordinary use. It was the sort of key that secured medieval dungeons. 'Our little secret,' he said with a wink, replacing the rosette.

D'Auburan showed me around inside. The ceilings downstairs were high with hand-hewn wooden beams. Uneven plaster walls painted white. Wide plank floorboards. The sparsely furnished main room had a huge fireplace, a long trestle table with six plain wooden chairs and a sagging velour sofa. The kitchen's tiny fridge and gas stove qualified as museum exhibits in the Betty Crocker Hall of Forgotten Appliances. On the plus side, everything worked and there was just enough bachelor stuff, knives, forks, plates and glasses to get by. My kind of set-up.

The bathroom was off the kitchen, so tiny it seemed the very definition of a water closet. An old-fashioned claw-foot bathtub took up most of the space. 'Not so posh as the Vendôme,' D'Auburan added, giving me one of his fake knowing winks.

There wasn't much more to see. The bedroom upstairs was really more of a garret, with sloping walls beneath the roof. I spotted a pile of folded threadbare sheets and a down-filled duvet on the brass bed.

The only other room in the place was the cellar, a small damp space with a dirt floor. 'Where's the furnace?' I asked.

'No furnace.'

'What about heat?'

The realtor led me back upstairs looking grim, explaining I'd have to use the gas boiler above the tub to heat water for bathing and a pre-war electric heater for the rooms. Probably figured he'd just lost a client. D'Auburan opened the armoire and took out the electric heater. 'This is it, I'm afraid,' he said with a wistful sigh. 'You must move it from room to room.'

'I'll take it,' I said.

'What?' D'Auburan looked puzzled.

'Not that piece of crap. I mean the house. How much is the rent?'

An expression somewhere between amazement and disbelief briefly contorted the suave businessman's face before he regained his everyday nonchalant savoir-faire and named his number.

'It's a deal,' I said. 'I'll pay you in cash.'

Another momentary jolt to D'Auburan's composure. The smile returned instantly. 'There is a telephone on the little desk under the stairs,' D'Auburan said. 'I will have the P-T-T connect it for you.'

'Don't bother. I'll handle it myself.' Fuck the phone. No way in hell I was having a listed number with my name and address printed in some public directory.

After I signed the lease and money changed hands D'Auburan offered to take me back to the hotel.

I told him I wanted to check out the neighborhood and would catch a cab later.

'As you wish. You will like this *quartier*,' he assured me. 'There is a little *café-tabac* right next door and an excellent *boulangerie* a couple blocks away. The Café de Flore is down the street in the other direction.' I said that sounded great. We shook hands and D'Auburan drove off.

I set off on a stroll around the quarter taking care to replace the cartoon-sized key behind the door-top rosette. The little café-tabac was two doors down on St Germain. Later I would talk to the proprietor about paying him to use his phone. When I passed the bakery D'Auburan had mentioned I did an about-face and went in. Why not stock up on provisions before I moved in?

Taking a different route on the way back to the little cottage, I saw 'LE JAZZ COOL!' printed in bold black letters on a poster affixed to an onion-domed advertising kiosk. 'Kenny Clarke – Zoot Sims, Le Club Saint-Germain-des-Prés, 13 rue Saint-Benôit. LIT 81-84. Mars 24 – 28. À partir de 21 h 30.' Boss news. Klook had a gig right in my new neighborhood. Made me feel right at home and gave me something to do tonight. Feeling enclosed in a cocoon of safety, I walked along the boulevard with a bulging sack in either hand. Just another anonymous Parisian heading home for lunch. My escape felt complete.

15

Moving out of the hotel was easier than pulling off my socks. In an hour my luggage was down in the lobby. I stopped on my way out to thank my favorite concierge, handing him ƒ5000 sealed in a hotel envelope. Why not make him a friend for life? Sometime in the near future, I might need his expertise once again. He wished me a safe journey, having no notion of the dangerous road I traveled. I tipped the bellman big after he loaded my bags into a waiting taxi.

Before heading over to the Left Bank, I had the cabbie stop at the costume shop where I returned the Red Death costume and the wolf mask. If the shop owner noticed any bloodstains, she made no mention of them. After a quick ride over the river, the cabbie delivered me and my luggage to my new home in the cobbled courtyard off Saint-Germain.

The house felt chill and damp inside. Getting out the map of Paris, I plotted my moves for the rest of the day, making a list of all the Métro stations closest to my destinations. Before leaving the Vendôme, I'd checked the Paris Directory for 'Nicola Dumas,' Fra Diavolo's offstage name according to Jérome Medrano, but the name wasn't listed. I still had more Natases to visit.

I set off on my rounds, descending into the Métro at the Odéon stop and, half an hour later, ascending at the Pont de Neuilly stop into unfamiliar territory. Someone named Dante Natas lived on Boulevard Richard Wallace. I worked out the shortest route and set off in that direction, wondering who this Wallace character might have been. Either a Yank or a Brit. Only some big shot got this kind of royal treatment from the froggies.

Turned out to be a long walk. The Bois de Boulogne ran along the left side across the street, a flat reach of lawn disappearing into the distance beneath even rows of trees. To my right elegant townhouses alternated with small balcony-fronted apartment buildings. A right-angle turn took me onto the street named for Dick Wallace. I came upon the Natas address a couple of houses down from the corner. It was an impressive white three-story residence with a gabled mansard roof and Palladian windows. A hedge fronted by an iron fence enclosed the property. I unlatched the ornate gate and let myself in. The front lawn's well-tended flowerbeds suggested the attentions of a professional gardener. I followed the flagstone pathway up to the front steps and rang the bell. After a long wait, I rang again, holding my thumb on the buzzer for the count of ten. This time, the door opened quickly. A skinny little woman in black with the sallow features of a dead nun glared up at me. How many of these hags must be guarding houses in Paris? I asked if Monsieur Natas was at home.

'Il n'est pas ici,' she spat at me, lips curling with scorn.

I asked when he might be back. Best as I could make out the biddy said she didn't know. Mr Natas was traveling and had not been at home in almost a year.

I dug the photo of Dr Cipher out of my satchel. 'Est-ce qu'il Dante Natas?' I demanded.

The crone shook her head. I didn't get all of it. The gist of what she said was that she had never laid eyes on Natas. She looked after the house only when he was away. He always sent a notice a day or two before his return and she and her staff cleared out. Natas had his own servants, none of whom she had ever met or seen. From the sounds of it, she worked for a ghost. I did my best with a final question. 'Combien de temps travaillez-vous pour Monsieur Natas?' I asked.

'*Vingt-trois ans,*' came her curt reply. '*Adieu, monsieur.*' She shut the door with the slow deliberate care of someone closing a coffin lid.

It was him. Cyphre. He lived here. I knew it without a doubt. Everything came together. The whacko name, the fancy pad with a staff that had never seen him in more than twenty years, the mysterious comings and goings. It all added up. My problem was what to do next. The park across the street offered perfect concealment but staking out the joint didn't make much sense. This cat hadn't been home in a year. How long would I need to hide in the woods spying on an empty house? A job like this meant snooping in shifts and there was only me on the payroll. I let myself out through the gate thinking about my next move.

Crossing to the other side of Boulevard Richard Wallace, I settled on a park bench and stared across at Louis Cyphre's palatial digs. My original plan for the day was checking out all five Natas addresses remaining on my list. I didn't expect to hit pay dirt on my first try. Slow down, I told myself. Maybe I wanted this thing so bad I was putting pieces into place that didn't belong together. Cyphre was a mysterious man. The cat who lived across the street was also a mystery man. Didn't mean they were the same guy.

Sitting on my ass wasn't going to solve anything. Good old-fashioned legwork provided my best option. I tramped all over the neighborhood for a couple hours, ringing doorbells and stopping in little shops. I showed everyone I encountered the Dr Cipher photo. Not one person recognized him. This told me everything and nothing all at once. Either Cyphre kept so deeply undercover that he never showed his face in public around his district or else Dante Natas wasn't the guy I was looking for.

I killed the rest of the afternoon running around Passy and Élysée, which I learned was what they called the 16th and the 8th arrondissements. Luck was on my side. Every doorbell I rang found somebody at home and I scratched three more Natases off my list of possibilities.

One more name remained on my list. Roland Natas lived in Nogent-sur-Marne, east of the city limits past Vincennes. It was a long haul and I decided to save the trip for another day. Two of the nightclubs on Warren Wagner's list, the Lido and Le Shako, were close by in the 8th. I hoofed it over to Place de la Concorde and took the Métro to the George V stop on the Champs-Élysées.

The Arc de Triomphe straddled the avenue like a squat colossus several blocks away. Dodging between eight lanes of passing traffic, I crossed over toward the Lido. I found the glass front door open. Inside, all was pure Copacabana. Unlit crystal chandeliers sparkled overhead in the shadows. Gilded mirrors created an illusion of spaciousness.

Halfway across the lobby, I got stopped short by an energetic little guy wearing a purple V-neck sweater and green corduroy pants. Taking me for a tourist, he unleashed a condescending barrage of English. 'I am ver' ver' sorry. You are too early. The club is not open at this hour.' I told him I wanted to talk to the manager, launching into my standard hokum about writing a story for *Life* magazine. He informed me with chilly disdain that an appointment was required.

'Look,' I said, pulling out the Dr Cipher photo. 'I'm interested in this character. He's a magician. His agent said he was once on the bill at the Lido.'

The pompous plum took a gander at the picture. 'I remember his act,' he said. 'Very skillful. Did he not call himself Doctor Zephyr?'

'Cipher.'

'Correct. He appeared on stage here perhaps three or four years ago. One night only. I remember because it was ver' ver' unusual.'

'No other performances here?'

'Not one. We try and book a return engagement. For an extended run. But no luck. He disappear like one of his trained mice.'

I said thanks and headed for the street. Was I missing something? A hidden pattern in these random one-night stands? Did Cyphre do this for kicks? Maybe his sporadic magical performances held an unknown key to his whereabouts. Crazy as it seemed, this off-chance theory was at least something to grab onto, a random chance worth taking. At least that's what I told myself as I headed around the corner toward Le Shako. Another fleshpot like the Lido but not as 'classy.' I was in and out of the place fast. When I showed the buxom blonde proprietor Cyphre's photos, she said she'd never seen him but knew his name. They'd booked him last July for the remodeled club's grand opening but he hadn't shown up. No notice. Nothing. She said it had caused quite a mess.

The time scheme she described made sense. Warren Wagner had booked Dr Cipher in for the opening of Le Shako last July. Natas hadn't been back in Paris in a year so he obviously cancelled. There was always a chance that Cyphre didn't live in the fancy digs out on Dick Wallace Boulevard but I doubted it.

Two of the clubs Jérome Medrano told me about were located in the Pigalle area. I figured I'd check them out and call it a day.

16

It was a short walk to the Place de l'Étoile where a buzz of traffic circled the Arc de Triomphe. Walking around toward the Étoile Métro station entrance, I caught a glimpse of the eternal flame flickering over the Tomb of the Unknown Soldier at the base of this triumphal gateway. Fire seemed the perfect memorial for a war victim. Destructive, fraught with danger, consuming everything it touches. I imagined Lucifer whispering in the architect's ear. 'Burn him… Burn him…'

It was rush hour. I crammed into the Line 2 train and got off at Blanche. The Moulin Rouge already glowed like a tropical sunset, never mind the show didn't start for two and a half hours. On narrow rue Pierre-Fontaine I found the Embassy. It looked pretty shabby. Showtime wasn't until quarter to eleven and the front entrance was covered by a rolling corrugated security door. The Embassy's locked red metal stage door stood on my right and I pounded on it, loud as a cop. After a bit, the door was yanked open and I was facing a burly bruiser in a rumpled black suit sporting a five o'clock shadow you could strike a match on. He looked mad as hell. I stepped back out of arm's reach as he barked a furious spew of guttural frogamania.

Once he simmered down, I explained my search for the mysterious magician, showing him the photograph. By some miracle he understood my rudimentary French. The gee was thug through and through, most likely a mobster, but he acted polite as a parish priest once he pegged me as legit. He owned the joint and personally hired all the talent, mostly girls and crooners. Over the years, he'd booked a number of magic acts but had no recollections of ever seeing Dr Cipher. I thanked him for his trouble and he shook my hand without breaking any bones.

Angling down Fontaine, I cut over to rue Pigalle. I paused for a moment on the corner by Le Can-Can restaurant. If ever there was an alley for pigs it was this sleazy street. Ablaze with vertical neon signs, it reminded me of 52nd Street after the war when jazz clubs alternated with strip joints all the way from Broadway to Sixth Avenue. It was early, the sidewalks nearly deserted. Staring straight ahead at the basilica of Sacré-Coeur high above the tawdry scene, bone white in the spotlights like a guardian angel, I imagined a drunken crowd of sinners carousing after midnight.

It all seemed so very familiar. How many streets just like this one had I prowled over the years in my nocturnal wanderings? I walked past number 58, rue Pigalle, La Lune Rousse, 'un Spectacle de Chansonniers,' and La Roulotte at number 62 with its painted gypsy caravan on one side of the entrance. Somehow I knew I'd been here before. Sphinx was a couple doors down at number 66, sporting its own gaudy vertical sign.

I stopped short at the entrance, gripped by a lurking terror. This was beyond déjà-vu. I knew I had been here before. Long-forgotten memories rose up like ancient gas bubbling from the depths of a tar pit. The arched entry with its surrounding garland of terracotta flowers remained exactly as it had been when I first saw it in September of 1938 on tour with Spider Simpson. It was called the Monaco way back then. It had been Bricktop's joint, the hottest nightspot in all Paris. Ada 'Bricktop' Smith ruled the royal roost, toast of the town since the twenties.

An icy prickling ran down the back of my neck. I remembered how green I'd been, thrilled to meet the redheaded mulatto queen. Everyone from the Duke of Windsor to Ernest Hemingway came to Bricktop's. Cole Porter wrote a song for her. That first and only night, she invited me up onto the tiny stage to croon a blues duet. The house band was the Quintet of the Hot Club of France, an acoustic string group featuring Django Reinhardt and Stéphane Grappelli. I swore I'd never forget that moment. For a while I did. Now it all came flooding back.

The entrance was unlocked and I went inside. It was a small room, no more than a dozen or so tables. It had looked huge to me as a kid. Waiters were setting up under lights brighter than the usual seductive nightclub dim. I stood and watched them arrange the chairs and silverplate. Bricktop's glittering metallic drapes were gone, replaced by large wall plaques shaped like playing cards, top hats and dice. A small stage stood where the dance floor used to be. I was barely eighteen when I'd last been here. Spider had hired me earlier that year after hearing me sing at a roadhouse up in Poughkeepsie of all places. I'd dropped out of high school my sophomore year. Changed my name to take a crack at showbiz. Next thing I knew, I was on the RMS *Queen Mary* sailing for Europe with a swing band.

I'd never seen anything like Bricktop's. All the swells decked out in evening clothes, white tie and tails, even the Negro couples. First time in my life I'd ever seen white women dancing with black men, graceful as Fred and Ginger. Truth was I'd never really known many Negroes. There were no black kids up at St Frances Orphanage in the Bronx where I was raised as Jonathan Liebling. Only old Horace, the custodian, a kind and gentle man who kept his head hung low whenever the nuns were watching. He took pity on the orphans, slipping us candy bars from time to time. All forgotten until now, my past lost in amnesia.

When I got older, I'd sneak down into the basement where Horace was king. He had an old ratty armchair and a reading lamp and a patch of tattered rug. Enthroned there, he sat smoking cigars, listening to music on a portable wind-up Victrola during his off time. A stack of 78s rested next to his chair. Blues, jazz, ragtime and boogie-woogie piano filled that basement with joy.

My real education began safe in the shadows behind the hulking furnace as Horace played his favorite sides, nodding his head to the rhythm and singing along in a hoarse whisper.

The old janitor's spirit soared up through me that night I sang with Bricktop. She worked without a stage or even a microphone. It felt like the real thing, music coming from deep in my soul. Not a drop of soul in the syrupy ofay arrangements I crooned for Spider Simpson's orchestra. The memory of this magic moment held me like a waking dream. That night twenty-one years ago was the reason I started going up to Harlem once the European tour was over. Why I started keeping company with Evangeline Proudfoot. My daughter, Epiphany, had been spiritually conceived right here at Bricktop's.

A waiter approached me. '*Pardon, monsieur,*' he said. '*Nous sommes fermé jusqu'à neuf heures.*'

I told him I knew the club wasn't open. I needed to speak with his boss, '*le propriétaire,*' about an important personal matter. He gave me a stern appraising look. My Sulka duds carried the day. The waiter told me to go up a flight of stairs behind the red stage curtain and knock on the first door to my left. I climbed up and knocked, hearing a muffled response from within.

I opened the door and looked into a tiny room only slightly wider than the cluttered desk filling the back end. Seated behind this imposing barricade, solid as a professional wrestler, a curly-haired dame with a faint mustache and a unibrow glared up at me. '*Que faites-vous?*' Gorgeous George demanded.

I jumped right in and fed her a line, starting with a compliment about her red dress. This won me some points. She listened to me mangle her mother tongue without complaint. The gist of my spiel was that I was writing a book about stage magicians and had been told she was the go-to gal. I dug the print of Dr Cipher's promo photo out of my satchel and slid it across her desk. '*Connaissez-vous cet homme?*' I asked.

She all but swooned. Not a pretty picture. '*Ah... Fra Diavolo. Il est magnifique! Un magicien unique de le monde; seul et unique!'*

When I asked if Diavolo the Magnificent had ever performed at her club, she looked like she was about to cry. She'd seen his act about fifteen years ago at a joint called Le Jockey over in Montparnasse. He'd been brilliant, *'formidable.'* She went backstage after the show to find he'd already left. I knew that trick. Cyphre had played it on me ten days ago at Hubert's Flea Circus. The club owner gave her the contact information for Diavolo's agent, some bloke in London at the time. She'd written several times trying to arrange a booking. No luck on that score. A number of dates had been scheduled over the years but the magician never showed. *'Quel dommage!'* she moaned.

I agreed it was indeed a great pity, thanking the broad for her time. She told me to come back tonight. A Punjab swami on the bill performed the best Indian rope trick she'd ever seen. No book on magic should be without this wizard. I promised to return and made for the door. *'À bientôt!'* she called cheerfully after me as I hurried out of her life forever.

On the Métro ride back to the *Rive Gauche* I checked my map and found Le Jockey, one of Warren Wagner's listings, at 127 Boulevard Montparnasse. I figured I'd check it out after grabbing something to eat. I'd intended to sample the chow at Brasserie Lipp but walking back toward the Place Saint-Germain-des-Prés, I spotted Le Canton down a tiny side street. The idea of eating Chink food in Paris hadn't occurred to me. I turned left toward the little chop suey palace. An order of barbequed pork, shrimp fried rice and moo goo gai pan took me straight back to Mott Street.

After paying my bill, I headed toward the intersection of Montparnasse and Raspail. I spotted the tall vertical neon sign thrusting from the side of a five-story corner building. It spelled out JOCKEY like a shout in the dark. A curved glowing arrow along its length pointed the way under an awning to the entrance on rue de Chevreuse.

I followed this neon imperative and found myself in a long,

low room with a bandstand at the far end where three French cats worked overtime trying to sound like the Nat Cole Trio. A cluster of small cloth-covered tables surrounded the dance floor. Several couples swayed sensuously to the music.

I made my way over to the bar at the other end of the room, strategically situated as far from the music as possible. Numbers of framed black-and-white photos hung on the back wall above rows of bottles. I ordered a Manhattan, straight up, and the barman shook one for me. 'You the boss here?' I asked after my first sip.

The cat struggled to come up with an answer in English. '*Êtes-vous le propriétaire?*' I repeated in semi-uncertain French. This broke the ice and got us croaking back and forth in frog talk. I figured out the owner usually didn't come in before closing time. No way I was sticking around for another three or four hours. I asked the bartender how long he'd worked at the Jockey.

'*Douze ans,*' he answered proudly.

Twelve was good enough for me. This cheerful mixologist probably knew more about what went down at the club than some fat cat who came in at closing time to count the receipts. I asked if the Jockey ever booked magic acts. '*Non,*' he replied. '*Musique pour danser seulement. Le jazz parfois.*' I didn't set much store by this. The heavyweight broad at the Sphinx told me she'd seen his act here.

I got my 8x10 photos of Cyphre out of the satchel and slid them across the bar top. '*Connaissez-vous cet homme?*' I asked. The barman had never set eyes on him before. I explained he was a magician who'd performed once at the Jockey. The cat told me it must have been before his time. That got us talking about the good old days in Montparnasse. He took a framed photograph off the wall behind him. Behind the dusty glass, I observed a nocturnal shot of an ancient two-story building with a row of tiled gables along the roof and cartoon figures of cowboys painted on the façade.

The barkeep kept up a steady patter about all the swells who'd tied one on there back in the good old days. Hemingway, James Joyce, Picasso and a barrage of others I'd never heard about. '*Regarde ça*,' he said, handing me another framed photo. I spotted Hemingway with his bold mustache right off, both hands thrust aggressively into his jacket pockets. He stood among a group posing against a wall plastered with tattered posters. All the others were nameless ghosts to me. And then, there he was, elegant in his evening clothes at the far end, that familiar leering smile parting his snow-white square-cut goatee. It was Cyphre!

My hands shook so hard I nearly dropped the picture. An icy numbness shuddered through me like fever chills. How could it be? Cyphre looked exactly the same, standing aloof and stylish as Cole Porter among this raffish bohemian crowd, flappers and bon vivants decked out in bobbed hair, tweed driving caps and baggy trousers. They were all dead or grandparents by now. Papa Hemingway had turned into a white-bearded senior citizen. A fine copperplate hand had written the date, 'May 5, 1924,' across the bottom margin in blue ink. Hemingway was in the photo but I thought of a book written before his time, *The Picture of Dorian Gray*. It was about a cat whose portrait ages while he remains untouched by time because he made a deal with the Devil. Cyphre hadn't changed a hair after thirty-five years. Must have made the same kind of deal.

My fingers trembled when I gave the framed photo back to the barman. Downing my cocktail in a long swallow, I half-expected Cyphre to come through the door at any moment.

17

I left the Jockey before ten and headed over to where Klook was playing. I hoped walking might clear my head. The basement jazz club was around the corner from the Flore on rue Saint-Benôit, a tiny, narrow street off the Place Saint-Germain. I made my way down the stairs into a fluid rush of jazz. The first set had started. I paid the cover charge and paused to listen to the last sixteen bars of Zoot's tenor solo before making my way to the bar.

With its arching brick ceiling the packed joint felt like rush hour in a smoke-filled wine cellar. Two energetic couples somehow found room to jitterbug in the crowded space. Klook took a snappy four-bar break with his brushes. He had the same ofay on doghouse along with an intense blond square-head playing guitar. I ordered a *fine à l'eau*,' leaning back against the bar to let the music wash over me like a sound massage. When the set ended, the band left the stage and pushed through the crowd to the bar. 'Solid work, Klook,' I said.

'Johnny Favorite! My main man.' Clarke greeted me with a put-on coon grin. 'Glad you could fall by. What happened to your specs?'

'Don't wear them all the time.'

The drummer introduced me to the other musicians. The blond cat turned out to be a Dane, not a Swede. 'You remember Zoot Sims, natch.'

'Four Brothers,' I said. 'Woody Herman's Second Herd. Caught the band at Café Rouge in the Hotel Pennsylvania in '47 or '48.' I didn't mention I was there tailing some big-time ad exec cheating on his wife.

'Think I saw you with Spider Simpson,' Zoot said. 'Year I toured with Goodman.'

'When was that?'

'1943.'

'Nope. I was out of the business by then. Went off to war instead.' I waved the bartender over and ordered the band a round. Amid a chorus of 'Thanks' we clinked glasses, forgoing conversation in favor of booze.

'Say what, Johnny,' Klook said, setting his empty snifter down on the bar. 'Why not sit in for a couple songs on the next set?'

'No way, man. My chops are long gone.'

'Bullshit! You still got the groove in you is what counts.'

'Maybe so.' I certainly had a lot more in me than I'd ever guessed. Maybe my groove was still in there, too. 'One thing I do know. My golden tonsils turned to brass.'

'Brassy 'n sassy better'n golden and olden, my man.' Clarke nodded at the bandstand and the boys downed the dregs of their drinks. 'We do a couple tunes first. Give you time to warm up in the john, if you need it.'

I watched them weave back through the crowd toward the bandstand in no particular hurry. Signaling the barman, I asked for another brandy and water. Time to wet my whistle. The band played a medium-tempo version of 'Billie's Bounce' as I sipped the drink. Even if I sang badly, it was no big deal. I cut off a rooster's head to send Cyphre a message. Let him know Johnny Favorite was making the scene again. Maybe crooning in public would help spread the word around town. The next number was a solid, sizzling 'Cherokee,' Zoot blowing his brains out and Klook driving everything along full-throttle on the ride cymbal, wrapping things up in an explosive exchange of four-bar breaks with Sims and the Dane.

When the applause died down, Kenny Clarke rose behind

his drum kit, holding up both hands for attention. *'Maintenant, mesdames et messieurs, pour nos prochain morceau une surprise agréable.'* Klook's French was more fluid than mine but his accent remained pure Pittsburgh. *'Le célèbre chanteur de* swing *Americain,* Johnny Favorite.'

The crowd gave me a modest hand as I made my way to the main kick. I knew they wondered just who the hell I was. 'Johnny Favorite!' Clarke called as I stepped up next to Zoot. This got me another ten seconds of acclaim. 'What'll it be?' Klook asked. 'How about "That Old Black Magic"?' He was pulling my chain because of that skull in my suitcase.

'After my time,' I said. 'Came out when I was in the hospital. Maybe "Dancing with the Devil." You cats hep to that one?'

'Memory lane,' Zoot said.

'Count it off, gate,' the drummer instructed, settling behind his kit.

After a nod from Zoot, I snapped my fingers to a long-forgotten tempo. The sax slid in for a languid opening chorus. I opened my mouth and the past came flowing out.

> *'She's got the face of an angel,*
> *A smile as sweet as sin.*
> *In my heart I know she's no angel.*
> *A prize I never can win.*
> *All her charms fill my arms*
> *As we twirl and dip*
> *And spin, spin, spin...'*

As the words returned to me, words I had written to a Vernon Duke melody, I felt transported into the past. I saw myself at twenty, in league with Satan and poised on the brink of enormous fame, a smooth young hustler in a tux without a drop of feeling for anyone. My voice maybe was gone but the black heart inside beat on to an eternal rhythm. I felt the crowd digging it. That connection with an audience stayed with you forever like knowing when some broad wanted to get laid. Looking out over the crowd, my old false smile pasted across my mug, I spotted this strange cat sitting against the wall on the left. He looked to be in his mid-forties, a gray man in a gray suit. His dead eyes stared straight up at me, magnified by the thick lenses in a pair of black horn-rimmed cheaters. He had the waxy complexion of an embalmed stiff. I made him for a cop, glad for the familiar pressure of the gat against the small of my back.

The pounder kept his corpse eyes fixed on me, mouth frozen in a stern frown. Maybe he was just here by accident, a cop on vacation looking for a basement sex show. Jazz was never high on the police hit parade. Letting the bastard know I feared nothing from him, I stared straight into his mortuary gaze and launched into the final verse.

> *'I thought that she loved me*
> *With a love so warm and true.*
> *When I dance with the devil*
> *I'm dancing, my darling, with you.'*

Zoot stepped up to solo for thirty-two bars, a soulful bluesy meditation on Duke's haunting melody. He got a nice round of applause. When the clapping faded, I launched in to a final reprise of the chorus. Glancing to my left, I saw the zombie cop had split. The empty space he'd left behind looked more substantial than his ghostly gray presence. I finished my number. The audience responded with enthusiasm. As the mitt pounding diminished, a handsome guy in rumpled trench coat with the collar turned up walked over. A smoldering cigarette dangled from the corner of his mouth. *'Bravo, Johnny,'* he said. *'Tu fais bien. Comme le temps jadis avant la guerre avec Araignée en la batterie.'*

'Who's that Bogie wanna-be?' I asked Kenny Clarke as the swell sauntered off. 'Some frog movie star?'

Klook looked at me like I was an idiot. 'That was Camus. The famous writer.'

'Yeah?' I answered his condescending smirk with my own scornful scowl. 'Never heard of him.'

'Nothing to be proud of. Cat won the Nobel Prize year before last.'

I let that one pass with a shrug. It never pays to be ignorant but apologizing for it only makes things worse. I hung around down in the cellar for the next two sets, buying drinks for the band during both breaks. After the final encore, Klook said, 'Say, Johnny, wanna fall by my pad? Get high and have some laughs?'

'Sounds boss,' I said, 'but I'm beat. Better cop a final and hit the sack.'

'Whatever. We're all staying at the La Louisiane. Sixty rue de Seine on the corner of de Buci. I bunk in room 20. We mostly party 'til dawn, so drop in whenever. The place ain't a shit hole. It's a classy flop. Sartre and de Beauvoir both have rooms there.'

'Who are they? Some tap dancing duo?'

'You're too much, man,' Kenny Clarke chuckled. 'You crack me up.'

'Gotta split,' I replied and hurried out the door.

18

I woke up with an aching back in a strange, sagging bed. It took a groggy moment to remember I'd slept in my new house for the first time. It was freezing cold. No way in hell was I ready to face that intimidating tub. I skipped bathing and shaved. Staring at my mug in the mirror revealed tiny dark roots showing under my golden mop. Human hair grows a quarter inch each month. It would really start to show in another week. I made a mental note to buy more hair coloring soon.

My first stop was the café-tabac next door where I introduced myself to the pot-bellied proprietor Alfonse Renard, told him I was a new neighbor without a phone, and made a deal to pay him ƒ500 for every call he took for me on his private phone. Of course I would use his public payphone for any calls I made. After buying a copy of the *Herald Tribune* from him I crossed the boulevard and angled toward Café de Flore. It was a beautiful, sunny spring-like day and several customers sat at tables on the sidewalk in front of the café. A waiter spotted me and came over. I ordered a *café complet*, and unfolded the newspaper on the small round table. The usual bad news dominated the front page. **Soviet Fighters Buzz US Plane in Dispute About Berlin Corridor**, a bold banner unfurled above **Franco Says Reds Still Are Peril as He Marks 20 Years of Rule**.

I had barely scanned the headlines when the waiter returned with my café au lait, croissant and preserves. I put on my reading glasses and looked for an obituary for Krusemark. Nothing. No news about the NYPD's hunt for Harry Angel or New York City at all, except for some kerfuffle at the United Nations. Reminding myself to get over to Le Mistral to buy the *Daily News*, I turned to 'PS from Paris,' Art Buchwald's column on the back page, taking my time, sipping coffee as I read. I dug Buchwald's off-beat humor. His column made me laugh. Not a common occurrence these days. Halfway through, I spotted the copper coming up the street. The corpse-like bull from the jazz cellar last night. In spite of the bright weather, he wore a drab woolen overcoat, neck scarf and a stingy-brim brown fedora. I saw that he'd made me and I eased the derringer out of my satchel, slipping it under the newspaper on the tabletop.

The gray ghost drifted my way. Up close, he looked taller than his slouched posture suggested from a distance. 'You're Johnny Favorite, right?' he asked, towering over me. He spoke in a mumbled monotone with the clipped diction of a make-believe tough guy. Certain he was the heat, I reached under the *Trib* and took hold of the two-shot.

'Who wants to know?'

'I heard you singing last night at *Le Club Saint-Germain-des-Prés*. I'm Bill Burroughs. Mind if I join you?' The stranger sat down opposite me without waiting for an invitation.

'What is it you do, Bill?' I asked, my finger on the trigger.

'Me? I'm just fine.' He'd misheard me.

'No. What line of work you in?'

'Well...' He seemed to think it over. 'I guess you could call me a writer.'

'You the cat wrote all those Tarzan books?'

'Nope. That was my distant cousin, Ed. So distant we're not even related.'

'Never read any myself. Saw some Johnny Weissmuller movies when I was in high school.' I relaxed a bit. Cops didn't talk like this bird. 'What kind of books you write, Bill?'

'Psychic travelogues into the subconscious mind,' he said in a flat monotone. 'Largely unpublished.'

'How do you pay the rent?'

'I'm a figment of the old adding machine dynasty.'

Burroughs was a middle-aged trust-funder, the worst kind of deadbeat, paid off by his family every month to stay away from home. The efficient waiter appeared at our table and while the remittance man ordered a coffee, I slipped the derringer back into my satchel. Turned toward the waiter, Bill rested his left hand on the table and I noticed that the last digit of his little finger was missing. When he looked back at me, I got out my cigarette case and offered him a Lucky.

I took one myself and set both pills on fire with my lighter. 'American…' Bill observed with a thin smile, exhaling through his nose. 'God bless 'em. You know, Johnny, I heard you once with Spider Simpson's band in Vienna. Summer of '37?'

'Nope. Started singing with Spider's outfit sometime that fall after they returned from Europe. Didn't get to Austria until next year. Late autumn, 1938.'

'Must have been in the States then. You look different somehow.'

'Don't dye my hair black anymore. What were you doing in Vienna?'

'Studying psychoanalysis and getting treated for the clap.'

My three days and nights in Vienna came back with sudden clarity. Cake-decoration architecture, sausages, beer. Nazis in their brown shirts and jackboots. Bold red swastika flags hanging everywhere. Plump little whore not much older than me. Two crazy krauts at the Wiener Rathauskeller where shouting drunks drowned out our noisy band. Pervasive dread. Menace lurking beneath the Gemütlichkeit. Last stop on a three-month European tour.

I started Burroughs talking about his time in Vienna living above a Turkish bath and his marriage of convenience to a Jewish woman, which allowed her to escape to the United States just in time before the Anschluss. As a detective, I'd learned the art of getting a suspect to spill the beans without revealing anything about myself. Before long, while I spread butter and jam on my croissant, Bill practically told me his whole life story. About his privileged boyhood in St Louis, his adoring mother and taciturn father who introduced him to an enduring love of guns. Burroughs built bombs in high school. One blew up in his hands, landing him in the hospital for six months. Maybe that's how he lost part of his finger. He talked about attending Harvard, where he kept a pet ferret and .32 revolver. He was some kind of character. Once nearly shot a classmate in the stomach, blowing a big hole in the dorm room wall instead.

Just when things were getting interesting, Bill turned the tables on me, asking, 'What are you doing in Paris, Johnny? Planning a big comeback?'

I decided to throw him a curve ball. 'Actually, I'm chasing the Devil,' I said.

'Aren't we all?' Burroughs stubbed out his cigarette and took a sip of coffee.

His blasé attitude pissed me off. 'You don't get it,' I said. 'I'm not into this stuff like some bookworm like you. This shit is real to me.'

Burroughs displayed no change of expression. I knew he was interested by his body language. 'I remember once reading a little dirt in some tabloid.' He leaned slightly forward, a vulture seeking carrion. 'You were supposed to be involved in voodoo. Black magic. Very intriguing. Frank Sinatra only cared about pussy.'

'Listen to me, Bill. This is not about bullshit intellectual blah-blah-blah. I've got a score to settle with Satan.'

I said it only to jab his superior intellectual attitude. Burroughs really dug it. He was hooked now. 'Johnny, I think I might be of some help,' he said. 'If you want to find the Devil you've got to know where to look. There's a book back in my room, not too far from here. It will show you where to start. Be happy to loan it to you.'

'Let's go,' I said, dropping a ten franc note on the table.

We walked together down the boulevard past the old church, Burroughs strangely silent after being such a windbag. We turned left on rue de Seine. There was so little traffic it was easier to walk down the middle of the street. This became a necessity a block later when we passed the Hotel de la Louisiane, a shabby corner building with paint peeling from the façade. Bustling housewives crowded around the sidewalk produce stands of M Fougeron on either side of the entrance. A row of skinned grinning pig heads hung from iron hooks along the wall of a butcher shop across the way.

'All the jazz musicians stay here,' Bill said as we turned right past the shoppers onto rue de Buci.

'Yeah, I know,' I said, not mentioning Klook as we strolled by.

Burroughs fell back into silence as we drilled across Carrefour de Buci onto rue Saint-André-des-Arts, a narrow street lined with small shops and bistros. Bill guided me to the left into rue Gît-le-Coeur, a lane barely the width of an automobile.

The hotel at 9, rue Gît-le-Coeur had no name. Burroughs called it 'the Beat Hotel,' a handle he said was invented by one of his poet buddies because of all the beatnik artists and writers living in this sorry fleabag. The ground floor felt cramped and dark. On the right, a door led into the café. We ascended a steep angled staircase. Burroughs lived in room 15 on the first floor. The place was dank, a miserable tomb lacking the essential comforts of most prison cells. Bill switched on a bare 25 watt lightbulb dangling from the ceiling, revealing the meager furnishings.

He sat at his worktable. I took the other chair. 'The Iron Maiden,' he rasped, gesturing at his Olivetti.

'What's that?' I pointed to four wire trays mounted to the dingy wall above his head.

'My book. Magazine in Chicago published a chunk last fall.'

'What's it called?'

'*Naked Lunch*. Jack Kerouac gave me the title down in Tangier couple years ago. Heard it wrong. I meant "naked lust." Know Kerouac?'

'Nope.'

'*On the Road*?'

'Beats me.'

A thin smile cracked Burroughs' waxed parchment features. 'I think you just wrote a poem,' he said. I didn't get his drift so I kept my yap shut.

Bill walked over to a shelf where he kept a few books and other odds and ends. When he turned around he was holding a tattered paperback in one hand, a revolver in the other. I reached instinctively behind my back for the holstered S&W. 'Tools of the trade,' Bill said, setting both the book and the pistol down on his table. I relaxed a bit, watching him strike a match and set fire to a foul-smelling frog cancer stick. 'Ever kill anyone, Johnny?' he asked, exhaling as he sat down.

I took my time, tapping a Lucky on my cigarette case before lighting up. 'No,' I said, 'not yet.' Lying comes almost as easy as killing.

'I shot my wife seven years ago in Mexico City,' Burroughs said with less emotion than if he was telling me about what he'd had for breakfast. 'It was an accident. We were playing our little William Tell game for some friends. Joan put a water glass on top of her head. I had a cheap .380 Star automatic that shot low. Way too low as it turned out.'

'Bad luck, Bill.'

'Not really. Joan's death is what made me become a writer.'

'Whatever it takes,' I said. 'Is that the book you told me about?' I pointed to the pocket book on the table.

'Oh, no. My initial publication. Sold over 100,000 copies the first year. I keep one around as a souvenir.'

I reached over and picked up the curling paperback. It was called *Junkie*, by William Lee, an Ace double-book original selling for 35 cents. The cover pictured a gent wrestling a syringe away from a hysterical blonde. On the back, another book was featured, *Narcotic Agent*, a reprint potboiler. 'You William Lee?' I asked.

'My mother's maiden name.'

'Guess you didn't want her to know about the *Confessions of an Unredeemed Drug Addict*,' I teased, quoting the book's subtitle.

'Always pays to spare mommy any bad news.'

'What about the gat?'

'.32 Colt Detective Special. No sculpture I've ever seen is more beautiful.'

'You shoot off the end of your finger like "Dingus" James?'

'Hell, no. I went on a Van Gogh kick and used a pair of poultry shears. Damn good ones. Stainless steel. Sharp as a razor. Set me back $2.71. Reminded me of my grandmother's Thanksgiving dinners. I felt euphoric. A lifetime's worth of hostility flowed out of me with all the blood.'

'Why show me the roscoe?'

'Thought it was something a Devil-worshiper might be interested in.'

'What makes you think I'm a Devil-worshiper?' I asked.

'Only know what I read in the papers. You said you had a score to settle with Satan. If I were a Devil-worshiper, I'd feel the same way. It's not just choirboys who get fucked by religion.'

'Help me out then. Where's that holy black magic bible you said you'd loan me?'

Burroughs set his cup down on the table and slouched back to the bookshelf. He rummaged through several stacks humming tunelessly to himself. 'Ah-hah!' he exclaimed at last, pulling a well-worn volume from the bottom of the pile. 'Eureka!'

Bill shuffled over and handed me a hardback book with a dirty pale blue cover, the gilt title barely legible along its cracked spine. *MY NAME IS LEGION: The Satanic Origins of the Christian Church,* by some bird named János Szabor. I opened it to the title page, surprised to find it was fairly new. Published in London by Chatto & Windus in 1951, translated from the Hungarian by Margaret Rushbrook Cobb, the dog-eared pages made the volume look decades older. Not the sort of thing I'd ever read under ordinary circumstances, Szabor's book had obviously been around the block a time or two. 'Translated into more than a dozen languages,' Burroughs said.

'Appreciate you loaning me the book,' I said.

'It's a connection,' Bill said. 'Szabor's a friend of mine. Lives here in Paris now. Teaches at the Sorbonne.'

'I'll give him a book report when I bring it back.'

Burroughs let that one pass him by. 'Want to fix?' he asked me.

'What?'

'Bought some very sweet horse from my pal Hadj over on the rue de la Huchette this morning. Cooking O from paregoric takes too much damn time. Better to score smack. Costs more but no hassle.'

'Not my thing, Bill,' I said, rising to my feet. 'More of a booze man.'

'Whatever gets you off.'

I gathered up my stuff and made for the door. By the time I split, Burroughs already had his jacket off and was rolling up his sleeve. This whole thing had been a waste of time, I figured. A junkie fantasy. Just another faggot scribbler pretending to be a tough guy.

19

The rancid smell from the squalid nameless hotel lingered in my nostrils as I retraced my steps along rue Gît-le-Coeur. I'd spent my life running away from bad-news joints like that dive. The orphanage, tour buses, cheap small town hotels bunking four to a room with snoring musicians, dreary railroad flat apartments after sweaty nights with sad faceless strangers. My final flight was from myself, ditching my identity in a futile effort to escape a bad deal gone wrong. Disgusted with the whole sorry business, I resisted an impulse to fling Szabor's book into the gutter. For a brief moment, I glimpsed an alternate future, one where I was no longer doomed, a wanted murderer chasing the Devil's ghost. A serene future of peace and security. I knew it was all pipedream bullshit even before the fantasy bubble burst. These sordid streets were the path I was destined to follow. A final confrontation with evil remained my only possible fate.

Using the street map, I worked my way back through a warren of medieval lanes to Brasserie Lipp on the Boulevard Saint-Germain. I was in luck, pushing through the revolving doors early enough to beat the lunchtime rush. The place glowed inside, a *Belle Époque* jewel box with a ceiling mural, intricate chandeliers, and tall mirrors between glazed tile wall panels. A waiter in a black jacket and long white apron led me to a row of tables running along the length of a nearly empty room. I sat against the wall on a long brown leather banquette. The mirrors were all angled to provide views in every direction. Just right for a gee on the lam.

The Michelin guide said the brasserie featured Alsatian cooking. When the waiter brought *la carte*, I asked about Alsace. He said it was a part of France to the northeast bordering Germany. Because their food had a Kraut connection, Lipp's featured a foaming beer mug on their sign outside. I ordered *Filet de Harengs Pommes à l'Huile* to start and the *Choucroute Lipp*, along with a *demi de blonde*.

Waiting for the food, I took a look at János Szabor's little book, starting with his 'Introduction.' Harry Angel had never been much of a reader, mostly the sports page and racing forms. Johnny Favorite was supposedly a scholar steeped in arcane knowledge. I didn't remember much of that. In my opinion, reading should be a two-way street, a dialogue with the author. This Szabor character came on like a pompous lecturing professor, embossing his text with ten-dollar words like 'Manichean,' 'Gnosticism,' 'Hegelian Dialectic' and 'parthenogenesis.' Just when I was about to give the damn thing up the waiter brought my herring and draft beer.

I was in hog heaven and ordered another draft when the waiter brought the *choucroute,* a heap of sauerkraut piled with pork loin, velvet-soft ham slices, salty smoked bacon and cumin sausages. Living on borrowed time felt good, knowing my last meal would be in a Parisian restaurant.

I declined dessert despite the waiter's insistent praise of '*le millefeuille magnifique*.' Between sips of coffee, I gave *My Name is Legion* another try. Szabor used one of those little quotes at the start of his book. Epigrams, I think they're called. Maybe it's epigraph or epitaph. 'There was only one Christian, and he died on the cross.' I dug it. This gem came from Friedrich Nietzsche, the same cat who said, 'God is dead.' Skipping the impenetrable Introduction, I dove straight into Chapter One. All the chapters had titles like the damp-stained boys' adventure books I read in the orphanage. I thought that was pretty cool.

The first chapter was called 'The Clandestine Library.' Szabor's opening paragraph got me hooked.

One clear December day in 1945, a murderer's hands pulled an ancient red earthenware jar from the ground at Jabal al-Tārif, a mountain near the town of Naj' Hammādī in Upper Egypt. Muhammad 'Ali al-Sammān would soon avenge his father's death in a family blood feud, hacking the killer to death and devouring his heart, but on this day he dug for fertilizer with his brothers in one of the 150 caves piercing the Jabal. Later, he acknowledged the murder 'had been written' just as he believed his extraordinary discovery was also preordained. The jar stood nearly a meter high. Muhammad 'Ali feared a demon might live inside and hesitated before breaking it open with his mattock. He was wise to harbor such suspicions. A peasant's mind dwells closer to the realm of spirits than more sophisticated imaginations. Greed overcame Muhammad 'Ali's fears. Hoping to find gold, he smashed the jar. The treasure it contained possessed far greater value than mere gold. Thirteen papyrus codices bound in leather had been hidden away in this cave for almost two thousand years. The reason for their concealment and the secrets they harbored held the clues to the most diabolic crime in the history of mankind.

Szabor grabbed me by my nuts like the start of a Mickey Spillane novel. Eating a man's heart was something I knew all about. I absorbed the opening chapter as my coffee grew cold. The ancient books became known as the Nag Hammadi Library. They survived their accidental discovery by the purest dumb luck. Muhammad 'Ali's mother used many of the papyrus pages to kindle her cooking stove. The remaining texts were sold on the black market in Cairo. A single book got smuggled out of Egypt and was offered for sale in America, eventually landing in Zurich as part of the Jung Foundation collection. The Egyptian government bought one of the remaining codices and confiscated the rest, depositing them all in Cairo's Coptic Museum. Public access was suppressed.

The codices were written sometime around 350 AD, all Coptic translations from the original Greek, the language of the New Testament. Szabor estimated the Greek texts dated no later than 140 AD. He was a specialist in antique languages, fluent in Latin, ancient Greek, Coptic, Aramaic and Hebrew. In 1947, Szabor traveled to Cairo with a colleague, French Egyptologist Jean Doresse. As the linguistic consultant, he was permitted a firsthand look at the collection. Szabor was also an anarchist who had fought with the Hungarian underground during the war. Trained in the art of espionage, he smuggled a Minox Riga into the Coptic Museum and photographed every page of the Nag Hammadi Library.

This Szabor came on like a cool cat close to my own devious heart. Secret agent Szabor worked like a total pro. When he developed the 9.2 mm film back home in Prague, Szabor made an important discovery. The Nag Hammadi Library preserved the texts of several long-lost Gnostic Gospels. Szabor explained that 'Gnostic' had its roots in the Greek word *gnosis*, meaning 'knowledge.' The Gnostics had been early Christians. Their forgotten texts recorded the parts that got left out of the Bible. Matthew, Mark, Luke and John, the 'official' New Testament Gospels, were written around the same time. The Big Four got the stamp of approval. The Gnostic Gospels were hidden away in a forgotten cave.

Szabor identified a few of them. *The Gospel of Thomas* implied Jesus had a twin brother. *The Gospel of Philip* suggested the Messiah loved Mary Magdalene more than the other disciples, even claiming He kissed her on the mouth. *The Gospel of Mary* taught the radical notion that Mary Magdalene was the first to see the resurrected Savior. This manuscript was previously known from an ancient Coptic text bought in Cairo in 1896.

Szabor ended his first chapter with unanswered questions. Why were the Gnostic Gospels sealed in a jar and buried in a desert cave almost two thousand years ago? What drove these ancient Coptic Christians to conceal their sacred texts? Who decided to leave the Gnostic Gospels out of the Bible? The answers, he promised the reader, altered the course of Western civilization. 'Like Adam and Eve, all mankind must forever mourn a lost paradise.' I closed the book in a numb trance. The tables around me buzzed with conversation. A lunchtime crowd had packed into Lipp's. Reading became impossible. I called for *l'addition*, paid up and split.

Back home in my blue-tiled cottage, I built a fire to take the chill out of the air. A nice long soak in the tub felt right for reading. After lighting the gas ring under the boiler and filling the tub I slid into the steaming water, a cold bourbon in one hand, Szabor's book in the other. Chapter Two was called 'Gemini.' I figured it was all about astronomy and that constellation shit but was dead wrong. Reading a chapter thick with philosophy felt like swimming upstream in a river of mud. Szabor introduced some bird named Georg Wilhelm Friedrich Hegel, a 19th-century German philosopher, who established the Hegelian Dialectic, a method of reasoning that included antithesis and synthesis. Everything grew so murky I nearly quit. Then something caught my attention: 'When probing into Hegel's reasoning one line from *The Science of Thought* rings with the purest clarion of Truth. "Just as little is seen in pure light as in pure darkness." Anyone grappling with the dialectic process will profit by keeping his words in mind. It contains the essence of the Universe.'

This bit rang a bell with me. I dug what Szabor had to say about Hegel and the concept of 'duality.' The way it struck me was that human consciousness can only comprehend the world by seeing it as split into polar opposites. Right and wrong, hot and cold, light opposed by dark, yin/yang, good versus evil, virtue and vice, sin and grace, all both sides of the same coin. Toss it in the air and call it. Heads or tails.

Szabor didn't make the toss. Instead, he launched a cool investigation into the origins of duality, tracing it back to an ancient time when the earliest ancestors of mankind were tiny arboreal primates who lived in trees because their enemies were large nocturnal predators. Fear of the dark became ingrained in Man's genetic makeup. Religion had its roots in overcoming primal fear. The first god was the Sun. Rituals developed to assure it rose again every day. On the flip side, duality demanded knowledge of darkness.

I read on about the early Paleolithic hunters who crawled into unknown caves and made art as a statement of faith; humankind's first deity, an earth goddess known to the agrarian ancient Greeks as Gaia; the emergence of a priest-caste; and the supreme religious offering of human sacrifice in the ancient world. The Jews had Abraham and Isaac. Greek mythology gave us Agamemnon and Iphigenia.

Szabor ended the chapter with an introduction to the origins of monotheism, tracing the belief in a single all-powerful god way back to Ahura Mazda, a transcendental supreme being worshiped by Zarathustra's followers in ancient Persia. 'The belief in one true God above all others set the stage for Satan's emergence as His spiritual adversary.'

I jumped straight into Chapter Five, 'Jesus and Satan.' Szabor found Satan in Leviticus, the Book of Job and the first book of Chronicles. 'It may be fashionable among modern biblical scholars to deny the serpent in the Garden of Eden as Satan. A cursory examination of the fourteen books comprising the Apocrypha suggests otherwise.' He hit one into centerfield on the next page. Fall of Lucifer. Isaiah 14:12. Challenging the Crown of God. Mutiny in Heaven. Fallen Archangel. What a story. Earth became Lucifer's dominion, the world his to rule. Archangels remained pure spirit. Gabriel a voice in Mary's ear announcing she carried the Son of God. Lucifer reigned over his kingdom through similar innuendo. 'Anyone seeking Hell,' Szabor wrote, 'need only look around him.'

Szabor had a field day with the New Testament. The Book of Revelations tagged the Devil as 'the dragon' (12:9) and 'the old serpent' (20:2). That same chapter and verse specifically identified Satan as the serpent in the Garden. Szabor quoted from Revelation (13:15-18): 'Here is wisdom. Let him that hath understanding count the number of the beast; for it is the number of a man; and his number is six hundred threescore and six.' I remembered Epiphany quoting it to me in the New York Public Library reference room. She'd looked so wise and beautiful in her rimless reading glasses.

'Is that a fact?' I'd said, teasing her.

'Don't you know anything?' she'd answered with a mock frown.

Epiphany had had it right. I didn't know anything. I'd learned a lot in the past ten days but I knew I'd better stick with Szabor's little book. The Hungarian traced Christ's lineage as a 'dying and rising god' back to the Corn King who'd proudly allowed the Iron Age Druids to sacrifice him in a bonfire to ensure a successful harvest. Others in the death-and-resurrection family tree: Osiris, Baldr, Quetzalcoatl, Adonis, Tammuz, Dionysus and Melqart, who adorned the ancient silver coin I'd taken from Krusemark's safe. 'Once again, modern scholars trample over one another in a fevered race to debunk the dying and rising god legend as the basis for Christianity,' Szabor observed. 'I stand with Sir James Frazer, who documented in *The Golden Bough* how the Crucifixion and Resurrection of Christ recapitulated early pagan beliefs. The fertility god demanded the ritual death of sacrificial kings who sanctified the harvest with their blood. Jesus of Nazareth, "King of the Jews," became the last to wear the crown.'

The rest of the chapter dealt with the temptation of Christ in the Judaean Desert. I might have given it a pass but something Szabor wrote grabbed my attention.

While many scholars dismiss the meeting between
Jesus and Satan as nothing but a parable, the Catholic
Church views it as a literal physical occurrence. Even
so, later religious paintings depicting the event always
portrayed Christ as an ordinary man and the devil as a
demonic creature. Curious, considering Revelations
clearly states 666 to be 'the number of a man.' If the
god called Jesus lived His life as a man why is it so
hard to imagine Satan taking a similar form here on earth?

Cyphre! Szabor knocked it out of the park. The Devil, eternal
source of all things evil, lived on earth as a man. I'd had lunch
with him once, in fact at a restaurant located at 666 Fifth Avenue.

Burroughs knew nothing about Cyphre. He didn't lend me
Szabor's book just to blow smoke up my ass. The junkie was trying
to clue me in. I thumbed ahead in the tattered volume at random.

Chapter Nine, the last one in the book, was called, 'Lord Satan's
Church.' The Hungarian launched straight into professorial
mode, turning back the clock to those earthen jars hidden in
the Egyptian desert. Szabor speculated that the Gnostics stashed
their sacred texts away in caves not long after the First Council
of Nicaea, convoked by Constantine I in 325 AD. The original
copies in Greek were considered dangerous 200 years earlier. By
the time of Rome's first Christian emperor, the Gnostic Gospels
had become downright seditious.

Szabor explained that by the start of the first century, a
schism had divided the pioneering Christians. What became the
Orthodoxy followed the teachings of Peter and Paul who preached
that apostolic authority derived from those who had witnessed
the Resurrection. Only the chosen eleven could ordain their
successors, creating a hierarchy of bishops, priests and deacons.
The church became divided between the clergy and the laity.

Gnostics saw things differently. These dissenters interpreted the
Resurrection as a spiritual event not a physical one. Their gospels

taught them to believe that spiritual illumination arose from dreams, visions and ecstatic trances. They had faith in personal enlightenment. For this they were denounced as heretics. Gnostic writing was burned. Two hundred years later, when Christianity became the official religion of the Roman Empire, the Gnostics sealed their sacred gospels in clay jars and buried them in the desert.

Where was all this leading, I wondered. It was duality all over again. Szabor reminded his readers that Christ and the Devil were personifications of good and evil engaged in an endless struggle. If the true message of Jesus Christ was to love unconditionally and find salvation within oneself what possible chance did the Prince of Darkness have to prevail? A world of introspection, selflessness and meditation permitted little temptation. Where no rules were set down none could be broken. As Szabor put it, 'The forces of evil could not allow Gnostic philosophy to take hold. Personal liberation must be stymied at all costs. The teachings of Jesus had to be perverted into dogma.'

How did this occur? According to Szabor, it was much more simple than one might imagine. All it took was one man.

20

The Hungarian fingered Saul of Tarsus as Satan's secret agent.

> Those who doubt an individual can redirect the
> course of time should bear in mind a number of
> men and women, most remembered by only a single
> name, whose actions permanently changed world
> events. Moses, Alexander, Caesar, Charlemagne,
> Joan, Elizabeth, Napoleon, Hitler and Gandhi all
> left behind their indelible mark. Stalin and Mao
> are current contenders to join that list. Even un-
> known nobodies have altered the flow of history.
> In 1914, Gavrilo Princip, a 19-year-old Bosnian
> Serb, fired two shots in Sarajevo and ignited the
> First World War.

Szabor admitted this to be an exception. Assassinations rarely changed anything in the long run. A single moment of violence might end the life of a head of state but the state continued to function. True and lasting change required a lifetime of effort. Such subversion became the 'clandestine occupation' of a man Szabor called both 'Paul the Apostate' and 'Saul the Deceiver.'

The Hungarian provided a quick thumbnail biography. Early in the first century AD, the Apostle Paul was born a Jew in Tarsus, an important ancient Anatolian trading city and capital of the Roman province of Cilicia. Saul was his Jewish name; Paul was the Latin moniker he alternately used after inheriting Roman citizenship from his father. Raised in Jerusalem, Saul was a 'zealous' Pharisee and as a young man 'intensely persecuted' early Christians in the years following the Crucifixion. He did everything within his power to 'destroy' the burgeoning religious movement, including participating in the stoning of Stephen, one of seven Christian deacons appointed by the Apostles. 'Acts 7:58-60 stated only that the witnesses to this execution laid their garments at the feet of a youth named Saul,' Szabor observed, 'but it is hard to imagine the angry young zealot not picking up a stone himself. If such a man converted to Christianity, would he not be the ideal candidate to become the Devil's double agent?'

Even I knew Saul's conversion took place on the road to Damascus. He was traveling there to arrest followers of Jesus, planning to return them to Jerusalem from Syria for interrogation and perhaps execution. Szabor went into greater detail, mentioning how Paul/Saul gave the matter 'short shrift' in his First Epistle to the Corinthians and his Epistle to the Galatians. Most of the story was told in the Acts of the Apostles. How just outside Damascus a blazing light from 'Heaven' flashed around the travelers. Saul was struck blind, hearing 'the voice of Jesus' ask why he persecuted Him. In this version, Saul's companions heard a sound but did not see the light. Later, when Saul was himself arrested in Jerusalem, he gave a speech offering another version of the event. Recounted in Acts 22, Saul told his listeners that those with him on the road to Damascus 'saw the light but did not hear the voice of the one who spoke to me.'

Szabor made a big deal out of Saul/Paul's conflicting accounts of his conversion. 'The surest mark of any dissembler is his inability to keep his stories straight,' the Hungarian observed, thinking just like a gumshoe again. Three days after his 'miraculous hallucination,' Saul had his sight restored by Ananias of Damascus. The New Testament claimed Ananias had been instructed to do this by his own divine revelation from Jesus Christ. The Messiah told him, 'This man is my chosen instrument to proclaim my name to the Gentiles and their kings and to the people of Israel.' Szabor found something fishy in all this.

> Satan is a great Trickster and what more devilish
> trick can be imagined than blinding a man with a
> flash of light and then sending another dupe to heal
> him? A tantalizing clue to this deception can be
> found within the pages of the Bible. Recounting
> the moment Ananias placed his hands on Saul,
> *Acts 9:18* states, 'Immediately, something like
> scales fell from Saul's eyes, and he could see
> again.' How strange. Something like scales.
> A most peculiar description. What comes
> 'immediately' to mind is a serpent. How like
> a trickster to leave behind some enigmatic clue
> as an eternal taunt to mankind.

It felt like I was reading a police report detailing the evidence of a crime. The lingo maybe sounded smarty-pants but the relentless logic was pure cop. Szabor went on to develop an impressive rapsheet against Saul/Paul. The missionary went exclusively by the name of Paul following his stay on the island of Cyprus sometime around 46 AD. Unlike the eleven surviving 'official' Apostles, he had never known or seen the living Jesus. Everything Paul taught came from visionary revelation. 'Divine inspiration provided a convenient cover-up for subterfuge,' Szabor pointed out. 'Perhaps Paul actually believed the voice whispering in his mind was that of Jesus and not Satan. Either way, it doesn't matter. The end result remained the same. The teachings of Christ as described by the Gnostics were utterly perverted.'

Szabor detailed these perversions like a prosecuting attorney laying out his case. In his First Letter to the Corinthians, Paul cemented the foundation of a paternal church, condemning woman to a subservient and submissive role in life. 'Women should remain silent in the churches ... it is disgraceful for a woman to speak in the church.' Szabor pointed out that besides putting women in their place, Paul's teaching undermined the Gnostic concept of a 'dyadic God who embraced both the masculine and the feminine aspects of life. Paul the Apostate drove the divine Mother Goddess from the temple.'

All four of the 'official' Gospels in the New Testament were written after Paul's beheading in Rome during the reign of Emperor Nero. They derived from an oral tradition in which the martyr had been well versed. Although never an actual participant in the events described in his letters, Paul wrote a quarter of what Szabor sometimes called 'the New Covenant.' Szabor argued that being first to record his thoughts, Paul's words carried the most weight in the formation of the early Christian church.

According to Szabor, among the many 'subversive' ideas introduced by the 'Apostate Paul' the Doctrine of the Trinity 'remained one of the most deviously pernicious.' What was wrong with the good old Father, Son and Holy Ghost trio, I wondered. Szabor quickly set me straight. 'By promulgating a tripartite god, Paul not only struck a vital blow to the Gnostic concept of God's oneness,' the Hungarian observed, 'he also aligned himself with the polytheistic pagan beliefs of his Roman oppressors. Satan thrived in a world of multiple minor deities. So much easier to spread evil when hiding among a crowd.' I dug it now. The Devil reshaped the new religion, making it a whole lot less spiritual and much more suited to his own designs. A triple-headed god was right up his alley.

The most satanic manipulation initiated by Paul's teaching was the establishment of the Eucharist. In *1 Corinthians 11:23-25*, Paul described the Seder dinner Jesus celebrated with his disciples on the

first night of Passover just before his trial and
crucifixion. Although Paul did not attend what
became known as the Last Supper, his description
of what took place there found its way into all four
of the Gospels and remains enshrined as the official
Christian sacrament called Holy Communion.

Szabor pointed out that by insinuating this sacrament into
the Christian religion Paul equated Christ with ancient pagan
divinites such as Dionysus and his Roman counterpart, Bacchus,
who demanded their devotees partake of ritual meals. Paul also
linked Christ to the Persian sun god, Mithras, a much beloved
deity in his hometown of Tarsus.

Szabor enumerated the many similarities between Jesus and
Mithras. Both born of virgins, both performed miracles and had
twelve followers, both died on a cross and were buried in rock
tombs, both resurrected, ascending into Heaven during the spring
equinox. The worshipers of Mithras also practiced baptism (they
favored immersion in bull's blood) and partook of a sacramental
bread and wine feast. Szabor went on to point out that when
Emperor Constantine I ordered the first basilica of St Peter to
be constructed on the site of the old Circus of Nero, the edifice
rose above an ancient subterranean *mithraeum* where the faithful
gathered for their ritual meal.

The Hungarian's words rang like an indictment. I read
on with near-maniacal fervor. Szabor zeroed in on Emperor
Constantine the Great, the first 'Christian' emperor. In 325
AD, the year after he made Byzantium the new capital of the
Roman Empire, renaming it Constantinople to honor himself,
Constantine, who still worshiped the sun god Mithras and would
not convert to Christianity until he was on his deathbed in 337
AD, convened the First Council of Nicaea. His stated purpose was
'to achieve ecumenical consensus throughout all of Christendom.'
Constantine's motives were purely political.

By the fourth century AD, Christianity had spread throughout the Empire with dozens of different competing sects 'claiming true authority and clamoring for power.' The 'pragmatic' emperor used the Roman Senate as his model when organizing the Council. He favored the orthodox establishment, the 'straight thinkers,' who were guided by the teachings of Paul. Essentially, he dumped the Gnostics on the trash heap of history.

I found myself reading faster and faster, gobbling up Szabor's book like fried food and almost before I knew it I was into the final paragraphs.

With the Edict of Thessalonica in 380 AD, Nicene Christianity became the official state religion of the Roman Empire. Government-sanctioned religion was nothing new. Old Kingdom Egypt developed this potent synergy five thousand years earlier. But now, for the first time in history all of the known world prayed at the same altar. Here was the most perfect instrument for universal mind control ever conceived. The retooled pagan sun worship that became Pauline Christianity was ideal for the purpose. A tri-part dying and rising god promised eternal life in exchange for unquestioning devotion. Blind faith was the answer to every despot's problems. Introspective Gnostics looking for salvation within themselves would never have tolerated the centuries of tyranny unleashed by the Catholic Church.

Having Satan's man crowned on the Papal throne gave the world the Crusades, the Inquisition, unending subjugation of women, the *Index Librorum Prohibitorum*, a universal ban on contraception which has resulted in

worldwide overpopulation and the perpetuation
of poverty and misery among the lower classes,
the enslavement and forced conversion of primitive
indigenous people everywhere, and, perhaps worst
of all, endless suppression of scientific knowledge.

Not every pope needed to be a devil worshiper.
The Prince of Darkness remains far too crafty
for such obvious manipulation. The right man
at the critical time did the trick. A few key
Cardinals, several select Bishops and a
scattering of devoted priests and monks
served as Satan's fifth column. At certain
malevolent times, the Renaissance being a
prime example, devious Popes wantonly
murdered one another and the devil overplayed
his hand. For the most part, however, he
remains safely out of sight, pulling the hidden
strings that control his evil Papist puppets.

At this point, Szabor digressed into a brief lurid history of those
popes he deemed to have been the tools of Satan, chronicling their
crimes and vices. I read it all with the sort of second-hand pleasure
nasty gossip always provides. After a couple delicious pages of this
stuff, Szabor returned to his savage indictment.

One last word on this insidious Satanic deception.
The Devil embodies all Seven Deadly Sins. Is he not
the master of temptation? Because his Vanity surpasses
all else, supreme Pride makes him mark every achievement
like a dog urinating on a lamppost. Satan left many
signs behind laying claim to his creation of the
Christian Church. The Mithraeum lying beneath
the Vatican remains a prime example. In Paris,

Notre Dame Cathedral is where the Prince of Darkness chose to leave his mark. This great edifice was built on the site of an ancient pagan Gallo-Roman temple, replaced first by a Christian basilica and next a Romanesque church before construction of the cathedral began in 1163.

While excavating in 1719 for a crypt beneath the nave of Notre Dame, workmen uncovered a rectangular limestone column originally erected (c.10 BC) to honor the Emperor Tiberius. It has become known as the Pillar of the Boatman. Carved on one side on the upper half of the third tier is the horned image of Lucifer. Some scholars have identified this carving as the Celtic fertility god, Cernunnos, but it is clearly the face of the devil. The column is housed today in the Cluny Museum in the ruins of ancient Roman baths. Go there and see for yourself.

Better still, climb the 387 steps to the top of Notre Dame's towers and take a close look at the gargoyles staring malevolently down upon the city. Can anyone doubt their demonic origins? One even devours an unfortunate doomed soul. Contemplate the narrow spire crowning the nave. See the rooster mounted at the top. Many claim this is the symbol of secular France, the triumph of the state over religion. I would argue that the rooster is a timeless symbol of the devil. Sealed within this copper *coq* is a thorn from the crown Jesus wore during his final agony on the cross. Satan mocks us all with this ultimate insult.

Paris
1950

I closed János Szabor's book with my heart racing and stared into the embers dying on the hearth. The crafty Hungarian had just shown me the way to find Cyphre.

21

It was just before midnight when I stepped outside. I'd read the afternoon and the evening away. The startling revelations in Szabor's book gave me plenty to think about. A long walk always got the cogwheels turning. The night air felt mild, maybe about fifty degrees. I carried my raincoat over my arm just in case. Springtime weather in Paris behaved like a beautiful woman with too much to drink. Trust her at your own risk. As I headed toward the Seine, I acknowledged there was every chance the brainy Hungarian was full of shit but everything he'd written made sense to me. I knew where to start checking out Devil-worshiping priests.

Despite the hour, the Place Saint-Michel was a lively scene of street musicians and milling groups of university students. I spotted an old woman selling flowers and bought a small spray of violets.

A taxi dropped me off less than ten minutes later in front of Baron Samedi's faux bamboo gate. The wild voodoo floor show was winding down when I walked into the darkened nightclub. I got to the bar and ordered a cognac just in time to watch the La Place cut a goat's throat. Very tough on goats in this joint. When the applause died down and the dimmed houselights rose to crepuscular semidarkness, I ordered a bottle of the best champagne in the house and told the barman to send it over to Mlle Jolicoeur along with my little bouquet.

I cooled my heels sipping brandy for another ten minutes before a waiter appeared and beckoned me to follow. He led me through the shadows to a little table by the back wall. Bijou sat regally there in her silver sequined evening sheath, making a mock show of sniffing my posies. The opened champagne bottle nested in an ice bucket, two full flutes effervescing on the tabletop. 'Very bad luck to drink bubbly alone,' Bijou sighed as the waiter held a chair for me.

I sat down across from her and we gently touched glasses. 'So,' she said after a first sip. 'What brings you *chez moi ce soir?*'

'Thought we might go out for a late dinner.'

'*Mais non, chéri.*' Bijou smiled like a seductive black cat. 'I have something much more delicious in mind.'

I awoke under a crimson-and-gold-striped eiderdown duvet, nested against plump cream puff pillows. Bijou lay asleep beside me, serene and beautiful as the Queen of Sheba. She had one ebony arm outside the covers, exposing her smooth shoulder and a roundness of breast. Dim gray light filtered through a brief parting of heavy velour drapes. I propped myself up on my elbows and had a look around, not remembering much from the night before when I carried Bijou in and tumbled onto the bed, blind with lust and drink.

I half-expected some Harlem Renaissance take on Voodoo mumbo-jumbo. Painted masks and shit. More proof snap judgements weren't cool. Mlle Jolicoeur's *boudoir* revealed gleaming hints of polished mahogany, gilt-bronze and beveled mirror. A tall ornate birdcage half-covered by a fringed purple velvet spread stood by the drape-enclosed windows.

My smokes lay on a round marble-top table to my left. I shook one loose and lit it. The lighter's flare danced firelight across Bijou's perfect flesh. Last night's urgent lovemaking had been surprisingly tender, nothing like the rough sex down in the catacombs. She'd pulsed softly beneath me, sighing, '*Doucement... Doucement...*' It felt so damn good that I said, 'I love you,' meaning, I love this feeling. If she was hip as she made out, she got my drift.

Bijou's hand slid along my quilt-covered thigh. '*Où caches-tu?*' she purred.

'I'm not hiding from you, sweet honey.' I took her hand, guiding it under the covers and between my legs.

'*Chéri...*' A murmuring as she stroked me. '*Un 'ti cadeau pour Minnou.*' She'd called her pussy that same nickname last night. I liked it.

'Mister Johnson's got everything *Minnou* needs,' I whispered, easing inside her.

Sweet and slow, gentle as virgins, we moved in unison, pressing close, a slippery film of sweat like silk between us. I savored her sumptuous body, luxuriant as midnight, while she mewed softly in my ear. We came at the same time just like the ending of a romance novel.

Fondling me, Bijou murmured, 'Be strong again for *Minnou*.'

'Sounds delicious, babe, but I've got to work today.'

'Work? What sort of work do you do, *menteur*?'

'I'm doing it now. What was the name of that priest at the Black Mass? You know him, don't you?'

'*Bien sûr. Il est Père Gustave.* Gustave Dumond.'

'What's his story? Disgusting, disgraced and defrocked?'

'The first two, yes, but not defrocked. He lost his *paroisse*, his parish, but is still a priest.'

'The Mother Church protects her wayward sons.'

'*Certainement.*'

'Know where I can find this fallen Father Gustave?'

'What do you want with him?' Bijou raised up on an elbow to look me straight in the eye. Her perfect breasts proved a distraction.

'Business.'

'What kind of business?'

'Private business.'

'This is why you behaved so badly *au sabat noir*?'

'Yes.'

'You are looking for *el Çifr?*'

'Yes.'

'I do not like this for you, Johnny. *Il est trop dangereux.*'

'Danger's my middle name, babe.'

Bijou gently traced her fingers across my chest, touching the bejeweled golden ornament I wore. 'Oh yes,' she cooed, 'it is your most attractive quality. Makes one not sée the nose so much.'

'Big nose means a big cock.'

'*Moi la chance*,' she said, reaching back under the covers to caress me.

'Yes, lucky you,' I said, kissing her, long and deeply. I got right to the point once our lips parted, 'So… where do I find faggot Father Gus?'

I caught the Line 4 train at the Les Halles Métro station and rode it all the way back to St-Germain-des-Prés. On the way, I thought about what Bijou told me when she explained how to track down Gustave Dumond. The disgraced priest was forbidden from ever again celebrating mass at the altar of Christ. He worked now in exile as a cook at the Orphelinat de Saint Hiöronymous Emiliani, out beyond the edge of the city in a suburban commune called Charenton-le-Pont. I choked back my rage when she told me this, cracking wise instead. 'Screw some choirboys and they give you an orphan's ass as punishment,' I said.

'*C'est la vrai justice catholique*,' she replied.

To hell with Catholic justice! I knew all about that shit. Back in my little blue-tiled hideaway in the courtyard off Saint-Germain, I changed into work clothes that were more appropriate for the old rough-and-tumble, clipping the .38 inside my waistband, and headed back out into the rain, flagging a cab.

We crossed the river on a bridge I guessed was the *pont* of Charenton-le-Pont. Another right took us down an avenue running along the other side of the Seine. Almost immediately, we took a left into a wooded area. A winding drive led to a gloomy three-story brick Victorian gothic fronted by a stagnant pond. Several surrounding acres of desolate trees made the place feel like an island of despair. I paid the driver what was on the meter, telling him to keep it running until I returned.

'*Combien de temps?*' he asked.

'*Vingt minutes, plus ou moins,*' I promised, slipping him an extra twenty-five francs to seal the deal. I didn't want to get left stranded in the middle of nowhere.

I walked along a graveled path toward the entrance. Since I was calling on the cook, the front door didn't cut it. Also, bad news to announce my arrival. I worked my way along the side of the building, spotting a rear door marked *Entrée de Service.* I saw no one in sight and tried the latch. Finding the door locked, I got my twirls out of the satchel and was inside faster than cats fuck.

It was a small dank chamber. Dim light showed through a frosted panel in the only other door. I went into a large pantry. An open entranceway beyond the shelves led into the kitchen, a spacious room with high clerestory windows. Several large pots were steaming on an ancient black iron stove. A concave butcher's block stood to one side and a long bleached table ran straight down the center. At the far end, a man sat on a stool, plucking chickens. It had to be Father Gustave.

With his shirtsleeves rolled to his elbows, he had on a blood-smeared white apron over one of those funny gray dickeys clergymen wear. A backwards collar was snugged-up under his close-cropped beard. Busy at his task, the renegade priest didn't notice my silent approach. When I was a couple yards behind him, I reached under my leather jacket and yanked the snub-nose from its waistband holster. In two strides, I was at his side and stuck the .38's muzzle into his ear.

'Remember me?' I growled, repeating it in French. 'Johnny Favorite?'

'*Oui,*' he said. '*Au sabbat noir.*'

I saw his hands trembling and took the gun out of his ear. *'Parlez-vous anglais?'*

'Non.'

I figured he was lying but didn't want to waste any time beating the truth out of him. 'Put your hands on the table,' I told him in French and he obeyed immediately. They taught these faggots obedience in divinity school. I unzipped the satchel and pulled out my S&W handcuffs, hooking the bastard up before he knew what was happening. He stared up at me, his terror magnified by the thick lenses of his specs. I pulled the photo of Dr Cipher from the satchel.

'Do you know this man? I asked, holding the menace steady in my voice.

'Non.'

'How about him?' I showed him the el Çifr picture. 'It's the same person. You worship Satan, just as I do, right?'

'Oui...' The priest shook his head sadly. *'Mais... Les photographes, je ne sais pas. Il est un inconnu.'*

I slid the duplicate prints back into my satchel. This scrawny prick was probably lying about Cyphre as well. I didn't really give a shit because it wasn't what I was after. It made sense in a way that low-level scum like Father Gus would never get to meet Mr Big in the flesh. 'OK,' I said, 'tell me the name of your superior.'

'Je ne comprends pas.'

Bullshit, I thought, Of course, he understood. Right now, he was more frightened of his boss in the church hierarchy than he was of me. I knew how to change that. Continuing in French, I snarled, 'For the last time, tell me his name. I need the name of your superior.' I added that if he kept his yap shut he'd be in a world of pain.

Threats didn't do the trick. I figured I'd have to knock out some teeth but didn't want to mess up his mouth before he spilled the beans. Glancing about, I spotted a pair of poultry shears lying on the table. Remembering what Bill Burroughs had said about his

Van Gogh kick, I grabbed the shears and took hold of the faggot Father's left wrist. '*Le nom, s'il vous plaît,*' I whispered. '*Ou bien... je coup votre doigt!*'

'*Je ne sais pas,*' he pleaded.

I pulled up his hand and placed the curved blades of the shears around the top joint of his little finger. '*Vite!*' I commanded. The fairy priest quivered with fear, pressing his lips so tightly together in a show of defiance that they drained of all color. I gripped the shears just enough for the blades to press into his flesh. '*Dernière chance,*' I grinned. '*Un, deux... trois!*' As I applied the pressure, I laughed and said, 'This little piggy went to market...' The poultry shears closed easily, almost without effort, and the last digit of Father Gustave's pinkie popped off like a Vienna sausage.

The skinny child abuser howled more out of shock than pain, I thought. I tilted his hand away from me so the spraying blood splattered his face and priestly collar. Gus talked plenty now, a fast and furious flow of frog babble I couldn't comprehend. '*Le nom, s'il vous plaît,*' I said with quiet calm.

He stared up at me, white with rage, his bulging eyes defiant. '*Monstre!*' he spewed.

'*Oui,*' I agreed, '*je suis un monstre diabolique.*' I moved the open jaws of the shears to his next finger in line. '*Encore?*' I asked. '*Le nom... ou le prochain doigt.*' Still, he gave no answer, looking away from the inevitable. 'OK, *petit pédé*... This little piggy stayed home!' *Snip!* The second joint of his ring finger popped off onto the tabletop beside the other severed digit.

This time he didn't scream. He sobbed like a baby, staring at his mutilated hand. I moved the shears to his middle finger. '*Encore?*' I asked. '*Un autre? Il y a plus de trois.*'

'*Non! Non! Avez pitié á moi. Je demande grâce!*'

He begged me for mercy. 'OK,' I said. '*Donnez-moi le nom.*'

'*Cardinal Vincent Latour,*' he blurted in a panic. '*L'archevêque de Paris.*'

'*Vous avez bien fait.*' I told Gus he did the right thing and set down the poultry shears, grabbing a dishtowel to wrap around his bleeding hand. '*Où habite-t-il?*' I asked. '*Cet cardinal?*' I needed to know where the bastard lived.

'*A rue Barbet de Jouy dans le sept,*' the priest sobbed.

'*Quel nombre?*'

'*Trente-deux.*'

'*Bon.*' I had what I'd come for. '*Courage. Il est seulement votre main gauche.*' I told the blubbering fag to cheer up as I unlocked my Peerless Number 4 bracelets. It was only his left hand.

'*Je gaucher!*' Gussy-boy wailed. He was left-handed.

'*Tant pis,*' I said. '*Votre malchance.*' Too bad. It was his tough luck.

22

I left by the service entrance and walked back through the dreary woods toward the waiting taxi. The cabby leaned against a front fender smoking a cigarette. '*Parlez-vous anglais?*' I asked, climbing into the hack.

'*Un peu,*' the driver replied. A little was good enough for me. I asked him the meaning of the word '*archevêque.*'

'Archbishop.'

I thanked him. Cardinal Latour was the Archbishop of Paris, a high ranking Devil-worshiper and just the man I wanted to see. We drove back to my place, taking almost the same route in reverse. Along the way, I practiced my French with the *chauffeur de taxi* and he responded by brushing up on his English with me. It was a game we played all the way until he pulled over by my building on Saint-Germain. I asked him to wait in the open space reserved for the driveway into the courtyard.

Inside the blue-tiled cottage, I ditched my satchel, making sure to take the twirls and monocular. I stuffed the red Paris street guide into my flight jacket's inner map pocket. It only took half a minute. On my way out, I grabbed the Leica with its telephoto lens. Back in the cab, I told the driver to take me to rue Barbet de Jouy and saw the look in his eyes in the rearview mirror. He knew the Archbishop of Paris lived somewhere on this street. What did it matter? When he dropped me off he'd be on his way with his fare and a big tip. I'd never have to see him again. My idea of a perfect friendship.

Didn't take long to get there. I gave my driver no street number and he dropped me off on rue de Varenne at the beginning of Barbet de Jouy, a long narrow street only wide enough for a single lane of traffic with parking on either side.

There wasn't much foot traffic and I sauntered along, the camera slung around my neck disguising me as an innocent tourist. The drizzle had let up a bit and felt more like a heavy mist. I spotted number 32, the first of two identical arched entryways with decorative blue-painted wooden double doors set into a long single-story building. Those doors probably led to inner courtyards. My twirls would get me inside in seconds but I didn't want to chance getting spotted. A quoin stack gave the near end of the building a fine architectural finish only slightly offset by the iron drainpipe running alongside it and provided an obvious access point it didn't take a cat burglar to spot.

After waiting a minute or so for two pedestrians to turn the corner, I slung the Leica over my back, took hold of the drainpipe, and started to climb. Everything was wet but it turned out to be easier than it looked. The Vibram soles on my boots provided a good grip on the slick angled surfaces in the spaces between the quoins and I went up quickly as if climbing a ladder, clutching the drainpipe for balance. I reached the cornice in a matter of seconds then hauled myself onto the roof.

It was a whole lot easier than playing window-washer outside of Ethan Krusemark's office on the 45th floor of the Chrysler Building. A white-clad chimney jutted straight up about fifteen feet away and I crawled toward it up the roof's gentle slope, keeping a low profile in case anyone might be watching on the other side. I scrambled over the ridge and slid down to the protection of the chimney, out of sight from both the street and the courtyard below. Turned out to be about what I expected, a parking area for the main house across the way. A couple big black cars were parked outside.

This was not where I wanted to be. I got out the monocular and scoped the place out. Behind the house was a garden with trees and beyond them more trees. A line of low structures separated the cardinal's backyard from what I assumed was a park. I pulled the copy of *Paris par Arrondissement* from inside my jacket. Turning to the little one-page map for the 7th, I saw that the park was probably connected to the Lycée V Duruy on Boulevard des Invalides, around the corner and down the next block.

Either way, the park provided access to the row of little buildings from where I could peek into Vincent Latour's private playground. No one down below to see me so I got to my feet and walked carefully along the roof toward the convenient drainpipe. I spotted a woman pushing a baby carriage coming toward me down the street. Two teenagers holding umbrellas approached from the opposite direction along Barbet de Jouy. I waited them out, making no effort to hide. From my experience, people rarely looked up in the city. They mostly kept their eyes fixed on the pavement before them. A rainy day made things even easier.

Once the pedestrians passed beneath me, I climbed quickly back down the side of the building. I drilled along Barbet de Jouy, catching up with the teenagers on the corner. They turned left and I swung right, strolling along, checking out the layout of the school I'd spotted on my guide map. A wall containing what I believed to be the park ran for half a block, connecting with the first of several conjoined four-story buildings. A name carved over the entrance gateway told me this was the Lycée Victor Duruy.

Easy enough to walk through the place pretending I had an appointment with someone and find my way to the park out back. I looked too old to be a student and wasn't dressed like a teacher. I'd stand out like Hitler at a bar mitzvah. Most of all, I didn't want to be seen or remembered and ruled out the easy way in. Walking back, I spotted something I'd missed going the other way, a three-foot gap between the wall around the corner property and a lower adjoining wall belonging to the Lycée.

A quick glance both ways up and down the boulevard showed no one approaching on my right and only a couple of students loitering far off by the entrance to the Lycée. Not rushing things but not taking my time about it either, I climbed up the decorative ironwork bars inset between the walls, swiveled my legs around to the other side, turned onto my stomach and slid down until I hung by my fingertips. It was a short drop to the wet dirt below.

Walking straight ahead, I found myself in the large wooded park behind the Lycée Victor Duruy that I'd spotted from the garage rooftop. None of the students talking and smoking beneath the trees paid any attention to me as I walked toward the row of buildings that hemmed in the cardinal's backyard.

I made straight for the last building on the left. Set back a couple feet and out of my sight, an adjoining structure half the height of the others came as a cool surprise. It was made to order. I dragged a garbage bin over close to the side wall, climbed up on it and clambered onto the roof. A pair of square waist-high ventilation vents thrust up close to the wall of the next house in line. I was on top of one quick as Peg Leg Bates tapping out a Double Buffalo. The edge of a roof came to the middle of my chest. A maneuver much like a vertical pushup lifted me high enough to get a leg over and I rolled onto my side taking care not to clobber the camera.

I crawled across the rooftop on my elbows and knees like a soldier scrambling under fire. A gap between this building and the next forced me to stand briefly and step across. Back on my belly, I wriggled to the other side and stared straight down into Cardinal Latour's backyard.

Using the monoscope, I stared into the wide windows of the archbishop's palace. That's what I mentally called the place. It was really just another millionaire's pad. The curtains were pulled back on every floor and I hoped for a glimpse of swishing scarlet robes. No such luck. Every instinct I'd honed in fifteen years of tail jobs and stakeouts told me that waiting would pay off in the end. Sometime today, sooner or later, Father Gustave would come moping along to pay his boss a visit. I felt it in my gut.

Killing time, I found myself mentally riffing Slim and Slam's

'Flat Foot Floogie,' repeating the nonsense syllables like a moron's mantra: *'floy, floy... floy-doy, floy-doy, floy-doy...'* Their novelty jive tune was a big hit in '38 when I toured with Spider's band. The guys on the bus sang it over and over through long nights on the road. By the time I was out of the army and the hospital and had become Harry Angel, private eye, the groovy duo had split the sheets. I caught them both separately in one or more of the many jazz clubs that flourished on and around 52nd Street after the war. Working as a dick often took me to those joints. I figured then it was just part of the job. In retrospect, I knew the music still had been in my blood, pulsing in my heart, drawing me back like an ebbing tide.

I lay watching on the damp rooftop, lost in my jump-tune memories, probably a couple hours or more. At one point, the low gray cloud cover opened up in patches, sending silver shafts of sunshine piercing through like searchlights. As if by divine command, His Eminence walked out the door into his backyard, followed by the cringing padre with his right hand swathed in bandages.

Vincent Latour was a plump, florid man possessing the smug porcine face of a cartoon tycoon. He dressed down in a black cassock with red buttons instead of the splendid scarlet outfit I expected. He did wear a broad scarlet sash belted around his waist and had on the little red beanie. A huge silver cross dangled around his neck.

Propped on my elbows, I got the Leica into position and focused the 135 mm lens, snapping a couple quick pix of the Devil-worshiping clerics in animated conversation. I couldn't make out what they were saying but got the gist of it from the way Father Gus waved his bandaged hand around. I knew they were talking about me. This was just what I wanted. But wait...! Things soon got even better.

Father Gus dropped to one knee and kissed the cardinal's big ring. I'd never seen that before except on TV. The skinny priest knelt before his superior on both knees and began fumbling with the lowest buttons on the cardinal's cassock. Using his unaccustomed right hand, his left now useless for the purpose, Gustave struggled with his task until benevolent old Latour reached down and helped out, unfastening all the buttons below the waist himself.

As I snapped shot after shot, the cardinal parted the folds of his cassock, revealing his thrusting hard on. The kneeling priest gobbled up the boner like a kid with an Eskimo pie, pushing its whole length into his mouth at once. I tightened my focus on this ecclesiastical blow job, getting it all on film as Cardinal Latour placed a benevolent hand on his supplicant's head and looked ecstatically up at the heavens above, his mouth wide in a silent howl of joy.

23

I spent the night with Bijou again. Our pillow talk mostly concerned recent events. She wanted to know if I'd been to see Father Gustave.

'*Mais oui, chérie,*' I replied.

'And was your meeting a successful one?'

'Everything I hoped for and a whole lot more.'

She didn't press for additional info and I kept the inside dope to myself. I knew she'd heard all about the finger chopping. News travels fast on the voodoo telegraph. Maybe even faster by black magic express. I'd shot a whole roll of film and asked a cab driver to take me to the nearest photographic supply shop. I knew what I needed because Ernie Cavalero had been a stickler about developing our own film. 'It's evidence,' he used to say. 'Would you send fingerprints you just dusted and lifted out to a drugstore for analysis?' Because our office had no bathroom, sharing toilet facilities with every other seedy business on the floor, I'd turned the crapper in my rooms at the Chelsea into a darkroom when there was exposed film to deal with. I'd done the same thing at my little Parisian house.

While I was waiting for the film to dry, I dropped by another restaurant on the Vendôme concierge's list, Lapérouse, a three-star Michelin temple to haute cuisine on Quai des Grands-Augustin. I regaled Bijou with a colorful account of my dinner and the friendship I'd struck up with the grizzled owner, Roger

Topolinski, who'd proved to be as charming as Maurice Chevalier once he learned I was Johnny Favorite. Turned out Topo wasn't just a genius restaurateur, he also spoke six languages, including being well versed in Latin, played the violin, and had an affection for American jazz. He'd insisted on accompanying me on his fiddle while I crooned a random selection of standards.

Working her wiles, Bijou got me to stay for *petit déjeuner* late the next morning. She didn't say much, smiling at me, catlike, content and serene as we drank coffee and ate croissants with blackcurrant jam. I felt her soft silken cords tighten about me. Better watch out. I was starting to like it.

Bijou had the Taj Mahal of bathrooms. I lingered in the shower, then shaved. Faced with the pathetic bathtub in my cottage, I could get hooked on this. Back in my double-breasted suit, I looked like a million bucks. Bijou snuggled up for a goodbye kiss.

Crisp and cool, perfect for a morning walk. I found my way to rue Saint-Honoré. I needed certain stationery supplies and located a fancy *papeterie*, buying a stick of red sealing wax and a large cream-colored envelope.

Ten more minutes at a brisk pace took me to Morgan Guaranty Trust. Alone in the little room with my safe deposit box, I slipped my exposed film inside and withdrew another grand. After changing my money into francs, I drilled across the plaza to the Hotel Vendôme, asking at the desk if any mail had come for me. The clerk handed me a monogrammed pink envelope reeking with perfume.

Back on the street, I lit up a Lucky and opened the perfumed letter. The pink stationery was embossed with the same ornate rosette monogram as the envelope. I guessed the intertwining initials to be ERM. The letter was written in green ink, the words vibrating against the rose-colored paper. Between the lines, Elizabeth Monteblanco's brief note became a bitter love letter to Warren Wagner Jr. After informing me she knew nothing of either Dr Cipher or el Çifr, the fragrant ERM concluded, 'Please tell

Mr Wagner how much I enjoyed our time together. The briefest pleasures often prove most memorable.'

I read the letter over a second time, amused by the thought of absurd little Warren Wagner Jr as a red-hot lover. I flagged down a taxi, which dropped me off by the courtyard entrance on Saint-Germain. I didn't hang around the cottage for long. I took the proof sheet prints down from the bathroom clothesline, putting one in my satchel and the other into the envelope I'd bought. Thinking about my next gag made me grin as I eased down the Windsor knot on my necktie. I unfastened a couple buttons and removed the gold medallion I wore. This bit with the sealing wax was a first. It bubbled and dripped onto the envelope flap, puddling like crimson lava. I pushed the face of my medallion into the molten wax. It left a perfect impression.

I headed for the archbishop's mansion, arriving at 32, rue Barbet de Jouy in under ten minutes. I pressed the button marked 'Diocèse de Paris' on the side wall of the main gate and was buzzed in. Having peeked down from the rooftop I knew what to expect and crossed the courtyard to the main residence. I rang another bell at the front entrance and was admitted by a gray man in a gray suit into a spacious walnut-paneled reception room. The somber gentleman asked me something in rapid-fire French that I didn't quite catch.

'I'm here to see the cardinal,' I told him in English.

This seemed to do the trick. The ghostly factotum led me silently up a wide flight of carpeted stairs to a second-floor hall. He opened a slab-like mahogany door and motioned me inside. A thin young priest wearing a simple black vestment stared at me without expression from behind a massive desk. A plain oak cross big enough to crucify a monkey hung on the wall behind him. I waited for him to speak. His blank stare told me nothing. This was how it worked at confession.

'I'd like a word with Cardinal Latour,' I said, speaking in English. Didn't want anything getting lost in translation.

'Do you have an appointment?' The priest knew I had no such

thing. He slowly opened a large red-leather bound day-runner to make his point.

'Here's all the appointment I need.' I handed the priest my large cream envelope with the bold red seal. He took it delicately between his fingertips. 'What are you waiting for,' I growled. 'Show it to him.'

'I am afraid His Eminence has a most crowded schedule today.' The priest avoided my furious eyes.

'Show him the fucking letter!'

'Are you threatening me?'

'I'm suggesting if you want to keep your cushy job here you better give the cardinal my letter *tout de suite*.'

'Very well,' he said, getting up with undisguised reluctance. 'Please wait here.' He walked to a door a few paces away and went inside, closing it in my face. I cooled my heels for maybe a minute before the servile priest reappeared. 'His Eminence will see you now.' His tone suggested stern disapproval as he held the door wide for me.

I heard the door close behind me. Stepping into this opulent office from the austere antechamber felt like going onstage. I took a moment to admire the set. A large mahogany desk, ornately carved as a medieval pulpit, stood dead center. The cardinal sat there staring down at the contact sheet, chuckling louder than a naughty choirboy hiding porn in his hymnal. Behind him, rich maroon drapes were drawn back revealing a pair of French doors that opened onto a small balcony overlooking the garden.

The archbishop glanced up. He wore his plain cassock with the red buttons and piping. 'Welcome, Mr Favorite,' he said, speaking perfect English in a hoarse whisper. 'I've been expecting you.' Latour gestured at an upholstered chair beside his desk.

'Yeah. Word gets around.' I sat down, still looking around. A triptych altarpiece depicting medieval souls pitched into Hell caught my attention. Grotesque monsters devoured the doomed as they fell.

'Perhaps I should call you, Mr Liebling.' The cardinal's scratchy rasp sounded so faint I had to lean forward to catch what he said.

'You've been doing some digging,' I said. Latour mumbled back at me. I didn't understand. 'Speak up. I can't hear a thing.'

'Impossible,' the cardinal whispered, tapping a scar on his throat. 'Larynx surgery.'

'What was the problem?'

'Esophageal cancer.'

'You're a lucky man.'

'Luck has nothing to do with it. As you are well aware, Mr Favorite, the Dark Lord rewards the faithful. All good things come to those who believe.'

'Yeah? Well, I believe in yours truly. That's my faith. I can understand how you found the dope on Johnny Favorite. I got a lot of press in my day. How is it you know my real name is Liebling?'

'The Mother Church excels at record keeping,' the cardinal whispered. 'We catalog our martyrs, maintain an index of forbidden books, list patron saints on the calendar and when an abandoned orphan boy rises from obscurity to achieve great success seemingly through talent alone, we never forget. How fascinating to learn this talented boy also worships Satan.'

'Certainly done your homework.'

'Whatever success I've earned I owe to diligence.'

'Bullshit! We both know you're just another Devil-worshiper like me.'

Cardinal Latour drummed his pudgy fingers on the contact sheet. 'Precisely. So why don't we get down to business? How much do you want for the film?'

It was my turn to chuckle. He thought this was all about blackmail. 'Not one damn *sou*,' I said. 'Those pictures allow me to pump you for information whenever I want.'

'Information…?'

I took the Cyphre photos from my satchel and placed two of them in front of Latour, watching him for the slightest twitch.

I'm good at this. Latour kept it deadpan. 'Know this character?' I asked.

'No.' The cardinal shook his head.

'The one on the left calls himself el Çifr. The magician goes by a few different names: Dr Cipher and Fra Diavolo.'

'I have never seen this man before in my life. In either version.'

Wasn't sure I bought that. 'You might run across him,' I said. 'You travel in the same circles.' I wrote the café-tabac phone number on the back of the el Çifr photo using one of Krusemark's fancy fountain pens. 'Call me at this number when you see him. If you work half as hard tracking down Cyphre as you did finding out about me, we'll have him in *un clin d'oeil*.' Didn't know if my brand-new French worked on Latour. 'I'll stop by from time to time and check on your progress. Make sure your snotty secretary lets you know when I call. I'm at the top of your list. All other business stops on a dime when I want to pay a visit.'

'You will have immediate access at all times, Mr Favorite,' the cardinal replied. 'I cannot promise results in "the wink of an eye,"' he said, winking for emphasis. 'I will do everything possible. Pull all the strings. Is that not the phrase?'

'*Oui.*'

'And… the film?'

'Safe for now. Find Dr Cipher and it's all yours.'

Cardinal Latour flipped over the contact sheet. 'Stay a moment, Mr Favorite,' he said, pulling a pen from an onyx-mounted set on his desk. 'This is for you.' He drew an intricate geometric pattern on the back of the contact sheet, displaying a skill learned only from much practice. 'A blessing from the Archbishop of Paris.' Latour jotted a couple lines beneath his drawing and slid the sheet across the desk toward me. '*Vade in pace,*' he said.

24

A final faint blue hint of day lingered in the darkening evening sky as I set out for La Tour d'Argent. This was a damn fine town once you got the feel of it.

I turned left on rue de Poissy and walked to the river's edge, continuing along the quai as brightly-lit bateaux mouches cruised past beneath me, trailing music in their wake like floating nightclubs. I reached le Pont de la Tournelle moments later. *Voilà!* There stood the famed Silver Tower restaurant across the street, top-floor dining room glowing fervently as a greeting card depiction of Heaven. This is where the Hungarian professor, János Szabor, had agreed to talk with me if I picked up the tab. Burroughs had arranged the meeting at my request when I'd returned Szabor's book to him. I crossed diagonally over to the unadorned entrance and a white-gloved footman swung open the door for me.

The receptionist took my name and said my guest was waiting in *la salle d'attente,* nodding his pomaded head in that direction in case I might get lost. I strolled through the empty waiting lounge past formally arranged antique furniture. A huge brocade carpet over twenty feet long hung from the ceiling. Finding my way into a small corner bar where glass showcases housed silver heirlooms from the restaurant's past, I spotted a curious little man sporting old-fashioned wire-rimmed glasses, perched on one of four tall bar stools, his lean lupine face blue with five o'clock shadow. A mop of gray curls made me think of the big bad wolf in a granny wig. The moss-green wide-wale corduroy suit, red plaid shirt and big blue bow tie with yellow polka dots exaggerated his clownish appearance. He stared into the middle distance holding a champagne flute effervescent with what appeared to be raspberry soda pop.

'János Szabor?' I asked, extending my hand into his daydream.

'Mr Favorite.' Szabor set his drink on the bar and climbed down to give me one of those wimpy European grips. 'A distinct pleasure.' His accent was impossible to place, a faint musical lilt spicing his perfect English.

'What's that you're drinking?'

'Kir Royal.'

I told the barman I'd have a Manhattan, 'Straight up.' He informed me in kindergarten French that this was not a cocktail bar, offering a complimentary glass of champagne instead. 'OK,' I said.

Szabor resumed his roost. I took the stool beside him. Distracted by the loud gunshot pop of a cork behind me, I missed some of what the Hungarian said, catching only, '… before the war, I remember reading that you used to be known as a Devil-worshiper.'

'So they tell me.'

'You don't remember?'

I tapped my noggin. 'Shell shock.'

'We are all still in shock from that terrible catastrophe,' Szabor said. The barman handed me a slim bubbling glass of something very far removed from a Manhattan. 'Chin-chin.' Szabor stared soulfully at me over the rim of his drink.

'Bottoms' up,' I said. Before my second swallow the maître d' appeared to say our table was ready. We followed him to a tiny four-person elevator and ascended to the sixth floor. The lift doors slid open and revealed a circular candlelit dining room topped by a glowing round glass ceiling. A crystal chandelier dangled from the center. Floor-to-ceiling windows formed a curving wall looking out on night-time Paris. Escorted across a carpet emblazoned with the restaurant's coat-of-arms logo, we were seated at an immaculate table set with white linen and silver water goblets. The back of Notre-Dame was bathed in spotlights before us, the Seine enfolding the islands in a dark sinuous embrace.

A waiter placed a volume twice as thick as the Manhattan telephone directory on our table. '*La carte des vins*,' Szabor said. He told me La Tour d'Argent had the most extensive cellar in all Paris. I glanced around. This was more than just another high-class joint adorned with tapestries and hand-painted wall panels. The view and the elevator ride made the place feel like an exclusive private club. Waiters all decked out in wing collars and tails. Affluent frogs everywhere, smoking and debating the inconsequential. A young Japanese couple held hands a couple tables away. I didn't spot any other obvious tourists.

Our waiter approached, solemn as an undertaker in his soup-and-fish, placing a silver tray of hors d'oeuvres on the table before handing us menus. Szabor wolfed down a canape and reached for a second. I took one, a perfect white slice of radish topped by salmon tartare. 'Eat here often?' I asked.

'Twelve years in Paris,' he said. 'Today marks my fifth visit. Poor academics don't often dine like kings. I am a mendicant monk, dependent on the kindness of occasional benefactors.' The starving professor grabbed two more hors d'oeuvres. Three remained on the tray. I ate a Madeleine stuffed with anchovy filling, leaving the rest for my voracious guest.

'What do you recommend?' I opened my menu.

'*Non!*' Szabor reached across and took the bill of fare from my hand. 'You must have the duck. There is no other choice at La Tour. The Terrail family raises every duck. On their family farm in Challans. Each gets a number! Six to eight weeks old only. They strangle them to preserve the blood for the sauce. You will see. *Il est magnifique.* Almost medieval.'

'I'm sold. Why don't you order our meal?'

'Everything?'

'The works.'

'*Le vin aussi?*'

'Be my guest.'

Szabor's smirking grin gave shit-eating a whole new meaning. Time for this bird to start singing for his supper. I pulled Cardinal Latour's mumbo-jumbo doodle from my satchel and placed it on the immaculate tablecloth in front of him. 'You read Latin, right?'

'*Bien sûr.*'

'Translate it for me.'

Szabor picked up the contact sheet, squinting at the inscription. I didn't want him to see what was on the other side and almost took the page away from him but he never turned it over. 'I am not well versed in witchcraft,' he said. 'The talisman means nothing to me.'

'What's it say?'

'A lucky charm, really.' He tapped a forefinger on the opening words. '*Bonam Fortunam.* Here right at the start: "Good luck..." Next, we see –'

'I don't need a private lesson,' I said. 'Just a translation.'

János Szabor blinked rapidly at me. 'I fear a literal translation might sound absurd. This charm is for seekers. Anyone on a quest. The text provides a guide. Every month, during the waxing of the final crescent, the supplicant must light a red candle at moonrise and burn a copy of this diagram in the flame while chanting, "*Adiuva me, Mater Luna. Viam monstra. Lux tua nos ducat,*" over and over, until the paper is reduced to ash.'

I handed him my fountain pen. 'Write it all down and give it to me again in English.'

'Help me, Mother Moon. Show me the way. Your light guides us,' Szabor intoned, mocking the whole business with his fake prophetic tone as he wrote the words at the bottom of the page. 'How fortuitous,' he added, his eyes lively with mirth. 'The phase of the moon for the next three nights is perfect for casting your little spell.'

I gave his sarcasm a pass and took back the contact sheet, slipping it into my satchel and bringing out Krusemark's silk-bound spell book in its place. Flipping to the page with the nearly identical diagram, I showed it to Szabor. 'What about this one?' I asked.

The Hungarian scholar took the book almost reverently. 'A *grimoire*. Late 18th century and printed in Geneva, I should guess. I have not seen this one before. You really are quite the black magician, are you not, Mr Favorite?'

'Call me Johnny.'

'Only if you call me János.'

'Deal.'

'Well then... the deal here, Johnny, as you must know, these two amulets, charms if you will, they are diametrically opposed despite their many overt similarities. See. Look at the start. "*Fortuna mala.*" Bad luck. The diagram appears identical to the other. I would guess they are different in marginal ways. Perhaps mirror images. The text also is very similar yet completely opposite in meaning. This dark charm is designed to prevent a seeker from finding the truth. The candle must be black not red, ignited at moonrise during the final quarter. A repeated chant is likewise required. Not so benevolent as the first. What we have in this instance is a curse laid upon the searcher.'

A different waiter stepped up to the table, this one the sommelier. I knew that from the little silver cup hanging around his neck on a chain. Szabor handed back my book of spells. Without ever opening the massive wine list, the Hungarian launched into rapid-fire frog discourse. After concluding our order, he assured me he had secured two bottles I would greatly enjoy. The first, a Chablis Montée de Tonnerre, '53, arrived in a little horizontal basket at the same moment our regular waiter set two small plates on the table, each holding several blanched caviar-topped stalks of emerald-green asparagus.

'Ah... *les amuse-gueules*,' János enthused, explaining these were complimentary and meant to enliven the palate. A brief mumbled consultation with the server concluded our order. I recognized the word '*canard*.' The clownish scholar looked very pleased with himself.

Once the crisp white wine had been uncorked and poured and we had a moment of privacy again, I told Szabor how much I had learned from his book. 'Until Burroughs loaned me his copy, I had no idea that you and I were on the same quest.' I slid the two pictures of Cyphre across the table toward him. 'I'm searching for this man.'

'Another Devil-worshiper?' he smirked.

'Someone much worse.' I gave him a little of the back-story and wrote each of Cyphre's aliases on the back of the appropriate photo, adding my phone number at the café-tabac. 'Call me if you ever run across him,' I said.

'What makes you think I might possibly keep company with some common music hall magician?'

'Nothing at all common about Dr Cipher. Don't ever underestimate him. Your book gave me a lot to chew on but I'm not really interested in the past. I want to know about what's going down now. Searching for Cyphre took me to a Black Mass in the catacombs on Easter Sunday. The officiant was an ordained priest, not some defrocked discard. I followed the trail from him to the man who gave me that lucky charm. High-ranking big shot in the Church hierarchy. The stuff you wrote about is not ancient history. It's happening here and now right under your nose.'

The flabbergasted scholar's eyes widened behind his spectacles, lips pursing like a goldfish as he groped for the words he wanted to say. Our waiter silently placed a gold-rimmed bowl in front of each of us. It held a pair of mysterious round broiled things smothered in Mornay sauce. Once again, food trumped all. 'First course!' János announced. '*Quenelles de brochet*. A fine fish dumpling, a mousseline, to be precise, bedded on mushrooms duxelle.'

'What kind of fish?'

'*Brochet*. How do you say in English? Pike!'

Light and satiny, the quenelles put me in mind of eating gefilte fish at the Carnegie Deli. Minus the cheesy Mornay sauce. 'Delicious,' I said.

'A recipe from the proprietor's father, a variation of Escoffier's original creation.' Szabor dabbed his lips with his napkin. 'I am interested to know the name of this priest,' he said. 'The higher-up as well.'

'Figured you'd be.' I polished off the last of my poached pike dumplings. 'Maybe we can strike a bargain.'

'I am working on a new book. One dealing with stuff right under my nose in the here and now. I can offer no compensation. Only the satisfaction of exposing an ancient crime.'

'Find Cyphre for me and we're square. I'll tell you everything I know.'

Szabor folded the photos and slipped them into an inside jacket pocket. 'I see. It is necessary now for me to *cherchez l'homme*.' He withdrew his wallet and extracted a calling card. 'Here.' He handed it over. 'Should you wish to reach me.'

I examined Szabor's card. Between his name and the trailing advertising banner of abbreviated honorifics and an address and phone number printed along the bottom, a single embossed word proclaimed: 'Philologue.' I placed it in my satchel. 'I know who to call when I need another Latin lesson,' I said.

'Whom,' János whispered.

I'd had just about enough of this little shit and muttered, 'Whom gives a fuck?' to shut him up.

We drained the last of the white. A busboy whisked our empty bowls away at the same moment the waiter and sommelier closed in. The service flowed smooth as choreography. Our waiter wore a long white apron under his tails. He carried a covered silver serving dish and lifted the domed lid with a dramatic flourish, presenting a perfectly roasted duck, crisp skin a mahogany brown.

'*Superbe!*' Szabor enthused. 'You must watch this now, Johnny.

La préparation du canard au sang. A magnificent, macabre piece of culinary drama.'

The busboy wheeled a white linen draped trolley over to the table. It held some sort of brazier or chaffing dish and a gigantic silver contraption topped by a huge handwheel. The Hungarian returned to his element, ranting about food. Did my best to ignore his rambling monologue as I watched our waiter set down the serving tray and go to work on the duck. After carving off the breasts and legs, he eviscerated and quartered the carcass. He reserved the liver and dumped the rest, heart and other innards included, into what I now recognized as an enormous press, turning the big wheel at the top to crush everything, bones, guts and all with an audible *crunch*. Blood and organ juices trickled out into a sauté pan.

'Madeira... *fine de Champagne* cognac...' Szabor droned as the waiter poured a glass of each spirit into the sauce warming over the brazier. Like the worst of bores, my pompous *philologue* took pains to describe exactly what his pained listener had already just observed.

The sommelier presented the wine to Szabor in its little wicker casket, got a nod of approval and uncorked the bottle with great care. A small tasting swallow was poured. János swirled the goblet of red under his nose, taking a cautious sip. His eyes rolled back like a man lost in the transports of love. '*Côtes de Nuits*,' he said in a sigh of pure pleasure. 'Romanée-Conti Grand Cru, 1940. You will never taste a finer Burgundy.'

The sommelier filled my delicate glass and I enjoyed a similar palate orgy. 'Delicious.' The Hungarian had picked a winner.

'The domaine uprooted all the old vines in 1945. Phylloxera. Romanée-Conti did not produce another vintage for seven years.' Szabor droned on about the marvels of his favorite wine. I tuned him out and focused on our waiter preparing the blood sauce instead. He mashed the duck liver into the thickening mixture and squeezed in some lemon juice. After slicing the breasts he poured deep puddles of his sauce, rendered dark as chocolate, around

them and brought the plates to the table. The busboy placed two
silver-wire baskets beside us. Some kind of fried golden puffs
nested inside. 'Ah, *les magrets*,' János enthused, '*avec pommes de
terre soufflées.*'

It wasn't much to look at, rare duck meat smothered in a rich
mahogany sauce. Just another hash house blue plate special. The
proof of the pudding always came at the end of my fork. *Canard
au sang* passed that test by a million miles. The duck meat moist
and tender, flavor enhanced by the metallic tang of blood in the
earthy sauce. Eating something tasting this wild and primitive in
such an elegant setting put me in mind of cannibals devouring the
royal family in the palace dining room. Szabor ate with his eyes
closed, making little moaning noises while he chewed. It was like
listening to someone getting laid.

Other than an excellent meal and a quick Latin translation,
I wasn't getting a lot of bang out of my buck with Szabor. He'd
learned a lot more from me than the other way round. We didn't
say much while we ate; an occasional purr of pleasure from János
and my nodded grunt in agreement. 'You will enjoy the next
course,' he said as the waiter cleared away our plates.

I made no reply, feeling foolish for having gone to this much
trouble for such meager results. 'What about the pope?' I blurted,
wanting to pry some info, any tiny scrap, out of my gourmet
scholar. 'Think he's a Devil-worshiper?'

'Saintly John XXIII? He wears a perfect mask of sanctity. A most
effective disguise, were he a Satanist. His predecessor, Eugenio
Pacelli, might well have profited from such pious camouflage.'

'Pius number twelve. Picked the right name.'

'That horrible man, so cozy with the Nazis. Who can doubt his
nefarious beliefs? Pacelli signed the *Reichskonkordat* when he was
Cardinal Secretary of State. The Holy See's pact with Hitler points
a finger of guilt his way. Pacelli made numerous anti-Semitic
statements while serving as Papal Nuncio in Germany, further
proof of his evil nature.'

'What about you?' I asked. 'You believe in God? Or Heaven? Hell? Any of it?'

'I believe in Pascal's wager.'

'What's that?'

'Blaise Pascal was a 17th-century French philosopher. Also a physicist and mathematician. His best-known work was his last. *Pensées*, unfinished when he died. It means "Thoughts." In it, Pascal postulated his "Wager." All humanity bets their lives on the existence of God. The stakes are infinite. Either a blissful eternity in Heaven or eternal damnation in Hell. Pascal argued if there is the slimmest chance that God exists a rational man should place his bet on God. He has everything to gain if he wins and nothing at all to lose if he doesn't.'

'I only bet on a sure thing,' I said.

'In that case, Johnny, your best bet is death.'

Szabor's palaver stopped on a dime when the waiter set a plate of food in front of him. This cat's mighty brain took its marching orders from his bottomless gut. I got the same dish, a crisp duck leg accompanied by Béarnaise sauce on the side and a small green salad. János began his low moan again as he tucked in. 'What makes you so sure Pope John has his hands clean?' I broke in.

'You've read my book, haven't you?' I couldn't tell if Szabor's look of displeasure resulted from having his meal interrupted or the thought of a reader misunderstanding his work. 'Not every pope need be in league with Satan. A good man with a pure soul might easily be manipulated by diabolic advisors. The right word whispered by a Devil-worshiping cardinal. It is the same with any head of state.'

'Makes sense. That big shot I told you about is a cardinal.'

János put down his fork, a sure sign he found the topic intriguing. 'I suspected as much. How can I persuade you to tell me his name?'

'You can't. You have to sit tight for a while.'

'I only ask for the sake of my research.'

'Listen, professor, I'm not your fucking assistant. I have my own business to handle. When the time is right, I'll share what I know with you.'

Szabor made no reply and we ate the rest of our second duck portion in silence. When only the leg bone remained, the Hungarian smacked his lips. '*Ah, délicieux,*' he sighed, pushing his plate away. 'Now, the cheese trolley and then we must consider dessert.'

That one pushed my button. I'd had my fill of this gluttonous son-of-a-bitch. 'Fuck the cheese!' I pulled my satchel onto my lap, needing to come away from this pricey feedbag hipper than when I'd walked in. 'Consider this,' I said, handing Szabor the sheet of Hotel Vendôme stationery with the rubbing of the old coin I took from Krusemark's wall safe. My favorite Hungarian's jaw dropped like he was about to swallow the paper whole as if it was some gourmet treat. The leaf trembled in his hands as he studied the dual image.

'Where did you get this?' he demanded.

'None of your damn business! I ask all the questions, remember?'

'Do you possess this coin?'

'Weren't you listening, doc? I'm picking up the tab tonight. Our deal was for me to tap your brain in return. So, spill it. What gives here? Why do you give a shit about this thing? And don't feed me a line about how it's just an old Tyrian shekel. I already know that.'

Szabor smoothed the page out on the tablecloth, tapping a forefinger against the first of my rubbings. 'This is indeed a Tyrian shekel,' he said, sounding out of breath, 'but not simply an old one. It is one of the thirty pieces of silver paid to Judas for betraying Jesus of Nazareth.'

25

I wanted to kill the little clown. No one I hated more than a con artist. I fought the urge to reach across the table and drive my fork into Szabor's tongue. 'Bullshit!' I hissed.

My compressed rage startled the little professor. 'N-No... No,' Szabor stammered. 'I assure you the thirty individuals who own these coins believe the story to be true.' He pointed to the I.I. die-stamped into Melqart's profile. 'These are the initials of Judas Iscariot. No letter for J in the classic Latin alphabet. His name was spelled I-u-d-a-s and pronounced *Yudas*, both in ancient Greek as well as Latin.'

'What about the Roman numeral on the other side? Number thirteen mean something special?'

'I might say to you that it is none of your business. These coins are at the heart of an important project of mine, hopefully my next book.' Szabor took a slow sip of wine. 'Perhaps it would be mutually beneficial if we did business together.'

'What kind of business?'

'I tell you the history of Judas Iscariot's silver, as much as I know at present. In exchange, you will divulge who owns coin number thirteen and the name of the cardinal you mentioned.'

'No deal, doc.' I took my own sweet time and lit up a Lucky. 'The way it looks from my angle is I've got more to offer.' Another pause for a deep drag. 'So,' I said, exhaling slowly, 'you give me all your dope. If I dig the sound of it maybe we can partner up.'

'You know nothing about the coin. I assume we pursue different goals. Tell me more about the man you search for, the one in the photos. What part does he play in our mutual drama?'

'I said no questions, professor, but I'll give you a pass this time. You're looking for Devil-worshipers, *n'est-ce pas?* Find Dr Cipher, alias el Çifr or whatever the hell he's calling himself these days, and you'll be up to your ass in Devil-worshipers.' The waiter approached, wheeling the cheese trolley our way. I waved him off.

'*Mais, le fromage...*' Szabor pouted like a kid sent to bed without supper. '*Quel dommage!*'

'Forget it,' I said. 'You can stuff your face with *beaucoup de fromage* after you spill the beans about the coin.'

The Hungarian stared wistfully at the departing trolley. '*Eh, bien*, no meal is complete without cheese. I will tell all I know. After the death of Judas Iscariot, whether he made a suicide by hanging or was crucified in place of Jesus according to Barnabas, Satan took possession of the blood money, the thirty pieces of silver. Christ had His twelve Apostles and disciples too numerous to count soon followed them. The Devil wanted his own apostles. An evil cadre spreading his message and serving as advisors. He picked thirty of the most wicked men alive and gave each of them one of the Tyrian shekels. Over the centuries these thirty met and held council. The coins passed to their successors, all chosen by Satan, down to the present day.'

'What makes you sure all this isn't just some wild bullshit fable?'

'Because I have seen it with my own eyes. Seven years ago, not long after my book was published, a young man came to visit me. He was personal secretary to an important European diplomat, the ambassador to France from a neighboring nation. Naturally, I cannot provide you with their names or nationality for the same reasons you will not share your own information with me. This young man had read *My Name is Legion* and sought me out because he knew I would believe his story.

'The ambassador owned a Judas shekel, one of those thirty

notorious pieces of silver. His was number 26. He kept it in his office in a gilt and crystal reliquary. As the ambassador's secretary, the young man prepared his daily appointment calendar and made all travel arrangements. He naturally noted any deviation from diplomatic routine. Four times each year, the ambassador left the embassy on unscheduled trips without consulting his secretary first. The young man kept a record and discovered these departures occurred like clockwork every solstice and equinox. Every time the ambassador left on one of these clandestine excursions the Judas coin went missing from its reliquary.

'Curiosity got the best of the secretary. He followed the ambassador on one of his mysterious journeys. Winter solstice, I believe. The young man disguised himself with a wig and false mustache, getting on a train to Rome with the ambassador. Curiously, this important dignitary did not take the Calais–Rome first-class sleeper but booked a first-class couchette in the slower train, which arrives more than four hours later. Perhaps he feared being recognized. A private car awaited the ambassador at the Nuova Stazione Termini. His secretary trailed him by taxi to the Excelsior on Via Veneto. Unable to afford a stay at such an expensive hotel, the young man sat in the lobby. Are you familiar with the Excelsior?'

'I've never been to Rome,' I said.

'Extremely palatial, the lobby enormous. Fit for a king. My young secretary being very well dressed did not look conspicuous in such surroundings. The ambassador's secret trips never lasted more than a day or two. His amanuensis told me he was prepared to wait all night long if required. He brought a book as a form of camouflage. The young man remained there for several hours. He was astonished to see the ambassador reappear sometime before midnight dressed like a priest in a floor-length cassock.'

'On his way to a Black Mass?' My own curiosity probably killed every pussycat in Paris.

'A far more intriguing destination, I promise you. Taxis always wait for passengers outside the Excelsior. The secretary hailed one and followed the ambassador's car. They crossed the Tiber via the Ponte Cavour. Their destination was Vatican City. When the ambassador's car turned into Porta Sant'Anna and stopped for the Swiss Guards, the young man exited the taxi. He drew closer and watched a passenger in the back seat show some very small object for identification.'

'The coin?'

'Yes. Although the distance was too great for the young man to be certain. A black limousine pulled up behind the ambassador's car. The secretary strolled past the entry gate in time to observe someone showing his silver coin to the Swiss Guard. Yet another long black car arrived and the secretary continued walking. Keeping a low profile, is that not how you say it?

'He managed to glimpse the ambassador getting out of his automobile in front of the Torrione di Niccolò V. It is a round 15th-century tower built against the walls of the Palace of Sixtus V. An ancient structure mostly hidden from view by the Swiss Guard barracks. At certain angles you can see it from the street. The secretary assumed it was the ambassador. The person he saw had his head covered by a peaked black hood and wore black gloves.'

'Hood and gloves?'

'Yes. Like a medieval executioner.'

'Clever. No fingerprints with gloves on. Perfect for a secret society.'

'The Council raiment certainly preceded the use of fingerprints for identification. A convenient coincidence nonetheless. They went inside the tower of Nicholas V, closely followed by a similarly hooded and gloved passenger departing the limousine waiting next in line.

'A long procession of luxury vehicles stretched down the Via di Porta Angelica, entering the Vatican one at a time. The young secretary found it prudent to continue walking. He took a taxi straight to the station and caught the first early morning train back to Paris.'

'What was going on inside that tower?'

'The Council of Thirty convenes there.'

'What the hell is that?'

'Most appropriate you should put it that way, Johnny. Remember, I told you how Satan picked thirty wicked men to be his apostolic council, giving each man one of the thirty pieces of silver paid to Judas. That was the original Council of Thirty and it persists to this day. When one of its members dies, his successor is chosen by the Devil and the numbered coin passes on to the next in line.'

'How can you be so damn sure? All your nosey secretary saw was the ambassador dressed up like a Klansman going into this tower. Maybe he was just a member of some secret fraternal Catholic men's society.'

János took a slow sip of wine. 'Excellent point, Johnny. If that had been all he had seen we would still be in the dark. As far as the outside world is concerned, the Council of Thirty does not exist.'

'What're you saying? The secretary got inside?'

'Be patient. Hear me out. My young man had been very confused when he returned to Paris. He, too, suspected he had merely witnessed a gathering of an ancient chivalric society such as the Constantinian Order of St George. He had no real knowledge of his employer's religious beliefs. Because the ambassador represented a predominantly Protestant nation, the secretary was surprised to learn he was a Catholic. That is what he assumed at the time. *L'Osservatore Romano*, the official journal of the Holy See, was among the many European newspapers the diplomat perused every day. After his return from Rome, my self-anointed secret agent made a point of checking the daily Italian edition.

'The secretary never again followed the ambassador to the Vatican. Instead, he discreetly searched for clues that might provide a plausible explanation for what he'd observed. The young man discovered a priest's vestment hidden with the black hood and gloves at the back of a bedroom closet. He kept a close eye on the embassy's travel calendar. Although trips to Rome were never officially recorded, the ambassador went there at every seasonal change.

'The equinoxes and solstices were the occasion of ancient pagan celebrations going back before the dawn of recorded history. Those are known as the "quarter days." The four midpoints between, the "cross-quarter days," are also time-honored pagan festivals. Beltane, otherwise called *Walpurgisnacht*, for example. What non-pagans know as May Day. The Council of Thirty meets on the cross-quarter holidays as well. To disguise her satanic origins, the mother church replaced them all with Christian holidays. Yule became Christmas. Ostara is now Easter.

'After certain trips to Vatican City, the ambassador returned to Rome the following week. His secretary noted that on these occasions a notice in Latin was printed in *L'Osservatore Romano*'s back pages announcing an additional meeting of the *Concilium de Triginta*.'

'The Council of Thirty?' I asked, needing to be sure I got things straight.

'Yes. After hearing the secretary's story, I myself traveled to Rome at every quarter and cross-quarter for the next year or so. I observed everything the young man told me to be accurate.'

'I still don't see how you can be sure you and this secretary saw a gathering of the Devil's council. Maybe it was only some Catholic mumbo-jumbo. Some secret deal like when they vote for a new pope.'

Szabor held up his index finger. 'Hear me out. At Litha, the Summer Solstice, the secretary told me he grew concerned when his employer did not leave the embassy that day in time for the Rome train's evening departure. He searched the embassy and found the man lying dead on the floor of his office. Heart attack? Stroke? There was no sign of violence. The ambassador and his secretary had the only keys to the office. Acting on impulse, the young man took the silver shekel from the reliquary, locked the office door and flew to Rome that evening with the black cassock, gloves and hood packed in his overnight case. Because he'd acted, how do you call it, spur of the moment, to satisfy a capricious curiosity, my young man felt no apprehension. Where was the harm in sneaking into a secret meeting of a Catholic fraternal society? It wasn't until a half-hour before midnight when the young man pulled on the black hood as the limousine sped across the Arno that he felt afraid.'

I sat captivated by the professor's account of what his young secret agent had witnessed at the Council of Thirty's meeting at the Vatican. 'I'd like to talk to this young man,' I said when he'd finished. 'How can I get in touch with him?'

'You can't,' Szabor said. 'After he came to me and told his story, he vanished off the face of the earth. I don't know if he went into hiding or was eliminated by the Council of Thirty.'

Before I could ask how the Council figured out the young secretary was an impostor, Szabor raised his index finger again, saying, 'You see, he made two serious errors. First, prior to the members' departure, a parchment and an athame were passed together around the table. Each member in turn pulled off his right glove and sliced open a forefinger to mark the document with blood. Some merely squeezed a drop of blood onto the parchment. Others pressed their wounds down on the vellum, smudging their mark without leaving fingerprints. Very nervous with the entire Council watching him, my young informant didn't think to imitate what he had just observed and left a clear fingerprint. He sealed his fate in blood on their document. Second, he flew home and as soon as he returned to the embassy in the morning, he returned the Judas shekel to the reliquary and phoned the authorities, reporting the ambassador's death.'

'Bad move. He should have given it more time. Made it look like the ambassador went to Rome and came back on the train before he croaked.'

'Once again, your assessments are most astute, Johnny.' Szabor sipped the pricey Burgundy. 'These are powerful individuals. You made rubbings from a coin belonging to a Council member. He certainly will have you killed if he finds out what you have done.'

'The man who owned that coin is dead.'

'In that case, the Judas shekel is gone.'

'What're you talking about?'

'The young secretary told me about the ambassador's last will and testament. He bequeathed the coin to the *Sancta Sedes.*'

'What's that?'

'The Holy See, the governing body of the Catholic Church. A representative of the Roman Curia was present at the reading of the ambassador's will. He left the same day in possession of the coin.'

I didn't get it. 'You said all members of the Council of Thirty were unknown to each other. Total strangers. A secret even within the Vatican. How would they know the meaning of the ambassador's Judas coin even if he bequeathed it to them?'

'A conundrum, to be sure. According to legend, the Devil, when he took the form of a man, handpicked his original Council and gave each of the chosen thirty a piece of Judas Iscariot's silver. This tale strikes me as no more implausible than the story of Jesus raising the dead or turning water into wine. Why not presume that the Devil still walks the earth today? Wouldn't he keep his eye on his chosen ones? If one dies, the Devil informs the Curia. An emissary is sent to retrieve the coin. So many secrets in the Vatican.'

I refilled my wineglass, my head buzzing with all Szabor had just told me. 'There must have been a recent Council of Thirty meeting.'

'Yes. The Ostara convocation, at the vernal equinox two weeks ago. March the twenty-first to be precise. There was also another meeting last week. I read of it in *L'Osservatore Romano.* What is truly remarkable, a third gathering is scheduled for tonight.'

'What?'

'Yes. At the stroke of midnight. It was announced in last week's *L'Osservatore Romano*. I have followed these announcements weekly for almost five years and have never before seen three consecutive Council meetings. I told you it was unprecedented. They must be planning something of enormous consequence. Hopefully, not the start of an atomic war.'

My heart sank like the *Andrea Doria*. I didn't want to believe it. Right there under my nose and I missed it. Twice in a row. 'What else do you know?' I asked without enthusiasm.

'Nothing more. That is the whole story, just as I heard it from my unfortunate young secret-agent secretary.'

'Well, then,' I said, sick with regret, 'I guess it's time for some cheese.'

26

I left the restaurant at twenty after ten and walked toward Place St Michel along the quai watching the lights dance on the river. My foul mood turned the picturesque into purgatory, fire-snakes writhing along the Styx. After a handshake, Szabor headed off without a word of thanks in the opposite direction, plunging deep into the shadowy bowels of the *Quartier Latin*. The big duck feast had set me back *f*15,000. Thirty bucks. Learning about Krusemark's coin made it a bargain. Number Thirteen on the Council of Thirty. Handpicked by Louis Cyphre himself.

I owned the Judas coin. It made me the thirteenth member. The Council of Thirty convened in an hour and a half. In Rome. Might as well be on the fucking moon. Why didn't I run into Szabor last week? I could have nailed Cyphre tonight or last week. The vernal equinox had come and gone. Week before Easter. The Last Supper had been a Passover Seder. Jews used a lunar calendar so things shifted around every year. Those satanic motherfuckers had convened their Ostara meeting two weeks ago. Why hadn't Krusemark been there? Why had he stayed in New York when he should have been in Rome?

Szabor said his spy secretary observed empty seats at the Council meeting he'd attended. Maybe it was no big deal if Krusemark didn't show. His daughter had just been murdered and a private dick was snooping into his personal affairs. Risking exposure as a Devil-worshiper trumped his need to get to Rome. Too late now.

He was deader than some throat-slit baby. I wondered why I hadn't seen his obituary in the *Herald Tribune*. I'd been reading it every day; well, most days. Surely an international newspaper would note the passing of a shipping tycoon who did business all over the world. Maybe Krusemark had only been reported missing. Maybe his corpse got torn into little pieces. Maybe rats ate the evidence. Fat chance. Like a wise guy, I'd mailed those film rolls of the Black Mass to the DA's office. They'd be down searching for Ethan Krusemark around the abandoned 18th Street station all right.

The Judas coin had value for me only as long as the millionaire ship owner remained alive. Presumed missing was OK. Alive, essential. The moment he was declared dead, his will would be read and the boys from the Vatican would come to collect the coin and they'd discover it had been stolen. From that moment on, whoever possessed number thirteen was a marked man. Showing up with it at the Bastion of Nicholas V would be signing my own death warrant.

I grabbed a cab over to the Baron Samedi. The voodoo floor show hadn't started yet. I found Bijou by the bar keeping an eye on things. She looked stunning in a strapless red sheath. I kissed Bijou long and hard in front of the bug-eyed bartender. '*Tu es mon trésor,*' I said.

'*Menteur,*' she replied. Liar had become her favorite term of endearment for me. How little she really knew. She pecked my cheek, nipping my earlobe with whispered promises of what was to come later in her bedroom upstairs.

'Couple favors to ask first.'

'*Parle français, chéri,*' she commanded.

'*Avez-vous un... un... je ne sais le mot propre en français. Un* candle *rouge?*'

'*Bougie,*' Bijou said. Without asking why I wanted a candle, she told me she had them in every color and sent a waiter off to fetch a red one. '*Quoi d'autre?*' she asked.

'Better speak English, *ma douce*. Where can I find the nearest all-night newsstand?'

'*Ah, oui*. The other side of Les Halles. On rue du Montmartre across from Saint-Eustache.'

A waiter materialized from out of nowhere and handed Bijou a squat red votive candle. '*Iras-tu prier pour moi?*' she teased, passing it on to me.

She asked if I was going to pray for her. '*Je t'adore seulement*,' I replied, wanting to say I worshiped only her. Wasn't sure I got it right.

'*Menteur...*' She smiled. I kissed her midnight cheek and said I'd see her after closing time.

I cut through Les Halles along rue Baltard between the glowing glass pavilions. The big wholesale market was just starting to jump with deliveries from all over France. Farther on, the open-front newsstand revealed an interior lined on three sides from floor to ceiling with newspapers and magazines displayed face-front. I asked the proprietor for a copy of *L'Osservatore Romano*. The Vatican rag was in Italian, a lingo I knew only from Mulberry Street menus. I went into a café and sipped brandy and water, slowly turning the pages. And there it was. Just the way Szabor told me. My heart skipped a beat. **XXX**. The Roman numerals headed a notice in Latin. None of it meant shit. I spotted *Concilium de Triginta* because the Hungarian professor used those words during his dinner table lecture. I had to know what the message said. I called Szabor from a payphone on the café's back wall. 'János?' I said. 'It's Johnny.'

'Johnny, I have been trying to reach you but can get no answer at your number.'

'My telephone service doesn't work at night. Have you seen the papers?'

'Of course. I bought a copy on my way home. The notice is there.'

'I saw it. Is there another meeting?'

'Yes, next Wednesday at midnight. It is unprecedented. Four in a row.'

'I'm attending that meeting. I have the coin. Judas shekel number thirteen. My problem is I don't know any Latin. Much as I hate to say it, I need your help.'

'This is all... *incroyable*. How can I believe you?'

'I showed you the rubbing. How the hell do you think I made that? I've got the coin to get me in. I need you and your Latin to get me out.'

'And what do I receive in return?'

'You finish your book. I'll share everything I learn with you.'

'And how much can that be when you won't understand a word?'

'I'll go in bugged. Your job is translating the tapes.'

'I know a few things about espionage, Johnny. Are you certain your experiences as an entertainer qualify you for the job?'

'Leave that end of it to me, professor.' We agreed to meet at Café de Flore tomorrow morning at nine.

I rolled up the papers and headed out into a night suddenly as good as it gets, walking toward the river. My mind raced with thoughts of Cyphre. Szabor called a fourth Council of Thirty meeting after Ostara 'unprecedented.' Something really big in the works. Something so enormous Lord Lucifer had to be there in person. Give me one clean shot across that round table and I'd blow His brains out. Like a kamikaze, I'd die happy.

I walked onto the quai downriver along the Seine's Right Bank to the Pont des Arts opposite the Louvre. I found the area deserted. Pairs of street lamps at intervals on either side of every span created alternate areas of light and shadow along the iron pedestrian bridge. To the west, a setting silver sliver of moon hung high above the Eiffel Tower. I lit the red candle with my lighter and placed it on the flat top rail of the iron balustrade. A gentle downstream breeze set the flame flickering.

I took Cardinal Latour's ink-drawn talisman from my satchel, holding one corner in the candle flame. The paper ignited. I chanted the Latin words Latour had written along the bottom of the page, 'Adiuva me, Mater Luna. Viam monstra. Lux tua nos ducat.' As I repeated the words over and over, an ancient power trembled through me.

27

Climbing the stairs up toward daylight at the Madeleine Métro station half past noon the next day, I thought of that legendary Greek cat who went down to Hell and back. A Tennessee Williams play about him flopped on Broadway a couple years ago. Orpheus descended into the underworld to save his sweetheart. I tried remembering the chick's name. No luck. Gone like my past. Things didn't work out the way Orpheus planned but he escaped from Hades with his soul intact. I sold my sorry soul to the Devil. Got the raw end of that deal. After I killed Cyphre maybe all bets were off. Maybe that bloody atonement would cancel my debt.

Despite Szabor's pompous, egghead manner, he had come through in spades that morning. Not only had he given me my first Latin lesson over coffee and croissants at the Flore and offered to continue the lessons at dinner tomorrow night, he'd recommended an ecclesiastical tailor who had just finished fitting me for the black cassock, cape and hood I needed for the Council of Thirty meeting. One item off my list. I still needed to stop by *Kreigman y Fils*, a purveyor of surveillance equipment, on rue Balzac that the professor had also recommended. But first I had to pay a visit to the bank in Place Vendôme, a short walk away.

Turning the corner off rue Saint-Honoré, I thought to check for mail at the hotel. My favorite concierge was engaged with a client when I walked in so I headed straight for the reception desk. The clerk asked me to wait when I gave him my name and requested any mail I might have received. He went back into the office and returned with a somber gent in gray business suit holding an envelope at both ends with his fingertips. He handed it to me without a word. It was embossed Hotel Vendôme stationery. Across the front, someone had written 'Favorite.'

I tore open the envelope, feeling the eyes of the manager, the desk clerk, even a pair of uniformed bellhops, all judging me. The verdict was in. I slid a business card out of the envelope. It was a cheap print shop job without embossed lettering. None of that mattered. It meant big trouble for me. I stared at the name and address, keeping my expression blank as a statue. Everyone behind the desk had certainly read the card several times. Probably had a big laugh that a '*déclassé*' New York City copper was after one of their classy guests. Like catching some big shot screwing the chambermaid.

Lt Daniel P Sterne
Homicide Division
23rd Police Precinct
134-138 West 30th Street
New York 1, NY
PE 6-5305

Sterne had written a brief note on back of his card:

'Mr Favorite, We need to talk ASAP re: a murder investigation. I'm staying at Hotel du Plat d'Etain, 69 Meslay St. Contact me there. ARC. 77-95.'

He signed it 'Sterne,' abrupt as a biting dog. Like a drowning man seeing his life flash before his eyes as he goes under, I dug what Sterne was up to in a split second. They found Warren Wagner Jr's body in the men's room at Idlewild. His father had been my agent. Johnny Favorite was aboard a flight to Paris the same day as Wagner Jr's murder. It took Sterne a couple weeks to connect the dots. 'Merci,' I said to the hotel manager.

'You must understand, Monsieur Favorite,' he replied, speaking in English and enunciating each word precisely as a diplomat, 'the Hotel Vendôme is not accustomed to rude policemen creating a disturbance in the reception area.'

I understood completely, picturing Sterne throwing a moronic shit-fit when a bunch of snooty frogs treated him like the dumb cop he was. 'My apologies,' I said.

'Most appreciated. We are very sorry the Vendôme can no longer keep your mail, Monsieur Favorite. All future correspondence arriving for you will be forwarded to the American Express Company at 11 rue Scribe.'

'Very kind of the establishment,' I said, holding back the urge to slap his smug face. 'One last question, if you'll permit me. When did the detective leave this message?'

'Sometime yesterday evening. I cannot state the exact hour with any certainty.'

'Bien.' I gave the majordomo a curt nod and turned on my heel, walking slowly across the lobby to show I wasn't getting the bum's rush. The concierge appeared unoccupied. I paused at his desk and exchanged the usual pleasantries. He assured me he had no news about Natas. I told him our deal was still on and sauntered out of the hotel like a man without a care in the world.

Crossing the square toward the bank, my mind raced with thoughts of Sterne. I knew he'd be back at the Hotel Vendôme sometime today to see if I'd got his message. Lucky break for me that he didn't walk in a couple minutes ago. I needed to stay two jumps ahead of him. While Sterne plodded along, one blind step at a time like a stupid flatfoot, I'd plan every move precisely as a chess puzzle. Smart money placed all bets on a winner. At the endgame, checkmate would be mine.

I left Morgan Guaranty Trust Company with two thousand bucks in my pocket, half-expecting to see Lieutenant Sterne clumping into Place Vendôme from the other direction. I needed to get in touch with him right away and make sure our meeting took place on my terms. It was lunchtime. Cops don't like missing meals. Good time for me to call his hotel.

Payphones were located in post offices all around town. I asked at the bank for directions to the nearest one. At La Poste on rue des Capucines I dug a *jeton* from my pocket, called the Plat d'Etain and asked for Sterne. A voice on the other end said, '*Moment.*' I waited while he rang the room. He told me Monsieur Sterne did not respond. Monsieur Sterne's room key had been left behind, so he must certainly be out. '*Voudriez-vous laisser un message?*'

No way in hell I wanted to leave a message. Didn't trust my French well enough not to screw the pooch. '*Non, merci,*' I said and hung up.

A quick look in my street guide told me rue Meslay was over in the 3rd. I backtracked to Place Vendôme and grabbed a taxi waiting in front of the Ritz. Usually, I like gabbing with the cabbie, asking questions about passing landmarks. On this ride, lost in thought, I ignored the driver. The view sped by unnoticed outside. Sterne was hot on the trail of Harry Angel. I had to keep him from connecting a fugitive private dick with a once-famous pop star. Cops always toed the line around the wealthy. My best bet was conning him into thinking I was a rich big shot. A man on the run doesn't shop at Sulka.

The cab dropped me off in a working-class neighborhood. Nothing posh in sight.

Hotel du Plat d'Etain was a plain five-story building with a dark, dingy lobby. A bald guy sat behind a curved wooden reception desk. He faced a telephone switchboard and the numbered pigeonholes for the guest mail and keys. I cleared my throat as I approached the counter and he got to his feet. I told him I was looking for an American named Sterne. The desk clerk turned and scanned the pigeonholes. The Hotel du Plat d'Etain had 46 rooms. '*Il n'est pas dans sa chambre,*' he said.

I already knew no one was home and told the clerk I wanted
to leave a message for Mr Sterne. He pulled an envelope and a
sheet of hotel stationery from under the desk. Seated at a little
table in the opposite corner, I wrote a brief note with Krusemark's
fancy fountain pen, printing every word in case he had a sample of
Harry Angel's handwriting:

SORRY I MISSED YOU. SUGGEST WE MEET
FOR LUNCH TOMORROW. AS MY GUEST OF
COURSE. NOON SHARP AT LE GRAND VÉFOUR,
17 RUE DE BEAUJOLAIS.
. SINCERELY,
John Favorite.

I sealed the envelope with care to let the clerk know it was
private. He took the letter from me with a show of indifference,
slipping it into pigeon hole number 33 where a lever lock skeleton
key attached to a brass tag dangled. Without knowing it, chrome
dome had just told me everything I needed to know.

Out on the street, I flagged down a cab and told the driver,
'American Express,' figuring he knew the address. I picked Le
Grand Véfour for lunch tomorrow because it was the kind of place
a cheap flatfoot like Sterne could never afford. I'd been there last
week. It was a glittering jewel-box, one of Paris's oldest restaurants.
He'd be completely out of his element. Exactly where I wanted him.
I planned to wear duds worth more than a month of his pathetic
salary. My nose presented the biggest obstacle. I knew Sterne would
focus on my bloated shnoz, maybe make a connection with Harry
Angel's deformed beak. Several options came to mind. I still had
mortician's wax and pan stick but reshaping my honker was not
an option. Sterne would spot any makeup in a flash. Maybe I'd
slap on a bandage. Pretend my nose had been injured. Dumb idea.
Why draw attention to the flaw I wanted to disguise? A bluff is
often the best move. Shove my big fat nose right in Sterne's face.

I also sported a grown-out version of Harry Angel's crewcut. Never mind it was platinum as Jean Harlow's mop. Sterne would mark me as a bottle blond first thing. Better off wearing a wig. The one matching the photo in my passport. Sure as hell he was going to ask to see that. The wig was first-class goods, genuine human hair. Set Ernie Cavalero back a pretty penny. No way Sterne would ever clock it as fake unless he yanked it off my head.

I'd have to study the fake stamps I'd pounded into my fake passport, trying to make it look like I'd been abroad at the time of all the murders pinned on Harry Angel. I needed to invent a plausible story to cover my imaginary travels over the past year. Easier than learning Latin.

We pulled up in front of 11 rue Scribe across from a sprawling wedding-cake pile the driver told me was *Le Palais Garnier, l'Opéra de Paris*. I suppressed an urge to crack wise about the Phantom and said it looked '*très jolie*.' I pushed through a set of double glass doors. The American Express office was crowded with tourists. I found the sign reading: INFORMATION and told a smiling gal behind the counter that I wanted to open an account. I said I also wished to buy a sizable amount of travelers checks and make some travel arrangements. Her smile brightened as she told me which departments would assist me. The corporate doors opened wide as the gates of Hell.

American Express boasted a top-notch travel agency. One-stop shopping for my upcoming trip to Rome: a one-way ticket on the all first-class Rome Express, which had overnight sleeper service; a reservation at the Excelsior on Via Veneto; and limousine service for the night of April 11. The pleasant young agent who spoke perfect English didn't blink when I told her I didn't want the driver to know my name. Her eyes sparkled as she passed me a handwritten itinerary detailing all my travel information. She thought I was off for a kinky sexual escapade. 'Have a most pleasant trip,' she said, smiling to beat the band.

I didn't look back, heading for the blood-red stairwell leading down to the lounge. I squeezed into one of the phone booths and fished out Armand Perrin's calling card. He was the waiter from Le Grand Véfour. I dropped in the *jeton* and dialed. '*Bon après-midi*,' a voice gargled. '*Le Grand Véfour. Je suis entièrement à votre service.*'

Entirely at my service sounded good. I asked to speak with Armand Perrin.

'*Moment, s'il vous plaît.*'

After a long wait, another voice replied, '*Oui.*' It was Perrin. I said he'd given me his card. It triggered an immediate boost in enthusiasm. He knew I was a big tipper. I told him I wanted a lunch reservation for two tomorrow at thirteen hours.

'*Bien sûr, monsieur.*'

I let Armand know my guest was '*un gauche américain de graisse.*' This was not news to Armand. He'd seen his share of fat rude Americans. Greet Sterne like royalty, I told him. King of the toads. He got my drift. Another *jeton* went in the slot. Two rings and an icy voice came on the line. 'Kreigmann Imports.' He spoke in English.

I pushed the connection button and said I was in the market for precision instruments.

'Kreigmann represents the most advanced developments in miniaturized technology.' The man had one of those undefined European accents sounding half-British public school and half-Hollywood Nazi. 'We are open only by appointment. Our hours run from ten hundred to sixteen hundred hours, every day except Sunday.'

It was quarter past three. Just enough time to make an essential purchase. I said to put me down for ten minutes from now, giving my name as John Favorite.

'Excellent, Mr Favorite. We will see you shortly. Please be advised certain items are available for purchase only by authorized law enforcement officials.'

'No problem,' I said, thinking of Harry Angel's honorary chief's badge from Schenectady in my satchel, and hung up.

Ten minutes later on the dot I was standing outside the Art Deco building at number 8, rue de Balzac. *Kreigmann y Fils; 1ère étage* was engraved into one of the brass plaques discreetly mounted to the side of the twin glass front doors. A small metal intercom buzzer hung on the right side of the entrance alcove. I pressed the button for Kreigmann and sons.

The intercom crackled. A distant metallic voice asked, '*Monsieur Favorite?*'

'*Oui,*' I replied. '*Ici.*' An answering electronic buzz unlocked the front door. I pushed against it and stepped into a lobby sterile as a hospital waiting room. Avoiding the claustrophobic elevator, I took the marble stairs up to the first floor. A lanky man waited by an open door across which bronze letters spelled out the name of his firm. He wore a perfectly cut gray suit. Everything about him was gray from his eyes and lank salt-and-pepper hair to the silver toothbrush mustache fringing his harelip. He looked like Hitler's ghost. '*Bonjour,*' he said, waving me inside.

'*Bonjour,* Mr Kreigmann…? Mind if we speak English?'

'Of course not. My name is not Kreigmann. I am Kurt Vital. Otto Kreigmann was my grandfather.'

Vital led me into a large ballroom with six large windows facing the street. So much light for such a shadowy enterprise. Fine Chinese carpets covered most of the parquet floor. Tall vitrines stood like sentinels along the walls. A row of glass-covered tables divided the open space. 'Might I see some identification?' Vital's voice flowed syrup-smooth. I fished my passport out of the satchel. Vital studied it, looking back and forth at me. 'I believe you said you were in law enforcement.'

'Retired.' I pulled out my wallet and let him peek at the Schenectady chief's button. 'I manage security for a multinational corporation. Can't tell you the name.'

'Secrecy is our business,' Vital whispered.

He let me browse around on my own for a while. It was an upscale supermarket for spooks. I came across a tall showcase housing dozens of different model Minox cameras, compact as packs of chewing gum. Another case held tiny spy cameras disguised as match boxes, lipsticks, pens, cigarette cases, and hidden behind buttons and stick pins. Vital glided silently up behind me. 'May I help you locate something?' he asked.

I told him about infiltrating a rival outfit's business conference, saying I couldn't reveal any further details. What I needed was something to record the proceedings without being detected. Kurt Vital had just the ticket. He led me to a long display table at the center of the room. Laid out like precious jewel boxes on its green velvet-lined inner surface were a number of miniature tape recorders not very much larger than paperback novels. Numerous accessories (earphones, mikes, foot controls, coils of electric cord) surrounded them.

'The Minifon series by Protona,' Vital said. 'A supreme achievement of German engineering.' He opened a side panel and reached inside, withdrawing the instruments one at a time. 'The P-55,' he intoned, setting each in turn out on the counter top, 'the Liliput, released just last year, smallest micro-recorder on the market. And, *la pièce de résistance*, the Minifon Attaché, newest in the line, a sample for display purposes only. Full production will not begin until next year. We are happy to take advance orders.'

'Can't wait until next year. I need something right away.'

'Understood. I show it as a courtesy. The Attaché is a great technological leap into the future. All transistors, eliminating the sub-miniature tubes. Only one battery. Instead of wire is the new magnetic tape sealed in compact plastic cartridge.'

I told Vital the gizmo sounded like the greatest thing since the first wheel rolled off a Babylonian assembly line. 'Right now,' I said, 'I'm interested in hearing about the little one.'

Vital launched into a rhapsodic praise for the Liliput, Protona's first all-transistor recorder. That was the main difference from the P-55 aside from size. Both machines were battery-powered, valve-based wire recorders with housings cast from magnesium alloy. I asked about recording times. Again, size made a difference. The Liliput used a smaller specially designed battery less powerful than the ones in the P-55. Here Vital leaned in close like a conspirator. The Liliput was not capable of achieving the four-hour recording capacity advertised by Protona. 'Three might be a more reasonable estimate,' he said.

'What about the P-55?'

'The standard model will record for more than two and a half hours. The long-play version is capable of five.'

'I'll take the long-play. How much does it weigh?'

'Eight hundred grams. Seven-fifty without the batteries. Twenty-six ounces avoirdupois.'

Almost two pounds. Not exactly featherweight. Like carrying a small brick in my pocket. Vital began a spiel touting all the accessories. An elastic cotton harness strapped the device to your chest. A small plugin external speaker allowed for easy playback. Stethoscope earplugs provided private listening. I bought them all, shelling out $230 cash, American. Biggest bargain: a crystal microphone disguised as a wristwatch for only six bucks.

As I walked out of the spooks' store, I felt almost ready for my face-off with Cyphre in Rome. If my luck held true, I wouldn't be the one getting fucked down in a secret Vatican cellar.

Now I had to get ready to deal with Sterne.

28

The next morning I spent a couple of hours playing with my new spy-gear toys before I donned the blond wig and dressed for the day in a blue double-breasted pinstripe suit, maroon silk shirt and deep green Sulka tie. Rich and successful but not like some square with a day job. The executive pictured in my passport wore a white shirt. I hooked the .38 on my left side. The derringer went into the ticket pocket above my right hip. My reflection in the bathroom mirror evoked prosperity. I wanted to check for messages at the café-tabac but sporting a golden mop like Liberace meant answering too many questions from Alfonse.

Distant noon-bells chimed the hour when I stepped into Le Grand Véfour. My personal waiter, Armand Perrin, loudly greeted me, *'Bonjour, Monsieur Favorite,'* warm and familiar, just as we'd discussed it on the phone. I glanced into the dining room while checking my coat and shopping bag. There sat Sterne, nursing a beer in a far corner. I knew he'd show up early. My message said noon sharp and I was right on the mark. Make the dumb flatfoot think I was some important honcho for whom time meant money. The kind of gee who kept waiting cops on his payroll.

Armand led me back making a show of servile deference. Sterne glanced up, his big beak leading the way, not rising to greet me as the waiter pulled out my chair. He wore the same ugly ill-fitting brown mohair suit he'd been wearing the last time I saw him. Probably the only one he owned. Armand inquired in French if I desired *'un apéro'*. I knew he meant an apéritif. The Frogs placed great faith in taking a little nip before eating as an appetite stimulant.

'Que me conseillez-vous?' I asked what he might recommend. My accent sounded right on.

'Un Lillet blanc, Monsieur Favorite. Il est très agréable.'

'Bien. Un nouveau goût pour moi.'

Armand replied that new tastes were good for the soul and departed with a crisp bow. Convincing a homicide dick I was fluent in jugarum just earned him a big tip.

'Lieutenant Sterne,' I said once we were alone, 'I'm John Favorite.' Sterne didn't respond, staring hard at me without expression. 'What should I call you, officer?'

'You can call me sir,' he growled.

'Up yours!' I snapped, pushing away from the table. 'Meeting's over.'

'Hey. Cool down. No insult intended.'

'Last time I called someone sir was in the war.' I brushed imaginary filth off my expensive tie.

'Yeah. Hated my topkick, too. The name's Dan. Where'd you serve?'

'North Africa,' I said. 'Show me some identification, Dan. Just to keep things legit.'

Sterne scowled, fishing his billfold from a back pocket as Armand returned with my drink. Another exchange of rapid-fire French blew more smoke up the detective's ass. Sterne's badge was pinned to one side of his drab simulated alligator wallet opposite the glassine window showing his NYPD ID. I made a show of reading every word through my drugstore cheaters. Meant shit to me. Just pulling his chain.

'Your turn,' Sterne hissed. Like some third-rate ventriloquist, his lips barely moved when he spoke. 'Show me what you got.'

I pulled my passport from my satchel and handed it to Sterne. He stared inside, turning the pages with apparent indifference.

This was bullshit. A copper's ploy to disguise the intensity of his search for clues. I sipped my Lillet. The faint citrus flavor offset a lingering bitter medicinal aftertaste. Not something I'd order again. 'Find what you're looking for?' I asked.

Sterne gave me back my passport. 'You seem to get around a lot,' he said.

'Business.'

'What kind of business would that be?

'Various kinds. Real estate. Money markets. Import. Export. Anything to make an honest buck.'

'How come you quit show business?'

I finished the Lillet. 'Truth is, it quit on me. Got wounded in Tunisia. Spent more than a year in the hospital. Another two in therapy.'

'What kind of therapy?'

'Psychoanalysis. Had a little shell shock. Shrink came on my dime. The army didn't give a shit. By the time I got my head back together, the big band days were almost over. I found another line of work.'

Sterne looked at me so hard I could almost hear the cogwheels turning inside his one-track mind. He focused on my nose, trying to make it all add up.

'You staring at my nose?' I snapped.

'Yeah. You might say that. Only ever seen one other beezer like it. What happened there, some kind of war wound?'

'Cancer.'

That shut him up. Nobody likes jawing about the Big C. Afraid it might be contagious. I wondered how Sterne twigged onto Harry Angel's botched plastic surgery. Gave him points for that one.

Armand returned to take our orders. Sterne glanced helplessly at his menu. 'You know the lingo, John. Help me out with this. I had a helluva time just getting a beer.'

'What do you want?

'A steak would suit me fine.'

I ordered *entrecôte à la bordelaise* for the flatfoot and *noix de ris de veau Brillat-Savarin* for yours truly. Also a bottle of St Emilion. 'So, what's up, Lieutenant?' I asked, with Armand out of earshot. 'You didn't come all the way to Paris just to get the autograph of some has-been crooner.'

'Bet your sweet ass on that one, Johnny. I wouldn't cross the street for your fucking autograph. Tell me what you know about Warren Wagner.'

I love cops. Predictable as puppies. They bring on the tough talk once they think they've got you cornered. 'Can't tell much,' I said. 'He was my agent. Haven't seen him since I got drafted in '43.'

Sterne reached down, picking a manila envelope off the ornate carpet. He pulled out a photograph and slid it over to me. 'This the guy?'

I took a long look at Warren Wagner Jr's Howdy Doody mug. 'Nope. Never saw that bird before.'

'He's Warren Wagner Jr.'

'Maybe so. Don't know any Junior. Warren was in his mid-forties twenty years ago when he represented me. All that came to an end when I got drafted.'

'His son, then. Ran a talent agency in the Brill Building.'

'Took over from the old man, I guess. What's this got to do with the price of beans?'

'Wagner Jr was found murdered in a men's room out at Idlewild couple weeks ago. Same day you flew TWA to Paris.'

'Coincidence is no crime.'

Sterne pulled a second photo from his manila envelope and handed it over. 'Tell me about this one,' he said.

It was a glossy publicity shot. I'd seen it three weeks ago in the city room of the *New York Times*. 'Talk about memory lane. Harlem. Maybe around 1940. Ran in *Life*. The Negro piano player is named Edison Sweet. Called him Toots. Fabulous left hand.'

'Not no more. Toots Sweet got himself murdered about three weeks ago.'

'That coincidence won't fit. I was in Tokyo.'

Sterne pulled another 8x10 from the envelope. A promo shot of me at eighteen with my slick black pompadour. 'You?'

'One handsome dog back then.'

'When you start bleaching your hair?'

'It's the other way around. Spider Simpson had me dye it black. So I looked more like a wop crooner. Russ Columbo. Perry Como. Louis Prima. All those goombahs.' I didn't like where this was going. Nosey cop caught the scent. I was back on the run. Armand saved the day when he stepped up and opened the Bordeaux. Sterne said he'd prefer another beer. Why waste good wine on this ignorant bastard.

'They seem to know you pretty well around here, Favorite,' Sterne snarled as I enjoyed my first sip. 'Eat here often?'

'Often as possible. One of the best joints in town. Been slinging hash since the seventeen-hundreds.'

'How long you lived in Paris?'

'I don't live in Paris. Just passing through.'

'Where do you live?' Sterne was getting pissed.

'Wherever I hang my hat.' I got a funny kick out of needling him. Probably wasn't my best move.

'And where the fuck is that?' he snarled through clenched teeth.

Armand approached, tray balanced on one shoulder. Time for another jab. 'None of your fucking business,' I said with a smile. 'This ain't New York City.'

Sterne glared at me. The formal ceremony of the service stopped him cold. First class was unfamiliar territory for cops. A fresh glass of beer appeared at his elbow. He grinned at the steak set before him. 'What's this stuff all over it?' Bitching as he cut his first slice.

'Wine sauce.'

'Shit! Fucking delicious!'

I watched Sterne tear into his meal like a starving man. No more third degree for the moment. I watched the flatfoot while I ate knowing he couldn't get his mind off my nose. No forgetting that shnozz. He'd seen it before, stuck on the mug of Harry Angel.

'Best steak of my life,' Sterne said, mopping up the wine-dark sauce with a chunk of bread.

'Glad you enjoyed it.'

'Couple more questions?'

'You're my guest. Why not?'

Sterne swigged his beer. 'You ever heard of a private dick name of Harry Angel?'

'Nope. Any reason I should?'

'About three weeks ago, this bird Angel drops in at Warren Wagner Associates. Guess who he was looking for?'

'Don't have a clue.'

'You.'

'Must not be a very good detective.'

'How's that?'

'He never found me.'

'Wagner's secretary said he was one rude SOB. Said she heard her boss tell Angel that Favorite was brain dead. Housed away in a private upstate sanatorium.'

'He was misinformed.'

'Maybe so. The records at Emma Dodd Harvest Clinic have you transferred to an Albany VA hospital in 1945.'

'All wrong.'

'We checked with Albany. The VA knows nothing about it. What's the real story?'

I smiled at Sterne feeling the noose tighten around my neck. 'Told you about my therapy. Up in Poughkeepsie at Emma Dodd Harvest Memorial. Checked myself in – and out. My dime, remember? Left in '45. That VA hospital crap? Bookkeeping error, maybe.'

'Any idea why Angel was hunting for you?'

'Beats me.'

Sterne leaned forward across the table, rasping, 'Maybe I can clue you in. Been digging a little myself. Seems like you was playing around with all kinds of voodoo and black magic shit back in the day.'

'Indiscretions of youth.'

'You was engaged to some society dame the press called the Witch of Wellesley. Shacking up with a nigger bitch in Harlem at the same time.'

'What can I say? Want me to apologize?'

'Don't get cute. So happens Toots Sweet, the jigaboo got himself murdered, was mixed up in Harlem voodoo. That witchy society broad also got bumped off. All the same week. Two weeks ago.'

'Can't help you out. I wasn't there.'

'You seem all broken up about it.'

'Look, Lieutenant. It was a long time ago. I was a kid. Confused. In over my head. Can you remember ever being that stupid? The war straightened me out. Got to really know the Devil up close in combat.'

'Very touching. Just don't add up is all. Why was Harry Angel looking for you? Why was he snooping into black magic? Got an answer?'

Sterne knew way too much. Bad news if the homicide boys connected me to a certain black mass down in the eastside IRT last month. They'd pin Ethan Krusemark's death on me. Dumb move sending the DA all that film. Hindsight always scores big on the eye chart. Two weeks ago, I'd never heard of the Council of Thirty. Whatever I did when I was Harry Angel meant less to me than a forgotten dream. Sterne breathing down my neck opened up an opportunity. Information was a two-way street.

'Sorry to hear about Maggie Krusemark,' I said. 'She was a swell kid. Just not a very good fortune teller.'

'In what way?'

'She predicted I'd make it big in the movies. Become a famous film star.'

'When you see her last?'

'Maggie? Not since I shipped out in January of '43.'

'You never tried getting back in touch?'

'What was the point? It'd been two years or more. Life moved on. I was a different person.' That last bit nearly cracked me up. No way Sterne would ever get the joke.

'It was doomed from the start. Her old man couldn't stand me.' I fed him that as bait, fishing for what he knew about Krusemark.

'Got three daughters myself.' Sterne kept his cool. 'I can see his point of view.'

'Never had any kids,' I lied. Maybe Sterne was holding out. Either he was in the dark about Krusemark and the subway Black Mass or he played his cards like a cop, keeping an ace deep in the hole. 'Not that I know of anyhow.'

'Life is empty without kids.' The slogan according to Sterne. 'Listen, Favorite, I'm here because Harry Angel is on your trail. He was at the airport same day as you. Same day Warren Wagner Jr got snuffed. I think Angel's in Paris. I think he's going to try and contact you.'

A chill rippled down my back. 'Am I in some sort of danger?'

'Harry Angel is a very dangerous character. Here's what he looks like.' Sterne pulled another picture from his manila envelope. It was a grainy blow up of my PI license application photo from back when I thought I was Angel. 'Probably shaved the mustache. If you see or hear from him you should let me know.'

'Count on it.' I gave him back the photograph and found Dr Mussey's card in my billfold. 'Unfortunately, I have a dental appointment in fifteen minutes.' I let Sterne look at the card, taking it away before he palmed it. 'I appreciate the warning about Angel.'

'How do I get hold of you, Johnny?'

'Got a pencil?'

Sterne fished a notepad and mechanical pencil from his inside jacket pocket. I gave him Alfonse Reynard's number at the café-tabac. He wrote it down. 'Not going to tell me where you live?'

'Nope.' I signaled Armand for *l'addition*. 'Don't look so glum, Lieutenant. You're in Paris.'

After that, only chitchat. I laid off the wise guy stuff. Sterne didn't have much to say when he wasn't grilling me. His sleepy eyes widened a crack when I peeled f10,000 from my bankroll to settle the tab. Thirty percent went to Armand. I'd told him earlier to clear away my place setting the moment I left. Glasses, flatware, napkin, ashtray, the works. Anything from which prints might be lifted. Didn't explain why to Armand. My money spoke for me.

When I stood up, Sterne also got to his feet. 'I'll walk you out.'

'Don't bother. I'm in a hurry.' Efficient Armand got busy clearing my place.

'Stay in touch, Favorite.'

'It's a promise. How long you in Paris?'

'Until I get some results.'

'Lucky you,' I said, making for the door. Sterne was like a bulldog. He had the scent in his nostrils, hot on my trail. He'd never give up until he sank his fangs deep into my heart. Sterne couldn't see the big picture yet. The deal with my bulbous nose nagged at him just below the surface. It would worry his copper's mind until he made the connection. I knew at that moment I had to kill him.

29

It was a short walk from Le Grand Véfour to rue des Pyramides. I thought about Sterne every step of the way, getting to Dr Mussey's office five minutes early. As the novocaine numbness set in, I closed my eyes and ignored his probing instruments, imagining Hell as eternity in a dentist chair without painkillers. While Mussey's pudgy fingers fumbled in my mouth, I concentrated on how to take care of Lieutenant Sterne.

No way the homicide dick would ever tumble to the real truth. Any notion of someone selling his soul to the Devil and sacrificing an innocent soldier in a satanic ritual to swap places with him was beyond the limits of his police-procedure mind. My deformed nose on the other hand was something he'd never forget. It wasn't good either that he could place both Harry Angel and Johnny Favorite at Idlewild the day Wagner was killed. In an ironic reversal of the facts, the conclusion Sterne would reach, although he didn't know it yet, was that Harry Angel finally caught up with Johnny Favorite, murdered him and took over the singer's identity. The motives were obvious. Angel wanted to elude the long arm of the law. He needed money and lots of it. Most of all, the fugitive private eye sought safety without fear of detection. Hiding in plain sight provided the best protection.

Sterne had to die before he figured all this out and wrote it up in an official report. Easy enough to knock him off. I knew where he lived. My problem was it couldn't appear to be murder. It had to look like an accident.

Before rubbing Sterne out I wanted a couple hours alone with him down in some subterranean chamber where no one could hear the screams. A pair of pliers and a blowtorch were all I needed to learn everything he knew about Ethan Krusemark. My imaginary interrogation was nothing but an amusing pipe dream. No way to pry the truth out of the bastard and still make his death look accidental. This quandary put me in a bit of a fix. If Krusemark's corpse had been discovered and his will entered into probate, the Curia was already aware that Judas shekel number thirteen was missing. Anyone showing up with it at the Council of Thirty in the Vatican was a marked man, the coin his death warrant.

It was a risk I'd have to take. Gaining entry to the Council didn't guarantee finding Cyphre right away. I had no idea how much time I needed. Having a pack of New York cops nosing around looking for Sterne's killer only meant trouble. Didn't need any more of that. The detective's death had to go down as an accident. End of story. By the time Dr Mussey finished with my caps and I settled the tab, I'd worked out all the details in my mind. Time to get busy putting the plan into motion.

I flagged down a cab at the corner of Avenue de l'Opéra and headed for home. The dentist never mentioned my new golden pompadour. He remembered me as a blond and that was it. Eyewitnesses always got it wrong. Learned that one the hard way over the years. Before I met anyone else who knew me as Johnny Favorite I needed to ditch the wig. Also wanted to change into more casual clothes.

My first stop was Reynard's café-tabac next door. Alfonse greeted me like a long-lost brother, a pungent Gauloise dangling from the corner of his mouth. A pair of noisy teenagers played foosball in the back. I ordered a Cinzano and he poured a second for himself, saying there was no charge. We shot the breeze for a minute or so before Alfonse told me I'd gotten a phone call about an hour ago.

'Sterne?' I asked.

'*Oui.*'

'*Tout message?*'

Alfonse didn't speak English. He struggled with a phonetic approximation. 'Kip een toosh,' he stammered.

'Keep in touch?'

'*Mais oui, bien sûr.*'

The flatfoot had wasted no time testing the number I'd given him. Wanted me to feel the heat. Let me know he'd find me whenever he wanted. Maybe it was a mistake to have told him Reynard's number. Hell, I had to give him something. Toss a bone to the rabid dog. Easy for Sterne to trace me back to the café-tabac. He'd find out where I lived. A rogue cop in Paris didn't need a search warrant. Once he turned up my wigs and makeup it was the end of the line. I had maybe a day or two before he came looking. I needed to string him along a bit longer before I killed him.

'*Pardon, Alfonse,*' I said, digging a *jeton* from my pocket. I dialed Sterne's hotel number on the wall payphone and slowly left a polite message in English with the receptionist. 'Got your call. Will keep in contact. Phone every day to touch base. Meet whenever you want.'

On my way out the door, I placed a 500 franc note on the bar top and told Alfonse to expect more calls from Sterne. He said, '*Le plus sera le mieux.*' The more the better.

'*Putain de droite,*' I replied and cut out. Wasn't sure I got the phrase right. Only heard it for the first time the other day. I wanted to say, 'Damn straight,' but maybe I'd just called his mother a whore.

I drilled through the quarter to the nameless hotel on rue Gît-le-Coeur. Peeking in the glass café door, I saw the junkie scribbler. I didn't know if Burroughs owned just one suit like Sterne or had several all in different shades of gray. He appeared drab and anonymous as always.

'Johnny Favorite, America's favorite has-been.'

I ignored his greeting and bought myself a cup of java and another one for him. 'How you feeling, Bill?' I sat down at his table.

'Little shaky.' Burroughs' hands trembled as he lit a cigarette. 'Clean out of smack.'

I pulled an envelope from my satchel and slid it across the table toward him. 'Get yourself straight with this.' Burroughs opened the flap and thumbed the greenbacks inside. 'Like to make five hundred bucks for a couple hours of your time? Half up front.'

'How many laws do I break?'

'None. You get the rest when the work is done.'

'Still in the dark about that.'

'Give you all the details the day after tomorrow. It's nothing risky or criminal. Just acting as a decoy.'

'Decoy for what?'

'Can't tell you too much right now. Maybe just this. Got someone tailing me. Need to throw him off my trail for a couple hours Monday night.'

'Sounds easy enough.'

'Piece of cake. But it's a two-man gig. Get someone you trust. What you pay him is up to you.'

Burroughs stroked his chin. 'Gregory just blew into town. He's always in need of a little extra scratch.'

'Don't tell me any names. Grab hold of your pal today so everything's set. Can't have any fuck-ups.'

'Count on me.'

'Know I can, Bill. That's why there's half up front.' Maybe giving Burroughs all that dough was a big mistake. Never trust a junkie. Might just shoot the works up his arm and OD. Leave me high and dry. 'Let me level with you,' I said. Threats were no good. Not with this cat. I needed to plug into his intellect. 'Remember how I told you I was chasing the Devil?'

Burroughs cracked a thin smile, sucking on his cancer stick. 'Tops my list of unforgettable remarks,' he exhaled.

'I'm hot on Satan's trail right now,' I replied. 'This little caper tomorrow is part of it.'

'Hot on his trail?' Burroughs' mirthless smile grew a touch wider. 'You certainly are droll, Johnny.'

'I'm not cracking wise with you. This is the real deal. You'd like that, wouldn't you, Bill, coming face to face with the Prince of Darkness?'

'There's no one else I'd rather meet.'

'It's settled, then. I'll call by Monday morning. Let's meet up in your room. Way more private. I'll explain the whole deal and bring what you need.'

Burroughs thoughtfully studied his long cigarette ash before flicking it onto the floor. 'Want to meet my friend? Size him up?'

'Nope. If he's good enough for you, Bill, he's jake with me.' I stood up. 'Gotta breeze. See you Monday at nine.'

It was a quarter past four. While there was still daylight I had time for some recon and took a cab north across the river to Montmartre. The driver dropped me off near the top of the hill at the corner of rue Cortot and rue des Saules. Across the way was La Maison Rose. This was the perfect spot. I walked down the narrow sidewalk alongside the sloping urban vineyard toward the Lapin Agile. It was a straight shot. Perfect.

Only one problem. I'd forgotten about three big stone bollards blocking the street at the intersection with rue Saint-Vincent. They upset my original plan. I looked around for other possibilities.

Diagonally across the intersection from the Lapin Agile, a set of stone steps rose up from the corner into a tiny wedge-shaped park dense with trees. I hadn't noticed it during my first visit in the dark a week ago. The place was perfectly situated for what I had in mind. Rue Saint-Vincent ran uphill from the Lapin Agile. Not as steep as the rue des Saules but still an incline suiting my plan. I walked past the little grape farm, checking things out. Cars parked on either side of the cobbled one-way street allowed only a single traffic lane down the middle. From halfway up the block, I couldn't see the cabaret. Instead, there was an excellent view of the tiny park. Wasn't exactly what I wanted but it would have to do.

I walked back downhill following rue Saint-Vincent past the Lapin Agile across rue des Saules and along the walled-in cemetery on my right. The street curved around the bone yard at its far end, running straight to the rue Caulaincourt. Not what I first had in mind. Perfect all the same.

The sky lost its light. Dusk draped the city in a filthy gray shroud. Brightly lit Caulaincourt, a curving street lined with shops, provided some relief from the misty gloom. I spent the next hour walking down narrow tree-lined streets and up steep sets of stairs as I explored the 18th arrondissement and memorized a bit more Parisian geography. Knowing my way around the *quartier* might prove very useful if my plan went wrong and I had to take off on foot. I crossed rue des Saules and de l'Aubrevoir became rue Cortot. I continued on past rue du Mont-Cenis up to the basilica of Sacré-Coeur and climbed the broad steep steps leading to the front of the church where I sat on a bench and took in the view. Paris spread out before me, an ornate dark carpet embroidered with a million glittering lights. Staring down at it gave me a rush of incredible power. I felt like I ruled the world. It would be easy to destroy the entire city with a single blow of my fist.

My imaginary omnipotence stayed with me for a couple minutes. Coming back to earth and the business at hand, I thought things over as I descended the basilica stairs. It struck me that planning to kill the Devil was every bit as absurd as imagining I could crush Paris like a bug. What made it all even remotely plausible was I knew Louis Cyphre to be a man just like me. A man the same as Lieutenant Sterne. Killing the cop topped my list. Simple as swatting a fly. Cyphre stood next in line.

30

The Brasserie Balzar occupied a small ground-floor space on the rue des Écoles. Open and inviting, it was a charming bistro with banquettes along the mirrored walls and another, T-shaped, running down the middle. No Siberias in this joint.

I was greeted by a pair of maîtres d'hôtel, one wearing a tux, the other clad in a business suit. I gave them János Szabor's name and the one in the tuxedo led me back to the tail end of an open table. Tucked into a far corner, the professor had his nose buried in a book, a glass of red wine at his elbow. We exchanged pleasantries without much enthusiasm. 'Colleagues need not be friends, Johnny,' he said, signaling for the waiter.

A bottle of the house Bordeaux arrived. I ordered herring to start and steak au poivre. For the first time in hours, I relaxed. The food turned out to be excellent, served on large oval platters and transferred to our plates with practiced formality.

'*Mon bistro habituel*,' Szabor said. Big deal telling me Balzar was his local joint. Anyone could find La Tour d'Argent. The perfect bistro proved a more elusive quarry. 'I eat here almost every evening. I teach just next door. *L'Académie de Paris*. The Sorbonne in the vernacular.'

We got to work. Szabor quizzed me on the numbers. I got them all, in random order, no hesitation or mistakes. Since the Council voted on its business – whether to assassinate certain world leaders or foment other types of mayhem that would assist their diabolical goals – János had taught me at our last session the words for the three possible responses: approve, *approbare*; disapprove, *improbare*; or abstain, *abstinere*. I showed him I had those down pat too. János looked very pleased with himself. 'Here's the deal,' I said. 'Number Thirteen missed the last two Council meetings. Don't you think they'll ask about that?'

'Very likely. Why was he absent?'

'His daughter was murdered.'

'Is this true?'

'Yes.'

'Then you must tell them the truth. That way, you have nothing to remember. Except Latin, *naturellement*.'

'How do I say "My daughter was murdered?"'

'*Filia mea trucidatus.*'

I wrote it down. Szabor helped with the spelling. He had me repeat the phrase over and over until my pronunciation became second nature. 'In all probability the Council will ask about the murder,' he warned. He offered several possible questions in Latin. I jotted them down phonetically. 'I have the perfect answer for all of them,' János said. '*Est enim mihi vindictam ergo retribuam*. It is from *Romans*. Vengeance is mine, I shall repay.' I memorized it on the spot. 'How do you know the real Number Thirteen will not also make an appearance this time?' he asked.

'I told you. Number Thirteen is dead.'

'Did you kill him?'

'What difference does it make?'

'None actually. However, if you killed to get the coin my prognosis for your eventual success in this endeavor improves substantially. Desperate tasks demand desperate measures.'

The grammar lesson ended and János turned the conversation to the Swiss Guard, *Pontificia Cohors Helvetica*, those legendary mercenaries protecting the Pope. 'A pair will be guarding the Porta Sant'Anna when you arrive,' he said. 'The Guards' barracks is the building immediately to the left of the gate. Do not be misled by their clownish Renaissance uniforms, all those red, yellow and blue stripes. These are highly trained soldiers. While the halberds they carry are ceremonial, they are not stage props. A guardsman can eviscerate you with one before you blink.'

'What's a halberd?' No percentage in faking it around Szabor.

'An ancient weapon favored by the Swiss. Something like a spear with an axe-head below the point.'

As we ate, János went on and on about the Swiss Guard and yakked it up about what he called 'a secular village' within the Vatican walls. Boasting a pharmacy, apartments for resident citizens, a large provision store called the 'Annona,' a post office, the newspaper offices and a printing shop, the miniature community stood just across from the Bastion of Nicholas V. 'Perhaps you don't know this, Johnny. The Bastion of Nicholas V where you will be going for the meeting houses the headquarters of the IOR, Instituto per le Opere di Religione, the Institute for the Works of Religion, more commonly known as the Vatican Bank. This pernicious institution was established in 1942 by Satanist Pope Pius XII who became Hitler's banker. Most appropriate for the Council of Thirty to share space with a holy bank, don't you think? Jesus Christ drove the moneylenders from the temple. The Catholic Church invited them back inside.' Szabor shook his head sadly. 'Yes, indeed, Vatican City is a medieval labyrinth of dead-end alleys and tiny streets.'

'What about if something goes really wrong and I need to make a getaway on foot?' I asked. 'I can't go back through the Sant'Anna gate. Not with those spear-toting Swiss. If I run into the little village, I'm sure to get lost. Which way do I go?'

János pulled a notebook from his briefcase on the floor and quickly sketched a little map. 'The only way is here,' he said, pointing with his ballpoint. 'From the tower (he made an X on a crudely drawn circle) you go to the left, past *L'Osservatore Romano* (another X) to this corner. Run to the right this way (he drew a long arrow on the lined paper) all the way to the northern end of the museums (a third X). Go left and you will find the tourist entrance here.' Szabor stabbed his pen down. 'The problem, Johnny, is you run not from the Swiss Guard alone. Also, the Papal Gendarmes. All crack troops. These men are armed with military carbines and automatic pistols. So are the Swiss beneath their colorful uniforms.'

'Sounds like you know the inside dope. Don't worry, I can take care of myself, professor,' I said, ripping the map page free from his notebook. This wasn't bullshit. I would have a little firepower of my own. 'Thanks for the intel.'

'We both survived the war, Johnny. Death is in our blood. Do whatever it takes to succeed. Only one thing is certain.'

'What's that?'

'Make a single mistake and you are a dead man.'

31

The next morning I stopped by Alfonse's café-tabac. Three guys stood drinking in silence when I entered. Nobody ever sat on the stools. I lingered a moment by a display of packaged snacks until the two beer drinkers departed and I took their place at the bar. Reynard told me I'd had another phone message from Sterne. This time he'd asked to hear it in French so nothing got lost. The flatfoot had put the desk clerk on the line to translate. The way Alfonse heard it was, '*Appellez-moi tout de suite.*' Sterne wanted me to call him right away. '*Important?*' Reynard asked.

'*Non,*' I said. '*Seulement une question d'argent. Il peut se faire foutre.*' I told Alfonse it was only about money. Sterne could go fuck himself.

'*D'accord, mon copain.*'

First time I'd heard Reynard call me a pal. His copain. I needed pals like a dog needs fleas. I smiled like I believed him and told him I'd be back before closing time.

I took the 12 train north under the river. Four stops later, I got off at Opéra and walked straight to American Express. Downstairs, I checked for mail, not expecting any, and found nothing waiting. I went to a telephone booth, and dialed the Hotel du Plat d'Étain, releasing the *jeton* when the desk clerk answered. After being told Lieutenant Sterne was not in his room, I told the clerk I wanted to leave a message '*en anglais s'il vous plait.*'

Bright boy clicked immediately into Berlitz-perfected English.

I took great care with my dictation, pronouncing each word like some old ham actor. 'I am at American Express. Someone calling himself Harry Angel left a note for me. He wants to meet. Will provide all details. Call me tonight, seven pm, at the number I gave you.' I told the clerk to sign it, 'John Favorite,' and had him read it back to me, word by word. He got everything down perfectly.

Figured Sterne would check in with his hotel before six. I had plenty of time to do a few essential errands to prepare for tomorrow night.

Strolling along the Champs-Élysées, I scoped out the fancy cars. It was the perfect place to hot-wire a set of wheels. Rows of trees on the pedestrian islands on either side of the broad boulevard provided the perfect cover. And it was much easier than you'd think to get away with crimes committed on a busy thoroughfare with lots of hotels, restaurants and nighclubs. Just past rue Marbeuf, I came to a men's store called Pronto. Something in the window caught my eye: a tan duffel coat like the one General Montgomery always wore during the war. I sauntered in and bought the same coat but in black and a black fedora to go with it. Just what I would need tomorrow night to cover my conspicuous blond hair. Then it was on to the *Trib* building on rue de Berri to buy a few of the back issues I'd missed. A long vertical sign hung out in front. HERALD TRIBUNE, four stories high. I got a better look at the place from across the street, near the entrance of the Hotel California. Someone told me the hotel bar was the *Trib* reporters' watering hole. Inside at the Subscription Orders desk I paid for several editions of yesterday's news. The gal handed them over in a canvas *Tribune* bag. Back on the Left Bank, I stopped by a hardware store for a few essentials, the most important being an 18-inch length of pipe. In order to look legit, I asked the owner to thread it for me.

I got back to my snug blue hideaway at twenty past six. Rush hour slowed things down. After packing the Ghurka bag with everything I'd need for tomorrow night, I sat at the trestle table and jotted a quick note on a Hotel Vendôme telephone pad. It took a couple tries to get it right.

A little before seven, I tore off the finished page and drilled up the street to the café-tabac. I found Reynard wiping down his bar and told him I expected a phone call soon. Would he mind hanging around for another ten minutes? 'Pourquoi pas?' Alfonse replied. 'Je dois nettoyer avant de partir.'

Why not, he told me. When I saw him reach for a broom and start sweeping the place, I figured nettoyer must mean cleaning up. He said he couldn't leave before he finished. No one likes being watched while he works so I pretended to examine a rotating display rack stacked with postcards while keeping one eye on the wall-mounted electric clock. The phone rang at five past the hour. Reynard grunted, leaned his broom in the corner and went around behind the bar to pick up the receiver. "Allo?" He listened for several seconds. 'Tout de suite.' Alfonse set the phone in front of me on the bar. 'Pour vous,' he said.

'You're late!' I barked before Sterne got in a word. 'Time is money. I'm not on the public payroll.'

'Calm down,' Sterne rasped. 'It's only five minutes.'

'In my world, five minutes can mean the difference between making a deal and blowing one.'

'OK. OK. I get it that you're a big shot. Now, tell me about this note from Angel.'

'You know I'm on the move all the time. I use American Express for my mailing address. They have offices everywhere in the world. I stopped by rue Scribe this afternoon. Among my business correspondence was a message from Harry Angel.'

'Handwritten?'

'No. Typed.'

'Read it to me.'

I pulled the note I'd composed from my jacket pocket. It was good having something to read. A nosey copper might tell the difference if I made it up on the spot. I cleared my throat and started in. 'It says, "Johnny Favorite," at the top. No salutation or anything. Goes on, "We need to talk. I have important information regarding your daughter Epiphany Proudfoot. Meet me tomorrow at midnight under the tree in front of the Lapin Agile. Come alone. This is your only chance. I won't contact you again." It's signed, "Harry Angel." That's all.'

Silence on the other end of the line. I could feel Sterne thinking things over. Trying to work it out whether to let me know Epiphany was dead. It was a gamble using her name.

'OK,' Sterne said at last. 'We need to talk face to face. Tonight.'

'Not going to happen.'

'Why's that?'

'I've got a date.'

'All right. Tomorrow then. You can buy me another lunch.'

'Forget it,' I said. 'I have a business engagement. Meetings scheduled all through the morning and afternoon. I will, however, act as your decoy at midnight.'

More silence from Sterne. 'You're a real prince, Favorite,' he replied at last. 'Where's this Lapp Anna Jeel joint?'

'*Lapin Agile.* L-a-p-i-n. Next word, A-g-i-l-e. Means nimble rabbit. It's a cabaret up in Montmartre. Very famous old place. Goes back to the middle of the last century. Deserted neighborhood. Almost rural. There's a grape farm across the street. Can't give you the exact address but any taxi driver will know. Ask the people at your hotel. On my end, there's just one concern.'

'And what's that?'

'You told me this character Angel was a killer. What makes you think he's not out to kill me?'

'Matter of fact, he probably is.'

'Listen, Lieutenant, don't mind being bait in a trap, long as I don't end up dead meat myself.'

'Relax. Angel won't shoot you on the spot. Son-of-a-bitch likes to do his killing slow and easy. Maybe a little torture first. You'll be plenty safe. I'll have my eye on you the whole time.'

'Plan on bringing a squad of French cops?'

'No way in hell! This is my collar. Ain't gonna have some noisy bunch what don't even speak English louse things up.'

'I don't know. Sounds risky to me.'

Sterne coughed. 'I'll be the one taking all the risks.'

'What the hell,' I said, faking a nervous laugh. 'You only live once.'

'Now you're showing some balls. We pull this off, the department owes you big.'

'Will they pay for my funeral if we fuck things up?'

'Maybe they'll send flowers.' Sterne said this without a trace of humor. 'One last thing. You really the father of Evangeline Proudfoot's bastard kid?'

'First I've heard about it. Got to run, Detective. I'll be inside the Lapin Agile tomorrow night. A little before midnight, I'll come out and stand under the tree in front like he said. Light a cigarette so you won't miss me.'

'Sounds like a plan. Hang onto Angel's note. I'm gonna need it after I slap the cuffs on him.'

'It's a deal,' I said and hung up.

After slipping Alfonse ƒ500 for the phone call, he insisted I stick around for a drink. He poured us each a brandy and we talked about horse racing. At a quarter to eight, I split. Had to meet Szabor. I decided to walk and work things out in my mind. The hour before sunset remained my favorite time of day, shadows filling the city's canyons and the sky above still a milky blue. I've always been a night person. Bandstand gigs ended long after midnight. All-night stakeouts kept me awake during my lost years as a private dick. My Lord Satan demanded rituals in the dark.

Ironic that a Devil-worshiper was on a mission to kill the Devil. It had nothing to do with destroying evil. Evil would always be around. What did János call it? The Hegelian dialectic? Opposing forces. Light and dark. Good and evil. Balancing them kept the universe in motion. Christ died almost two thousand years ago and his message of love survived. After I rubbed out Cyphre witches and warlocks would still gather at midnight to celebrate the Black Sabbath. It's what made the world go round.

I turned down rue des Écoles about five after the hour having spent my walking time thinking about philosophy when I meant to calibrate a mental schedule for everything on deck tomorrow. To hell with it. I knew what needed to get done. Plans can go wrong no matter how often you think them over. A smart schemer knew when to let go. Some things were best left to chance.

Szabor waited at the same table at Brasserie Balzar where we'd eaten last night, nose stuck deep in a book. I hung up my duffel coat and left the Ghurka bag and pillowcase by the circular metal rack. '*Bon soir, János,*' I said, placing my satchel beside the chair as I sat down.

'*Salve, Ioannes.*' Szabor greeted me in Latin. '*Quid agis?*' He said, hello, John. How's it going?

'*Bene sum,*' I answered. '*Gratias tibi.*' I was well, I said, thank you.

We played this little game until the waiter took our orders. It was no contest, the heavyweight champ in the ring with a bantamweight Golden Gloves contender. János gave me easy replies. I still ran out of vocabulary in a hurry. Forgotten Latin bubbled up out of distant memory. Words familiar twenty years ago. *Sacrificium. Tormentum. Sanguinem. Malum.*

We kept at it. Me asking for translations while we ate. I wanted to say things like 'I don't understand,' and 'Repeat that, please.' Handy stalls when things got hot. János gave me the answers, cutting his *gigot* into bite-sized pieces like some prissy fruit, knife in his right hand, fork in the left, tines curving downward. Pissed me off. I tore into my *poulet rôti* with my fingers, ripping off chicken hunks like a barbarian. Here's how we do it in America. I wiped grease from my lips with the back of my hand.

Fastidious and prim, Szabor ignored my atrocious manners. 'No need to learn all and everything all at once, Johnny,' he said, spearing a delicate morsel of lamb. 'Two evenings remain at our disposal. Language grows easier to digest when absorbed in small doses.'

'You're way off, János.' I licked my fingers clean. 'This is our last session for now. I've got business tomorrow night. Tuesday, I leave for Rome.'

'Why so early?'

'Taking the train.' Szabor's sour schoolmarm expression told me he was displeased. 'Can't make someone fluent as the Pope in a couple days,' I said.

'*Sans doute, mais...* he is always best served when most prepared.'

We finished our meal. I ordered a second bottle of wine. János had lost all faith in me. His eyes held no hope. We nursed the wine. I coaxed more lingo from him. Szabor barely went through the motions. He had no heart invested in it. When we shook hands at the door, I could see in his eyes he thought I was a dead man. 'Good luck, Johnny,' he said.

'Thanks.' I squeezed his hand. 'See you next week.'

'*Peut-être,*' Szabor replied with a sad little smile.

That doleful 'perhaps' stayed in my mind all the way to the Baron Samedi. I brooded during the taxi ride about János. He thought I was unprepared for my undercover caper. Szabor considered himself the better man for the job. He'd been a spy and was fluent in Latin. He didn't know I'd worked as a shamus in New York for fifteen years. The professor figured me as some has-been pop singer. Did his pathetic smile simply indicate regret? Poor old Johnny walking into a death trap? Were there more sinister implications? Did Szabor somehow sell me out?

I went upstairs to Bijou's apartment and stashed my bags in the hall closet. No plausible reason for János to betray me. If I pulled it off, he'd benefit from all the inside dope. I tossed the newspapers onto a sofa in the parlor. Even if I bought the farm, no big deal.

Szabor stayed out of it. He had no skin in the game. Always a mistake letting fear rule your judgement. What I needed was a drink. Finding Bijou in her dark nightclub was next to impossible. I waited at the bar, sending word through a waiter. After a few minutes, glorious in a gold lamé gown, she burst from the shadows like the rising sun.

We exchanged a chaste kiss. Bijou signaled the barkeep for a bottle of champagne. I wanted something stronger but settled for bubbly because it made her happy. She had other work to do and slipped back into darkness after a single glass. I took a double pour snifter of cognac back upstairs with me and settled on the sofa with my newspapers. I read them all carefully. Not every article. Who gave a shit if the Chinese swallowed up Tibet? Why should I care that Fidel Castro planned a visit to Washington later in the month? The headline told me at a glance whether or not I needed to read the piece below it. I searched for anything I could find about Ethan Krusemark.

Had the Devil-worshiping shipping tycoon's body been found in a subway tunnel, it would be worldwide news. I didn't come across a single word about him. Nothing. *Rien.* After double-checking the names in every obituary column, I still came up empty. No news was the best news. With Krusemark officially alive, Judas shekel number thirteen was not an invitation to my own beheading.

32

I woke abruptly from a dream of killing Louis Cyphre. He lay stretched on his back dressed in his Dr Cipher music hall soup-and-fish. Leather straps bound his arms and legs to a thick stone sacrificial slab. Cyphre laughed as I cut the buttons off his white evening vest with the point of my athame. A single swift stroke opened his abdomen revealing a tangled pudding of guts. His viscera pulsed and throbbed. A cloud of enormous flying insects burst from his intestines. Fanged and hideous, they swarmed about my face, big as birds. I screamed, swatting at them. I sat up sweating, my heart pounding in my chest.

In the bedroom's twilight, Bijou slept gently beside me, her breathing even and slow. She came to bed around 3:00 am after closing her nightclub. When I told her I had to leave early in the morning, she made no protest. Bijou enjoyed starting the day getting a leg over. She cut me some slack this time.

Half past seven when I padded to the shower. By eight o'clock, I was clean, shaved and on my way, casually dressed in chinos, a sweater and my suede windbreaker. I pulled on the duffel coat because I didn't want to carry it. On the street, it was cloudy but pleasant and dry for the moment. Leaving yesterday's duds hanging in Bijou's hall closet should have made me feel like a sap. Getting comfortable with the old ball and chain took a man one step closer to total Dagwood Bumstead.

I walked to the Les Halles Métro station lugging the Ghurka

bag, my satchel hung over my left shoulder. After taking care of business this morning, my afternoon looked wide open. I paid fifty centimes at the newsstand for a copy of *La Semaine à Paris* to see what was going on around town. Morning rush hour meant standing up to read for the short trip under the river. From Boulevard Saint-Germain it was an easy walk to rue Gît-le-Coeur through the maze of narrow streets intersecting this ancient quarter.

I climbed the stairs in the nameless hotel at ten minutes before the hour, knuckle-rapping on door number 15. Burroughs opened up, dressed in his rumpled gray suit and narrow tie. I wondered if he slept in those shabby threads.

'Morning, Johnny,' Bill drawled as I slid past him and placed the Ghurka bag on his unmade bed. 'I was trying to remember what they called you back when you were a rising star. You know, like Mel Tormé was "The Velvet Fog" and Sinatra "The Sultan of Swoon." Vaughn Monroe, I think, was "Old Leather Tonsils." What were you called?'

'Don't remember.'

'Sure you do.'

And I did. The nickname had been gone, like most of my past, until that very moment when it came bubbling up out of nowhere. 'OK,' I said to Bill. 'It was "The Fabulous Fave." Happy now?'

Burroughs cracked a mirthless smile. 'Funny. I always thought you were called "The Devil's Choirboy."'

'That came later. With all the bad press at the end of my singing career. Listen. Maybe you want to stand around jawing like some bobbysoxer. I'm here to talk business.'

Burroughs sat down by his tiny desk and set fire to a stinky French coffin nail. 'I'm all ears, Johnny,' he said, shaking out the wooden match as he exhaled.

'You line up one of your pals to join in?'

'All set.'

'Perfect. Like I said yesterday, you guys are my decoys. I'm being tailed. Need to throw the nosy bozo off my trail for a couple hours tonight. He thinks I've set up a meeting with a business rival. That bit is true. Only the meeting is going down someplace else. Your job, Bill, you and your buddy, is to fool him into thinking I'm where I said I'd be.'

'And just where does this grand deception transpire?' Burroughs made no effort to conceal his condescending smirk. I needed him now and let it pass.

'Know a place called Lapin Agile?' I asked. 'An old-fashioned cabaret?'

'Heard of it. Over in Montmartre, I think. Picasso's hangout fifty years ago.'

'That's the joint.' I paused to fire up a Lucky. 'There's a big tree out front. My tail thinks the meeting is set for midnight underneath it. He'll be watching. I want him to believe you're me.'

'Highly unlikely.'

'We'll get to that later. First off, you need to find the Lapin Agile. I want you inside the joint by eleven.' I got out my copy of *La Semaine à Paris*. Cabaret listings were in the back of the little publication, grouped numerically by district. Grabbing a pencil off Bill's desk, I drew a circle around the listing and tore the page free, memorizing the address, '4, rue des Saules,' in the process. 'Here.' I handed Burroughs the page. 'Take a cab. Get there before eleven.'

'What about my partner? What's his role in this intriguing endeavor?'

Burroughs looked more interested than his sarcastic manner implied. 'OK,' I said. 'Here's the plan. At five minutes before midnight, you come out of the cabaret and stand under the tree in the front yard. Light a cigarette so my tail can see you from a distance. I want your buddy to walk up rue des Saules from rue Caulaincourt. At twelve on the dot, he approaches you outside the Lapin Agile. Just stand there jawing for the next ten or fifteen minutes. When it's over, both of you take off back down rue des Saules.'

'When what is over?' Burroughs sounded uncertain.

'You'll know. Not really your problem. Do it right and it's worth that extra two hundred and fifty clams.' I knew the promise of more dough would calm any misgivings.

'All right,' Bill said. 'Sounds good to me. Big question is making someone who knows you believe in the deception.'

'Got that covered,' I said, unbuckling the Ghurka bag. 'Wear this.' I shook out my Aquascutum raincoat and draped it over the iron footboard of his rumpled bed. 'And this.' I set the blond wig on the brass ball-knob of the bedpost. 'Don't ask. I know it's not like my hair. Just pull it on. Doesn't have to fit right. No one's gonna look real close. And, Bill, be sure to wear your horn-rim cheaters. Cat on my tail knows me as someone sporting specs. Make sure to wear your black horn-rims.'

'Yassuh, boss.' Burroughs mimicked a minstrel show coon. Took me by surprise. He mocked me. Got a big kick out of it. I wanted to backhand him across his stupid hangdog face. Not a smart move. I needed him now and had to eat his wise-ass shit like it was fruit salad.

'Listen, Bill,' I spoke slow and easy. 'This may all seem like a big joke to you but it's very serious business for me. I'm paying top dollar for a job well done. Are you up to it?'

Burroughs blinked and blinked again. He badly wanted that extra two-and-a-half yards and saw it slipping away from him. 'Sorry, Johnny,' he said. 'I have this bad habit. Sarcasm. Like a poison. Hope you're not offended.'

'Nothing offends me, Bill,' I said, my voice flat and hard, 'except a double-cross.'

'No one likes a two-timing rat,' Burroughs said, falling back into the role of a make-believe underworld insider.

'We're on the same page then unless I'm hearing it wrong.' I pulled my war surplus flight jacket and knitted navy watch cap from the Ghurka bag. 'I want your buddy wearing this shit,' I told him. 'If it doesn't fit right, no big deal. It's gonna be dark.'

'Perfect,' Burroughs said. 'You can count on us, Johnny.'

'Good. Got the plan down straight?'

'Want me to recite it back to you?'

'You're a Harvard man, Bill. Figure you know how to pay attention in class. I'll drop by tomorrow afternoon, let's say around two o'clock, pick up my things and give you the rest of the dough. Just so long as everything goes down without a hitch tonight.'

I decided to while the day away at L'Hippodrome d'Auteuil, the racetrack in the Bois de Boulogne. On the train ride out there I read a copy of the *Trib* I'd bought at a news kiosk. I skimmed through the international headlines. None of them held any interest. Not a single line about Ethan Krusemark. At the track I placed a couple of bets guided by stuff I used to know about numerology. Side trips from my distant past. I won and won and kept winning, doubling down every time. I walked away with over nineteen grand. A good omen for the night ahead.

It was going on eight when I walked into my blue cottage. Time to get ready. I changed into dungarees, a woolen turtleneck and the Vibram-soled hiking boots, all dark as midnight shadows. After clipping the gat on my left hip, I pulled the derringer from my satchel and slipped it into the right outside patch pocket of the duffel coat.

I took a wire coat hanger out of the armoire and used the pair of pliers I'd bought at the hardware store to snip one side of the hanger free below the hook's twisted stem. The needlenose worked like a charm, bending the hook straight, twisting a nickel-sized loop into the wire at the end. All the tools, the bent hanger, and the length of pipe went into the *Herald Tribune* carry bag.

After stuffing my winnings from the track into the money belt and strapping it around my waist under the navy blue sweater, I slung the carry sack over my left shoulder. When I pulled on the duffel coat it was roomy enough to conceal what I carried underneath. Hooking the coat toggles through the rope loops, I headed out into the night.

33

I climbed the stairs of the George V Métro station beside the Lido around nine-thirty. The Champs-Élysées was bustling. I spotted a pink Cadillac Eldorado convertible parked at the curb. A great big brute. Just the ticket. Only the color looked all wrong. Much too light. Time enough to stroll down to the Étoile and see what else might be available. If I didn't find anything, I'd risk taking the Caddy if it was still there when I got back. Most of what I saw was worthless European junk; puny Fiats, Renaults, Borgwards, Dauphines and a bunch of crap I couldn't identify. About every third car turned out to be a sardine can Citroën *deux chevaux*. Why not just build them out of tinfoil and chewing gum wrappers?

It had started drizzling. Umbrellas popped open all around, black flowers blooming in the night. I pulled the hood of my coat up over the woolen cap, keeping the strap-hung satchel clenched tight to my side under my right arm. Fewer pedestrians prowling the sidewalk in the rain was a plus for me. I glimpsed the pink Eldorado from a block away gleaming through the gloom like a boil on Miss America's nose. Just what I feared. Time was running out. Beggars take whatever drops into their open mitts.

I waited for the moment to make my move. Half an hour had passed since I first saw the Cadillac. Who knew how long it had been there or when the owners might return? Just then, a big black car pulled up, parking on the other side of the tree-lined

pedestrian island across from the Lido. A '55 Oldsmobile Super
88 coupe. Made to order. My lucky day didn't end at the track. A
slim man in a gray Chesterfield coat got out and went around to
open the passenger door for a platinum blonde wearing a silver fox
stole. They hurried through the drizzle across the inner traffic lane
toward the nightclub.

I watched them go inside and sauntered over to the traffic
island. The set-up looked perfect. Trees and distance and the Olds
itself screened me from bystanders on the sidewalk. Traffic sped
along the Champs. Who would notice some guy getting into his
car?

Standing beside the driver-side door, I checked the traffic
moving in both directions and pulled on a pair of rubber gloves
from my satchel. I unfastened the duffel toggles, reaching beneath
the coat into the carry bag to withdraw the putty knife and bent
coat hanger. The coupe lacked a central post and my knife blade
slipped easily between the two side windows. I pried the front
window open a crack, inserting the coat hanger. A moment later,
I had the little wire loop lassoed around the lock button. Tugging
up, I eased it into the unlocked position. I was inside the Olds in
less than a minute.

When I tossed my satchel onto the passenger side of the red-and-
black vinyl seat, I noticed a small silver-sequined clutch glittering
in the corner. The lady had forgotten her purse. Bad news. As soon
as she wanted a cigarette or needed to use her lipstick lover boy
would be on his way to fetch it for her. Working fast, I took the
screwdriver and rubber mallet out of the carry bag. I inserted the
screwdriver's tip into the dashboard ignition switch and pounded
on the handle with the rubber mallet, driving the blade deep into
the key slot.

This was it. I turned the screwdriver handle hard to the right
and tapped the gas pedal. The big V8 kicked over immediately.
Lover boy kept his ride well tuned. Even better, the gas tank looked
almost full. I switched on the headlights and windshield wipers,

put the Olds in drive, signaled a left-hand turn and pulled out into the flow of traffic.

A few minutes before eleven, I parked on the right-hand side of rue Saint-Vincent about halfway down the hill across from the little urban vineyard. Plenty of parking spots on either side of the one-lane street. More cars lined up down at the end of the block near the Lapin Agile. I pulled in six feet behind a VW bug and switched off my headlights, leaving the motor running. The V8 purred soft as a sleeping kitten. I turned the radio down and cracked the vent window to light a smoke. I dug the hip flask from my back pocket and settled in for another stakeout. The French songs were mostly cornball stuff, lots of accordions and broken hearts. Every so often they'd play a tune from back home. A cut of Pops and Ella doing 'April in Paris' came as a happy surprise.

During the first half-hour no one strolled past along the sidewalk. Not a single dog walker. To my right, the windows in the houses were all dark. The quarter felt like a ghost town. Only the glow from the Lapin Agile at the bottom of the hill provided any sign of life. After fifteen minutes or so, a car sped by toward the graveyard on the other side of rue des Saules. In a moment, it rattled around the corner and out of sight. The set-up was everything I had hoped for.

Around 11:30, I spotted someone in a drab overcoat walking down the far side of rue des Saules. It was Sterne. I watched him slouch along like some loser without a hope in the world. At the corner, he turned left and went up into the shadows of the tiny park just like I figured. I turned off the car radio. This part I liked. The quiet waiting. Predators lurking in the shadows. Kind of a joke really. Sterne staked out the cabaret while I staked him out. Dumb bastard didn't have a clue.

After a few minutes, I saw a match flare down in the little park. Sterne was lighting a smoke. Shit for brains made no effort to hide it. I also passed my time smoking. A dashboard lighter inconspicuous in the darkness. I cupped my fags in my hand the way I'd been taught in the army. Also disposed of my butts the GI way, field stripping them, scattering loose tobacco out the window and flicking away the rolled-up paper. Didn't want to leave anything American in the dashboard ashtray.

Another car rolled past along rue Saint-Vincent. One every half-hour seemed to be the drill. I'd have to gamble on that and hope my luck held true. A few minutes before midnight, I put the big 88 in drive, moving out into the street with the headlights off. My left foot pressed hard on the brake pedal while I waited. Straining to stay focused on the bottom of the hill, my eyes darted to the rearview mirror every few seconds, checking for approaching traffic.

I didn't need to check my watch to see what time it was when Sterne stepped out of the shadows. He moved with slow deliberation down the steps of the park. I eased up on the brake and the Oldsmobile started downhill as I pressed the accelerator. Didn't want to rev the engine and alert the slow-moving lieutenant. Cops never rush in to collar an unknowing suspect. They like surprise on their side.

Sterne reached the middle of the intersection and I floored it, pumping all 200-plus horsepower. The speedometer pushed up past forty. When the flatfoot heard the onrushing car, he stared in my direction, a look of disbelief illuminating his ugly mug. At that moment, I switched the high-beams on. The rain-slick paving stones gleamed before me. Sterne stood transfixed in the headlight's glare, dumb as a deer on a country road. I hit him dead center, pushing sixty. Sterne tumbled up over the hood, his overcoat ripping on the saber jet ornament before his head struck the windshield with a sodden *thump* and his body flew off to the right.

I jammed hard on the brakes. The Olds fishtailed, swerving down the wet street. It came to a stop across from the graveyard wall about thirty yards from Sterne's crumpled body. In other circumstances, I'd have put the car in reverse and backed over him to finish the job. This time, it had to look like a hit-and-run accident. I pushed the selector into park and took that length of pipe from my carry bag, getting out of the 88. I heard the distant echo of footfalls. Burroughs and his buddy running in a panic down rue des Saules. The sounds of their escape faded as I walked toward Sterne. An unseen dog barked in a backyard far away. Muted piano music and discordant song came from inside the Lapin Agile. Such happy nocturnal noise.

Sterne lay on his belly, head turned to one side in an expanding puddle of blood. Translucent blood bubbles blossomed from his nose. He was still breathing. I looked all around, making sure I was unobserved. No one had come out of the cabaret. Not a single light went on up the street. Things unseen go bump in the night. I leaned over Sterne, bending my knees like a back alley crap shooter. My only shot had to be a good one. Gripping the pipe with both hands, I brought it down full force against the side of Sterne's head. Made a sound like hitting a pumpkin with a baseball bat. Music to my ears. Son-of-a-bitch had dogged my trail long enough. I watched the large bubble forming on his left nostril slowly deflate.

Walking back to the purring Oldsmobile, I wished I'd given Sterne another knock with the pipe. One might look like part of the accident. A second would definitely be suspicious. I knew he was dead, so what did it matter? A quick check of the car's front end showed both headlights unbroken. The only damage was a bowl-shaped dent in the hood's snout where the Olds emblem hung loose. Black paint job made it hard to see. A large round spider-web of cracks on the right hand side of the windshield was of greater concern. Back home they'd pull you over for that.

Time to move. Inside the 88, I wrapped the bloody pipe in the threadbare towel, selected drive and cruised around the boneyard's corner on Saint-Vincent. Figured finishing off Sterne took no more than a couple minutes. I wanted to ditch the Olds in a hurry but not too close to Montmartre. Dark night-time streets provided refuge. Zigzagging east from rue Caulaincourt, I stuck to a safe legal speed. Lover boy had probably reported his car stolen by now. A big American rig, easy to spot in Paris. Busted windscreen only made things worse. Not knowing my way around this part of the city didn't help much.

After a quarter hour's meandering, I happened onto a concrete wasteland, an area of railroad yards and warehouses. Somehow I came across a dead-end street called Impasse du Curé jutting into the yards. It looked perfect, desolate and decaying. I parked in the ass-end of nowhere, yanked the screwdriver from the ignition and collected my stuff. Before walking out of the cul-de-sac, I locked the Oldsmobile like a proper citizen.

At the corner, I turned left, pulling off the latex gloves. In the distance, a clang of unseen freight cars coupling provided the only hint of human activity. A train whistle pierced the night. B flat. I soon found my way onto rue Marx Dormoy, dead as Main Street in a ghost town. Not a taxi in sight. My second big mistake. Making no plans where to dump the hot jalopy. After a few blocks, the neighborhood changed character. Young men lurked in shadowy doorways. Arabic script curlicued across the shop windows. I passed a couple cafés open late. Glancing in, I saw all the patrons were male. Sipping coffee or tea. No wine or booze. Without knowing it, I'd entered a foreign country no longer France.

Continuing along, I sensed I was being followed. No need looking back over my shoulder to make sure. All those years as a private dick gave me a sixth sense. My second mistake looked to be a beaut. Alone in a strange land with twenty grand strapped around my middle. I unfastened the toggles on my duffel coat. Wanted my roscoe in easy reach. The Smith & Wesson held five rounds, plus another two in the derringer. That should be enough. Kneecap one of the bastards and the others would take off like startled roaches when the lights go on.

'*Savez-vous où vous êtes?*' a voice called from the roadway. I looked over and saw a medium-weight box truck had pulled over. The driver leaned across the seat. He asked if I knew where the hell I was.

'*Perdu.*' I told him I was lost.

'*Entrez,*' he said, opening the passenger door. '*Cherchez et vous trouverez.*' The truck driver said something along the lines of 'seek and you will find.' I turned for a look at the four dark-skinned young thugs following me. They stopped in their tracks, staring hard, waiting to see what I would do.

I wanted to kill them all. Craved it. So damn sweet seeing them sprawled out dead on the sidewalk. Instead, I hissed, '*Fous le camp!*' telling them to piss off, and climbed into the truck cab.

As we cruised south, the truck driver told me I'd blundered into a district so densely populated with Algerians that the FLN hid their local headquarters within its crowded streets. I'd been lost in a war zone. We were passing a large railroad terminal, Gare du Nord, the truck driver informed me, and I told him to drop me there. I'd catch a cab down to the Place de la République, I said. This much I'd planned in advance not wanting a cabbie to remember taking me to Sterne's hotel after midnight. '*Pas de problème,*' the driver replied. He let me off near a large bronze statue of a woman holding an olive branch aloft at the center of the huge square. '*Marianne,*' he shouted before speeding off. '*Symbole de la république!*'

34

I walked west from the Place de la République along rue Meslay. At the end of the second block, I came to the Hotel du Plat d'Etain. The little lobby looked deserted when I peered in through the glass front door. A small engraved plaque mounted above a push button instructed hotel guests in both French and English that the entrance was locked after midnight and to ring for admittance. I pulled my latex gloves back on. The door lock was foreign made but of a type I recognized. Selecting the closest match among the twirls from my satchel, I slipped it into the key slot. Fit like a charm. Inside the lobby quick as a magician palming cards.

Ghost-silent on my Vibram soles, I drifted past the desk clerk counting Zs in his swivel chair. I spotted Sterne's room key dangling from pigeonhole number 33. Nobody home anymore. Bypassing the coffin-sized elevator, I took the stairs landing-to-landing around the grille-enclosed shaft. Halfway down the hallway on the fourth floor, I found Sterne's room. Locks using skeleton keys were child's play. I had it picked and the door open in under fifteen seconds. Even knowing I would not be disturbed, I pulled the security chain into place as an extra precaution.

Sterne's room was small, spare and simple. Several notches above the shit-hole Burroughs bunked in but still a pigsty compared with my digs at the Vendôme. Made me laugh that the fugitive lived better than the copper hot on his trail. Aside from a bed tucked against the wall, two plastic chairs, and a combination bureau and desk in the corner, there wasn't much to look at.

I wanted to split in under an hour. Had no way of knowing how long before *les flics* traced Sterne's body from Montmartre to this two-bit room. A gray typewriter stood on the desk. A stack of hotel stationery was piled on one side of the Olivetti. Several manila folders rested on the other. I sat down at the desk and had a look.

One folder was Harry Angel's jacket. It contained several blow-up copies of Angel's PI license application photo along with many sets of his fingerprints from the same source. Far as I remember, Johnny Favorite never had his dabs taken. A number of the license picture copies doctored by a police artist showed him or me, whoever I was, without a mustache. Lucky thing they didn't draw Angel wearing horn-rimmed specs. I read a condensed version of my alter ego's fake life story, much of it lifted from that same license application. A separate page contained a compendium of all the recent murders Harry supposedly committed: Edison Sweet, Margaret Krusemark, Epiphany Proudfoot. No mention of Ethan Krusemark or the Black Mass. Sergeant Edelio Deimos made the list. His body had been found in the basement of the Chelsea on 3/26/59. Death by strangulation.

The next folder held several copies of those glossy publicity photos Sterne brought to our lunch. In with them were several Thermofaxed pages from Warren Wagner's office files. The originals were over twenty years old. I recognized Warren's handwriting. One page outlined the stops on our European tour. 'London (two weeks), Paris (two weeks), Brussels, Amsterdam, Copenhagen, Stockholm, Berlin, Vienna (one week each) and Rome (two weeks).' A side note read, 'Focus on schmaltz in Germany and Austria. The Nazis consider jazz degenerate music.'

I stared at the list of cities without remembering any of them. Paris remained smack dab in the present. Only glimmers of pre-war Gay Paree flashed back from the fall of 1938. I tried picturing London in my mind's eye, coming up with only the image of a red double-decker bus that I probably once saw in a magazine ad.

Bits of Vienna had come back a week ago when Bill Burroughs asked me about performing there. Staring at Warren Wagner's photocopied handwriting made me hear the sound of his voice again and see his cheerful grin, brimming with false optimism. His advice about playing schmaltz brought up snatches of Berlin. All those menacing swastikas. Two years later, after Cyphre came into my life, I understood their evil beauty.

We played four nights at the Femina-Palast ballroom on Nürnberger Strasse. I remembered a huge ornate casino with columns and curving balconies along the sides and an immense beaded chandelier hanging overhead like the hull of a crystal ship. Spider took Wagner's advice. We used our corniest arrangements, sounding more like Guy Lombardo's outfit than a swing band.

The last night, after Hesch Geller overheard a customer praising the Reich for banning 'nigger-jew jazz' in 1935, he stood up for his solo and blew six blistering choruses, hotter than Lips Page at the Reno Club in KC and added a Ziggy Elman frailach flourish at the end to rub their Aryan noses in pure Yiddisher joy. All that kike jazz led to a brawl with a bunch of Brown Shirts after the show. The band got the best of it and split from Berlin a day early.

Hard not daydreaming about the past with so much of it outlined on the pages I held in my hand. Wagner wrote a note at the top of our Paris schedule way back in June of 1938. 'Tell Carl and Ben. Take Johnny to after hours sessions at clubs on list.' I saw Club Monaco (Bricktop's), 66, rue Pigalle on the list. I'd been to Bricktop's old joint a week ago and remembered most of it. That same day, I'd passed by the Moulin Rouge, all gussied up now, and thought only about cancan dancers. I tried my damnedest but nothing more came back about the Moulin Rouge.

Sterne had pencilled short notes on the after-hours list. Most clubs had check marks next to them. Club Monaco was marked, '(now called the Sphinx. No longer a jazz club).' Le Jockey's note read, '(Staff doesn't remember seeing Angel).' Le Boeuf sur le Toit:

'(Nut-hatch music. Checked with staff. No one recognized Angel. Some knew Johnny Favorite by reputation. Said he was before their time. A has-been).'

I rolled the photocopied sheet into the typewriter. Below Sterne's last entry I typed: 'Lapin Agile, 4, rue des Saules. (Word at Jockey Club is Favorite and some of the Simpson band hung out here long ago).' It looked legit. Provided a reason why the lieutenant ventured alone at midnight to some out-of-the-way cabaret in Montmartre. I unrolled the altered Thermofax and returned it to the folder. My heart raced. I felt more anxiety than I did stealing the Olds. My wristwatch told me I'd been inside the Hotel du Plat d'Etain for only about ten minutes. It felt like hours. Calm down, I told myself, you've got plenty of time.

The next folder contained a few hotel stationery pages detailing Sterne's daily reports. I was most interested in the notes about French law enforcement and his lunch with me.

'4/6/59. Arrived Orly 9:00 am local time. Met with French customs. Got John Favorite's local address: Hotel Vendôme, 1 Place Vendôme, 1st. 2:00 pm, cab to Paris Police Prefecture Headquarters, Île de la Cité. 2:30 pm, meeting with Inspector Edmond Lenoir. Briefed him on Angel case. Angel after J Favorite in Paris? No record Angel's entry. Left photos and prints. 6:00 pm, dinner. 8:30 pm, cab to Boeuf sur le Toit (jazz club), no one remembered Favorite or Angel. Left Angel photo and hotel number. 11:00 pm, cab to hotel. Phone message from John Favorite. Meet for lunch tomorrow. Noon.'

Sterne was thorough. Give him credit for that. His next entry on 4/7 was of great interest to me. 'Early start. Métro train to 9:15 meeting with Interpol Senior Agent Oskar Schrober at ICPO headquarters, 37, rue Paul Valéry, 16th. Gave him all info (plus prints/photos) on Harold R Angel. HA entered Europe through another country? Provided list of possible aliases. Angel coming to France? Searching for Favorite in Paris? Schrober will notify all border and customs officers. 12:00 noon, subway to lunch at

Grand Véfour with John Favorite. Classy place. Favorite a regular. Well known to staff. Speaks French. Expensively dressed. Blond hair. Peroxide job? Claimed to be traveling businessman. No fixed address. Lives in hotels. Won't reveal current local address. Gave me a phone number, ODE. 31-27. Passport looked OK. Returned from Tokyo, 3/22/59. Favorite didn't recognize photo of Warren Wagner Jr. Victim's father was Favorite's agent. Claimed no contact since 1943. Last saw Margaret Krusemark in January 1943. Something fishy about all this. Favorite has deformed nose identical to Harry Angel. Coincidence? Asked about it. Favorite said it was cancer. 1:30 pm, subway to American Embassy, 2, avenue Gabriel. Meeting with Ralph Ingolsby, passport division. Have him check Favorite's SF entry date from Tokyo.

The stuff about my nose, 'something fishy,' and Mr Ingolsby at the embassy looked like big trouble. Several entries for 4/8, running over onto a second sheet, ticked like time bombs. Skimming through the Métro rides and meals, my eye caught on '5:00 pm, phone hotel for messages. Favorite called at 3:30 pm. Said Angel left a message for him at American Express. Angel wants to meet with Favorite. I phone Favorite at 7:00 pm for details. Ingolsby called 4:15 pm. No record of Favorite entering San Francisco from Tokyo on 3/22. Perhaps an oversight by passport control. Ingolsby will follow up. Curious. Called Favorite at 7:00 pm. Said Angel wants to meet tomorrow midnight outside a place called Lapin Agile in Montmartre.'

I rolled a clean sheet of hotel stationery into the typewriter. Never had bèen much of a typist. Two-finger hunt-and-pecker. Took me almost forty-five minutes to retype Sterne's report. Most of it I left exactly the same, omitting only the incriminating stuff like my 'fishy' nose and all those phone calls about a midnight meeting with Harry Angel at the Lapin Agile. I left out Ralph Ingolsby, the American Embassy and only mentioned Sterne saying my passport 'looked OK.' Figured Ingolsby was a one-way street. When he tried reaching Sterne again and got no reply he'd let the matter drop. Anyone reading the report on this end wouldn't have a clue. Hocus-pocus. No more passport problem.

The lieutenant's original took up three pages. I slipped them into my satchel. My condensed version reduced the report down to two and a half. They went into a manila folder beside the typewriter.

I left his sad little room, locking the door with my picks from the outside. Only silence at the bottom of the stairs. The night manager snoozed on as I tiptoed past on my rubber soles. I unlatched the front door. It locked behind me when I closed it. I sashayed off down the street. Turning south, I spotted a taxi pulling up in front of a small hotel on the far corner. I ran and jumped in, telling the driver to take me to the Pont Notre-Dame.

As we drove through deserted streets, I thought about Warren Wagner's handwritten itinerary. Now I knew the names of all the Paris venues where I'd performed on tour with Spider Simpson. Only twenty years ago. Might as well be ancient history. I ran the names through my tattered memory again, letting my thoughts float freely through my mind, hoping I'd remember something if I didn't try too hard. That's how memory works. You don't force it. Forgotten moments bubble up unexpectedly from the past. Drifting along in a hazy recollection of the Moulin Rouge from long ago, I suddenly saw Louis Cyphre clear as gin in my mind. All alone, dressed in white tie and tails like a year later when we first met. He had a ringside seat at a small table on the edge of the dance floor. I remembered his gleaming black hair, ermine goatee and perfect smile. One other thing I recalled. Cyphre winked at me.

When we reached the bridge, I paid the driver and descended the steps to the riverbank pathway along the quay. All was quiet as I walked west along the river. When I was underneath the next bridge I reached inside my coat and took out the bloody pipe and towel and threw them into the Seine.

After a half-hour walk I spotted the welcoming glow of Bijou's nightclub. I went upstairs to the apartment first, stashing my white canvas carry bag at the back of the hall closet.

Bijou stood by the bar drinking champagne as I found my way through her shadowy joint. She wore a shimmering green sheath iridescent as a beetle wing. At 2:30 am it was close to closing time, the club mostly empty. 'Ah, Johnny,' she smiled, tapping the shoulder of my black duffel coat when I pulled her into my arms. 'Why do you dress like a university student?'

I kissed her hard, feeling her ripe body beneath the clinging dress. 'Had a job to do,' I said.

'Yes? What manner of job? Some dirty work down in the catacombs?'

I didn't answer, kissing her long and deeply instead.

35

In the morning, once I'd showered and shaved, the high-yellow girl served me coffee. Bijou slept like an angel in the other room. She'd screwed like a she-devil a few hours earlier, war whooping in savage ecstasy. Not a word about the money belt I kept strapped around my naked waist. Just like she never mentioned the .38 I wore on my hip and stashed under the pillow at night. Think she got off on grinding her belly up against so much moola. Bijou knew I was a strange bad boy. She liked me that way. I waited until after banging her twice before breaking the news about leaving town for the weekend.

'Take me with you,' she murmured.

'No can do, babe.'

'*Pourquoi?*'

'Strictly business.'

'Dirty business?'

'*Bien sûr.*'

I was out on the street at twenty minutes past ten, dressed in the camel hair jacket, brown cardigan and twill trousers I'd left hanging in the closet two days ago. The red silk necktie made me feel respectable. Nothing I could do about my hiking boots and duffel coat. The eccentric tastes of an unconventional man of means. Feeling like I owned the world, I walked over to the ecclesiastical tailor's shop on rue des Pyramides. I thought about how much I owed János for all his help. The somber cassock fit perfectly. Also the hood and cape. I stuck my hand through the right side vent pocket, reaching across for the roscoe on my left hip. Plenty of room for a smooth draw. Good thing my cardigan concealed the gat.

Next stop, my bank to retrieve Krusemark's Tyrian shekel. I arrived at Morgan Guaranty Trust Company just before noon. Alone in the little room with my safe deposit box, I pulled up my sweater and shirt, unzipping the money belt. I carried a ton of francs in my wallet so I put the rest of my racetrack loot into the box. The Judas shekel in its little velvet sack went straight into the money belt. I zipped up and rearranged my clothing, walking out of the bank barely fifteen minutes later.

Lunchtime. I drilled across the square, making straight for the Ritz. Michel greeted me like a long-lost friend, the headwaiter's sham affection reinforced by a ƒ500 note I slipped him, explaining I had no reservation. Michel arranged for a two-top by a window. I checked my duffel coat and canvas shoulder sack. Showing me to my table, he expressed his regrets. He had not seen Monsieur Natas since my last visit. What he really regretted was missing out on another tip.

I skipped the prix-fixe luncheon in favor of ordering à la carte, enjoying an excellent *noix de veau Brillat-Savarin* and a fine bottle of Côtes du Rhône. Wiping my patrician lips, I signaled Michel over and asked to make a local call. He hurried off, returning with a telephone. He managed to kneel and plug the four-pronged connector into a wall receptacle set into the baseboard molding without any apparent loss of dignity.

I dialed the number of the café-tabac. I didn't expect Alfonse to have any messages for me. If he did, it meant big trouble.

'*Allô?*' Alfonse came on the line.

'*C'est moi, Johnny,*' I said, asking if I'd gotten any messages.

'*Oui. Un seulement.*'

I froze. '*Qui?*' I asked. Had the French cops connected me to Sterne's hit-and-run?

'L'imprésario du cirque. Jérome Medrano.'

Medrano! The circus big shot. He had news about Cyphre. I asked if Mr Big left any message. Reynard burst into croaking overdrive, essentially telling me Medrano wanted me to call back.

I found Medrano's card and dialed his private number. The circus impresario answered on the fourth ring. I told him I got his message. 'The reason I telephoned you, Mr Favorite,' he said, 'was because I received a telegram from Fra Diavolo yesterday afternoon.'

'You're kidding!' I blurted, sounding like a cartoon American from the funny papers.

'I must assure you I am not. You expressed interest in this amazing magician. His wire arrived from Vienna. He returns to Paris next week and wishes a performance at Cirque Medrano.'

'When? Have you booked him?' My mind raced. Could Cyphre really fall in to my lap like this? 'I want to catch his act.'

'Fra Diavolo is one of a kind. A privilege having him on the bill anytime. For that reason I am keeping the circus open all of next week. He said he will perform on Monday. I hope he will play the entire week. But even only one performance will make me very happy.'

'Next Monday?'

'Very likely.'

'When will you know for sure?'

'With Fra Diavolo nothing is certain. If he comes to my theater on Monday, I will include him on the program.'

'Save a ticket for me.'

'But of course, Mr Favorite. I hope you succeed in persuading him to join your comeback act. Having it headline at Cirque Medrano would be an honor. A ticket waits at the box office.'

I heard the receiver click on the other end and hung up my

phone. Staring blankly into empty space, dumbfounded, I felt like I'd just been sapped. Could my legwork have paid off? Did the wide net I cast ensnare the Devil? Ernie Cavalero once told me shoe leather was a PI's best investment. Maybe Ernie was right. Why risk my neck going undercover in Rome?

Looking for an easy way out most often found the shortest route to failure. There was no guarantee Cyphre would show up for Medrano's circus. Fra Diavolo welched on his commitments most of the time. Cyphre might show up in the Vatican. Make an appearance at the Council of Thirty. Maybe he was chairman of the board. Made sense. Even odds at best. I had no way of knowing. One thing was sure, even if Cyphre proved to be a fake, I'd get the inside dope on Satan's inner-circle. I owed that much to Szabor for setting me straight on the path.

I settled the tab and caught a cab outside the Ritz. The taxi dropped me at the nameless hotel on rue Gît-le-Coeur. I rapped on Burroughs' door; I knew he'd be in there. No way Bill was missing out on the payoff. 'It's open,' his gruff voice growled and I went inside.

Burroughs sat on the edge of his sagging bed, hunched in his gray suit. He stared straight at me, cold dead eyes magnified by his specs. 'You are a very dangerous man, Johnny,' he said in his trademark monotone.

'Don't know what you're talking about.'

'Hit and run.'

I shrugged. 'Haven't a clue. Something bad go down?'

'Why ask?' Burroughs said. 'You were there.'

'Not true, Bill,' I replied with a straight face. 'Over in Clichy concluding a business deal. You were just my decoy.' I pulled the Hotel Vendôme envelope from my satchel and tossed it onto the bed. Burroughs glanced at it, almost with disinterest, making no move to pick it up.

'Your stuff's by the door,' he said.

I glanced over my shoulder, spotting the Ghurka bag in the

corner. 'See you around,' I said, grabbing it on my way out and catching one last glimpse of Bill Burroughs, a silent cadaver seated in his dank, dark tomb.

36

The overnight train to Rome was surprisingly comfortable and elegant. I had a tidy little compartment with a couch that converted into a bed and the Rome Express still boasted an elegant dining car that served sublime food and wine. Aside from a passport check when we crossed the border in the middle of the night and a cursory customs check a few hours later, no one disturbed me.

I took a cab from the Termini to the Excelsior. The hotel occupied an entire corner at the intersection of Via Vittorio Veneto and Via Boncompagni. A hulking white six-story building studded with small balconies and crowned by a tall cupola borrowed from some ancient tabernacle, it was the sort of splendid palatial pile I'd grown accustomed to in my new life as a Devil-worshiping criminal. My spacious room looked out on the Via Veneto from the third floor. Made me feel like I owned the world. Crime most definitely did pay. Paid off big time.

Took a long hot shower and got to work. I fitted the black wig with bobby pins and split the lace mustache with scissors the way Ernie taught me. Daubing spirit gum on my upper lip, I stuck each half in place and applied a dusting of neutral face powder to take the shine off the glue. Harry Angel stared back at me from the mirror. Tough luck for Sterne that he was no longer around to see this.

I'd given the idea of using makeup a lot of thought. Big risk, turning myself back into the man I was running away from. On the other side of the coin, I didn't want the limo driver knowing what I looked like. Even worse, if my hood came off in some terrible mishap at tonight's secret meeting after I punched Cyphre's ticket, better if the surviving Council members thought someone else pulled the trigger

After killing a few hours walking through the Villa Borghese and catching a view of the dome of St Peter's silhouetted against a sky set aflame by the setting sun, I headed back to the Excelsior. On the Via Veneto by Via Sicilia I came across a simple sign hanging over the door at number 155. BRICKTOP'S. Could it really be? Was this gin joint owned by the same Ada Smith I sang the blues with so long ago? Maybe it was like Birdland, named in honor of Charlie 'Yardbird' Parker, a junkie who almost never performed at the club. This was a good omen. Bricktop alive and still swinging with the swells might be my lucky charm, a magic bridge back into the forgotten past, a portal leading to an unknown future. .

Like Birdland, Bricktop's was down in the basement. I descended the stairs not knowing what to expect and stepped into an elegant room, plush with thick carpets and heavy drooping chandeliers. A headwaiter stopped me at the entrance. He said something in Italian that I didn't understand. I replied in French. The headwaiter asked if I had a reservation. When I said, 'Non,' he started telling me that he was very sorry but – and I cut him off. 'Please tell Miss Bricktop that Johnny Favorite is here to sing with her again,' I said in English.

Bricktop treated me like visiting royalty. Second nature to her. 'Call me Bricky,' she said. Dumpy, freckled-faced, high-yellow, she had a Southern accent unblemished by thirty expatriate years. In her mid-sixties, Bricky's famous red hair looked thin and streaked with gray. She said I looked just the same except for the mustache and asked about my nose, clucking sympathetically when I told her it was a war wound. 'That why you got outta the business?' she asked. 'Disfigured? You was a big star, child. Could've got even bigger, funny nose and all.'

I didn't dispute this although she'd never guess the real story. Bricky ran a piano bar. A coal-black professor in white tails tickled intricate stride riffs out of the eighty-eight. I dined on *saltimbocca alla Romana* with a fine bottle of Barolo, refusing to let Bricktop pick up my tab. 'You're gonna sing for your supper no matter what, Johnny,' she said, taking my hand and pulling me in front of the piano, long black feather boa trailing behind her.

As the applause settled, Bricky greeted her customers in Italian and French. Me, she introduced in English. 'Special treat tonight, my darlings. Y'all remember Johnny Favorite. Big star back before the war. Some said he met with Satan at the crossroads just like Robert Johnson.' Bricktop gave me a hug. 'How 'bout one a' your own tunes?' Piano man didn't know 'Dancing with the Devil.' We settled on 'Voodoo Queen.' Hoagy Carmichael wrote the melody. Bricktop harmonized, her long cigar a smoldering baton.

'*Voodoo queen,*
My lovely voodoo queen
Came to me in a dream.
Loved her sight unseen,
Black magic voodoo queen.
Work your magic on me.'

Bricky wanted to hear all about my life since she'd last seen me. I made most of it up. Even so, my lies often touched upon the truth and many more forgotten moments from the past were revealed to me. She jokingly pleaded for me not to go, 'sing more songs and make a party of it.' I told her I had another engagement. This time it was the biggest party of my life.

I was back in my room at the Excelsior by eleven. Didn't take long to change. Shedding my suit jacket, I got the Judas coin out of my money belt and strapped the Minifon to my belly in its elastic harness. I set the Omega aside and buckled on the phony watch, plugging the mike into the wire recorder. Plenty of cord allowed my arm free movement after I tugged on the black cassock. Before fastening all those buttons, I put the derringer and pair of Pachmayrs inside the specially tailored front pocket. Shekel number thirteen went into the vent pocket on my right side. I checked myself out in the mirror. The vestment fit perfectly. No bulge on the left where I packed my heater. I practiced my draw through the vent. Smooth as Vaseline on a hand job.

The front desk called at half past eleven. My car waited outside. With the black cape draped over my shoulders and the hood clenched in my right hand, I headed for the elevators looking like a man of the cloth. My two sweetly smiling fellow passengers seemed not to notice that I wore a red and blue striped necktie instead of a clerical collar. I half-expected them to say, 'Bless us, Father.'

Passing through the opulent lobby, I encountered my driver dressed in a gray business suit leaning against the front fender of a black Alfa Romeo limousine. 'American Express,' I said. He nodded and held the back door open for me.

'*Dove vogliamo andare?*' the driver asked, pulling away from the curb.

He wanted to know where we were going. I guessed this from studying my Italian phrase book on the train last night. '*Alla Vaticano. Via di Porta Angelica,*' I replied, having memorized my answer in advance. '*Porta Sant'Anna.*'

On hearing this, the driver made a quick U-turn without a signal. We cruised through dark mysterious streets. I'd spent two weeks here with Spider's band in early November of '38 but remembered nothing. Maybe I'd roamed these same shadowy boulevards way back when. We crossed the river over some nondescript bridge. I pulled on my hood in the darkness remembering another bridge lined with tall statues of angels. Maybe I saw a picture of it once. Just as likely, I walked across it twenty years ago. Not that it mattered anymore. I was far beyond any help angels might provide.

We drove straight up a broad boulevard, looping around a nondescript piazza and turning right at the corner of what my guidebook photos taught me were the walls of Vatican City. Up ahead a row of fancy black cars formed in a long line along the brick wall on Via di Porta Angelica. '*Accostare!*' I barked. '*Giusto qui.*' I told the driver to pull over, words memorized from the phrase book.

'*Allora che cosa?*'

I think he wanted to know what to do next. '*Aspetta.*' I told him to wait. '*Seguire gli altri.*' Follow the others. I hoped he understood.

'*Si,*' the driver replied.

We didn't wait long. Another limo pulled up behind us as the line of cars started slowly moving forward. We crept ahead, headlights off, a one-lane traffic jam. I knew what to expect from Szabor's tale of the young secretary's undercover adventure and slipped my Judas shekel from its velvet pouch. The big Mercedes in front of us turned and stopped midway through Saint Anna's gate. I rolled down my window, watching the Swiss guardsman in his clownish tri-colored outfit step up, halberd in hand, to examine the coin an unseen passenger offered to him. The guard stepped back, waving the car through as he shouted, '*Numero diciassette.*' Seventeen. I remembered János saying this was an unlucky number in Italy.

My number was thirteen, unlucky the world over. Bad luck followed me everywhere since the day I was born. Always managed to outrun the black dog up until now. Maybe tonight the beast would catch me at last. My driver turned in and stopped by the gate. The Swiss guardsman stepped forward. He didn't look quite so funny up close. I handed him the silver shekel. He stared at it in the palm of his hand for a moment before giving it back. '*Numero tredici,*' he shouted, waving us through.

I watched through the windshield over the driver's shoulder as the Mercedes ahead of us paused by the round dark tower of Nicholas V. Light spilled through an open door framed by a tall archway. A guy in a blue uniform wearing a holstered automatic strapped to his waist marked something on the clipboard he carried before stepping forward to open the rear limo door. His round visored pillbox cap had a badge pinned on the front. Some kind of cop. Figured he was one of the papal gendarmes. A hooded figure in black emerged from the car. The cop gave him a crisp salute and bent to say something to the driver. A moment later, the Mercedes pulled away.

Our turn next. The Pope's copper opened the car door for me and snapped off a brisk salute, bending to tell my driver something in Italian. I walked into the gray stone tower, all gleaming marble inside, following Number Seventeen.

37

The hooded figure in black walked past the central stairway that led to the ultra-modern Vatican Bank, went around an unoccupied blond-wood reception counter and disappeared from sight. Behind the counter, I found an open trap door designed to look like a marble floor slab when closed. An ancient spiral stone staircase wound deep into darkness. After I'd descended about twenty-five steps, I looked up and caught a glimpse of another black-clad Council member heading down behind me.

The stairs twisted deep into the earth, fifty feet or more by my rough calculation.

I emerged into a rectangular vestibule with a vaulted stone ceiling. The rough walls were studded with iron bolts. It was hard to believe that this subterranean chamber that resembled a dungeon at Madame Tussauds existed beneath a bank every bit as modern as Chase Manhattan. I watched the man ahead of me hang up his cape. I did the same. Other capes and black overcoats dangled from the walls. When I walked into the domed Council chamber it matched the young secretary's description. Demonic statuary leering from wall niches. Flaming torches angled in iron sockets. Hanging chains. The huge round table at the center of the room was decorated with the Sigil of Baphomet, the pagan idol that looked like a winged muscular human figure with the head of a horned goat enclosed by a star pentagon.

Several Council members sat at their designated places in

black robes and hoods, somber as Inquisitional judges. I didn't stand around gawking. Every calculated step I took indicated complete familiarity with my strange surroundings. Spotting the golden numeral XIII on a seat-back, I walked over as if I'd done it hundreds of times and sat down, inserting my silver coin reverse side up into the gold receptacle on the table rim by Krusemark's place.

I glanced around the chamber calculating a possible escape route. The eyeholes in the hood restricted my vision. Off to my right, I spotted the gleaming, grotesque carved marble throne black as obsidian. It stood mounted on a dais, the arms and seat a tangle of intertwining snakes, the back formed from a pair of giant unfolding wings, an inverted golden pentagram set dead center. The young undercover secretary's description didn't do it justice.

My mind raced with possibilities. Had to be the Throne of Satan. No other explanation. None. Was Cyphre coming to tonight's meeting? That nest of snakes had been built for Lucifer. If el Çifr really was the Devil, his ass would be a perfect fit. Maybe my search had reached its end at last. A big surprise awaited the guest of honor.

No good wearing a fake watch if you want to know the time. I fought the urge to look at it. Like an itch I couldn't scratch. A good snoop never calls attention to his spy gear. I watched the Council members file into the circular chamber one at a time. When I heard a distant clock toll midnight, every seat around the table was occupied. Not a single no-show tonight. At the final stroke of twelve, Number One rose to his feet and all twenty-nine others, me as well, stood up with him. He began a low sonorous chant in Latin. The rest of the Council joined in or so it seemed. Hard to tell if someone was singing or not when he wore a hood. I mumbled along behind the beat, grunting in double-talk like I used to do during Mass back at the orphanage.

When the chanting ended the black-clad klan sat down in

silence. Numerus Unus seemed to be the de facto chairman. He cleared his throat and began a sonorous spiel in Latin. Concealed by the table's edge, I reached my left hand discreetly under my cassock through the vent pocket and switched on the Minifon. My right arm remained resting on the tabletop, the dummy watch exposed. Didn't want to miss a single word.

The chair addressed *'Octo,'* Number Eight, as I'd learned from Szabor. *'Explicare vestra absentia.'* Explain your absence. Eight launched into a lengthy alibi. The dog ate my homework, blah, blah, blah. I noted how he stayed seated during his testimony. Next, came my turn. Number One asked me the same question. Only he said something about *'duo congressi.'* I guessed this meant 'two meetings.'

'Filia mea trucidatus.' I gave my memorized answer.

'Quid facis?' I figured Number One was asking what I planned to do about it.

'Est enim mihi vindictam ergo retribaum.' I gave him that quote from *Romans* about vengeance being mine and repaying my daughter's killer.

'Quando?'

I knew this meant 'when?' *'Mox,'* I answered. Soon.

Number Twenty-Five, *'Viginti quinque,'* suffered the final interrogation. He gave another convoluted answer. I didn't understand a single word. All down on the wire in any case. Three members absent from the last Council meeting. A full house tonight. The stage was set. Demonic throne on prominent display. Something big was definitely in the works. Lucifer had to be waiting in the wings for his cue. Ready to make a grand entrance. I had no idea what his show was going to be. All I knew was the last line. The final curtain. When the fat lady sang, Louis Cyphre was going to die.

The hooded strangers conversed in a language I didn't understand. Almost an hour passed, I estimated. I sat stock still, not saying a word. Waiting for the big star to make his appearance.

Adrenalin surged through me. Burning pitch from the smoky torches scented the air.

Suddenly, the leisurely Latinate rhetoric grew more heated. Council members began interrupting the speaker. Everybody talked at once. Shouting. Stepping on each other's lines. When I saw Number Nine point at the Devil's throne and scream something about *'Dominus Luciferi,'* I felt my trigger finger start to itch. This was it. Lucifer.

The first angry outbursts settled into more orderly debate. I listened hard, not understanding a single word. Paying close attention to the dynamics in the room, I thought I'd somehow learn something. All that Latin got in the way. Everything sounded like Solemn High Mass. Number Three, *'Tres,'* spoke, his words so low that everyone at the big table leaned forward to hear. I did as well, not wanting to be the odd man out. Three was barely audible, speaking in a hoarse, scratchy whisper. I knew that voice. It was Cardinal Latour, the Archbishop of Paris.

Being in the dark about the subject under discussion didn't keep me from learning something of vital importance. I decided after killing Cyphre, I'd shoot Latour as well. Too bad I couldn't kill the lot of them. Didn't have enough bullets. Needed some to fight my way out of this rat hole. It wasn't about doing the world a favor. I didn't give a shit how wicked and corrupt they all were. For me their only crime was being handpicked by Cyphre. The whole rotten bunch had been tainted by his touch.

The wrangling and palaver dragged on for at least another hour. At the end of it, they all sat silent. Nothing left to say. The winged throne sat empty. Lucifer was a no-show. Cyphre had stood me up. I felt sick at heart. Tricked one more time by the Great Trickster. Number One raised his hand. *'Alia disputato?'* he asked. No one made any reply. Number One rose to his feet. *'Opertet suffragii,'* he said, crossing to the far wall where he pulled on a hanging chain. Somewhere far in the distance a bell chimed.

Moments later, after Number One resumed his seat, a young

priest appeared bearing a leather-bound ledger with a golden clasp. He sat at a small wooden table and opened his massive book. He asked Number One something in Latin and the hooded figure replied, '*Vero.*' I didn't understand the question but heard the word '*suffragium,*' which Sabor taught me meant 'vote.' One's answer was '*etiam.*' I guessed that meant 'yes.'

The priest uncapped a pen, '*Unus,*' he called out. Voting had begun.

'*Approbare,*' Number One approved.

'*Duo.*'

'*Approbare.*'

When '*Tres,*' was called, Cardinal Latour abstained.

And so it went. '*Quattuor... Quinque... Sex... Septem... Octo,*' all voted to approve. When my number, '*Tredecim,*' was called, I followed Cardinal Latour's example and voted to abstain, not knowing what was going on in the first place. The roll call continued. One after another, most of the Council of Thirty voted for approval. Only six abstentions. Me, the two who were absent from the last meeting, the Archbishop of Paris, Numeri *Septemdecim,* the cat who walked in ahead of me, and *Viginti.* Not a single nay.

Number One spoke again. His voice sounded stern and precise. No one replied. Finished, he held up both hands and said, '*Sermonem consumere.*'

At this, the priest stood. He held a narrow carved ivory box. I hadn't seen it with him when he entered the chamber. Numerus Unus stood as he approached. The priest bowed, handing him the box. Our chairman bowed in return and sat back in his place. Once the priest was also seated, Numerus Unus opened the box, taking out a dagger and a parchment scroll. '*Sigillum meum et al Luciferum pignus,*' he intoned, slicing the tip of his left forefinger and pressing a bloody smudge mark onto the scroll.

Once the dagger and scroll reached me, I had the Latin phrase memorized. The athame looked very old. Not as fine as the one I stole from Krusemark's office. Limned like a medieval manuscript by skilled scribes, the parchment had ornate letters at the top, reading: CONCILIUM TRIGINTA. Below was the date, Dominica XII Aprilis MCMLIX, and a long descending list of Roman numerals running down the left margin. I cut my fingertip, chanting, '*Sigillum meum et al Luciferum pignus,*' as I pressed out a drop of blood beside the number XIII before passing the parchment on to the man on my left.

Other Council members fished handkerchiefs from their pockets to staunch the bleeding. I forgot to bring one and made do with my little velvet sack. Ten minutes later, Number Thirty passed the parchment back to Number One and bound up his finger. The meeting was over. I stared at the empty throne, angry as hell. Number One rose from his seat, handing the rolled parchment to the priest on his way out of the arched entryway. Number Two was right behind, followed closely by Number Three.

I saw the drill and waited my turn, getting up after Number Twelve to retrieve my cape from the vestibule. By the time I emerged into the Vatican Bank lobby a single line of twelve hooded black-clad figures stood in front of me, while seventeen others ascended the central stairway behind me. The simple ingenuity of the system impressed me. All the limousines had been parked in numerical order, pulling up out front one after the other. There was no confusion. Each mysterious anonymous Council member climbed into his car and was gone. It wasn't long before I sat in the back seat of the Alfa Romeo. I asked my driver the time in my clumsy Italian. '*Due e mezzo,*' he replied as we cruised off into the night. The whole damned Council of Thirty meeting had only taken two and a half hours.

38

I was on a 6:00 am flight back to Paris. Three hours later, I landed at Le Bourget, much smaller than Orly. A snappy double-breasted suit works wonders with customs officials. I caught a cab outside at the curb and got dropped off on Saint-Germain around ten o'clock, hanging out at the pad only long enough to leave my two-suiter and grab the earphones and mini-speaker for the P-55.

Szabor told me he taught a few classes at the university and did his research and writing at his home office. I wanted to call the Professor to see if he was in but I spotted a cab and gave the driver the address printed on Szabor's card as I climbed into the back seat. Rue de la Clef was not that far over in the next arrondissement. We made it in under ten minutes. Number 25 looked to be centuries old. The wooden doors beneath a tall central entrance archway were locked. A shabby open portal to the left led into darkness. I stepped inside and saw no sign of any concierge. I galloped up the worn steps two at a time excited as a kid on Christmas morning.

The thunder of my urgent knocking echoed inside Szabor's apartment. Loud enough to wake the dead. No one responded. The professor wasn't home. I figured he must be teaching or out enjoying some petit déjeuner with friends or students. Any other time, I'd come back later in the day. Maybe leave a note on his door but I itched with anticipation. What would I do to kill the time? Wander around the Latin Quarter like a headless chicken? Waiting here for the professor's return made more sense. Without another thought, I fished my set of twirls from the satchel and let myself in.

At first glance, the place looked trashed. That didn't ring my alarm bell. Eccentric professors lived like bums among stacked books, crumpled paper and ashtrays overflowing with butts. None of that bothered me. Something else caught my attention among all the chaos. A plate of uneaten food on a low table by the sagging couch. Neat wedge of cheese, a browning apple cut into segments, fresh baguette along with butter and jam next to a brimming cup of coffee. Nobody sets out a meal and leaves it untouched unless something goes wrong. Adrenalin flowed through me like a nitroglycerine transfusion.

Standing stock still, I looked slowly around the room not wanting to disturb anything. Crowded bookshelves, Moroccan rugs, art resembling dried vomit. Carved Buddhas, terracotta figurines, framed papyrus fragments. Ancient relics crowded the mantle over a smoke-stained marble fireplace. A large wooden cross hung above them. It was a simple thing maybe a yard high, plain weathered boards fastened crudely together. Something bloody had been nailed to it. A chunk of meat dead center. I stepped up for a closer look. It was a tongue.

Part of me wanted to believe it came from a sheep or a pig. Some exotic gourmet treat bought at the local boucherie. A rational mind seeks reasonable explanations for the unexpected. Deep down, I was kidding myself. This hideous gory thing was a human tongue.

Without moving an inch, I took the latex gloves from my satchel and pulled them over fingers suddenly grown cold. Mentally retracing my steps through the apartment, I felt sure I hadn't touched anything except the outside lock and doorknob on my way in. I've seen a lot of spilled blood over the years. Didn't mind much when it wasn't my own. Ernie Cavalero gave me a few simple tips on estimating how long since the plasma splattered the pavement. One look at that impaled hunk of flesh and the congealing dribbles down the cross told me the blood was less than eight hours old.

My every instinct insisted it was time to breeze. I was still enough of a snooper to want a look around first. Stepping carefully through the clutter on the floor, I made my way to the tiny kitchen. Unlike the front room, it was neat and orderly as a surgical hospital. Geraniums on the window ledge added a perfect Fanny Farmer touch.

The only other room turned out to be where János slept, really more of a book-lined study with a cot in one corner. He was sleeping forever now, stretched out on his back in his clownish bow tie and corduroy trousers. Szabor's mouth yawned wide as a dental patient. Blood filled his oral cavity to the lip-line and ran across his chin to puddle beneath his head. No sign of any struggle other than the wrinkled duvet beneath his body. I knew his killer had kneeled on top of him to cut out his tongue, holding him down while he bled to death.

An involuntary shudder ran through me. Not revulsion or even terror. I'd seen plenty of stiffs over the years. What I felt was dread. This butchery was the work of Louis Cyphre. He'd sent me a message written in blood. Szabor talks too much, it said. I know he's been talking to you. Cyphre probably also knew I killed Krusemark and had the coin. Maybe he was hip that I crashed the Council of Thirty meeting last night. Might even have been there wearing a hood. If he'd watched me enter Szabor's building, he could be calling the cops right now, setting me up as the fall guy for a murder rap as he'd done in New York. Better split while I was still in the clear.

On my way out, I took a peek at János's desktop, spread with photocopies of an ancient language looking like chicken tracks in the mud. Rough translations into French on a legal pad sat atop them. All gibberish to me. I tiptoed back through the front room and took care to wipe the doorknob and lock on both sides with my pocket square. Meeting no one going down the stairs, I lingered in the darkened entrance passage for a peek along the street. No automobiles or pedestrians in sight. I slipped out and was around the corner in a matter of moments.

Sick at heart, I walked slowly home through the winding rabbit warren of medieval streets. All the soaring elation from pulling off the Rome caper without a hitch crashed inside me like the *Hindenburg* crumpling in flames on the Lakehurst tarmac. Szabor was dead like those sacrificial corn kings he'd written about. Maybe he'd dig the irony of his own ritualistic demise. Me? I didn't give a shit. Tough luck for the professor. Maybe worse for me. What sort of game was Cyphre playing? Cat and mouse? The rodent wins only in the Tom and Jerry cartoons.

Without János, the wire recording of the Council meeting was useless unless I found another Latin translator. Didn't Burroughs say he knew the lingo? Bill probably would avoid me like the clap because of the Sterne business. I felt too tired to think straight about any of it. Last sleep I'd had was Tuesday night on the train. Maybe a little shuteye at the pad might do the trick.

A little before noon, I let myself into my secret blue house with the hidden key and spotted a pale blue envelope lying on the floor just inside the entrance. It was a pneumatique, one of those telegrams sent within the city of Paris via underground tubes of air pressure. In my haste, I'd missed it when I dropped off the suitcase. For some absurd reason, I thought the message might be from Cyphre when I picked it up. It was postmarked yesterday. I tore off the pneu's perforated edges and read the message inside.

Cher Johnny,
Forgive the short notice. I learned only this morning that el Çifr, the magician of whom you spoke, will give psychic 'readings' tomorrow at a party to which I am invited. I mentioned your interest to my hostess (Mme Yvonne de Lucenay) and she insisted I ask you to come.

17:00 to 21:00 hrs. Cocktails and hors d'oeuvres. 40,
Boulevard de la République, Saint-Cloud. I will look for
you there.
    À bientôt,
       Chris

My hand trembled as I read D'Auburan's letter a second time.
Could it really be this easy? After all my fruitless searching was
Cyphre simply being served up on a cocktail party platter? Part of
me wondered if the pneumatic might be a clever trap engineered
by Dr Cipher himself. Absurd thought. I'd met Chris by accident
on a plane and rented this little house through him. By some
miracle of coincidence, his path had crossed with el Çifr's. Things
worked out that way sometimes. Every so often you rolled a seven.
Lady Luck had just smiled on me. Tonight Louis Cyphre was going
to die.

At a few minutes past five, I was dressed and ready to go, wearing
chinos and my tweed sports jacket. A striped silk Sulka tie added
a touch of class. I looked inconspicuous, a well-heeled college
prof. Along with wads of cash, the money belt strapped under my
clothing held the Judas shekel and the spool of recorded Minifon
wire, two things I wanted to hang onto even after knocking off
Cyphre. I wore the .38 on my left hip like always and carried the
over-and-under in my right-hand outside jacket pocket with one
of the Pachmayrs. My twirls and a pair of rubber gloves went in
the pocket on my left side.

I waited on the sidewalk less than a minute before spotting a cab
coming down Saint-Germain. The driver chuckled appreciatively
when I gave him the suburban Saint-Cloud address. A long haul
meant a big fare. We turned left toward the river and left again
on the quai, crossing the Seine on Pont Royal. Then along the
Right Bank quai to the Place de la Concorde and straight up the
Champs to the Étoile where we angled off onto Avenue Foch. My

first glimpse of the famous broad boulevard lined with chestnut trees and gilt-edged real estate.

'*Avenue Boche*,' the driver remarked.

I asked what he meant. He explained it was a wartime Parisian joke. During the occupation the Gestapo located its headquarters on this luxurious thoroughfare.

We entered the Bois de Boulogne at the far end of Avenue Foch, driving in a straight line through the park. I stared out the cab's side window, gripped by sudden apprehension, thinking about Louis Cyphre and our last terrible encounter three weeks ago. The night he broke into Harry Angel's office, knocked me out, and, after I came to, taunted me before he disappeared. I didn't realize quickly enough that he was on his way to murder my daughter Epiphany.

All the old hatred and anger boiled up inside me. The humiliation and pain. I remembered Cyphre's taunts and mocking laugh, clenching my hands into fists to keep them from trembling. My face burned feverishly. If I'd walked into the cocktail party at that very moment, I would have gunned Cyphre down in a blind rage the second I laid eyes on him and damn the consequences. I needed to get a grip.

What good was revenge if it brought me only grief? Killing el Çifr in front of all those witnesses meant a one-way ticket to the guillotine. A death sentence was just what Dr Cipher had planned for me in the first place. Why give him the satisfaction of knowing he'd won? Much better to bump him off in some dark out-of-the-way place and get away free and clear. The moment of Cyphre's death would be mine forever in memory. What more perfect revenge?

The cab driver interrupted my musing. '*Nous sommes arrivés, monsieur.*' I paid the fare and stood on the curb as the taxi drove away. The weather was mild and fair with wispy clouds striating the pale blue sky. Saint-Cloud looked to be an affluent suburb, no Algerian slums in this neighborhood. Number forty was a pleasant two-story house set well back from the street and screened by several large shade trees. I walked up a flagstone path through a well-tended flower garden to the front door and rang the bell.

After a moment, a pretty young maid wearing a black dress and white apron opened the door. She looked just like a stock character in a bedroom farce. After getting my name, she politely asked me to wait and left the foyer. She clearly didn't recognize the name Johnny Favorite. I looked around the comfortable antechamber, well furnished with antique art nouveau furniture, listening to the surf-like murmur of distant conversation. Before too long, the maid returned and said. *'Par ici, s'il-vous-plait.'*

I followed the sweet wiggle of her perfect ass back through the posh house toward the party's noise. The maid led me into a dining room furnished by an interior decorator in the Directoire style. A temporary bar stood in one corner presided over by a server in a white jacket. The long central neoclassical table boasted a variety of cheeses, pâtés and various appetizers. Several noshers circled around it stuffing their faces. A tall woman in her mid-fifties observed the proceedings like a field commander. She wore a tweed skirt and tan cashmere sweater with a mauve silk scarf complementing her silver hair, tied casually around an elegant neck. *'Monsieur Favorite,'* the maid announced, steering me toward her.

'Enchanté, Madame de Lucenay,' I said, taking her hand.

'You must call me Yvonne,' she replied in perfect English, 'if I may call you Johnny.'

'I prefer it that way.' I brushed a dry kiss across her fingertips. My hostess smiled and spoke to her maid in French, instructing the girl to find Monsieur D'Auburan and tell him that his American friend had arrived. 'Would you care for a cocktail or perhaps a glass of wine?' she asked as the maid walked away.

'Un Manhattan serait parfait,' I said and she took my arm, leading me to the bar where she gave *'Georges,'* the barman, my order. The Manhattan he shook for me was better than perfect,

it was *'sublime.'* I said so to my hostess. I took a second swallow as D'Auburan, holding a big-bowled burgundy glass, stepped up to join us. 'Hello, Johnny,' he said, 'Happy you could make it.' We clinked rims in lieu of shaking hands.

Yvonne asked Georges for *'un peu de champagne.'* Once served, she steered the conversation toward her guest of honor. El Çifr was *'trés magnifique, n'est-ce pas?'* He was *'incroyable!'*

'Étonnant!'

'Ahurissant!'

Their praise sang like slogans on a circus poster. The man of the hour was telling fortunes in the back garden. Yvonne didn't put it that way. She said, *'Le sage regard profondément dans votre coeur... dans votre âme.'* Surely, I wanted to experience this miracle first hand? Have the swami look deep into my heart and soul. Did I not come all this way seeking the master?

I smiled and smiled as they spoke, feeling the urge to kill simmering deep inside. Mustering every ounce of smarmy fake charm, I told Mme de Lucenay and Chris D'Auburan about my 'true interest' in the garden wizard. I said I'd started singing before an audience again, quite a surprise really, although I'd secretly been thinking about a comeback for some time. Performances in Paris and Rome had gone well, I lied. I wanted to put together a big act. Dancers, comedians, perhaps a backup choral quartet. A talented magician seemed just the ticket to fill out the bill.

I had them in the palm of my hand as the saying goes. They ate up every false word like dogs licking bacon grease from my fingers. When I told them I'd seen Dr Cipher perform in New York, they both nodded in agreement although it was clear Mme de Lucenay had no clue what I was talking about. I wondered what she'd think if she knew her beloved sage performed on the basement stage of Hubert's Flea Circus, a two-bit 42nd Street shit-hole. I had never seen the magician appear as el Çifr, I said, and was curious about his mentalist act.

Yvonne, clearly upset when I implied the Arab magus was a

phony, more of a vaudeville act than an oriental prophet, tried to hide her feelings behind a patrician mask. 'I don't want Mr Cyphre to know he's being auditioned,' I explained. 'Better if he doesn't think I'm watching. I'd like to observe unnoticed from a distance.'

They bought my line, hook, sinker, rotten bait and all, swallowing it whole like bottom feeders. 'Perhaps Johnny will entertain us with a few songs,' Yvonne said. 'Now that he is once again an entertainer.'

'I would be honored, Yvonne, but must unfortunately decline your gracious invitation for the same reason. I want to remain anonymous to my potential magic act.'

The silver fox smiled at me. '*Pas de problème*,' she mewed, 'el Çifr must leave in...' she glanced at a slim wristwatch bright with diamonds, 'an hour or so. Won't you reconsider and sing for us after he has gone?'

'Of course,' I said, sounding as if I meant it. 'I'd be delighted. Right now I'll just take a look at the wizard at work.'

39

I helped myself to a couple canapes and sauntered further into the de Lucenay residence carrying my cocktail glass. Most of the guests stood outside in the formal back garden. Dark maroon drapes had been pulled aside on a broad multipane window and the crowd was visible through the sheer white under-curtains. I drifted over for a furtive look. Louis Cyphre was the center of attention. He sat on a high-backed chair, all decked out in his Sheik of Araby outfit. Very like the one he wore when I saw him preach at the New Temple of Hope up in Harlem less than a month ago. A long white robe flowed from under his red and gold embroidered kaftan, the blood-red turban providing a crowning touch. I wanted to blow his fucking brains out.

A young woman in a little black Chanel dress sat facing him, a look of enthralled wonder lighting up her face as el Çifr spoke to her. I couldn't hear what he said but I understood the gist of it without knowing his words. The Great Trickster seducing the innocent, weaving his evil spell about her. And all around among the topiary hedges, the other suckers stood waiting their turn.

For a single moment, Cyphre looked my way, his sapphire eyes bright through the scrim. Don't think I got made. The sheer curtain provided a partial shield from that penetrating stare. Even so, I felt a shiver of terror and backed away from the window. Blond hair and shaving my mustache might have conned Sterne but no disguise would ever fool the Prince of Darkness. Watching my quarry from an exposed position struck me as a dumb ploy. Yvonne said her prize soothsayer was sticking around for another hour. No need to keep an eye on him all that time.

I made a beeline for the little bar in the dining room and timed it perfectly, nursing each of my next two Manhattans for nearly an hour as I shot the shit with strangers in awkward French, do-si-doing through the crowd. I passed the large living room window several times, always catching a glimpse of the seated swami weaving his poisonous web around a fresh gullible victim. I had a brief chat with the pretty girl in the little black dress. She glowed with spiritual rapture yet the diabolic glint in her sparking eyes declared a more sinister purpose. Cyphre had found another convert. So much I could have told her about the deal she'd made. Why bother. Let her find her own way. The solitary path to wisdom was always walked alone.

My final peek through a veil of sheer curtains into the back garden revealed el Çifr on his feet holding Yvonne de Lucenay's hands in both of his. He was thanking her, bidding a fond farewell. A jolt of electricity shot through me. I walked out of the house, crossed the street, and took refuge beside a tall beech tree.

It was a time of day the French called 'l'heure bleue,' the blue hour, that bit of dusk with the sky not yet dark and the gathering shadows a deep cobalt hue. A brief, haunting moment, no longer daytime but not yet night, a time of mystery and melancholy. I saw no cars in sight. Figured Cyphre would have a limo with a driver. Maybe he was phoning for a cab. Finding my own ride might prove difficult. Didn't matter. Dr Cipher was heading home and I knew where he lived. My twirls provided a way inside the mansion on Boulevard Richard Wallace. The Smith & Wesson held five death pellets. Epiphany's killer would receive them all tonight.

Louis Cyphre strode down the pathway from the de Lucenay house, his white robe distinct in the twilight. I didn't see any taxis or limos approaching. Instead of waiting at the curb, Cyphre turned left and walked off down the avenue. I tailed him from the other side, moving silently through the shadows. Nighttime tail jobs on foot were tricky. Without the cover of a crowd you bucked the odds of getting spotted. I used the trees lining my side for cover. It turned out to be a piece of cake. El Çifr never looked behind and would have seen nothing if he had. We passed an occasional dog-walker. None of them took any notice of the Thief of Bagdad striding past. Parisians were blasé just like New Yorkers. Every so often, automobiles slid by along the avenue. Mostly we had the deserted avenue all to ourselves.

I followed Cyphre for nearly twenty minutes, turning every corner he did, sticking to the shadows on the other side of the street. I passed up several opportunities to knock off Dr Cipher. Gunshots would roar like thunder in the nearly deserted suburban streets. Citizens brain-dead from television, suddenly alert, rising from their torpor to phone the police. I didn't know the area and had no getaway plan. So long as Cyphre kept walking, I'd follow until the right spot turned up.

Cyphre turned right and disappeared from sight. I hurried to catch up. At the corner, I spotted him strolling over a narrow one-lane footbridge over the Seine. He started across. Following him, I had no cover. If Cyphre looked back, he'd spot another shadowy pedestrian like himself. My blond hair might provide an extra moment before he knew the jig was up. The bridge looked as good a spot as any. No turning back. Only one way to go. After I killed him, I'd dump the body in the river.

I pulled the .38 free, holding it by my side as I picked up my pace. The snub nose wasn't very accurate at a range over fifty feet. When I got closer, I'd start running and call his name. I wanted Cyphre to see me. Needed him to know. The gap closed. Maybe eighty feet separated us. I started jogging but put the brakes on right away. A young couple came toward us holding hands. I slipped my gat back into the holster. By the time they passed and I nodded a greeting, Cyphre had reached the other side.

All at once, he was gone from view. I ran to the end of the footbridge where a flight of steps descended into the Bois de Boulogne. Across the dark wood to the east, the lights of Paris gleamed like the rising sun. Cyphre was nowhere in sight. I cursed myself for having lost him and rushed down the steps. He could have gone anywhere in the darkness. I gambled on my instincts, doubling down on a bet that el Çifr was calling it a night and going home. Dick Wallace Boulevard ran along the northern edge of the park. I walked in that direction along the edge of a two-lane road paralleling the river.

Figuring Cyphre would not walk along the curb like some wayward hitchhiker, I crossed the road and angled onto the grass under the trees. I spotted el Çifr a hundred feet ahead, a sudden wind gust flaring his kaftan like the tail of a preening pigeon as he retreated back into the woods. I caught up with him along the bank of an oval pond. It was quiet here, shielded from the sparse passing traffic on the outer roadway. Not another soul in sight.

I silently closed the distance to about twenty feet and drew the .38. 'Cyphre!' I called. The tall Arabian in the shadows stopped in his tracks. El Çifr turned and stared straight into the barrel of the snub nose. '*Est enim mihi vinidictam*,' I said.

'*Salūtō, Ioannes Dēlicātus*,' Cyphre replied with a sardonic smile. 'Nice to see you've kept up with your Latin.'

'On your knees, you fucking bastard!'

Cyphre's smile widened. 'Why soil my clothing?'

'Kneel!' His cool demeanor inflamed my rage.

'I like your hair, Johnny. Do blonds have more fun?'

'Keep on joking, motherfucker. The hangman loves gallows humor.'

'Gallows humor?' Cyphre grinned. 'Am I condemned?'

'I'm judge, jury and executioner.' The Smith & Wesson held steady in my hand. Felt cool as Cocaine Bill. I'd waited for this moment. Dreamed of it. Now it was mine. 'My roscoe holds five pills,' I said, calm and easy. 'One for János. One for Doc Fowler. Another for Toots. And for Maggie. The last for my daughter, Epiphany. You killed them all. Now, I'm going to kill you.'

'Poor Johnny. Can't remember anything. Forgot his famous crooner past. Forgot the poor dumb GI whose heart he ate. Doesn't recall killing those innocent people. All five of them. Must ease your conscience blaming every death on me.'

'Kneel, motherfucker,' I shouted, kneecapping the son-of-a-bitch with my first shot. Cyphre howled in pain, kneeling quickly as a supplicant acolyte. I wanted him genuflecting at my feet. Praying for mercy.

El Çifr bared his teeth. A wolf in a trap. 'The man without a past,' he snarled at me. All he had left. No bite in his bark. A Latin phrase I hadn't learned from Szabor returned from out of the blue. Without thinking, I said, '*Ut sementem feceris ita metes*,' and shot Cyhpre in the stomach. As you sow, so shall you reap.

He clutched his mid-section, grunting. A wave of joy surged through me. I shot Cyphre again, three times in the chest, straight to the heart, quick as I could pull the trigger. The impact spun him backward. '*Ad mortem te, Lucifer*,' I yelled above the roar of gunfire. More Latin emerging out of nowhere from my forgotten past. Death to you, Lucifer!

Louis Cyphre lay on his side in the grass, wide unfocused eyes gazing at oblivion. Vengeance was mine. An eye for an eye. Five or six strides closed the short distance between us. I stood over Cyphre's body, looking down into his vacant ethereal stare. A reflection of eternity mirrored in those sky-blue pupils. Dumb move when a murderer hangs around the crime scene, but I wanted the glory just a little bit longer. This moment of triumph. My crowning achievement. 'Welcome back to Hell,' I muttered.

The empty revolver hung in my right hand. I noticed it the way one discovers a pencil stuck behind one's ear. Flipping open the cylinder, I pushed the ejector rod and dropped five empty shells into my left hand. Dumped them into my left jacket pocket, reloading with a quick push of the Pachmayr before slipping the .38 into its holster. Killing Cyphre wasn't enough. Happened too fast. I wanted to see him crawl. Hear him beg. He'd died with a sneer on his lips.

I unzipped my fly and pissed on Cyphre's corpse. Golden shower. All over his sneering face. Louis Cyphre blinked. I froze. Maybe I'd imagined it. Postmortem spasm. Unexpected reflexive muscle action. He blinked a second time. With curious athletic grace, Cyphre rolled into a sitting position. 'Why, Johnny,' he groaned, looking straight up at me with my pecker in my hand, 'Never knew you cared.'

I gasped, stuffing my cock back out of sight. Cyphre was dead. I knew it. Three lead pills had torn his black heart into stew meat. I groped blindly for my heater. Blow his fucking head off, I thought. Cyphre's next move stopped me cold. He stood up in a single fluid motion, nimble as the Nicholas Brothers rising from a pair of splits in a tap dance routine. Impossible, I knew. A man with a shattered kneecap doesn't dance.

Cyphre smiled, amused by my astonished expression. 'You look exactly like Yusupov and Pavlovich the night they murdered Rasputin,' he said. 'They fed him poisoned cake and wine. Rasputin loved it. Asked for more. *Incroyable!* Shot him next. Left the mad monk lying dead. He revived. Tried to escape. They shot him again and again but still he lived. In the end, they stuffed his still-breathing body through the ice of the frozen Malaya Nevka River. A pity really. December 1916. Terrible loss. Rasputin was one of my favorite disciples.'

'Enough bullshit!' I shouted, my mind whirling faster than a ride at Coney Island. 'Christ died on the cross!'

'Wrong, Johnny. Jesus of Nazareth, the humble carpenter, was crucified, died and was buried.' Cyphre spoke calmly like someone dealing with an angry dog. 'Christ was the Messiah. Son of God. He wore the Crown of Heaven and will never die. Lucifer wears the crown of Hell. He, too, is immortal. The man you know as Louis Cyphre may die. You just killed him. I have died many times over the centuries. Lucifer, Lord of the Underworld, always resurrects. As a mortal, I know death like all men. As the Prince of Darkness, I am eternal, a force of nature.'

I had no words to express my dismay. Not a single wisecrack about fables and fairy tales. I stared at Cyphre in silent disbelief. It was like looking at a ghost. 'Do you feel pain?' I asked as he fussed with his Arabic outfit.

'Of course. I endure pain,' he replied. 'All men suffer.' Cyphre unbuttoned the front of his bloody robe. 'You've ruined my very best kandura, Johnny. Handwoven in Medina.' He bared his chest for me to see. Three bullet holes made a nice tight grouping around the area of his heart. Lower down, a single shot pierced his abdomen above the navel. The white fabric had absorbed most of the blood like a bandage. I saw his wounds already healing over, sealing shut, becoming scar tissue before my eyes. It was like watching a lizard regenerate a missing tail. Cyphre's upper torso was a patchwork of old scars, gnarled and corrugated like an ancient tree trunk.

'I'm not the first,' I said. 'Am I?'

'Oh no, Johnny. Far from it. Many better men than you sought my death. They are dust while I abide forever.' Cyphre touched the welts and puckers crisscrossing his body. 'These are my stigmata. Christ suffered injuries only to his hands and feet. A spear wound on his side. I bear dozens of such trophies. They say everyone awaits the Second Coming. If Christ ever returned as a man he would most certainly be killed once again. Mankind remains evil at heart. You worshiped a stronger power years ago, Johnny. Never too late for the faithful to return to the fold. All men are sheep. Why not be a black one?'

Cyphre laughed at his own lame joke, a deep robust belly laugh. It grew louder and louder, filling the night with demonic mirth. Lucifer was not just laughing at me. His derision took in all of humanity. I stood watching in bleak dismay, helpless to stop el

Çifr as he strode off into the night. Deep in what was left of my soul, I knew that for the Devil the whole wide world was nothing but a joke without a punch line.

40

I stared into the flames in the blue cottage's fireplace, seeing nothing but emptiness. My drink offered no comfort. It tasted dead. Spiritless. Hollow-eyed Yorick, the skull I'd taken from the catacombs, grinned at me from down the length of the trestle table, his ivory dome aglow with firelight. For the first time in my life I lacked all ambition. Lost the fire burning in my belly since I was a kid. I no longer gave a damn.

Cyphre was not a con artist. I'd marked him as a fake because Ernie Cavalero taught me never to buy into bogus claims. Like the doubting Apostle Thomas who had to touch the wounds of Jesus before believing He'd risen from the dead, I'd needed all the facts. No denying what I'd seen. The gunshots in el Çifr's body healing before my eyes. Impossible, yet I saw it with my own eyes. Cyphre was Lucifer incarnate. I'd killed him and still he lived on. Dr Cipher the flea circus magician remained immortal. Not a fucking damn thing I could do about it.

He had been ahead of me every step of the way. I'd thought I was hunting him when all along I was his prey. What I didn't know was why. The joy of torment most likely. Outing Harry Angel as Johnny Favorite, the Devil-worshiping pop star, had to be a stroke of diabolical genius. What a great joke, sending my sorry ass to the electric chair for crimes I didn't commit. I heard Cyphre laughing at that one. I remembered Krusemark telling me Johnny Favorite had tried to duck out on his bargain with the Devil by becoming someone else. Was Cyphre punishing me for trying to trick him? Was my escape from New York part of his plan? Why kill Szabor? Did he know where I lived? Trying to figure things out only mired me deeper in the unknowable. Maybe I should just cut out, split Paris for good, run off to some remote island in the middle of nowhere. After cleaning and reloading my heater, I stretched out on the sagging velour couch, wrapped in the ratty duvet, falling fast asleep almost immediately, adrift in confusion.

At 6:00 am I woke up with a splitting headache. Any urge to run away had left me. Where could I go? No place to hide where the Devil couldn't find me. Whatever Louis Cyphre had in store for me I'd find out in due time. Nothing I could do about it in any case. Might as well go on living my life in Paris. I had plenty of dough. Why not enjoy what time I had left? I'd been bullshitting when I told people about making a comeback as a singer. Maybe it wasn't such a dumb idea. If I was going to hell in the end anyway, living out the rest of my life in the lap of fame, adulation and luxury struck me as a winning proposition.

A little after seven, I headed next door to the café-tabac. One other customer stood at the bar drinking a hair-of-the-dog brandy. Alfonse grunted a brief greeting, took my coffee order and resumed conversation with the stranger as he prepared the espresso. I bided my time, sipping the black brew, waiting until we were alone. There was a call for me on Friday afternoon, Reynard said. From Inspector Edmond Lenoir of the 'Préfecture de Police.' Clearly troubled, he told me this in a grave tone as he slid the inspector's phone number across the counter.

I said not to worry. There was no problem. A New York cop had come to Paris last week looking for a man he thought might be after me. I'd never heard of the guy, I said. Lenoir probably was just following up on the matter. I'd handle the whole thing, I told Alfonse. Make the call from someplace else so he wouldn't be involved. I dropped a ƒ1000 note, double our agreed rate, on the bar top on my way out. Everything was cool. We were *bons amis* once again.

I knew what to do. No way *les flics* could learn the address of my little hideaway. Back in the blue-tiled cottage, I packed my fancy duds into the Ghurka bag along with my dirty laundry from Rome and the back issue *Herald Tribunes*. I needed a new address *tout de suite*, thinking it through while waiting for a cab out on Saint-Germain. It was 8:35 am. The Ritz came first to mind. I ruled it out. Too expensive and probably fully booked. The less fancy hotel by the *Herald Tribune* building with the bar where reporters went to drink struck me as the perfect choice. 'Hotel California,' I told the driver. 'Rue de Berri.'

Fifteen minutes later, I strolled beneath the domed glass canopy above the entrance to the California. The polished wood front desk, plain and functional, stood to the right of the entryway. This joint was half the price of the Vendôme.

I wanted things to seem like I'd come straight from the airport yesterday. Tried sweet-talking the desk clerk into registering me a day early. He was all nose and no chin. Looked like Andy Gump in the funny papers. He said it was against the law. I told him no law would protect me from my wife if she found out I wasn't here last night. Andy Gump got a big kick out of that one. Still cost me a *f*5000 bribe for the phony night.

My room on the third floor was pleasant and quiet, looking down into the central courtyard. After a shower and a *café complet* from room service, I sat at the desk by the window and made some phone calls. First one was to L'Espadon, the seafood restaurant at the Ritz Hotel. I spoke with Michel, the headwaiter, making a reservation for two people at 12:30.

Second call got Alfonse on the line. I told him it was all OK. If anyone ever asked, he should say he gave me Inspector Lenoir's message during this conversation, not earlier in the morning. Reynard got my drift. '*D'accord, Johnny,*' he said and we hung up. Last of all, I phoned the Prefecture of Police and asked to speak with Edmond Lenoir. I gave my name and said I was returning a call from the inspector. After a few moments, Lenoir came on the line. He spoke in English and asked if I could come to his office at 11:30. I already had an important luncheon engagement, I said. Expected to be free '*après quatorze heures.*'

Would two o'clock work for me, the inspector wanted to know. I said that would be fine and he gave me the address of *la Préfecture de Police* on the Île de la Cité. We exchanged cordial *au revoirs* and disconnected. First order of business concluded. If the cops traced my calls or checked with the hotel switchboard, they'd conclude I made my lunch reservation first, then called for messages and immediately after phoned Lenoir. Everything looked legit.

Maybe Cyphre was behind all this. Maybe not. Either way, I had to stay one step ahead. A single mistake meant losing my freedom. Something I valued far more than my worthless life. I spent a half-hour tearing business articles out of the copies of the *Trib*, writing notes and calculations in the margins that an eccentric investor might make. I left them on top of the desk for all to see.

After dressing in my gray suit with a blue shirt and dark blue tie, looking like a conservative businessman who didn't fit the mold, I took a square of toilet paper and tore it into small pieces, each half the size of a three-cent stamp. I moistened these tissue bits with my tongue and stuck them to the sides of the bureau and desk drawers right next to the dovetail joints. They stayed in place when I slid the drawers carefully shut. Another Ernie Cavalero trick.

On my way out, I snooped around downstairs toward the back of the hotel. I found an exit leading into what looked to be a small private park. Perfect place to take a powder on the double when the chips were down.

Thinking they'd frisk me down at the cop shop, I played it safe and put my holstered .38 and the other tools of the trade that I carried in my satchel in the safe deposit box at Morgan Guaranty Trust.

Across the square, at the Ritz, Michel acted happy to see me. Not overjoyed. Too cool a customer for that. A pleasant smile lit up his expression when he said, '*Bonne après-midi, Monsieur Favorite. Très agréable de vous revoir.*'

. I said it was very nice seeing him again, too, slipping a ƒ500 franc note into his palm as he showed me to my table. He had very good news, he told me. Monsieur Natas made a dinner reservation for '*vingt-et-un heures dimanche soir.*' This information cost me another five hundred francs. I informed Michel I had already seen Natas and would not be coming Sunday evening.

After fortifying myself with the prix-fixe luncheon, *espadon grillé aux asperges*, the namesake dish, grilled swordfish with asparagus, and a half-bottle of Sauvignon, I walked over to the towering arched entryway to the *Préfecture de Police*, an edifice so grand you'd think French cops were kings. Asking directions from some spiffy bluecoat head-beater, I was quickly informed this was not the way in. The public entrance was around the corner on rue de Lutèce. A guard behind a counter looked into my satchel. No surprise considering de Gaulle's position on Algeria and the FLN rebellion. The much-expected frisk never happened. So much for frog security.

By the time I finally found the open door to Inspector Lenoir's office, I was fifteen minutes late. He was a somber man, thin and bald, engrossed in paperwork. Looking my way when I knocked, his walleyed stare gave me the creeps. You never knew which eye was watching. He listened stone-faced to my awkward apology in garbled French. A moment of silence followed. I figured he was working up an insulting flatfoot wisecrack, the sort I learned to expect from New York's Finest. Instead, he said, 'Passport, please,' in crisp efficient English. I dug the document out of my satchel and handed it over. Lenoir leafed through the pages, jotting notes on a pad. 'Sit down.' He nodded his head at a wooden chair beside his desk without looking up. I obeyed his order.

'Thanks,' I said when the inspector handed back my passport.

'You have returned from a recent trip to Rome?' He was not interested in small talk.

'Yes.'

'Very brief.'

'Yes.'

'And the purpose?'

'Business.'

I expected he'd ask the nature of my business and was prepared to blow him off. Instead, he changed the subject. 'What is your current address in Paris?'

'Hotel California, 16, rue de Berri.' I smiled, adding 'Eighth arrondissement,' to show I was hip.

'You previously resided at the Vendôme, a hotel of a much higher quality.'

'Not so much, really.'

'Certainly more expensive. Is there a reason for the change? Some financial difficulty?'

'Listen, Inspector, I can afford the Ritz or the Meurice or the George Cinq. Any place in town. I choose my residences strictly for business reasons. Depends on the impression I want to make.'

'Impression?'

'A tactic. Where I stay has everything to do with who I'm meeting. Sometimes I book a room in a dump.'

Again, no small talk. Lenoir shuffled through a sheaf of papers on his desk. He paused, tapping his forefinger on a page. 'You left the Vendôme on 31 March…' the inspector consulted his notepad, '… and entered Italy on 9 April. Were you in Paris between those dates?'

'Yes.'

'At what address?'

I squirmed in my seat, feigning discomfort. 'Listen, Inspector,' I said in a confidential tone, 'this is a delicate matter. I was with a woman. Staying at her place.'

'And the name of this woman?'

'Surely, as a Frenchman, you understand my need for discretion.' Lenoir permitted himself a slight smile. 'Her husband is an occasional business partner. To share this information would hurt my pocketbook as well as my heart.'

The inspector nodded, consulting his file. 'All right. For the moment, you may keep your little secret. On Saturday 5 April, you met with Lieutenant Daniel Sterne of the New York police at Le Grand Véfour.'

'That is correct.'

'What was the purpose of that meeting?'

'Detective Sterne wanted to know if I'd seen a man he was looking for.'

Lenoir pulled a picture from his file and slid it across the desk toward me. 'This man?' It was Angel's old PI license application photo.

'Yes. Sterne said his name was Harry Angel. Some kind of private detective.'

'And?'

'I told Sterne I never saw the guy before in my life.'

'Since meeting with Lieutenant Sterne, has this man Angel approached you?

'No.'

'Why did Sterne think Angel might have an interest in you?'

Lenoir already knew the answers to all his questions. He'd been working with Sterne right from the start. For some reason, the inspector was trying to trip me up. 'Twenty years ago when I was a singer,' I said, easy as dealing off the bottom of the deck, 'I had an agent named Warren Wagner. He's dead now. His son took over the business long after my time. Never knew Junior except as a little kid hanging out in daddy's office. Seems this Angel character came snooping around the Wagner agency about a month ago. Asking all sorts of questions about me. Soon after that, Angel gets arrested by Lieutenant Sterne for a bunch of killings. He escapes from custody. Don't ask me how. Sterne didn't give me the details on that one. A couple days later, Warren Wagner Jr, is found dead at Idlewild. Same day I flew to Paris. Sterne called it murder. Pinned it on Harry Angel. Thought my connection to the Wagner Agency was somehow mixed up in all of it.'

'What do you think?'

'Haven't got a clue. Last time Warren Wagner represented me was in 1943. Kraut dive-bomber in Tunisia put an end to my showbiz career. When Angel went on his killing spree I was out of the country.'

'You were traveling from Japan?'

'That is correct. Everyone Angel murdered was part of my past. Like some kind of mystery novel. Sterne thought he was after me, too.'

'Why?'

'Got no idea. The lieutenant didn't explain that part.'

Inspector Lenoir pulled an 8x10 glossy from his file. I knew without looking it was the promo picture of me at eighteen. 'You were a handsome young man, Monsieur Favorite.' He placed the picture on the desk in front of me. 'A certain type of psychopath seeks out celebrity. Perhaps they believe if they kill someone famous, or kidnap them, or rape them, they inherit some part of their essence, a piece of their soul.'

'I'm not famous,' I said. 'Maybe I almost was, once upon a time. Why would someone want to go after a has-been?'

'The criminal mind is an unknown labyrinth,' Lenoir replied. 'Why do these monsters rape infant children? Or torture their victims for hours, even days? The depraved are capable of any monstrosity.'

I knew this was true. I killed a man and ate his heart. 'Lucky for me, I only deal with crooked bastards trying to screw me out of my share of the profits.'

'Such a handsome man.' The inspector picked up the publicity photo. 'When did you start bleaching your hair?'

I fed him the line about Spider wanting me to look more dago.

Don't think he bought it. Not that he let on. Lenoir was way too cool. 'I assumed you were Italian. What is your heritage?'

'German, probably. My birth name was Liebling. I grew up in an orphanage.'

'Your story is so very American. Rags to riches.' The inspector slid the photograph back into his file. 'That is all for today, Mister Favorite. How long will you be staying at the California?'

'Depends if my new deal works out or not.'

'Please keep me informed of any change in address. Thank you very much for your time.' That was it. Dismissed in under twenty minutes. I left Lenoir's office and wandered the corridor, trying to remember the way I'd come in. My mind buzzed with unknown possibilities. What was the inspector's angle? I'd seen him studying my bloated nose but he'd never mentioned it. Never said how much it looked like Harry's beak. Didn't even let on he knew Sterne was dead. Didn't mention Szabor either, although he might not know Szabor and I were acquainted. The crack about my blond hair was a clue. Lenoir was up to something. Too bad I couldn't just bump him off and be done with it. I needed to go someplace quiet and think things over.

41

Leaving the *Préfecture de Police*, I had the feeling someone was following me. Made sense Lenoir would have my ass tailed. Walking along rue de Lutèce, I clocked a Métro station to my left and beyond it, the colorful bustle of the flower market. Considered losing my tail among the warren of stalls under the long art‑nouveau pavilions but made no detour. No dodging through throngs of shoppers for me.

The blunt twin towers of Notre-Dame promised seclusion if not salvation. I hurried across the Place du Parvis to rue du Cloître Notre-Dame along the north side of the cathedral. Pausing at the tower entrance, I checked out nearby loiterers, fixing them in memory. No way my tail would follow me into the north tower. Only one way out. He'd wait for my exit at street level. I paid the small admission and started climbing stairs. At the end of Szabor's book, he wrote about the resident gargoyles being demonic images. Seemed a perfect spot to think things through.

János also mentioned the exact number of steps. Nearly 300 as I recalled. I labored up all of them, emerging in the tower's upper chapel where a gaggle of Japanese tourists gawked at a collection of ancient statues. More steps led up to the south tower platform. Another cluster of sightseers stood around enjoying the view. I wandered along the parapet admiring the carved monsters looking down on Paris. 'Can anyone doubt their demonic origins?' János wrote about these medieval gargoyles. Uglier than the Hunchback, they'd be right at home in Satan's dungeon under the Bastion of Nicholas V.

I liked them. Cool cats every one. Thought of going on tour with a gargoyle band. Johnny Favorite and his Hell Hounds. Each grotesque statue had a different personality. One winged character cupped his chin in his hands, lost in wicked thought. Another clutched a victim by the waist and legs, a long tongue lapping out to slurp him up like cotton candy. I lingered by each in turn, trying to find my soul mate. The right demon might give me some insight. Provide a clue to solve my dilemma.

These bastards all had one thing in common. Unbridled malevolence. No matter what they'd never shed a single drop of mercy. Never quit. Like Moray eels and Gila monsters, their jaws stayed clenched once they sank their fangs into you. A lesson to be learned here. I couldn't kill Cyphre. Why not cause him endless suffering? Be a constant grievance. Inflict continual pain for the sheer joy of doing it.

I had the means at my disposal. The secrets of the Council of Thirty provided a powerful weapon. Their clandestine meetings revealed secrets Cyphre surely wanted kept. Every word of the last Council was down on my wire. Who knew what poison the recording contained? My problem was not remembering much Latin. Without Szabor, I had no one to translate the ancient language for me. The proceedings of the Council of Thirty were gibberish as far as I was concerned.

Brooding on this, I wandered onto a projecting corner balcony and leaned against the balustrade, flanked by a pair of dubious hairy-shanked monsters. Lost in thought, I stared west down the river at the distant pinprick spire of the Eiffel Tower. The leaden Seine flowed sluggishly below. I saw the Pont Saint-Michel and the medieval tower of Saint-Germain-des-Prés, my Left Bank neighborhood spread around them like a gray patchwork quilt.

Along the quai above Pont Neuf, I spotted that old restaurant, Lapérouse, where, while waiting for the Cardinal Latour photos to develop, I feasted and sang the night away with the owner backing me on his fiddle. Topo, he was called. Quite a character. Spoke six languages. Something he said popped into my mind: 'The Romance languages present no problem for anyone well-versed in Latin.' Topo spoke Latin!

I checked my watch. Five minutes past three. If I hustled, I'd get to my bank to pick up my valuables before it closed at four and make a reservation at Lapérouse at whatever time the proprietor could join me.

First thing when I got to my room, I checked the floor by the dresser. Tiny bits of toilet paper confetti littered the carpet around the curving legs. Someone had opened the drawers. No reason for the maid to have opened it. My stack of annotated newspaper articles on top of the desk looked as if someone had flipped through them.

My phone rang. The concierge called to confirm I had a reservation at Lapérouse tonight at nine. Monsieur Topolinski was delighted to be my guest. He would supply the wine and bring along his violin. As I hung up, I figured Lenoir's boys were keeping track of my phone calls at the hotel. From now on, I'd only use the blower in my room to blow smoke up their asses.

My fancy threads and classy address carried the day when I asked the cabbie to wait outside for me. He didn't balk as I ran out of sight through the arched courtyard entryway to my cottage. I grabbed my P-55, along with the earphones and mini-speaker, took the wire recording from my money belt, locked up the pad, and returned to the back seat in under three minutes. After years of getting the bum's rush it felt boss being treated like a king for a change.

The taxi dropped me off on the quai outside Lapérouse at five minutes before nine. Topolinski's daughter stood behind the marble-topped counter when I entered the restaurant. She told me her father waited upstairs in 'le Salon de la Chasse.' I said I knew the way, climbing the winding stairs. I found Topo in a little bonbon box *cabinet particulier* where ornately framed hunting scenes hung on the paneled walls. Decked out in a green brocade waistcoat and bright butterfly tie, he sat behind a white linen-spread oval table glittering with crystal and silver. Four red candles flickered in a candelabrum. The slender neck of a wine bottle poked up from an ice-filled bucket. '*Bon soir, Johnny,*' Topo said. Any politician would kill for his smile.

I took the other seat as Topo popped the cork and filled two tall flutes with sparkling wine. 'The magic of champagne,' I said, trying to flatter him. 'Bubbles of hidden laughter.'

'*Pas de Champagne, mon ami.*' He tapped the label with a pudgy forefinger. '*Crémant de Bourgogne.* Crown jewel of white Burgundies.' We touched glasses and drank. We shot the shit. We talked about my trip to Rome without any mention of the Vatican. Topo dug hearing about my singing with Bricktop again after twenty years. My fairy tale about making a comeback really yanked his chain. Topolinski begged for a couple of duets before dinner and rang a bell for service. When one of his ancient waiters appeared, coughing discreetly outside the door before entering, Topo insisted on ordering for us both.

I went along for the ride. Topo cranked out second-rate Grappelli riffs on his fiddle while I groaned through half-remembered arrangements of 'Someone to Watch over Me' and 'Blues in the Night.' He smiled like we were the Benny Goodman band onstage at Carnegie Hall and insisted on an encore after dinner.

A steady procession of trays bearing covered plates began arriving. Topo announced each dish one by one as he lifted the lids. '*Timbale des Augustins... Homard américain avec filets de sole pochés et quenelles de brochet... Les rognons de veau braisés... Poularde poêlée Docteur... La selle d'agneau Delorme...*' My host wanted to eat family style, sharing everything, and served our portions with finesse. I knew he'd never let me pick up the check. It all tasted *très* boss, every course accompanied by a splendid wine, Chablis, white Burgundy, Bordeaux.

When the cheese platter came, I knew it wouldn't be long before Topolinski reached for his fiddle and I'd have to start singing for my supper again. 'Topo, I need a favor,' I said.

'You have but to ask.'

'I remember you told me you were fluent in Latin.'

'What the Jesuits teach is never forgotten.'

'Here's the situation. I have a friend, more of a business associate really, who's a member of a secret society that conducts all its meetings entirely in Latin. Got the idea there was some sort of Satanism involved, sex orgies and that sort of thing.'

'Like the Hellfire Club?' Topo asked.

'What's that?'

'A notorious pagan organization in 18th-century England. Founded by noblemen, all make-believe Devil worshipers, and given over to boozing, debauchery and banqueting. Sounds like our kind of club, eh, Johnny?'

Topo didn't have a clue how close to the bone his little joke hit. 'People used to call me a Devil worshiper,' I said with a grin. 'That's why my friend's secret club interested me so much. I'm afraid I can't tell you what it's called. Can't tell you my friend's name either. You'll understand why in a minute. What happened last week is that this friend comes to me and says he can't make it to the next meeting. However, it's very important for him to know everything that's going on. Wants me to go in his place. Undercover like. Everyone wears an animal mask. No names, only numbers. Secret society stuff.'

'Did you go?'

'*Naturellement.* The deal is there was no orgy, just talk. And all in Latin. My friend gave me a little wire recorder to sneak into the meeting. Figured I was safe because I don't know the lingo.'

'Lingo...' Topo echoed with a chuckle.

'So, I recorded the whole damn thing. I'm supposed to give him the wire tomorrow. Here's where you can help out, Topo. I figure there's stuff on the wire that would be helpful to me, you know, in a business sense. Stuff this guy doesn't want me to know. Maybe you think that's unethical?'

'On the contrary. I have on occasion secretly arranged for a young nephew to work as an apprentice at rival establishments, Lasserre, let us say, or the Lucas Carton, in order to learn their techniques. Running a restaurant is like fighting a war. Most especially when you have three Michelin stars and wish to keep them.' Topo rubbed his hands together. 'I like this very much. It is like being a spy.'

'*Vraiment*,' I said. It truly was war. 'I want you to translate what's on the wire. Maybe there's something I can use next time I do business with my so-called friend.'

Topo spread some soft cheese on a bit of bread. 'How long is this recording?'

'About two hours. It's not all talk. Many long boring stretches when everybody sat around saying nothing. Fast-forward through those parts. Maybe an hour or so total of Latin in all.'

'Very well. I translate for you. Play the spy.' Topo rang his service bell. 'I have a fine old bottle of vintage cognac. Croizet 1908. Perhaps half remains. I have been waiting for the perfect moment to share what is left.'

'Perfect for me,' I said. 'Drinking excellent brandy while you do all the work.'

I pulled the Minifon from my satchel and slid it across the table. The restaurateur studied the miniature recorder like it was an unfamiliar kitchen appliance. I could tell he thought of it as a toy. Better that way. Safer. Innocent as snooping on the competition to steal their recipes. I got several sheets of Hotel California stationery out of the satchel along with the Minifon's accessories. 'So small,' Topo said, admiring the P-55. 'Perfect for a spy.'

I plugged in the external desktop speaker and showed my eager translator how to operate the little machine. Topo waved away my offer of a fountain pen, saying he preferred to use his mechanical pencil. Without another word, he pressed the 'play back' button, leaning intently over the speaker and got to work.

It was past midnight when Topo switched off the P-55. '*Fini,*' Topolinski said, pushing the densely scribbled pages across the table toward me. '*Certainement pas orgie.*'

'Nowhere near an orgy,' I said, glancing at what he'd written. It was all in French. 'Let's talk about this.'

'The Council?'

'That what the club's called? The Council?' I played like I was real dumb.

Topo nodded. 'Not even a sexy name. What was your number, Johnny?'

'Thirteen. *Tredecim.*'

He pulled the pages back toward him and consulted his notes. 'Was your daughter murdered?'

'My friend's story. I don't have any children. He taught me what to say in Latin. I hoped to learn the truth about his daughter at the meeting.'

Topolinski rang his service bell. 'No help for you there, I am afraid, Johnny. It was not mentioned again after you explained Number Thirteen's absence from the previous two meetings.'

'Damn!' I frowned with fake concern. 'Thought I had something on him. What was the rest of the meeting all about?'

'Deposing their leader. Lucifer they called him. Sometimes Lord of Darkness. Like the old Hellfire Club where diabolic titles often were used in jest. Blue bloods play-acting as Satanists. Fancy banquets pretending to be a Black Mass. Whores dressed as nuns.'

My heart raced. 'No nuns at this shindig,' I said, finding it hard to keep my cool. After a deep breath, I asked, 'What do you mean, "deposing"?'

'This meeting involved voting to remove the club's leader. The verb *deponere* was used. Latin for depose. To get rid of. More frequently they said, *abdicare*, which means disinherit or to dethrone. Surely, you knew that?'

'No. Not a clue. Don't speak Latin. My friend insisted I abstain at every vote.'

A knock on the door signaled the arrival of the elderly waiter. Topo told him to bring up a vintage magnum of Roederer champagne. *'Brut, s'il vous plaît,'* he said. 'A '47 if there is a bottle well-chilled.'

I waited until we were alone. 'Only six abstentions?' I asked, already knowing the answer.

'Including your own. Not a single no vote.'

'What was all the wrangling about? What did the Council debate?' I asked.

'You have it word for word in my transcription. The failure of this so-called Lucifer to face the music. How do you say it?'

'Face what music?'

'The rules of your modern-day Hellfire Club demand the leader appear in person at any meeting involving a motion to depose. Lucifer, so called, missed two sequential meetings. All detailed in my transcript. If he does not attend the next meeting, he will be summarily removed from office.'

'Automatic dismissal?'

'Apparently so.'

Had I put Topo in danger over this? Would I one day find his severed head baking inside the coal-fired cast-iron oven? An apple stuffed in his mouth? Wild manic thoughts raced through my mind. Cyphre's immortality lasted only while he wore the anointed Crown of Hell. Twice the Council of Thirty voted to dethrone him. He ignored their official summons both times. If Cyphre failed to show at the next meeting, he'd be uncrowned without another vote. Expelled. Cast out. Dethroned. No longer Lord Satan. Louis Cyphre once again would become a mortal man. Just another average Joe Blow same as me. Born to die. Die like a gut-shot dog.

A polite cough outside announced the waiter who carried in a huge bottle of champagne on ice. He placed the tray on the table and left without muttering a word. '*Alors*, Johnny,' Topo said, 'have you further questions for me or is it time now for wine and song? Alas, no women.'

'The women wait at home while the men sing and drink,' I said with a smile, feeling like a retired middleweight stepping back into the ring still capable of delivering powerful surprise uppercuts. What more could I ask? Topolinski had already answered the biggest question of them all.

42

The Baron Samedi was closed when the taxi pulled up outside. I figured Bijou was still counting her receipts, so I let myself into the building with my key and went upstairs. Adrift in a booze buzz, jubilant, but dead tired, I crawled into her big bed. Bijou's shouting woke me up an hour later. Still groggy, I caught only a few familiar words: 'menteur!' and 'salaud!' and 'connard!' I muttered, 'Whoa. Slow down, babe,' blinking up into her fury. 'Call me a lying bastard shitass, that's OK, but do it in English.'

'Lying bastard shit,' she sneered. 'Où étiez-vous?' Where were you?

'A business trip, like I told you.'

'All this time? What sort of dirty business?'

'Show business. Dirtiest of them all.'

'You are such a lying cheat.' She sat on the edge of the bed. 'You were off with other women, I know for true.'

'I was in Rome. You're right, I was with a woman. Name of Bricktop. Know her?'

'Everyone knows Bricky,' Bijou snorted. 'She is old enough to be your mother. What pleasure do you find in such ancient flesh?' Bijou's underlying corrosive insecurity at being ten years older than me augmented her dismissive scorn.

'I sang with her. At her club on the Via Veneto.'

Her smile transformed Bijou's furious mask into a mug you wanted to kiss. 'Is this really true? You were singing at Bricktop's?'

I kissed her, a quick peck on the lips. Pulled her down beside me, sleek as a seal in her shimmering black sheath. 'I'm thinking of making a comeback,' I said. 'Starting up as a crooner again. Did some warbling at a basement jazz club over in the Left Bank last week. With Klook Clarke's outfit. Sort of testing the water.'

'Did you sink or swim?'

'Little of both.' I kissed her harder this time. Reaching behind her back, I ran the zipper open along its track down the length of her dress. Bijou shrugged out of it like a snake shedding her skin. She wore no undergarments other than some kind of black corset. Sexy as hell. Reminded me of naughty postcards I peeked at as a kid. Dangling garter straps attached to sheer stockings. Those chocolate breasts brimmed in the bustier, overflowing. I ran my tongue along the rim of fabric tasting her dark perfumed nipples. Too many intricate fasteners. When I slid my hand up between her legs, I found *Minnou* moist and dripping.

'Sing to me,' she whispered in my ear as I entered her. Slowly, smoothly, our bodies flowed together.

Later, corset and hose discarded, I sang softly as she lay cradled naked in my arms. A little Gershwin, some Rodgers and Hart, wonderful slow ballads. Bijou drifted into sleep while I moaned my way through what I remembered of 'Voodoo Blues,' a Toots Sweet tune I heard for the first time up in Harlem at the Red Rooster a month ago. Ten minutes later, I sawed wood myself. When I got up to take a leak a little after nine, I wanted to crawl back under the covers with Bijou. The sweet, soft warmth of her body offered sanctuary. Her fierce *voudon* love protected me. I turned my back on this refuge. Too much on my plate for the day. Needed an early start.

After leaving Topo's last night, I'd gone to the all-night newsstand near Les Halles and bought a copy of *L'Osservatore Romano*. The notice was there. The next Council would convene on Wednesday at midnight. Cyphre was bound to show up. Otherwise, he was a dead man. He didn't know I was hip to that. Also not savvy I'd be at the meeting counting votes. The membership wanted to wrest away Lucifer's crown. Twenty-four had voted yes. Six abstentions. One was me. The other five had to be looking for an angle. Why not a single no vote? Cardinal Latour had abstained. He knew what was up. Time to call the Archbishop of Paris.

Before I entered my hotel I bought a copy of Friday evening's *Trib* and looked for Krusemark's obituary. Wasn't there. I could still play the role of *Tredecim*.

I showered and messed up the bed as if I'd spent the night, figuring the maid reported everything to Gump. I took my time heading through the lobby. Outside the Hotel California I picked up the pace. At the George V Métro station, I bought a handful of *jetons* and stuffed myself into a phone booth.

My first call was to Cardinal Latour's office. The secretary answered. No snotty backtalk from him this time. Once he heard Mr Favorite wished to speak with the archbishop he put me right through. Latour's hoarse whisper was barely audible over the phone. I told him it was very important I meet with him today. 'In what regard?' the cardinal rasped.

'Something of great importance. Can't talk about it on the telephone. Needs to be in person.'

Latour explained he had a lengthy lunch meeting with '*le préfet du département de la Seine*,' scheduled to begin at noon. There was no getting out of it. He could fit me in anytime before. 'Come straightaway and I will make room for you.'

I said that would work for me.

Fifteen minutes later the cab let me off in front of 32, rue Barbet de Jouy. I was ushered straight through to Latour's office on the second floor. The cardinal sat behind his big carved desk, splendid in the scarlet robes of state he wore to lunch with big-shot bureaucrats. 'Mr Favorite,' he purred, half-rising to greet me. 'Such a pleasure to see you again.' Easing his bulk back into his padded chair, he gestured for me to sit. 'Afraid I haven't had much luck locating your elusive Dr Cipher.'

'Forget about it. I've already found him.'

'But…' Latour wondered where this left him. 'What about our… arrangement?'

'Still stands. Only now, I want to talk about this.' I pulled the graphite rubbing of Judas shekel Number Thirteen from my satchel and handed it over to the archbishop. His hand trembled. This one snuck up behind him. 'Do you own this coin?' His hoarse whisper lacked any haughty disdain. 'Are you *Tredecim*?'

'Nope. I work for Number Thirteen.'

'He sent you to me.'

'Correct. He knows you are *Tres*. Knows your name. Figures each of the abstainers knows one of the others. All have their own reasons for not voting. What's yours?'

Latour rested his elbows on the desktop, touching his fingertips together like roof beams on an imaginary chapel. 'I believe in prudence. He who acts first perhaps gains some advantage. He who acts last always profits from his rival's mistakes.'

'You figure your advantage here might be what?'

'I expected the Council member… the one you might call my friend. I won't tell you his number. I expected something in return for my vote.' The cardinal balled his hands into pudgy fists. 'And now…'

'And now?'

'It appears I must go to him with your employer's offer.'

'Looks that way.'

'What does *Tredecim* bring to the table?'

'He'll do anything, anything at all. Whatever your connection desires in exchange for a yes vote.'

'It will take nothing less.'

'One more problem. Convincing the last hold-outs.'

The cardinal sighed. 'That is not a problem,' he said. 'Those three always vote in tandem with my friend.'

I got to my feet. 'Then, it's aces.' I walked behind Latour's desk to the glass doors opening onto a small balcony. 'Find out what your buddy wants for a yes vote. Do it now!' I stared out at the garden, noticing a uniformed guard wearing an exposed sidearm patrolling the garden. Latour must have beefed up security since I took those pictures of him and Father Gus.

'Impossible. The person in question is out of the country. Returning later this evening. The earliest I can have an answer for you would be tomorrow afternoon.'

'Not good enough. Get started on it,' I barked. 'I'll phone you tonight and see how you're doing.'

'A bit premature, Mr Favorite. Might take more time.'

'I'll call every hour on the hour. Keep you honest.' I walked toward the office door. 'Why do you want to depose Lord Lucifer?'

'What makes you think I wish to depose Him?'

I set fire to a smoke. 'Just going along with the lynch mob?'

'Always the best move,' Latour rasped. The cardinal got the last word.

43

I spent most of the day in my room at the Hotel California with Topo's translation of the Council of Thirty meeting and my pocket dictionary. I had to know exactly what the Council members had said about Cyphre.

I learned Number Eight missed the previous Council because he had to have an impacted wisdom tooth removed. Number Twenty-Five had a more elaborate excuse. Something about a crucial cabinet meeting requiring his vote. No specific government was mentioned. From what I gathered, the fate of a president in some unknown banana republic hung in the balance.

By the time I'd roughed out the English translation, I saw that János Szabor had gotten one thing wrong about Satan. He wasn't immortal. Once upon the dawn of time, a first Lord of the Underworld had been crowned by some pagan priest cult that worshiped the power of darkness. Jesus walked the Earth as a man for three short decades before being crucified, dying, being buried, and ascending into Heaven three days later. So the story goes. For almost two thousand years the faithful have awaited the Second Coming of a celestial Christ while the Devil reigns here among us in perpetuity. Lucifer is of the Earth. It is his domain. He never descends into an abstract Hell. Mankind supplies all the hell required.

If Christ was the Son of God, divinely chosen by God for his mission of peace and love, Lucifer must be the son of man chosen by other men to wear the Crown of Hell. Over the centuries, how many men have been so anointed? When the powers behind the throne deem the Devil unworthy of his wicked task someone new is crowned. The Council's main beef with Cyphre concerned his thinking, which they argued was fixed forever in the Renaissance. Machiavellian to the core, whatever the fuck that meant. For over five hundred years, since the rule of the Medicis, el Çifr had called the shots. Intricate alliances and betrayal. Conquest. Foreign colonies. The art of the double-cross. Right up through two epic world wars. Evil triumphed. On the surface this all looked great for business.

The Council was pissed because the majority believed Dr Cipher's strategies had led inexorably to the phenomenal recent growth of evangelical Christianity and fundamentalist Islam throughout Latin America, the Middle East and Africa. Millions of devout new converts were in league against Satan. The Mother Church had lost ground. The Council of Thirty wanted new crusades. Holy wars. More use of the doctrine of Papal Infallibility established by the First Vatican Council in 1870 and invoked only once in nearly a century nine years ago by the Devil-worshiping pope, Pius XII. Number Fifteen suggested renewed corruption on the grand scale of Indulgence selling. He called for a new take on old ideas. Straightforward, businesslike arrangements. No more intricate 15th-century intrigue. The Council sought a modern, forward-thinking sovereign. Someone to protect the faithful. Connect with the masses. All those fornicating Black Mass true believers sporting animal masks.

It made me laugh. The Council of Thirty had it in for Cyphre not due to any failure on his part. They sought to depose him because his grand schemes no longer fit their vision of the future. Dr Cipher had been too busy fucking over small-timers like me to pay any attention to what was going down behind his back. That's how it looked from my perspective. Who could really understand the secret motives of a cabal of evil men? I didn't really give a shit why the Council wanted to dethrone Cyphre. All I cared about was his being an ordinary mortal like me again. I'd do anything in my power to make that happen.

I gathered Topo's translation and put the pages away in my satchel. After mussing up the bed, I slipped out into the shadows.

I went to a local bistro for a dinner of *omelette aux fines herbes* and *pommes frites*, washed down with the house Côtes du Rhône. The best thing about the place was the payphone in the back. Time to check in with Cardinal Latour. Had to keep the pressure on. I got out the cardinal's private number and dialed. The phone rang and rang, no one answered.

The evening was still young. While strolling around the side streets off the Champs, I knew what I really needed was a drink. I remembered two small hotels facing each other across rue Lord Byron straight ahead. Maybe one had a bar. Near the top on the other side of the street, I spotted a little joint tucked into the lower end of the corner building. Chez Suzy Solidor. I cut over for a closer look. Turned out to be a small nightclub, the kind the French call a *chansonnier*, an intimate place like Bricktop's, showcasing the music of the resident talent.

This gin mill belonged to Suzy Solidor. Her glossy photo hung in the small glass-covered menu case. A butch-looking dame in her fifties sporting a flaxen pageboy. Showtime was 21 h. Dinners starting at 19 h. The door was open so I went inside. Took a moment for my eyes to adjust. Dim as twilight, the place was decked out in 1930s décor. Several well-dressed couples were seated at dining tables. A mute baby grand occupied the far corner. Straight ahead, a lesbian couple made out at one end of a curved bar, while an elderly gent at the other end chatted animatedly with the bartender.

I took a spot in between and ordered a *'fine à l'eau.'* A shot of bourbon cost the same as a bottle of champagne in joints like this. Settling back, elbows on the bar, I took a long look around. Every wall was closely hung with paintings, all of the same subject: Suzy

Solidor. Some were nudes. Others showed her wearing evening gowns. Classy stuff. Museum quality. All showed Suzy twenty-five years younger than the woman framed in the menu case outside. This place was her shrine.

I drank a second brandy and water before it was time to go. Heading across Lord Byron, I thought about my so-called comeback. All bullshit like my folder of newspaper clippings. But a comeback story would provide extra cover. Chez Suzy Solidor was located only a couple blocks from the California. Smart move falling by one night during the week to sing a song with her. Not likely she'd share the mike with me on a Saturday night.

Down in the George V Métro I squeezed into a phone booth and tried the cardinal again. Barely made out his raspy voice. His Eminence sounded pleased to hear from me. He'd made contact with the Mystery Guest within the past hour. 'I proposed your offer to him,' Latour said. 'He expressed interest. I will learn his decision on Monday before *le midi*. How do you say it? Noon?'

'Why not tomorrow?' I pressed.

'Is not Sunday a day of rest for the faithful, Mr Favorite?'

'I'll call you at noon on Monday.'

'Call at eleven.'

I didn't argue.

44

'Tell me about Suzy Solidor,' I said to Bijou as she cuddled in my arms, her smooth darkness glistening with sweat after marathon sex.

'She's not your type.'

'Too blonde?

'Too lesbian,' Bijou murmured. 'I know you favor older women. Solidor is old enough to be your mother.'

'I don't want to fuck her. She any good as a singer?'

'The Boche liked her.'

'What's that supposed to mean?'

Bijou wriggled free from my embrace and sat back against the pillows. 'She was a collaborator. During the occupation all the big-shot kraut officers flocked to her nightclub. Not the little cabaret she has now. La Vie Parisienne near l'Avenue de l'Opéra. *Très chic. Très cher.*'

Hip and expensive sounded boss to me. 'Her new joint still draw a crowd?'

'*Bien sûr.* Suzy is a Paris institution. *Comme la tour Eiffel et presque aussi vieux.*'

'Meow,' I said. Bijou showed her claws when she called Solidor an institution almost as old as the Eiffel Tower. 'You must be close to speak so fondly of her.'

'We have a professional connection. Very cordial.'

'Do me a favor? Remember what I said about making a

comeback? Ask Suzy if I can sing at her club one night.'

Bijou traced a red-lacquered fingernail across my chest. '*Tout pour toi, chéri*,' she said. Anything for me.

With Baron Samedi closed on Sunday Bijou and I buzzed the morning and afternoon away with shave 'em dry sex and sweet hugging affection. Moments when I felt safe. All my anxieties surrendering to her warm dark embrace. A happy fantasy free from Cyphre's menacing shadow. Bijou glowed in my arms. I wanted this to last forever. Instead, we went out for dinner.

When I got back to my room in the California on Monday morning, I hit the shower first thing. I liked having a clean white-tiled bathroom all to myself. Sharing Bijou's made me feel like an intruder. Enjoyed room service delivering my morning coffee and drinking it alone while I went over last evening's *Herald Tribune*. No mention of Krusemark. Much as I craved the sex and sleeping beside Bijou's warm, sumptuous body, I knew I couldn't linger this morning. No denying Mme Jolicoeur had a hold on me. When I reminded her last night to try to set up a gig for me with Suzy Solidor, I asked if Solidor was 'a true believer' like us. Bijou made me laugh, saying, 'Solidor believes only in Solidor. You have been to her temple. Not even the baby Jesus had His portrait painted so many times.'

Time to get dressed. Cardinal Latour expected a call from me at eleven. First turn of the thumbscrew. Walking to a payphone while residing at a first-class hotel provided an enormous pain in the ass. Price paid for police surveillance.

Looking sharp in my gray suit, I checked the place over before stepping out. Bed looked slept in. Yesterday's marked-over *Trib* sat dead center on the desk. Everything in order. The phone rang as I closed the door. It was Edmond Lenoir. 'What can I do for you today, Inspector?' I asked, wanting to strangle him with the cord.

'I would like to see you in my office at your earliest convenience.'

'My schedule's full,' I lied. 'Listen, Inspector, with all due respect, I'm a very busy man. You can't just call at the last minute and expect me to cancel all my meetings.'

'Would sometime late this afternoon fit into your crowded timetable?'

'Afraid not. I'm booked up to a dinner engagement I expect will last until midnight.'

'All right. We shall make it tomorrow. What time might accommodate your crowded schedule?' He pronounced it *shed*-ule like a Limey.

'Any time you like, Inspector.'

'Be here *midi*. On the dot.'

'You got it, chief,' I said but he had already hung up.

I made straight for the George V Métro station. Down into the subway. Best place in the world to lose a tail. I rode the Métro for the next hour, changing trains at random, traveling in arbitrary directions. Lenoir smelled something fishy but couldn't put his finger on the stink. I couldn't shake the feeling of being followed. Started thinking I saw the same cat over and over. Always some drab Frenchman in a gray coat.

It was close to eleven when I got off at the Odéon station and called the cardinal. His secretary answered. Latour came on the line right away. 'Our Lord and Master guides us,' rasped the Archbishop of Paris. His Eminence wasn't talking about Christ. 'You must come quickly. I made contact with the interested party within the past hour. Your patron will be most pleased. His answer was affirmative. There are certain conditions I cannot discuss on the telephone. I will disclose them in person.'

'On my way,' I said. '*Tout de suite.*'

Vivid in scarlet regalia, Cardinal Latour sat behind his fancy carved desk. 'Forgive the pomp and circumstance,' he rasped. 'Full panoply for a breakfast reception at the Ministry of Culture. All in honor of Charles Chaplin's 70th birthday. Are you familiar with Chaplin?'

'Silent movie clown?'

'Here in France, he is considered a great artist. André Malraux, our Minister of Cultural Affairs, treated him as an equal.'

'That where you make contact with your pal on the Council?' I tamped a Lucky against the flat surface of my cigarette case. 'Fancy receptions?'

'A public government function provides the least appropriate location for such delicate transactions. Beyond that, how I initiate and arrange contacts is none of your concern.'

I flicked my lighter and tipped a fag into the flame. 'He tell you he was changing his vote?' I asked out of the corner of my mouth.

Latour nodded. 'On one condition.'

'I take orders from *Tredecim*. He said to accept any terms for cinching the deal. On our end, we need a unanimous Council vote.'

'I assume the dirty work falls upon your shoulders.'

'Don't assume a damn thing.' I blew a smoke ring over the Cardinal's desk. 'What does your guy want?'

We watched the drifting smoke circle dissolve like mist. 'Are you familiar with an ancient punishment the Romans called *deglubere*?' Latour asked.

'Fill me in.'

'Flaying the condemned alive. Peeling off his entire skin in slow strips. Not an easy death. Agonizing. Torture so extreme it sends a powerful message.'

'Who to?'

'Not your concern. The price for the votes *Tredecim* desires is the flesh from one of our benefactor's enemies. The "goods" are to be delivered Wednesday evening in Rome.'

'Where, exactly?'

'A location not yet disclosed to me. My colleague plays his cards very close to the vest, as the saying goes. He bid this hand brilliantly. Trumped me at every trick. Revenge and magic in the same winning hand.'

'Magic?'

'An enemy's skin holds great power. Invaluable for someone with the Knowledge. I have among my few possessions a *grimoire* bound with the flesh of the famed 17ᵗʰ-century warlock, Tournier. Three hundred years after Tournier's death his spirit lives on in that little book.'

I stubbed out my smoke in the silver seashell on Latour's desk. 'Who gets skinned?' I asked.

'I don't yet know.' Latour offered a pallid smile. 'Further information will be provided tomorrow morning.'

'That's bullshit! How the hell am I–' I caught myself and took a deep breath. 'How are we supposed to track and snatch someone, some complete stranger, in only a day?'

'Not my problem, Mr Favorite.' Elbows on the desk pad, the Cardinal leaned forward and touched his fingertips together. 'I suspect my colleague wants to test *Tredecim*'s mettle. His determination. See if he's capable.'

'I understand your man wants some wet-work as proof of loyalty. What kind of fucking test rigs the rules up front?'

'None of this is by my design.' Latour stared at his hands, pressing his fingers together as if praying. 'I envy *Tredecim*. Sacrificial flaying honors Our Dark Lord. The Greek god Apollo flayed the satyr Marsyas alive for boasting of his musical prowess. The ancient Aztecs worshiped a flayed god. Xipe Totec. The challenges facing *Tredecim* only enhance the value of the sacrifice.'

'Why beat around the bush? Call it murder.'

'Slaughter in a dark alley is murder. Make the required ritual preparations. Appropriate chants and salutations. It becomes sacred sacrifice.'

I stood up. 'Better get started. Skinning someone alive sounds like a job needing a lot of prep work.'

'I am sure you will prove a most capable assistant.'

'What time do I get the name tomorrow?'

'I arrive at the office every morning before eight. *Tredecim* will have his answer then.' I started for the door. 'One more thing, Mr Favorite.'

'What's that?'

'Do you own a tape recorder?'

'Sure.'

'Very good.' The cardinal's whisper rasped with menace. 'My colleague insists his victim be skinned alive. He requires physical proof. A recording of the man's final agony.'

'I'm your guy,' I said on my way out. 'Know all about cutting records.'

45

On the street, I turned left and made tracks searching for a cab. Remnants of Harry Angel's soul lingered inside me nagging like a bad hangover. His suspicious country boy cop instincts warned me to watch my step. Look out for a double-cross when events started moving too fast. Something felt wrong. I didn't have time to fit all the pieces into the puzzle. Ten past noon. *Midi.* Eight hours maybe before all the stores closed. I made a mental shopping list not really knowing what I needed. Surgical implements? Rubber sack? Never skinned anyone before.

I hoofed it till I caught a cab that took me to my favorite hardware store Dugrenot et Vedrenne on rue de Luynes. The old-fashioned interior felt like a sanctuary, a timeless refuge from the cares of the modern world. Back in the day, Lizzie Borden bought the axe soon to deliver eighty-one whacks in a shop just like this one. My purchases were of a similar nature. I bought a spade, a pickaxe and a 25-kilo sack of quicklime. Harry's inner voice told me to buy each item at a different store. His instincts warned me to cover my tracks. I had no time for playing it safe. The Council of Thirty met again in less than a day and a half.

The staff at Dugrenot et Vedrenne helped me haul my goods out onto the street and load them into the trunk of a taxi. A short ride took me around the corner and into the courtyard of my building on Saint-Germain. Harry Angel did not approve. I left a trail hotter than Hansel and Gretel's. The cabbie did most of the unloading. I tripled his tip, waiting until he pulled out onto the boulevard before I reached for my key. In and out on the double, tossing the tools inside and dragging the sack of quicklime after them. Locked back up in less than a minute and hailed another cab.

At Champs, Ruisseau et Sommet, Harry Angel's inner voice scolded me. It was my third visit to the sporting goods store. I bought a large rubber sack and a handsome khaki canvas tackle bag with brass fittings.

At 2:00 pm on the nose I walked into American Express just as the doors reopened after their midday break. Already had plenty lire and traveler's checks, so I made a beeline toward the gasser chick at the Travel Desk who took care of me last time. Made like she didn't remember even as she booked a room at the Excelsior and hired the Fratinelli limo service using only the company name. Without blinking an eye, she reserved a seat for Johnny Favorite, Wednesday, on the 11:00 am Air France flight to Rome. 'One way?' the doll asked, handing over my ticket. Her knowing smirk let me know she'd been hip the whole time.

One final item on my shopping list. I stopped at the Information Desk and asked a well-dressed young man where one might buy medical equipment in Paris. After double-checking in a thick directory kept under the counter, the eager factotum suggested an outlet of Delacroix-Chevalier, a noted manufacturer of surgical implements, located at 13, rue Ambroise Paré across the street from Hôpital Lariboisière.

I'd eaten nothing since nibbling half a stale brioche with this morning's coffee. Time to grab a bite downstairs in the coffee shop or snack bar or whatever the hell they called it. The lounge buzzed with conversation. Hearing those twanging American accents put me in mind of home. I ordered a ham and Swiss on rye along with a bottle of Jenlain blond. The meal came with a dill pickle. I was in heaven. Chewing, eyes closed, savoring familiar tastes and sounds, I enjoyed a pipe dream of being back in the Apple.

New York was my town in a way Paris would never be. Lost in deli memories, I indulged a fantasy of killing Cyphre and escaping from the Vatican alive. Long odds, I knew. What is life without hope? Harry Angel remained a wanted man in New York. Johnny Favorite, a forgotten has-been. No coming back ever for a two-bit PI on the lam. The Fabulous Fave's fallen star at least had a long shot at rising once again.

Back in a cab at ten before three, heading for the medical equipment store, I thought about how to skin someone alive. Didn't have a clue. A suppressed memory from Harold Angel's rural Wisconsin boyhood bubbled up like swamp gas out of a past not my own. Little Harry raised rabbits. His 4-H project. Images of slaughter flickered in flashback. The swift stroke of the club. Pegging each hind leg to a sharpened 10-penny nail thrust from the barn wall. A butcher knife lopping off bunny's head. The decapitated body jerking against the boards. Warm blood spraying against my face. Harry's face.

The rest was easy. A tug on the pelt peeled it from the rabbit like pulling off a glove. Did human skin come off just as easy? Indians scalping Custer's men came to mind. Those cardboard Budweiser 'Last Stand' lithos decorating two-bit saloons back home. The redskins lifted the troopers' hair gleeful as farm boys peeling rabbits. Looked easy in the beer ad. The cavalrymen depicted were all dead or dying. Not much fight left in a corpse. Problem for me was my guy had to be alive. Lucky thing I had two pairs of cuffs.

I expected someone dressed like a druggist in a white jacket to greet me at the entrance of Delacroix-Chevalier. Instead, a smooth-talking salesman wearing a dark blue three-piece suit ushered me inside a small wood-paneled space set up like an art gallery. Freestanding vitrines displayed glittering silver implements arranged with a care usually bestowed on hand-crafted jewelry.

I spun a yarn about my brother setting up practice as a plastic surgeon in Geneva. He'd finished his residency, I lied, and finances were tight. I knew nothing about what he might need but wanted to give him some of the best equipment money could buy.

The slick young salesman took the bait, laying out a gleaming assortment of stainless steel gadgets: scissors with tiny blades, dissecting forceps, scalpels, various hemostats and clamps. He identified and explained each item with robust enthusiasm. Twenty minutes later, I walked out with two hundred bucks worth of top-end medical gear wrapped in my satchel. Also had a rough idea how to use the stuff. I fed the salesman a final whopper about wanting to understand the tricks of my brother's trade. A whole lot easier than first year of med school.

It was close to five before I got back to my hidden blue-tile cottage. A wild goose chase in a cab from one pharmacy to another as I looked for a rubber sheet ate up the time.

I had the cabby go the long way round on the quai and drop me off by Reynard's café-tabac. Inside, Alfonse leaned his elbows on the bar, jawing with a customer wearing a beret. A smoldering Gitanes dangled from his lower lip. The flick of his eyes told me to wait my turn. I stood in back by the baby-foot table until the customer downed his brandy and headed for the door. I stepped up to the counter. Alfonse set a clean glass down, poured a shot of cognac and refilled his own short-stemmed snifter. A silent salute, glasses held at eye-level before we drank. 'The police came here asking about you,' he said in French.

'*Qu'est-ce qu'ils veulent?*' What did they want? He wasn't happy about *les flics* paying him a visit.

'They asked where you lived.' Reynard slowed the frog-lingo down to a croak so even Yankee Doodle Johnny could catch every word.

'What did you tell them?' Nailed *le francais* that time around.

'*Je dis que je ne sais pas. Vous êtes un client. Comment puis-je savoir où vous habitez.*' Alfonse told the cops nothing. I was a customer. How should he know where I lived?

'*Bien,*' I said. '*Appels téléphoniques.*'

No phone calls, Alfonse told me.

'OK,' I said. '*Pas plus d'appels téléphoniques.*' No more phone calls. I knew the cops would drop by and snoop around. Put the heat on Reynard. I'd made it easy for them, leaving his number where I knew they'd find it. I'd needed to know if Alfonse, *mon vrai copain,* was a rat or not. Lucky thing he passed the test. Didn't have to kill him. Already had plenty on my plate as things stood. I dropped a ƒ10,000 note on the zinc bar top. '*Au revoir!*' See you around.

I started for the door.

'*Non,*' Alfonse replied. '*Adieu, Johnny.*' Farewell, he said.

The packed dirt floor in my tiny cellar proved hard as concrete. Each swing of the pickaxe sent trembling shockwaves up through my arms. After half an hour, I'd barely scratched the surface, chiseling out a rough rectangle six feet long, a couple feet wide and maybe four inches deep. The flickering kerosene lamp perched on a board shelf cast shifting shadows across the stone walls. My highball Manhattan radiated a sunset glow. I reached for it and took a belt.

Stripped to the waist, I slaved like a gandy dancer laying track in August. Unaccustomed to manual labor, my soft pink hands blistered. Those fancy pigskin gloves I bought in Hartford provided a measure of protection. When I knocked off for something to eat a little after seven, I had a primitive grave gouged down a foot into the cellar floor.

I spread my meal of bread, cheese and cornichons and my last bottle of Bordeaux across the trestle table before the welcoming fire. I felt safe in my secret sanctuary. Only Chris D'Auburan knew where to find me. When Alfonse said the cops had been snooping around I knew Inspector Lenoir had the café-tabac staked out. *Le Préfet de Police* wanted to know where I went after making clandestine payphone calls.

Leaving Reynard's place, I didn't spot a tail, but I knew he was there. Years living as Harry Angel gave me a sixth sense about things like that. I'd taken the long, circuitous route home.

Now I had to face the music. Consider the flaw in my plan. What might go wrong. Cardinal Latour thought I was *Tredecim*'s legman. Part of a big operation. Like the ones he and his pal on the Council of Thirty controlled. Like fat-cat shipping tycoon, Ethan Krusemark, the genuine *Tredecim*. These men would have no problem snatching anyone – even a big shot – in a single day. My target had to be someone important like them. Their one-day notice just another power play. Maybe I was out of my league. Couldn't pull it off on my own. I put my back into the pickaxe. Brute force always the best medicine for anxiety.

When I knocked off around half past eight, the rectangular hole in the cellar floor was almost two feet deep. I pulled my flannel shirt back on, leaving the tails hanging to cover the snub-nose holstered on my left hip. Didn't change my dirty work jeans. No dress code at the circus. Heading up Saint-Germain, I passed Reynard's joint, locked up and dark. Empty as the inside of my heart.

I got off the Line 12 train at Pigalle just before nine o'clock. The place blazed like a tawdry carnival. Blinking neon all around. Moulin Rouge. Cyrano. Eve. Pigalle's. Walked away from the razzle-dazzle and spotted the lights of the circus a couple blocks off. No neon. Old-fashioned lightbulb letters from another era spelled out MEDRANO.

The big street-level billboard boasted a brand-new horizontal two-sheet posted below FERNAND RAYNAUD's star billing. '*Incroyable! FRA DIAVOLO!!! Étonnant! MAGIE DIABOLIQUE!! Ce Soir Seulement.*' Dr Cipher on the bill tonight only with his special brand of 'diabolic magic.' I'd gotten a taste of that in the park. Little did the suckers know just being there was Cyphre's greatest trick. I wished I could kill him onstage. Perfect finale for his devilish act.

I entered under the central arched door into a small foyer housing the box office. Only a few jostling stragglers pushed past me. A ticket in my name waited inside an envelope bearing Jérome Medrano's embossed logo. My ducat was for the *loge*. Best seats in the house. A distant blare of band music echoed from inside. Pretty young usherette wearing a colorful frock instead of some corny brass-buttoned circus uniform showed me the way to the box seats. Mine was on the aisle in the first of four short rows.

I looked over the rail at an arena about 40 feet in diameter. Curving rows of seats rose steeply all around. A packed house even on a Monday night. Standing in the spotlight at the center, a tux-clad ringmaster introduced the first act, the bareback-riding tiger. The band blared oom-pa-pa at its best. Big cat's doggy friends leaped and cavorted. Other animal acts followed, including a baby elephant named Berolina that spun a hula hoop and played a set of chimes with her trunk. Then came Colette Duval and Gil Delamare who turned out to be married stunt parachutists who did a quick aerial turn. In between the big acts came the clowns.

I started dozing off. A sudden geyser of flame erupted at the center of the ring. The bright flash took the audience by surprise. Silent as an apparition, a figure cowled in a hooded monk's cape stepped through the smoke and fire. Wisps of smoldering vapor drifted like poison from the folds of his cloak. He carried a worn carpetbag in his right hand. Setting down the bag, he shrugged his cloak to the floor. It was Cyphre.

He wore a vivid floor-length crimson vestment so boldly red it seemed dyed from all the battlefield blood spilled since man first picked up a club. He raised his arms toward the domed ceiling. '*Mesdames et Messieurs*,' Fra Diavolo proclaimed. '*L'enfants de tous âges*.' Classic Big Top intro. Children of all ages. Cyphre wore no makeup under his red skullcap. The square-cut white goatee flared in the light. Speaking in French, his deep baritone voice resonant with the melodic cadence of song, Fra Diavolo described a recent journey to Hades and back.

Didn't listen too close. Mostly showbiz palaver, a magician's lead-in to his first big trick. 'I've brought back a few things from hell to show you,' Cyphre intoned, bending to open the carpetbag. Pale misty smoke flowed from the bag, spreading like ground fog around the red-clad wizard in the spotlight. Dry ice steaming inside.

Presto-Chango! Dozens of tiny imps clamored out of the carpetbag. Medieval creatures with fish heads and scorpion tails. Film images projected onto the smoke. The tiny animated monsters scampered around Fra Diavolo. He apologized to the audience, ululating a demon's command to the swarming imps. They rushed to the carpetbag. Tiny battalions pulled out a pair of gaudy barber poles. Corinthian pedestals to be exact. Not bone-white like you'd think but painted in bold primary colors. The little demons positioned the pedestals, one on either side of the ring. A rooster crow from Cyphre sent them scuttling back into the carpetbag.

The audience applauded. Pretty good trick. What if I jumped down into the arena and pumped Dr Cipher full of hot lead? Rising from the dead has always been the best trick of all. Fra Diavolo had the crowd in the palm of his hand. He orated on the wonders of the underworld like a tour guide. 'Eyes that have seen Hell see all,' he said. 'My eye does not offend me,' Cyphre continued, 'yet I pluck it out.'

Fra Diavolo hooked his thumb into the corner of his right eye, gouging out the orb quick as Jack Horner with his plum. Made it look so easy. The audience screamed in horror. A trickle of blood ran from the hollow socket like a ruby tear. Cyphre placed his eye on top of the pedestal. Bigger than a golf ball. Brilliant blue iris staring like the Pinkerton logo. 'This eye never blinks.' Fra Diavolo walked back across the ring toward the opposite pedestal, calm as if nothing extraordinary had happened. A frigid wave of terror flowed from the audience like a January wind up Fifth Avenue. 'Nor does this one.' Cyphre yanked his left eye free with a sudden tug. Everyone was screaming. He set the startled eyeball upon the other pedestal.

Fra Diavolo circled back to the center of the ring, arms spread wide, vacant red eye sockets transforming his face into a tragic mask. 'I see much better now,' he proclaimed. Where once he merely observed the world, Cyphre told us, he gazed now into eternity. His eyes watched everything in both directions. Cyphre invited audience members on either side of the arena to hold up random items for all to see. Pocket watches, lipsticks, eyeglasses and umbrellas thrust into the air.

Fra Diavolo, sightless, identified every object in turn. He also described each thing's owner, pointing out bald men and those wearing mustaches. Admiring a young lady's decolletage, he identified the color of her dress and the color of all the neckties on the men in the row beside her. Amazing trick. Yet so ordinary at the same time. Took the edge off the terror. Dr Cipher transformed a moment of grotesque violence into just another mundane mentalist act. He turned his vacant gaze toward the loge. 'If you think this just another mundane mentalist act you are wrong!' Diavolo said.

Had he read my mind? I think in English. Fra Diavolo pushed the blade in to the hilt. 'All magic is mundane to a magician,' he said in English.

I felt a chill tremor deep within. Whatever Cyphre had coming was meant for me. He spun a yarn about doves. Their soft throaty cooing. Their sleek streamlined bodies and supernatural homing instincts. The ancients sacrificed these birds for augury, Fra Diavolo explained. Probed their spilled entrails for glimpses of the future. 'I also use doves for prophesy,' Fra Diavolo announced, 'without killing them.'

A red-sleeved gesture toward the open carpetbag sent a flock of doves whirling two at a time into the air from deep within. A dozen or more. Black birds and whites together. 'Here is the future,' eyeless Fra Diavolo intoned. 'The white ones bring good luck. Blacks fly straight toward the doomed.'

The birds turned in a whirling cloud under the girdered dome of Cirque Medrano. Old Italian guys flew pigeons off tenement rooftops in lower Manhattan. Some kind of dago Renaissance sport. Always dug how the flock turned all together like a single creature. The synchronized tilting of wings. Diavolo's doves did something different. The flock veered apart. Many birds, black and white, roosted on guys and cables supporting the high wire. The others raced in circles above the audience. One by one, the remaining doves either perched with the others or soared to land on someone's shoulder.

Only white birds landed. Good luck angels. The black doves settled onto the rigging overhead. All but one. It flew with two white companions, round and round the arena. I watched the white pair flutter down, each in turn, landing like blessings from heaven on a couple smiling patrons. The last black bird made a final solo circuit of the arena. All heads followed his dark progress. A messenger of doom gliding silently in, claws forward, flying straight for my shoulder.

46

All eyes were on me when I grabbed the black dove from my shoulder, broke its neck and tossed the feathered corpse soundlessly onto the stage at Fra Diavolo's feet. The audience sucked up half the oxygen in the arena. My loge companions recoiled. The eyeless red monk turned in a half-circle, speaking to the crowd. I knew his words were meant for me. 'Never mistake the messenger for the message.'

I didn't leave the Cirque Medrano until after the end of Cyphre's turn. He said some more stuff about fate before gesturing at the open carpetbag. A miniature tornado spun out of the yawning sack. It twisted in the air, sinuous as a fakir's cobra, growing darker and larger as the whirling funnel reached up toward the domed ceiling, devouring everything close at hand, perching doves, eyeballs, pedestals, even Fra Diavolo himself at the end, sucked down out of sight into the carpetbag. The well-worn piece of oriental rug luggage closed by itself and sat alone center stage for a long moment after the applause died down. A clumsy Auguste clown wandered onstage with a broom, sweeping away at a retreating pool of spotlight. He noticed the carpetbag and went over for a look. Picked it up. Nothing underneath. Unfastened the clasp. Looked inside. Empty.

I rode the train from Pigalle to Les Halles thinking about Cyphre at every stop. I replayed Fra Diavolo's act in my mind. Cyphre knew I was in the audience. What else did he know? The

Council of Thirty had summoned him twice. One more no-show and he was out. No doubt he was hip to all that shit. One thing for sure. Lucifer had no idea of the vote count against Him. I'd bet the farm on that. Another safe wager: I'd skin a thousand strangers alive for the chance to pump five fatal slugs into Louis Cyphre.

'*Fais-tu toujours rechercher ce magicien?*' Bijou loved pillow talk almost as much as sex. '*El Çifr le chiffre?*' She asked if I still looked for that magician, El Çifr the cipher.

'*Mais oui, chérie.*' I kissed her ear. '*J'ai besoin de quelque chose à faire quand je ne suis pas avec toi.*'

'*Menteur.*'

Said I needed something to do when I wasn't with her. Bijou called me a liar. The usual tease. Led to a conversation about what I did all day. '*Pas de profession,*' she taunted, saying I had no job. '*Où obtiens-tu ton argent?*' Where did I get my money?

'*Je vais te dire tous,*' I said. 'Tell you the whole story. Has to be in English though, babe. Don't know enough French slang to get it all straight.'

'I do not believe your story will be whole or straight. Amusing, I hope.'

'Here's the lowdown. Most of my dough comes from playing the ponies. Got a faith-based system I use at the track. The Dark Lord rewards the faithful.' I pulled her closer. 'How about we make a date of it some Sunday? Watch the nags run?'

'You speak such nonsense,' she said. '*Mais, j'aime les courses de chevaux.*'

Said she loved the races. We could do it this Sunday.

I told her watching the ponies had to wait because I was going back to Rome for a few days.

'Bricktop's?' Bijou asked.

'Yes. Hope so,' I lied. 'Also, an important business meeting. Tell you the whole deal if I pull it off.'

Bijou smiled at me. 'Why don't you tell me where you wandered today?'

I gave her an edited version. Couldn't say anything about the cardinal, my strange shopping spree, and what I'd been doing at my blue-tiled cottage. I'd never mentioned the pad.

Somewhere in my bullshit, curiosity got the best of Bijou. She asked where I was living. She'd called the Vendôme today and the operator had told her I was no longer there.

Told her I had a room at the Hotel California on rue de Berri. 'Only change my clothes there, doll. Your bed's where I sleep.'

'*Sauf pour un plaisir de l'apres-midi!*' she scoffed, jabbing my ribs with her elbow. She accused me of using the hotel for afternoon quickies. A kiss cooled her down. Had to give her some kind of yarn.

'This is part of your hunt for el Çifr?'

'Yes.'

'Why do you look so hard for this man?'

'He murdered my daughter.'

'*Non. Impossible!*' Bijou couldn't believe it.

'*C'est vrai. Je t'assure.*' I assured her it was true. 'Didn't even know she was my kid until after she was dead.'

Bijou sat up beside me. 'But you must go to the police about this. Tell them what you know.'

'It's no good. The cops, *les flics*, already pinned the whole deal on some two-bit private eye named Harry Angel.'

'Two-bit private eye?' She didn't catch my lingo.

'*Détective privé pas cher.*' Did my best to explain. Said the law would never buy into a black magic murder. 'Lord Satan teaches us to stand alone. To be strong. Never surrender personal power. Seek revenge for every injustice. Punish your enemies. *Tu crois donc.* This is what you believe. That's why I... I –'

'Ay, yi, yi. Afraid to say the word love?'

Bending down, I kissed her hip. '*Je t'aime,*' I whispered. Told her I loved her. I lied. She yearned to hear me say it.

Gave her what she wanted. Maybe that was love after all.

'*Menteur,*' Bijou murmured. Before drifting off into sleep she whispered in my ear, '*Un cadeau pour toi.*' She had a gift for me. Turned out, Bijou had gotten in touch with Suzy Solidor and set up a singing gig. Tomorrow night, I'd croon a couple at Solidor's club. Maybe this comeback shit was the real deal. Big joke without a punch line. Comebacks blessed cats owning a future. I figured on dying in the Vatican early Thursday morning. Down under the Bastion of Nicholas V. Right after Lucifer's dethroning when I busted a cap on Citizen Louis Cyphre.

A vivid nightmare tore me awake around half past six. In the dream, screaming black doves swarmed about my face pecking out my eyes. Less than four hours of sleep didn't feel so bad. Gave me a nervous edge sure to prove useful with the job at hand. Bijou's soft distant breathing followed me out the door. I caught a train out of Les Halles station and walked into the Hotel California just before seven.

A midnight phone message from Inspector Lenoir waited at the front desk. '*À midi,*' it read, reminding me of our noon meeting at the *Préfecture.* After a long, hot shower and a *café complet* from room service I thought about what to wear. Nothing too flashy. Needed to blend in. Snatching a stranger called for stealth. I dressed in khakis, brown tweed jacket, a cardigan and crepe-soled loafers. Not a hip outfit for Chez Suzy Solidor.

With everything I had to do to satisfy Latour and his pal there was no way I'd make that gig. *Tant pis.* Would've knocked 'em dead. Johnny Favorite. Headliner. Comeback kid. Maybe if I returned from Rome alive, Bijou'd sweet-talk Solidor into giving me another try. Fat chance. After standing her up tonight I'd never see my voodoo queen again. Funny how things turn out. I'd gotten it all back. Money. The power of darkness. Beautiful black lover. Promising singing career. Poised for a second time on the brink of stardom. Didn't doubt I'd make it big again. Top of the charts.

Everything smelled like roses. Except for the stench of Louis

Cyphre. A poison toad stinking up the flower garden. Cyphre had made me a box office sensation way back when. Payback came tomorrow night. Killing him was worth more than all the rest of it put together. Sold my soul for fame. This time around, I was giving it all up to watch Cyphre die. A double sacrifice. Hail, Satan! We who are doomed salute Thee.

I got to 32, rue Barbet de Jouy at five before eight and found the arched wooden street gate locked tight. The engraved brass plaque said office hours started at '8h30.' Pressed my thumb hard on the buzzer button. Standing in the misty drizzle for half an hour was not on my agenda. After a minute or two, someone got pissed off enough to buzz me in. No cars in the courtyard. A short Asian priest in a floor-length black cassock held open the townhouse door. He stopped me at the foot of the grand staircase after I demanded he inform the cardinal that Johnny Favorite was on his way up.

'*Son Éminence n'est pas encore arrivé,*' he told me. '*Attends ici s'il vous plaît.*'

The flunky said 'His Eminence' had yet to arrive. I should wait for him in the reception room. I shucked off my raincoat and sat on one of the high-backed brocade upholstered chairs lining the wood-paneled walls. This was horseshit. Latour said he'd have a name for me first thing this morning. Something smelled fishy. With the cards already stacked against me why start dealing off the bottom of the deck?

Fifteen minutes later, I heard a car pull into the courtyard. At a window, I pushed the sheer curtain aside and watched the chauffeur open the rear door of the black Peugeot for Cardinal Vincent Latour, bright as blood in his vivid scarlet paraphernalia. Maybe he'd come from another breakfast with the cultural minister. He carried a rectangular black leather dispatch case flat out in front of him like a bakery box. His chauffeur held the front door open. Latour caught my eye, striding in like a prom queen. 'Mr Favorite,' he whispered hoarsely. 'Very sorry to keep you waiting. Please come with me.'

'My apologies, Mr Favorite,' he rasped once he was seated behind his desk. 'What should have been a simple matter became somewhat more complicated for reasons which don't concern you.' He patted the leather case's flat top. 'Nevertheless, I have the information.'

'Fork it over.'

'Patience, Mr Favorite.'

'No more fucking time for patience, padre,' I growled. 'Got work to do.'

'Indeed. *Tredecim* found a most capable man. Before rushing off to work, you need further information.'

'Spill it!'

'I do not understand this colloquialism. Spillette? What can this mean? My colleague has selected a time and place for our meeting tomorrow night. *Vingt et une heures précisément.*'

'Nine o'clock sharp,' I repeated in English.

'Exactly. *Tredecim* must bring his offering to the Baths of Caracalla before the Council meeting. To the *mithraeum* by the south wall.'

Got a pad and pen out of the satchel. Started taking notes. 'Give it to me again,' I said. 'That bit about mytherium?'

'Are you familiar with the ancient cult of Mithras?'

'An ancient resurrection god, something like Christ. Constantine built the first St Peter's above a subterranean sanctuary dedicated to Mithras.' I remembered this from Szabor's book.

'A scholar as well, Mr Favorite? Your manifold talents provide continual delight. Thirty-five *mithraea* have been unearthed in Rome to date. The one at the Baths of Caracalla serves well for clandestine Council caucuses.'

'My boss'll be there,' I said. 'Nine on the dot with a sackful of skin.'

'Of that I have no doubt, Mr Favorite.' Cardinal Latour opened the diplomatic case. 'Especially with your capable assistance.'

'Cut the crap. Just give me the name.'

Latour picked a black 8x10 envelope off the top of the papers stacked inside. He held it with both hands, reluctant to surrender the sacred object. 'Everything you and *Tredecim* need to know is sealed inside,' he said. 'Special instructions included.' The Cardinal handed me the envelope. 'One last thing…'

'What's that?'

'You are not to break the seal anywhere in this building. That is imperative. Disobeying nullifies our arrangement. Do you understand?'

'Yes.'

'Good.' His Holiness pushed some hidden button. The skinny priest appeared at the office door seconds later. 'Father Junot will see you out.' The archbishop turned his attentions to the contents of the diplomatic case.

I walked down the marble stairs with Junot beside me, watching my every move. Red wax impressed with the Sigil of Baphomet sealed the black envelope. I slipped it in into my shoulder-slung satchel. The ecclesiastical escort paced beside me across the courtyard all the way to the front gate. Once I stepped out onto the street, he slammed the little entry door behind me. A bolt rasping closed inside told me I'd never be readmitted. I broke the wax seal and slipped a photo from the envelope. A beautiful black woman smiled at me from its glossy surface. Bijou Jolicoeur.

47

Cracked me up. Busted a gut standing out on rue Barbet de Jouy. Laughed my goddamn ass off. Cardinal Latour must've heard it up in his insulated second-floor office. What a great fucking joke! All this time, I feared a suicide mission. Instead they planned for me to skin my lover alive. Perfect punch line. No way Latour knew Ethan Krusemark was dead. Or anyone else on the Council. To them, Johnny Favorite was *Tredecim*'s flunky. The cat who did the wet-work. Right from the start, Latour had had me tailed. Knew everything about Bijou. The mystery guest's challenge was a loyalty test. How much control did *Tredecim* have over his right hand man? What line wouldn't I cross to serve my boss? Funny, if you like gallows humor.

I turned the photograph over. 'BIJOU JOLICOEUR' written across the top in ballpoint. Below that, 'AGE, 52.' Her occupation listed as 'ENTERTAINER, NIGHTCLUB OWNER.' The address on rue des Innocents for 'BIJOU'S BARON SAMEDI' along with the club's business hours and phone number came next. They knew Bijou lived upstairs and had her private unlisted number. At the bottom it said: 'IMPORTANT! Take great CARE with her TATTOO. Remove the entire design intact. Leave sufficient surrounding flesh for suitable display.'

I drilled up the street to rue Babylone. I had lots of time on my hands. Didn't have to plan a big-time snatch today. Maybe the joke was on them. Why Bijou? Why not someone else? Any black chick fit the bill. No telling who the victim was just from the skin. Even the tattoo offered no big problem. Jailbirds got inked with sewing needles and bottles of black shoe polish. Cartoon skull wearing shades and a top hat. Easy tattoo. How close would anyone look in a torch-lit *mithraeum*? At most, it would take me an extra hour before the peel.

Walking against the flow of one-way traffic headed towards Raspail, I mulled things over. Where do I find another black woman? Maybe pick up some stranger on the street. Lots of dough made seduction a breeze. Only Negroes I knew in Paris were American musicians. Except for the Baron Samedi crew. All those hot voodoo dancers. Bijou worshiped Satan. True believer. Get her to help. Beltane came at the end of April. Celebration to herald the start of summer. Bonfires and orgies. Blood sacrifices to the Beast. Ritual offerings demanded of the faithful two weeks prior to the festival. How did I just remember all that?

No problem feeding Bijou a line about the need to sacrifice a black woman. Make a big deal about Beltane. Enlist Bijou's help. Get her to name the victim. Must be someone working at the club she doesn't like. Some sassy little bitch with a bad attitude. After I spun my yarn, she'd think the whole damn thing was her idea. Lying came second nature to me. Easy as scat singing.

Au Bon Marché, a cast-iron 19th-century department store across rue du Bac, filled an entire block like Wanamaker's in downtown Manhattan. All the stuff I needed under one roof.

Bought candles, colored chalk, a bottle of India ink, an eyedropper, two bottles of Mumm, a cheap plastic compass in the toy department and a perfectly matched string of cultured pearls. Why spend a fortune at Van Cleef & Arpels? Pricey gift might look suspicious.

Back at the blue cottage, I changed into work clothes and hurried to get everything ready for tonight.

Two hours later everything was set. Time to leave for my meeting with Inspector Lenoir at noon. I peeled out of the work clothes and put on my khakis and brown tweed jacket again. Not the coolest threads. I'd change again later. Had to look fly tonight for the Suzy Solidor gig. Parade around the Baron Samedi like a big star at closing time. Let Bijou fix me up with one of her sexy voodoo dancers. Bring a little piece of strange back to my secret pad and teach her an important lesson. Beauty is only skin deep.

I walked into the *Préfecture* hearing the Notre-Dame bells ring the Angelus. On my first visit to the *Préfecture* I went unarmed. Didn't know the drill. Thought they'd frisk me. This time I wanted an edge, a shot at walking back out if things went wrong. I'd fastened the two-shot derringer inside my left calf with strips of adhesive tape. My trousers covered it with no telltale bulge. The gendarme behind the desk took extra time going through my leather satchel. He held my little Swiss army knife for a long count before dropping it back inside. '*Bien*,' he said, handing the shoulder bag over. Heading upstairs, I slipped on my reading glasses.

Felt boss waltzing into Lenoir's office armed. Anything went wrong, I'd blow him away first.

'Come in, Mr Favorite,' he said, not a glance in my direction. 'Right on time.'

I took a seat by the inspector's desk. A small stack of manila file folders sat next to his left elbow. I glanced over and read the name on the top tab. Even upside-down it was easy to make out: ANGEL, HAROLD R.

'Punctuality is the most admirable Teutonic trait.'

'Yeah. We make the trains run on time, but don't make too much of my Kraut-sounding name. It was pinned to my baby blanket when I got left at the foundling hospital. For all I know, maybe I'm Jewish.'

'I am not concerned with your lineage, Mr Favorite.' The inspector spun his chair around to face me. 'I care only about your activities in Paris. Do you know Professor János Szabor?'

Figured they'd found János's body by now. Burroughs must

have told the *flics* he'd introduced me to the professor. 'Somewhat. Had dinner with him a couple times last week at the Balzar.'

'For what purpose?'

'Research.'

'Please be more explicit.'

'I read a book he wrote about religion. Interested me so I contacted him. Turned out he was researching another book. Vatican politics. I was going to Rome on business and did him a favor. Delivered a message.'

'Did you read the message?'

'Of course not!'

'To whom was it delivered?'

'I can't tell you that. My deal with Szabor means now it's his turn to do me a secret favor.'

'What sort of favor?'

'Wouldn't be a secret if I told you.'

'Professor Szabor has been murdered.'

'What?' I tried to make my surprise appear genuine. 'I ate with him only last week. He was teaching me Latin.'

'Whatever for?'

'Fun.'

'Not at all funny, Mr Favorite.' The inspector's uneven eyes burned with fanatic zeal. 'What favor did Szabor promise you?'

I ducked my head in mock chagrin. 'This is a bit embarrassing,' I said. 'After many successful years as an international speculator, I'm thinking of making a comeback.'

'A what?'

'In show business.'

'Comeback? As a singer?'

'Foolish as it must seem. I've worked a few times in public. Very low key. No publicity, front or back. That's why I went to Rome. To sing at Bricktop's on the Via Veneto. Sang with her once here in Paris when I was a kid back before the war.' I got out my deck of Luckies. 'Mind if I smoke? Lenoir nodded his head. I offered him one. Negative shake this time. Set fire to a cancer stick. 'Szabor's favor was asking Suzy Solidor if I could sing at her club,' I said.

Lenoir drummed his fingers. 'Have you performed recently in Paris?'

'At a cellar off Saint-Germain-des-Prés. With Kenny Clarke. The drummer. Lives in the Hotel La Louisiane. He'll give you the lowdown.'

The Inspector jotted a few notes on his pad. 'At what time did you return from Rome?' I gave him my flight number and the arrival time at Le Bourget. He wrote them down. 'Since our last conversation, have you had any contact with anyone claiming to be Harry Angel?'

I shook my head. 'You'll be the first to know, Inspector.'

Lenoir picked up the top file folder, glancing briefly at the cover before setting it aside. He reached for the next atop the pile. I caught a glimpse of the inverted name printed on the tab: FAVORITE, JOHN X. The Inspector opened the folder, leafing methodically through its contents. 'You lived quite an extravagant life as a young man, Mr Favorite,' he said, placing the closed file before him on the desk.

'Just sowing some wild oats,' I replied, experimenting with an innocent grin.

'You are far too modest, Mr Favorite. The information in your dossier indicates otherwise. Did you learn about *voudon* from the Jesuits at the Catholic orphanage where you grew up?'

Damn. Should have seen that one coming. 'No,' I said. 'A beautiful black woman was my teacher. No finer classroom than a big brass bed.'

'What did she teach you about black magic?'

'Don't know a damn thing about black magic.' How smoothly that glib lie slid off my serpent's tongue. 'What you call *voudon* has nothing to do with black magic. Obeah is a spiritual celebration of the natural world. Its followers never hung a man on the cross.' I paraphrased what my daughter, Epiphany, had told me. 'Obeah has no Inquisitions. No such thing as an Obeah holy war.'

Lenoir reopened my folder. He cocked his head, reading the contents. 'The victims of Harold Angel, according to Detective Sterne's report, were all known to you. You were engaged to Margaret Krusemark. Sang with Edison Sweet. Epiphany Proudfoot's mother had been your Negro lover. All were murdered in a ritualistic, sacrificial manner. Sterne referred to them as "voodoo murders."'

'First off, I've never met anyone named Epiphany. My time with her mother was twenty years ago. Ditto, Toots Sweet. Can't help you out on that score. If Harry Angel tried getting at me by killing them, he was way off the mark. They were part of another life.' Lenoir didn't mention Ethan Krusemark when he listed Harry Angel's presumed victims. No news was good news. If the French cops didn't have Krusemark in their report, either the NYPD didn't know shit or they were holding out for unknown reasons. I only needed another day. After Cyphre's dethronement he was a dead man and none of it mattered any more.

The inspector tapped a telegraphic forefinger on the file cover. 'Yet you say you wish for, what was the word? A comeback?'

'True enough. Only this time around, I'm doing it without Obeah.'

Lenoir smiled. On him it looked weird. 'Do you know Lapin Agile?'

That one took me by surprise. 'Old time cabaret,' I said. 'Far side of Montmartre. Picasso's hangout long ago.'

'Were you a customer, Mr Favorite?'

'Went there once. Looking for a magician named Natas. Didn't find him but an artist named Natas at the Lapin Agile took me to the Cirque Medrano. Introduced me to Jérome Medrano. The magician Natas performs there from time to time as Fra Diavolo. Caught his act just last night.'

'Did Fra Diavolo agree to take part in your comeback?'

'Nothing decided yet. I may go out as a solo.' I swelled with pride. 'Tonight I'm singing at Suzy Solidor's club.' Wanted to bite my tongue off as I said it.

Lenoir made a note. 'At what time do you perform?'

'Around midnight.' I regretted every word. Last thing I needed was a cop's ugly mug staring at me when I sang.

Scribble. Scribble. 'When exactly did you visit the cabaret Lapin Agile?'

The inspector caught me off balance a second time. Used my supposed comeback like a shell game misdirection. Took my eyes off the pea. 'Couple weeks ago,' I said, faking a thoughtful expression. 'Can't say for sure exactly.'

'This… artist? The one also called Natas. Where do I find him?'

For a cat who can't remember half his life my immediate answer surprised me. '20, rue Ravignan,' I said. Harry always had perfect pitch remembering dates, addresses, numbers. 'Found him in the phone book. Concierge told me Natas was at the Lapin Agile.'

Lenoir scribbled more notes. 'Have you frequented the cabaret on other occasions?'

Knew he had a witness. Someone placing me at the joint the night Sterne died. 'No,' I lied. 'Only there that one time.'

The inspector stared at his notes a beat too long. 'Mr Favorite.' He set down his pen. 'I need to see you again tomorrow. At the Lapin Agile.'

'When?'

'This same time. *Midi*.'

'I'll be there.' I got up. 'Anything else?'

'I wish you *merde* tonight. How the French would say break a leg.'

48

Walking south along rue de la Cité after leaving the Préfecture, I spotted a striking colored woman headed my way across the broad plaza in front of Notre-Dame. Not dark like Bijou or light-skinned like my daughter Epiphany. Wore a chic red woolen cape, hair bound up turban-fashion in a vibrant multicolored scarf. I fell back a dozen paces and tailed her over the short span of le Petit Pont's single arch.

My African queen angled left across the Place after crossing the bridge. Stayed right behind as she veered into a crowded rabbit warren of narrow streets with shish-kabob, couscous joints and Arab faces all around. Not only did I lose my tail from the Préfecture, I found my hunting ground. Moroccans. Algerians. Dark discards of colonial France. Wait for the right woman to come strolling along. Fox in the henhouse.

I had to weigh my options. Picking up a stranger meant seduction on the double. Eight hours max before my date with Bijou. No idea how long the skinning would take. A black hooker might fit the bill. I could offer extra dough to skip the cheap hotel and head straight back to my pad. Nice work if you can get it. Whores turned very few tricks at lunchtime and some packed shivs and razors. Finding a stray black chick looked like a long shot. Odds stacked against me. My best bet was to make Bijou my partner in crime. Perfect stalking horse among the nightclub dancers. After-hours party with the boss. Night out on the town. Maybe a threesome? Having a plan lifted a ton of bricks off my shoulders. Now I had to take care of a few more details to put it into action.

When I returned to the California at close to six I almost laughed. The copper sitting stakeout in the lobby looked about as inconspicuous as a baboon high-stepping in a Broadway chorus line. Lenoir really wanted to nail my ass. Must cost the Préfecture a bundle keeping some flatfoot posted at the hotel twenty-four/ seven. I luxuriated in a hot shower for fifteen minutes and dressed in my double-breasted blue pinstripe suit and a red Sulka tie. Wanted to look sharp. A different cop slouched in the lobby when I strolled back through, satchel slung over my shoulder.

Madame Jolicoeur was all dressed up and ready to go when I walked into her apartment at a quarter past seven. She wore the tight silver sequined sheath she'd had on the first night we met. Looked good enough to eat with a spoon. We spoke in French. 'Very beautiful,' I said, kissing the hollow above her collarbone. The tattoo peeked above her decolletage.

'You, also.' Bijou slowed down the lingo. Like talking to a child. Or a dog. 'Why do you carry that ugly sack? You look so handsome in your suit.'

'Certain things I need inside. For… unexpected circumstances.'

'Like the pistol you wear on your belt?'

She'd never mentioned the gat before. One of those unspoken things. 'My gun is for protection.'

'Do you need to be protected?'

'Not from you.' I pulled the gift-wrapped pearls from my coat pocket. 'A small present to mark the occasion.'

Bijou smiled, tearing off the paper. She opened the oblong box. Her smile lit up her eyes. 'They are very beautiful. I adore them.' Bijou reached behind her neck to connect the pearls.

'Here. Let me help.' Stepped up close, fitting the clasp. Kissed Bijou's ear.

'Are you in danger?' She turned and touched my cheek.

'Tell you all about it at dinner.'

We ate at Bijou's favorite snail joint. She got the usual red carpet treatment. Red carpet night. She hired a car and driver to ferry us around. Wore a long black mink coat. Maître d' gave us the best table in the house. Bottle of vintage Krug. Feasted on plump oysters and escargots oozing herb butter. Along the way, I spun my web. Told Bijou a yarn about why I went heeled. Twisted tale featuring hired assassins, hidden Nazi gold, a murderous black magician.

'Çifr?' Bijou took my hand.

'Yes,' I said. 'My sworn enemy.' I looked deep into her eyes. 'How strong is your faith?'

'Born in my heart. Forged by fire.'

'Do you sacrifice at Beltane?'

'I have my birds.'

I told her this deal was bigger than birds. 'Beltane celebrates rebirth,' I said. 'Fresh starts. There must be something you want.'

'Bad luck to tell.'

'Maybe so. Me? I want to sing again. Want you in my life. Finish all that other business with el Çifr forever. I've got lots to sacrifice for.'

'As do I,' Bijou lifted my hand. Kissed my fingers. 'Why does the magician wish you harm?'

'Bad luck for you to know. Too dangerous. I need your help. Be my partner in this sacrifice. I found the perfect Beltane ceremony in an old *grimoire*. A man and a woman officiate together. Do this with me. Seal our love with blood. Find strength in our union. We both need rebirth. Pray for something big as dreams.'

Bijou clasped my hands in hers. 'Prayer is a song from the soul. I feel your power, Johnny. Together, no magician can stop us.'

'You'll do it?'

'Of course.'

Our searing kiss sealed our pact. 'Here's the deal,' I said. 'This may not go down so easy. The subject must be female...'

'I have no problem–'

'And black.'

Bijou flinched. Anger flashed in her eyes but it was gone in an instant like lightning. A total pro, this woman. She never betrayed her emotions. Not in front of customers. Never to a lover. 'Why not an infant?' There was no hint of rancor in her voice. 'The orphanages overflow with unwanted bastards.' Her fingertips traced along the shining strand of pearls. I avoided her penetrating gaze. Had to think fast or it all went down the drain.

'I wish it was that simple, Bijou,' I said, speaking English. Didn't think my French could handle a complex lie. 'Some little orphan brat might fit the bill just fine for a Missa Niger. This Beltane ceremony is more specific. Not just a faith celebration.'

'So... a black woman for the sacrifice?' She said this in French.

'Symbolic,' I said. 'Queen of the Night. New day dawning.' I reached for her hand. 'This ceremony dates back to Solomon and Sheba. Selection is an honor. I thought of looking for a whore, but –'

'Too risky.'

'Yes.'

'Better coming to me.'

'No other choice. Out of all the dames on your payroll, must be a couple you'd like to get rid of.'

Bijou pulled a cigarette holder from her clutch bag. I stuck a Lucky in for her and thumbed my lighter. She exhaled. 'I own these girls. Buy them from their families in Haiti. When I get a bad one, I sell her to the brothels in Bucharest. Black ass brings top dollar in Romania.'

'How much?'

'One hundred thousands francs.'

'What if I double that?'

'I do not understand.'

'I'll pay ƒ200,000 for one of your girls.'

'You must be crazy.'

'Like a fox, maybe. We honor Lord Satan with this sacrifice. Why tarnish our offering? The Spirit of Darkness deserves the greatest possible gift. He will reward our generosity.'

Bijou smiled. 'You make it sound like a business transaction,' she said. 'We are not bankers.'

'Don't talk like a Christian. Jesus drove the moneylenders from the temple. Who do you think put them there? Bankers are Satan's chosen ones. Dealmakers. Manipulators. Driven by greed. Making a profit on this only enhances your participation in the sacrifice.'

'You are the Devil's own press agent, Johnny.' Bijou slid closer on the banquette and kissed my cheek. 'Part of why I love you. One of my girls is yours.' Another kiss. This time on the lips. 'For the price you mentioned.'

'Always a businesswoman at heart,' I said. 'That's what I love about you. Have you already made a choice?'

'Let me think about it. I have several candidates in mind.'

'Give me one with big tits.'

Bijou arched an eyebrow. 'This pleases Satan?'

'Can't speak for our Lord. I know what I like.'

49

We arrived at Chez Suzy Solidor on rue Balzac around eleven o'clock. Bijou told the driver to wait. He backed several yards downhill into a parking space. The little joint was packed. I caught Bijou checking out the crowd in the smoke-filled main room. Suzy Solidor, closer to sixty than fifty, leaned back against the bar by the entrance. A sleeveless floor-length pale blue chenille gown stretched across her broad hips. Bottle-blonde hair curled by her ears like a schoolgirl's perm. The pale painted face a mask of horror.

Bijou swept into Suzy's arms, false smiles, cheek-kissing all around. A brisk introduction from Bijou. No frills. She'd already sung my praises to Solidor to get the gig.

'May I call you Johnny?' Suzy asked in French, taking hold of my hand. I nodded. 'Remember you from before the war. Your recordings. I am very pleased you will perform with me tonight.' She gestured for a waiter, instructing him to set up a table and two chairs down front. 'I begin in five… ten minutes. After my show, I introduce you. We sing some duets and the stage is yours.'

'Dyke collaborator,' Bijou hissed as we followed the waiter to a small round table close to the piano. 'Convicted by *l'Épuration légale*.'

Close quarters. There was no stage to keep the audience at bay. We sat down, ignoring the displeasure of those displaced by our arrival. Paintings of Suzy hung all around. 'What's a little treason matter?' I said. 'She's immortal.'

We both ordered cognac. Watching the waiter depart, I spotted Inspector Lenoir seated against the back wall with a drab woman in a plain brown dress. 'Pardon me.' Quick whisper to Bijou in French as I stood. 'I see someone I know.'

I wove between the crowded tables over to Lenoir's observation post. We shook hands and he introduced me to his wife, Isobel. 'I was a boy during the swing years,' the inspector said in English. 'I look forward to revisiting my youth.'

'Don't bet on it. No swing band behind me tonight.' Lenoir loved our game of cat and mouse. His best case in years. Here he was in a nightclub. 'Hope you enjoy the show.'

I strolled back to our little table by the piano. Two glasses of brandy sat waiting. Bijou leaned in close as I sat down. '*Qui est-ce?*' she whispered, picking up a snifter, handing me the other. Who is that?

'*Un flic,*' I said. A cop. We touched rims the American way. A first fiery swallow burned its way to my core. Told her Lenoir was investigating the death of an American policeman in Paris. Someone pursuing a fugitive private detective suspected of murder.

'What has this to do with you?'

'This detective, Harry Angel, was poking around New York, digging into my past. Seems like everyone he talked to ended up dead.'

Bijou frowned and started to say something but just then a young man in a dark suit slipped past us, sliding onto the bench behind the baby grand piano's keyboard. The pianist switched on the lamp attached to the music rack.

Suzy Solidor entered to a polite smattering of applause. Haloed by backlight, she smiled into the single Fresnel spot mounted on the rear ceiling. Mere feet away, Solidor talked about times gone by and sang her greatest hits surrounded by wall-to-wall images of herself. I wasn't listening. I had other things on my mind. Most of the songs I'd never heard before. Then came 'Lili Marlene,' sung in throaty throbbing French. The bitch loved rubbing the audience's noses in this kraut song.

The chumps gave her a big hand. Solidor bowed her head like a Valkyrie queen. Her bare arm reached languidly toward me. She spoke my name, beginning a brief spiel. I rose when the applause started and stepped to her side. We bantered about Paris before the war. Sang a duet. 'The Man I Love.' Not bad for no rehearsal. Suzy kissed my cheek, gliding off into the shadows.

'I'd like to start with a blues tune,' I said, alone in the spotlight. 'This one's by Edison "Toots" Sweet. Want to dedicate it to my sweetheart.' I gave Bijou a big smile. No way I'd speak her name out loud with Lenoir listening.

'I got them voodoo blues,
Them evil hoo-doo blues.
Petro Loa won't leave me alone;
Every night I hear the zombies moan.
Lord, I got them mean ol' voodoo blues.'

The piano player noodled behind me until he picked up the chords. Had a good ear. I sang some Cole Porter and 'Dancing with the Devil.' About a half-hour's worth.

Got a nice hand. Not enough for an encore. 'Think I'm in the running?' I asked, sitting back down.

'You have a pleasant voice,' was all the praise I got from Bijou.

'Maybe that and the Beltane sacrifice will do the trick.'

Over my shoulder, I caught Lenoir rising to his feet. He approached our table, leaving his wife behind. 'Don't forget our rendezvous,' the inspector said, looming over us.

'À midi,' I replied. I checked my watch. Almost 1:00 am. 'Aujourd'hui.' At noon. Today. I made a point of not introducing him to Bijou.

'Good.' Lenoir said this in French. 'Regarding your "comeback," my advice would be do not give up your business career.'

'I'll take that under consideration,' I said in English. 'Policemen always being so hip about music.'

'Hip?' The inspector pronounced it 'heap.' 'This word is some slang I do not understand. Just as I do not understand you, Johnny. Not yet. When I finish my investigation, I will know everything about you.'

'That's what I love about cops...' I lit up a Lucky, blowing a plume of smoke at Lenoir. 'Know everything. Understand nothing.'

'Patience. Persistence. That path approaches wisdom.' The inspector bowed to Bijou. '*Enchanté*,' he said, turning back toward his mousy wife who was standing by the entrance.

'Why torment him?' Bijou asked once they'd left. 'It is like kicking a hornet's nest.'

'Lenoir's on my turf tonight. Down at the Préfecture he calls the shots.'

Suzy Solidor marched up to our table waving a bottle of bubbly. A waiter followed bearing a trio of champagne flutes. He set the glasses down and fetched a chair while Suzy deftly twisted off the wire, popping the cork with her thumbs. Solidor sat beside us. The waiter poured the wine.

'Bijou tells me you sang with Bricktop,' she said following our European look-in-the-eye-over-the-rim toast.

'I was just a kid,' I said in French. Suzy's red lips grimaced like those painted on the waxworks in Danny Dreenan's Coney Island dime museum. 'Eighteen. Only a couple songs late one night.'

'I adore Bricky.' Suzy waited for me to light her cigarette. 'You had a reunion with her in Rome?'

'One song this time.' I needed to get my own show on the road. 'Make-believe comeback.' I stubbed out my smoke and turned to Bijou. 'Made the decision we discussed earlier?'

Bijou giggled into her Moët. 'Monday,' she said. 'Let us enjoy tonight. I need time to think about it.'

Those words rang her death knell. 'Sure you can't decide tonight?'

'What's the rush?'

'No rush.' I lit another fag and settled back. Bijou and Suzy traded catty remarks. Something about goats and the Baron Samedi. I'd run out of options. If I insisted on tonight and Bijou still said no, she'd smell a rat when I suggested a visit to my mystery cottage. There were no more strings to pull. No dice to roll. I sat still and quiet, gathering strength. The first tendrils of love I'd felt had to be ripped from my heart like noxious weeds.

'We should go soon, my darling,' I said, interrupting the women's bitchy conversation, 'I have a surprise for you.'

50

We left Suzy's place just before two in the morning. Our driver slumped fast asleep behind the wheel when we slid into the back seat. Bijou waved off his groggy apologies with a laugh. 'Stay awake when you drive,' was all she said.

Bijou had already settled her tab with the driver. 'Do me a favor,' I said, handing him a ƒ1000 tip. 'Drive to the top of the hill and turn right on Lord Byron without a signal. After fifty meters, pull over quickly and let us out. Keep on driving for another twenty minutes. Go anywhere you like.'

The driver never let on what he thought but he followed my instructions to the letter. Dropped us off where Lord Byron curved to the left. I hustled Bijou across the sidewalk. 'Is this your surprise?' she asked as I guided us into a shadowy doorway.

'First of many,' I whispered, peering back down the street. A car with no headlights turned from Balzac just as the taillights of our hired car disappeared down Lord Byron. I ducked back into the shadows. The dark car sped past. 'There goes our tail.'

We walked to the Hotel California. I ordered a bottle of champagne sent up when I collected my key. The cop on stakeout in the lounge fronting the courtyard dining area looked inconspicuous as a neon sign. Up in the room, Bijou draped her mink across a striped divan by the wall and took a look around. She checked out the bathroom and peeked into the closet, sizing up my limited wardrobe. 'What are you looking for?' I asked in French.

'Some clue about Johnny Favorite. My mystery man.'

'Find anything?'

'*Rien*,' she said. Nothing. Bijou wandered over to the table by the window. She picked up the manila folder, shuffling through the newspaper clippings inside. 'What is all this?'

'Business research.'

'You said you were a gambler.'

'Real estate. The stock market. Biggest gambles on earth.'

'*Johnny, le flambeur*,' she laughed, adding in English, 'Risk-taker, a high roller.'

A knock at the door. Moët in an ice-bucket. The waiter set the tray on a bedside table. I signed for it, flinching when Bijou popped the cork behind my back. The waiter left and she handed me a glass alive with rising galaxies of tiny bubbles. 'Here,' she said. 'Tickle that big nose of yours.' Bijou spoke French again.

'This stuff would taste like piss without the fizz.'

She smiled. 'Champagne is a fine white wine. The effervescence gives it magic. The laughter of angels.'

'Who are they laughing at?'

'Us, naturally. Foolish mortals.' Bijou gave me another mysterious smile, gliding away like a dark swan across the room. Queen of the Night. 'Like you,' she said. 'You gave up Le Vendôme for this place. Like a fool.'

'Left Le Vendôme when I started sleeping with you. This room is to throw the cops off track. So they don't start snooping around Le Baron Samedi.'

Bijou slid into a tight embrace. '*Tu es mon vrai chevalier*,' she whispered, kissing my ear. You are my true knight.

'My armor's a little rusty.' Didn't have the lingo for this so I spoke in English.

She replied in French, keeping me on my toes. 'When the heart is gold,' she said, 'nothing else matters.'

My heart was stone, I thought. A blank tombstone marking the grave of an unknown corpse. No point stalling any longer. 'I have another surprise,' I said.

'You are going to strip off my clothing and make love to me in your big soft bed?'

'Yes. But not here.'

Bijou laughed. 'Where then? In the bathroom?'

'I have another place. My real home. Secret home.'

'What nonsense are you talking?'

'Tonight I share all my secrets with you. No one knows about this other place. Not even the police. Come on. Get your coat.' I helped Bijou into her mink, grabbing my Aquascutum and the bottle of bubbly. 'We're going to cop a sneak.'

'You talk gibberish, Johnny?'

'A little adventure.' I held the door open for her. 'We're going on the dodge. Ducking out the back way. Cops won't have a clue.'

Bijou suppressed an unladylike giggle. She dug it. Her idea of fun.

We held hands, running down the carpeted hallway past the elevator. I led Bijou to the fire stairs at the rear of the building. Took a big slug of champagne. Handed the bottle to my midnight queen. She guzzled like a teenager on a prom date. We emerged from the stairs into the hall behind the darkened courtyard and slipped out the door into the little park I'd found earlier. Dark trees towered over us. We angled to the right into darkness and stepped out onto a little street. Less than five minutes later we were on the Champs-Élysées where I flagged down a cab.

Settled in the backseat, we passed the champagne to each other. 'You know a whole lot about me,' I said. 'All I know about you is how you came to Paris with a sugar-daddy when you were a teenager. Tell me more.'

'*Bien.*' The whites of Bijou's big eyes gleamed in the shadows like opals. 'I didn't stay with *mon papa gâteau* very long. There were other men. Paris is the city of love. I found a job dancing at the Congo Club in Montmartre, across Place Pigalle from the Moulin

Rouge. Gone now but *très chic* back in the Jazz Age. In less than a year, I land in the chorus line of *La Revue Nègre* at Théâtre des Champs-Élysées. Josephine Baker was the headliner.'

'Become a star?' Like me, I thought, polishing off the Moët.

'*Non*. I lacked the magic of the divine Baker. I opened a little club, *Le Ti-Bon Ange*, in Saint-Germain-des-Prés.'

'What happened to your nightspot?'

'The Third Reich did not welcome young black women. Like the Jews. And fairies. Gypsies. When Poland fell, I made plans to depart. I had friends in French West Africa. Closed my bar the day after the German tanks rolled into the Ardennes. I heard the news of Dunkirk on the radio aboard a freighter bound for Senegal.

'I stayed in Dakar six months, then traveled south to Dahomey. Among the Fon people, I discovered the true spirit of *voudon*. Four years later, *la Libération*. I was *ounsi kanzo* in the *société* of the most powerful *oungan* in the territory. I had been reborn. Upon my return to Paris in the autumn of '45, I established my own *ounfò* and became a *mambo*. Le Baron Samedi opened three years later. A celebration of my faith for a public ignorant of its beauty.'

'What of your true faith?' I asked. 'Is Lord Satan not your Master?'

'Of course. *Voudon* provides a public outlet for my private beliefs.'

'Would you sacrifice your life for Satan?

'When my Master calls, I will offer everything I have to Him.'

She didn't see me smile in the darkness.

My blue-tiled cottage glowed cool as foxfire under the courtyard lights. '*Incroyable*,' Bijou sighed as I led her toward the door, our footsteps echoing in the enclosed space. 'Like in a fairy tale.'

I found the hidden iron key. 'Where you live happily ever after?' The door opened, complaining on its ancient hinges.

'Perhaps an ogre eats you,' Bijou said, walking inside into darkness.

I switched on the lights. Bijou looked around in wonder like Goldilocks in the three bears' house. A damp chill held the downstairs in an icy grip. 'Keep your coat on,' I told her. 'I'll get a fire going.'

Didn't take long. I'd set everything up beforehand. Struck a match. Started a blaze roaring in the fireplace. Bijou stared into the flames, astonished at finding herself in a country cottage magically transported to the center of Paris. I went into the kitchen and opened a bottle of champagne. Brought it and two wine glasses back into the living room. My mink-clad minx rested a ring-bright hand on Yorick's ivory dome and gave me a coquette's smile. 'I see you still have your stolen souvenir.'

'Keeps me company when I'm alone.' I handed her a drink.

We killed the bottle standing by the fire as the room warmed around us. Bijou shrugged off her fur, letting it fall onto the trestle table. I stroked her bare shoulder and arm. She relaxed into my arms for a long probing kiss. 'Where is your bed?' she whispered when at last our lips parted.

'Don't have electricity upstairs,' I said, lighting the white candle I'd stuck into the neck of a wine bottle. I led Bijou up the narrow stairs, holding the bottle to illuminate the way.

I set the wine bottle on the bedside table and drew Bijou into a tight embrace. 'Je t'aime,' I breathed into her ear. I found the zipper behind her silver sheath and tugged it down to her ass. She kissed me like the bite of a lion. No girdle. No panties. No garter belt or nylon hose. I cradled her sweet plump cheeks in my hands.

As I fumbled with the hooks on her bra, Bijou pushed me away, shedding her dress and brassiere like a snake's skin. She tore at my clothing, ripping the buttons off my shirt. I wriggled out of my suit jacket. She had my pants down around my ankles. Pushed her onto the bed, kicking off my shoes and trousers. We were all over each other. Sucked her nipples tight as walnuts. She gripped a boner about to explode.

I reached her right hand up over her head and clipped my S&W

Peerless Model 4s around her wrist. 'What are you doing?' she gasped.

'A little game.' I kissed her, stroking between her legs. 'Trust me.' Pulled her left arm over to the bedpost, hooking the other wrist to another set of bracelets. Licked and kissed her all over then tied my woolen scarf over her eyes.

'Johnny!'

'Our game is about pleasure. Surprises. I'm lighting more candles. The magic starts the second your blindfold comes off.'

'Are you my magician?'

I walked to the corners of the pentacle I'd drawn on the floor that afternoon and lit each of the five black candles. Satan's spirit flickered into the room. 'I have the power of the loa. When I mount you tonight,' I crooned, running my lips along her thigh, 'your joy will be complete.' Bijou moaned. I threw a double half-hitch around her ankle with the Goldline.

'Johnny, no!'

'Take it easy.' A second pair of half-hitches secured the other ankle to the footboard. 'Only a game.' I kissed the pouting coral lips of her vagina. 'I have warm scented oil to rub all over your body.' I opened the table drawer. Turned on the Minifon wire recorder. 'It will feel so nice,' I said, reaching for my scalpel.

51

The noon flight to Rome was full. Heavy weather obscured the continent. We flew above the clouds, aluminum wings gleaming with reflected sunlight. Staring down at the gray cloud cover from my window seat, I thought of Inspector Lenoir waiting outside the Lapin Agile in the drizzle. By the time he figured out I was a no-show and ordered his men to check the airports and train stations, I'd be safe in Italy.

Decked out in my pinstriped suit with my money belt around my waist, I looked like a traveling businessman. One with an edge. With a .38 on my hip, a two-shot derringer and a leather sap in my jacket, a speedloader in each trouser pocket and my sacred athame strapped to my left leg with adhesive tape, I was a walking arsenal. Didn't want any heat in my luggage. At Le Bourget, I'd checked the Ghurka bag, stuffed with extra clothes, black vestment, cape and hood. The leather satchel and canvas fishing tackle bag were stashed under the seat in front of me. Papers, passport, maps, guidebook, Minifon P-55 and its external speaker were packed into one, strips of Bijou Jolicoeur's flesh in the other.

It wasn't as easy as you'd think. Human skin doesn't just peel off like rabbit fur. Connective tissue under the top layer refused to let go. Bijou screamed louder than any rabbit. I chanted the sacred invocation, the ancient ritual transporting me beyond the sacrificial chamber. '*In Nomine Dei Satanas, Luciferi Excelsi...*' My Latin rose up from the past. Knew every word. Skinned Bijou in long strips. Got her tattoo together with the nipple all in one piece. After a couple hours, I thought about knocking her out. I had feelings for Bijou. Did my damnedest to find someone else. Tried like hell to get her to give me one of her voodoo gals. In the end, I had no other choice. My deal with Latour included recording all her suffering. Never welch on a deal.

Bijou lasted more than four hours. Things got easier after that. Took my time with the face and scalp, getting almost all of it in a single mask-like piece. Didn't bother with her hands and feet. Too much trouble. Naked, drenched in blood, I carried the raw red corpse down to the basement wrapped in a rubber sheet. Half past nine in the morning. I doused her with quicklime and shoveled a mound of dirt into the grave.

Packed her torn, stripped skin in the waterproof sack and stuffed that into the tackle bag. Put a bottle of wine and a couple tins of pâté on top as camouflage. Cleaned up in the tub. Plenty of hot water. Started the boiler when Bijou stopped screaming. I felt nothing afterward. No remorse. Looking at the other passengers, I thought of the revulsion they would feel at what I had done. The guilt they'd suffer if they were in my shoes. For a moment, I envied them. They experienced emotions I'd never comprehend. Was I missing out on something? Did these squares have one up on me?

At Ciampino, after collecting my bag and clearing passport control, I breezed through customs without a nod from the uniformed officials giving me the eyeball. In a taxi at 4:00 pm. Headed north for the heart of the city on the Via Appia Nuova. The road ran parallel to the old Appian Way. All along the route, ancient ruins thrust from the countryside like rotten teeth. Rome was a town overcrowded with decaying buildings. Maybe New York will look the same after a thousand years.

Arrived at the Excelsior well before five. I went straight to my room, showered and called room service. Soon the evening sunlight was gilding the room. While I ate a steak dinner, the favorite last meal of condemned men, I slipped back into memory. I quit Spider Simpson in August of '39. Signed with Warren Wagner right away. Ferocious little weasel. He had Walter Winchell yak about me on the radio and booked me into El Morocco and the Copa. Played the Paramount, Saturday night, May 11, 1940. I remembered the screaming teenage girls like it was yesterday. Had a return engagement that September. I was on top of the world. Never made it to Rome when my star was rising. The war got in the way.

It didn't take long to want out of my deal with Cyphre. I knew the best of what fame offered was finished even as it started. That first-time rush. Getting rich overnight. I'd never enjoy such feelings again. The downside included endless rehearsals, long recording sessions, sycophantic staff, bullshit in the gossip columns, a performing schedule more exhausting than big band one-night stands. Everybody knowing who you were got old in a hurry. Money flowed in and out like the toilet flushing. I had a fine library in my Waldorf Towers apartment. Occult volumes hundreds of years old. Greek papyrus scrolls. I combed through these books looking for an answer. Endless invocations and rituals. One night, there it was in front of me on a fox-freckled page: '*Transmutatio Animae*.' Transmutation of souls.

The Hammer of God, an alchemist's *grimoire* handwritten in 1438, contained this obscure sacrifice. I read the Latin text from *Malleus Dei* out loud. A bird bursting into song. The ancient ceremony would save me. An ace in the hole. My fiancée, Maggie Krusemark, seemed eager to assist. No big deal right away. Not with my career going great guns. Wanted to make a pile of dough first. Everything changed early in November 1942, when I got drafted.

Left boot camp a month later as a newly commissioned second-lieutenant in the Army Special Services Entertainment Branch who'd skipped OCS. I knew my time had run out. Still a crooner but with different gigs. USO clubs, War Bond drives, galas for the top brass. Singing every night. All for a shavetail's paycheck. Plans for the Transmutation Sacrifice went into high gear. The offerant had to be a man my age and size and born under the same sign of the zodiac. Someone I didn't know, picked at random. No abductions. The stranger must become my friend.

Maggie and I spent hours talking it over. She said Times Square on New Year's Eve fit the bill. It would be crowded with half-drunk strangers looking for a good time. Easy pickings. We prepared my library for the ceremony. Used the room often for occult rituals. Kept the windows covered with heavy drapes. Never let the cleaning ladies inside. We moved the furniture out. Covered the floor with a rubber mat. Charcoal brazier in the corner. Candles all in place.

I owned an antique athame with a hilt of carved walrus ivory. *Grimoire* demanded an unused blade. Knowing a custom cutler upstate, Maggie brought me steel fresh from the forge. She insisted I wear my uniform. Maggie's old man agreed to serve as our witness. He always called her Meg. Don't know why. We took a cab over to Times Square together a couple hours before midnight. No spectaculars lit up because of the blackout. People wandered around in a twilight gloom. My second-lieutenant's uniform provided camouflage. Nobody recognized me.

I spotted him right away. Maybe ten minutes after weaving into the gathering crowd. A young corporal exactly my age. Same color hair. Maggie got the conversation going. Ethan Krusemark faded into the shadows. Harry acted nervous at first because of the butter bars on my shoulders. 'You outrank me,' I said, nodding at the bandaged arm showing below his cuff. 'You've seen combat.'

Angel pulled the sleeve up over his white plaster cast. 'It's nothing,' he said.

'Million dollar wound?'

'Maybe for now. They'll ship my ass back soon enough.'

'Hope not. This brand-new Sears Roebuck roots for a desk job.'

'Holy shit!' Corporal Angel's surprise was so genuine and innocent. 'You're Johnny Favorite.'

'Lieutenant Favorite,' I said with a conspirator's wink.

By the stroke of midnight we were all best buddies. Learned he was a Gemini, just like me. My psychic twin. No ball drop on Times Tower. First time in decades. Fucking war. Started off the new year with a round of barhopping. Plantation Club, White Rose, Leon & Eddie's. Got Harry tipsy. Slipped a mickey into 7&7 number eight. No knockout drops. Something to make him feel sick. Nauseous. Corporal Angel said he wanted to lie down.

Maggie asked where he lived. Bunking with army buddies out in Flatbush. 'Long subway ride,' she said. 'Better come home with us.' Bundled him into a cab. Crosstown to the 50th Street entrance of Waldorf Towers. Elevator up to my pad at 38C. Five floors above Cole Porter. Maggie made Angel comfortable in the guest bedroom. Gave him something she said would settle his stomach. She lied. Administered a triple dose of Seconal. The corporal was out cold in minutes. No screaming needed for this ceremony.

Ethan Krusemark phoned from the lobby just as I lit the altar flame. We undressed Harry Angel and bound his ankles with long strips of adhesive tape. Secured his wrists to his hips in a complex harness of bandages. Carried him into the library. Twelve tall black candles encircled the *Sacrificium Altaris*. Maggie and I danced naked with her father. Chanted invocations in Latin. In Hebrew. We'd rehearsed it for days.

Burned a large pentagram into Angel's bare chest with a branding iron heated cherry-red in the brazier. Made to order by a Devil-worshiping blacksmith over on Staten Island. Incense sweetened the skillet smell of charred flesh. Maggie brought my new dagger right on cue. Purified the blade in the altar's fire. Cut the young soldier across each breast, tracing a circle in blood around his body. Maggie chanted the invocation. Sprinkled powdered chemicals into the candle flames. Rainbow colors flared around the room.

I drove the dagger deep into Angel just below his sternum. Couldn't split the rib cage open. Made a deep cut, reaching up inside to the left. Found his beating heart. I wrenched it free. Easier than you'd think. The pulsing muscle spurted in my hand. Final hot spray. I ate Harry Angel's heart. Try eating a catcher's mitt. I tore at the still-throbbing organ with my teeth. Savage beast swallowed gory hunks without chewing. Blood glistened on his lifeless body. Maggie and I fucked in the spreading gore. Her father watched, howling like a wolf. Later we dismembered him in the bathtub. Maggie and I hauled the body parts to a farm her father owned in the Catskills.

All memory of that night had been lost for years. Staring out at Rome in the settling dark, I recalled every moment. Johnny Favorite. Big star. In the flesh. I didn't turn into Harry Angel on the spot after making a meal of him. The ceremony gave me possession of Angel's essence. Every moment of his past. I planned to make the switch when the time was right. Only one more invocation needed to complete the transfer.

South America was our escape plan. Brazil or Argentina? Buenos Aires sounded like a hip town. Maggie loved tango rhythms. Stashed bundles of cash south of the border. Ready and waiting. What's that old line about mice and men? I got shipped to North Africa two weeks after the sacrifice. A Stuka dive-bomber strafed the troop show I was performing in, ending my military career and robbing me of my memory.

The rest of the story I knew from what Cyphre and Krusemark had told me. Two sons-of-bitches but what they'd said made sense. I was shipped back to the States shell-shocked, living like a forgotten discard of the war in a veteran's hospital in New Hampshire until my agent Warren Wagner used some of my earnings to get me into a private hospital in Poughkeepsie. Even though I recovered my senses and the use of my limbs, I still suffered from acute amnesia. If it hadn't been for my former fiancée, Maggie, I would have sat in that hospital for the rest of my life. She rescued me, honoring an agreement we'd made before I went overseas. With a $25,000 bribe to Dr Albert Fowler and using a false name, her father got me discharged from the Emma Dodd Harvest Memorial Clinic and persuaded my doctor to maintain the pretense that I was still a patient there. Without telling me my name or anything about our past relationship, Maggie and her father drove me to the city and set me loose at Times Square on New Year's Eve 1943. I was back at the starting point, the last place the soldier named Harry Angel remembered before Johnny Favorite drugged him.

Louis Cyphre killed Maggie Krusemark. My daughter Epiphany, too. Tonight, vengeance would be mine.

Dressed in suit pants, white shirt and tie beneath the long black vestment, I was packing all my heat for my final showdown. No black wig or paste-on mustache. Didn't leave the room until the front desk phoned to say my limousine had arrived. Why tempt fate? Owed it to Bijou to get this done right. At eight-thirty, I strode through the lobby of the Excelsior, cape swirling, tackle bag over one shoulder, hood clenched in my gloved right hand.

A sleek black Lancia Flaminia waited at the curb. 'Terme di Caracalla,' I told the driver. The limo slid through unknown night-time streets. I fingered the Judas shekel in my pocket. Tried to keep from thinking. Somewhere along the route, I tugged on the black hood. We pulled over near a grove of trees. The driver gave me basic directions. Said he'd wait for me.

I set out through the trees and across a grassy lawn toward the vast shadowy ruins of the ancient Roman bathhouse. Scattered lampposts provided scant illumination. Thought I saw another hooded figure slipping through the darkness ahead.

I walked toward a faint glow in the distance that turned out to be a votive candle flickering at the top of a narrow flight of stone stairs angling into the earth under the crumbling outer walls. I started down. At the bottom I followed a sequence of votive lights along a wide arched tunnel to a small dim chamber. More light spilled into another antechamber two steps down. Was this the *mithraeum* where worshipers of Mithras had sacrificed bulls, crouching below the animals in a pit so they could be purified by the hot blood flowing down upon them?

'*Octo*,' a voice called out around the corner. '*Ave Satanas!*'

'*Ave Satanas*,' answered several muffled voices.

Turning a corner, I looked into a candlelit vaulted rectangular chamber about seventy feet long and thirty feet wide. I stopped when I saw five black-robed hooded men standing by a large hole in the ground. I was only expecting Latour and his buddy who called the shots. Why were three other Council members there? In case of a trap, I reached both hands into my vestment, gripping the concealed two-shot in my right and pulling the Judas shekel out with my left. '*Tredecim*,' I called, showing the coin. '*Ave Satanas!*'

'*Ave Satanas*,' the others replied in chorus.

One of them stepped forward. '*Tres*,' Latour's raspy voice announced. He spoke to me in Latin. I understood every word. First time in years. I was fully in the present. For almost two decades, thinking I was Harry Angel, I'd been a captive of the past. Now I was Johnny Favorite who lived in the moment.

The cardinal motioned to the other Council members. One by one, they identified themselves by number. '*Octo.*' '*Viginti.*' '*Septendecim.*' '*Viginti quinque.*' Why the extra trio? How did they know to come here tonight? I gripped the derringer in my pocket.

Before I could phrase the question in a way that wouldn't blow my cover, Latour introduced Number Twenty as '*noster conlega et benefactor*'. Our colleague and benefactor.

Number Twenty stepped toward me. '*Tibi partem meam?*' he asked. Have you brought my tribute?

Holding tight to the two-shot, I slipped the tackle bag's strap off my left shoulder. '*Spero quod placuerit vobis*,' I said, handing it over. I hope it pleases you. Didn't give a shit as long as I got the votes.

'*Gracias tibi*,' he said, unfastening the leather buckles. '*Tale negotium bene gessit Satanas noster celebret.*' He thanked me. Said such a task performed well celebrates Satan. I gave him a curt bow. *Viginti* pulled out the wire recorder and speaker, handing them to me. He clutched the waterproof rubber bag, letting the canvas sack fall to the floor. He tore the rubber bag open. Somber as plague doctors, the other Council members made a show of not watching. Pulling out Bijou's corvine hair, Number Twenty stared for a long time at the ragged mask of her face. Next he fished for her tattoo. I knew he dug seeing the nipple. '*Nunc autem sonitu!*' barked *Viginti*. Now the sound!

I plugged in the speaker, switching on the P-55. No amplification. Tiny treble squeaks. Bijou's agony no more than the screaming of a mouse. We listened to Bijou's recorded suffering down in the *mithraeum* for over two hours. Didn't bother me much. I'd heard the real thing. The chirping rodent pain sounded so far, far away. Closer at hand, Number Twenty stroked his hard-on through the straining fabric of his black vestment.

52

Number Twenty switched off the P-55 at 11:35 pm. *'Optimum. Suffragia ad vos.'* Excellent. The votes are yours. I pictured him smiling under his hood.

'Approbare omnes?' All approval?

'Certe. Ut dictum est.' Certainly. As agreed.

Ten minutes later six black limousines cruised like marauding sharks through the heart of midnight Rome. We pulled into Vatican City under the Porta Angelica at five before the witching hour. Swiss Guardsmen shouted out Roman numerals on the double. The Pope's policemen ushered us inside the Renaissance tower headquarters of the IOR. I followed a black hooded lineup around the reception desk and down the trapdoor dungeon stairs like before.

I knew this was the end of the line. A kamikaze assassin with no way out. My previously planned escape route looked impossible tonight. The minute Cyphre lost his crown I'd kill him. And face the wrath of twenty-nine enraged Council members. I had seventeen .38 rounds. Also my sap and athame. Not enough. Funny thing. Dying meant nothing to me if Dr Cipher went down first. Just might get carried away and put four pills into him. That left thirteen. My lucky number.

Hung my cape in the vestibule and entered the dark Council chamber, a phantom merging into the shadows of his tomb. My eyes adjusted slowly. Torch smoke hung in a fogbank above our heads. I glanced around at the last arrivals before I found my place at the big table and took my seat, setting Krusemark's Judas shekel tails up in its golden receptacle. I saw Satan's black serpentine throne was unoccupied. A sensation of relief and liberation jolted through me. A stay of execution. Tonight's Council meeting was no longer a suicide mission for yours truly. Cyphre's no-show tonight meant immediate dethronement. Without Satan's crown he was just another dumb SOB waiting to die.

The distant clock chimed midnight. All the Council members rose to their feet, chanting in unison. This time, I knew every word of *Hymnus ad Satanas*. 'Hymn to Satan.' I sang the Latin verses loud as Frankie Laine belting out 'Mule Train.' Out of the corner of my eye I caught a glimpse of something moving. Hard to see much wearing a hood. Turned for a better look. Something moved in the darkness. Swirls of mist caught a faint red glimmer of torchlight. The crimson shimmer coalesced, taking shape faster than blinking. Wrapped in a scarlet cloak, Lord Satan stepped from the shadows.

Our chant quavered for a half note. The choir caught its breath. *Numerus Unus* picked up the tempo bringing the Council's convocation to a harmonious conclusion. '*Ave, Satanas!*' the members shouted in unison. Everyone but me. Cyphre wore Satan's Crown, a horned golden helmet shaped like a goat's head that covered half his face. His white square-cut goatee gave him away. He stared at us, implacable behind the mask. Without a word, he unfastened the red silk cape, which slid to a vivid pool around his feet. He was naked underneath. I saw a Charles Atlas physique with bone-china white skin. A patchwork of scars striated his torso. Wounds maybe hundreds of years old. Five puckering pink welts bloomed where I'd shot him last week. Three marked his chest. One on his belly. Another inflaming his right knee. Cyphre limped up the dais steps, taking his seat on Satan's Throne. The Council of Thirty sat in a single body as if choreographed.

Numerus Unus stood, holding a slender golden scepter, and

began a rambling Latin sermonette. Something about the powerful roots of our ancient faith. I didn't give two shits for the fucking Council of Thirty. Settling my score tonight with Louis Cyphre was all that mattered. Number One caught my attention when he mentioned 'casus Luciferi,' the Fall of Lucifer.

'Archangel Lucifer, cast out of Heaven to Earth, was given dominion over His prison,' Number One said. 'Lord Lucifer. Exiled. Composed of pure spirit. An invisible force of nature. For countless millennia, the ancients worshiped Lucifer. Paleolithic man had his Horned God. Civilization gave us Bel-Marduk. Pazuzu. Moloch. Set. Many others. Lucifer remained invisible. An ethereal spirit influencing mankind through storms and pestilence. Flood and fire. Master of catastrophe. Ruling by fear.

'Yahweh anointed the Nazarene as Christ and a living god walked the earth. Lucifer understood this threat. He found an avatar to walk among men Himself. The Crown of Satan solemnized the incarnation. Who was the first man crowned? Forever a mystery. Lord Lucifer made His choice before establishing the Council of Thirty. Eleven men have worn the crown. The last coronation, 1737...'

Why preach to the choir? The Council members knew this shit by heart. '...much honor to you, Satan, for all you have achieved. The Reign of Terror. Two World Wars...' Too bad János Szabor couldn't hear Number One's ramble. '...awesome responsibility. We have called you before us, O Satan, to hear our grievances.'

Cyphre seemed not to listen. Hard to tell with half his face covered by a gold goat head. A Council member rose to speak. 'Testimonium,' they called it. Unus handed the serpentine scepter to Quinque and took his seat. This guy's beef concerned the Dalai Lama's escape from Tibet. Six months earlier the Council had voted for him to die. Cyphre crossed his muscular arms, staring above Number Five's head into the middle distance.

The sceptre passed to Number Nine. He bitched about the revolution in Cuba. A month ago Castro rode victorious into

Havana. The Council's plan called for a Communist state ninety miles from American shores. Satan had not worked behind the scenes to help establish this, amusing himself instead with mass executions. 'World War III at our fingertips,' *Novem* said, 'and Satan distracted by a firing squad.'

Number Fourteen was next on his feet. I didn't like being so close to the action. Staring eyes all around the table. *Quattuordecim* spoke of Eisenhower sending troops into Little Rock. The Council had discussed the opportunities offered by segregation for two years. 'Did Satan implement any of our strategies?' Fourteen raised the scepter above his head. 'Not one lynching!' Cyphre ignored him.

The scepter passed to Number Seventeen who complained about what was going on with the spread of Communism in Southeast Asia, proclaiming 'it is not sufficient to have the American president mouth the words "domino effect" if no military intervention is proposed.'

Anger boiled beneath the calm surface of their polite *testimonii*. Nineteen wanted the Algerian uprising brought to the streets of Paris. Terrorism. Assassinate de Gaulle. Number Twenty-six was all for promoting a secret Soviet plan to build a wall across Berlin. Thirty complained about last year's merger of Egypt and Syria into the United Arab Federation. The Council voted for a war with Israel not a UAF coup d'etat against Jordan and Iraq's Arab Union.

Turned out the Council of Thirty was behind the failed Blair House assassination attempt on Truman and Operation Ajax, the CIA coup in Iran putting the Shah back on the throne. The Council had coined the phrase 'Godless Communism' around the time they got Congress to adopt 'In God We Trust' as America's national motto.

At last, the gold scepter returned to *Numerus Unus*. My adrenalin surged. Time to vote. Number One asked the Council if anyone else wished to speak. *Viginti* stood. Number One handed over the scepter and resumed his seat. I wanted to hear every word. This cat had demanded six pounds of flesh for his vote. Plus the soundtrack.

'O Lord Satan,' *Viginti* intoned in sonorous Latin, 'I come before You in homage. Your achievements are many and magnificent. But you indulge Yourself. I don't understand Your choices. The Council decided an American Catholic president would best serve our purposes. We suggested cultivating the young senator from Massachusetts. One on one. Make him Your disciple. Instead of influencing world events, You dally with a treasure-hunting sailor stranded in Macao and an ambitious young American entertainer. Lucifer intended that You seek the advice and guidance of His Council. Our purpose here on Earth is to serve as Your guide. You have lost Your way, Lord Satan.'

Number Twenty walked the scepter back to Number One who waited for *Viginti* to be seated before speaking. 'You have heard our grievances, Lord Satan. The Council of Thirty wishes to listen. Anything You want to say.' Silence from Cyphre. 'Have You no comment regarding these proceedings? No argument in Your defense?'

Satan laughed, a half-heard chuckle at first. A private joke trembled through his scarred sculpted body and burst into loud scornful laughter. Cyphre's contempt echoed in the domed chamber. The mirthless sound sent prickles down my spine. The man wearing Satan's Crown got to his feet laughing like mad. He stepped to the edge of the dais roaring with laughter, a rigid erection leading the way. Dr Cipher leaned back, spread his legs, and pissed an arcing stream into the darkness above the Council table. Urine splattered like rain across the inlaid tabletop. The nearest Council members ducked for cover. Reflected torchlight glinted on the spreading puddle. No more laughing.

Stunned silence engulfed the windowless dungeon. Satan's scorn turned inside-out. Everyone sat motionless in its power. Cyphre slumped on his obsidian throne. Number One walked away without speaking and pulled the hanging chain on a wall.

The distant bell chimed. *Unus* waited until the young priest arrived with his ledger. Couldn't hear their brief whispered conversation. The priest set up on his little table. Number One rejoined the Council. '*In tempore ad suffragium*,' he said. Time to vote.

'*Unus!*' the priest called.

'*Approbare*,' Number One answered.

'*Duo.*'

'*Approbare.*'

So it went around the Council table. A loud '*Approbare*' after the priest proclaimed each number in turn. I cast my own approval with a lusty shout. Followed the escalating tally with total concentration, mouthing a silent '*approbare*' before each member's vote. When *Viginti* gave his '*Approbare*,' I reached inside my vestment and slipped the Smith & Wesson from its clip-on holster.

The final ten approval votes crescendoed in my mind. A longhair symphony climax. Crashing cymbals. Up-tempo heartbeat. *Approbare* all the way. Thirty votes for dethroning Satan.

Number One stood, holding the golden scepter. With slow painful reluctance, the man wearing Satan's Crown rose to his feet, naked before us on the gleaming black dais. Head held high in defiance, he listened to *Unus* proclaim the terms of Satan's forced abdication. A lot of blabber about dedication and responsibility. I got itchy. Old Number One might drone on all night. He started talking about the rewards of a mortal life. I'd had enough. Cyphre had lost Satan's Crown. Now he was just a man like me. Time to die.

I jumped to my feet, pulling the heater out from under my black robe. '*Satis!* I shouted in Latin. '*Mutim loqui!*' Enough! Too much talking! I yanked off the hood with my left hand, wanting el Çifr looking me straight in the face when I rubbed him out. 'It's me, Cyphre,' I yelled in English. 'Johnny Favorite! Cat with the golden tonsils! Your favorite crooner!' That shut up Number One pronto. All the hooded Council members turned my way. I kept the gat trained on Cyphre. 'Show's over,' I shouted. 'Lost your crown, Devil-man! Just another dumb citizen like me.' No more words. I'd spoken my piece a week ago in the Bois de Boulogne.

'I am at your mercy, Johnny,' Cyphre said, cool as a corpse. 'The Council voted for my abdication. I must comply with their decision. Until I crown my successor, I wear Satan's Crown and remain immortal. Were you a Council member, you would be more familiar with protocol. *Numerus Unus* will explain.'

I kept my .38 trained on Cyphre, glancing over at Number One.

'Whoever you are,' one said in heavily accented English, 'your intrusion into the sanctity of our Council is an outrage'. His voice trembled with contained rage. 'It shall not go unpunished. Nor will we allow you to harm Citizen La Croix.'

'That your real name?' I barked at Cyphre. 'La Croix?'

'Count Eugène Alexander Jérôme de la Croix, at your service,' Cyphre said with a slight bow. 'For as long as I wear the crown, I remain your Lord Satan.'

'Abdication occurs only after a successor is crowned,' *Unus* growled at me.

'Not so heavy a burden as you might suppose, Johnny.' La Croix spread his arms wide and stepped down from the dais. 'I accept the Council's decision. It has been my great honor to serve. May the next to wear Satan's Crown be as faithful.'

I kept the roscoe trained on Him as he approached the Council table. The moment Cyphre passed the crown to the next in line, he was dead meat. The golden goat head gleamed with reflected torchlight. The naked demigod circled the table, arms spread like a welcoming lover. He walked counter-clockwise passing one disappointed hopeful after another. La Croix/Cyphre strode past Number One without a glance.

Satan stopped in front of me. 'John Favorite,' he intoned. '*In nomine Dei Lucifer, ego te dominus corona Inferos, Rex Damnatorum.*' I understood every word. In the name of Divine Lucifer, I crown you Master of the Underworld, King of the

Damned. '*Salutant te, Dominus Satanas.*' Hail to thee, Lord Satan!

Cyphre lifted the horned helmet-shaped crown with both hands, holding it high in the air. Jet-black hair. Empyreal blue eyes. I should have shot him right then. Didn't pull the trigger. He fit the crown on my head.

A lightning bolt of pain blasted through my body. Excruciating torment drove me to my knees. The snub-nose clattered across the cold stone floor. Overwhelming agony beyond anything I'd ever imagined. Shock so great I was unable to scream. My open mouth emitted a soundless exhalation from Hell.

'Lord Satan, Your subjects salute You.' I heard Cyphre's voice from a great distance. I didn't know if he spoke Latin or English. 'You possess the power of darkness. The forces of terror and desolation are at Your command.' I fell onto my side, writhing. 'The Crown of Satan demands much from those who wear it. All suffering known to mankind must be borne. Torment lives within you. Agony is the source of your strength. Christ died for the sins of his followers. Satan lives for His, wracked by eternal pain. That is His sacrifice.' Cyphre laughed. 'I waited a very long time for you to come along, Johnny. Don't disappoint me. You will learn to live with the torment in time.'

Fueled by indescribable suffering, rage and fury burned deep within me. Every fiber of my being screamed, electric with misery. Shouldering this burden, I rose up slowly to my feet and began my reign.

FIN